MT. CARMEL MEMOIRS:
THE CYCLE

LARRY PAYNE

JourneySoul Christian Ministries
Amarillo, Texas
www.journeysoul.org

MT. CARMEL MEMOIRS: THE CYCLE

Copyright © 2006 Larry Payne

All rights reserved. No portion of this book may be reproduced, stored in an electronic system, or transmitted in any form by any means, except for brief quotations in printed reviews, without the prior permission of the publisher.

Published by JourneySoul Christian Ministries, 3300 S. Coulter Dr., Ste. 3-155, Amarillo, Texas 79106

Scripture quotations used in this book are taken from The Holy Bible, New International Version, copyright © 1973, 1978, 1984 by International Bible Society. Used by permission of Zondervan Publishing House.

This novel is a work of fiction. Any resemblance to actual events, organizations, persons, living or dead, is coincidental and beyond the intent of either the author or publisher.

Library of Congress Cataloging-in-Publication Data

Payne, Larry
    Mt. Carmel Memoirs:The Cycle/Larry Payne
    p.   cm
    ISBN 13 978-0-97724450-8
    ISBN 10 0-9772445-0-4
    LCCN   2005907685

PSALM 59

Deliver me from my enemies, O God;
Protect me from those who rise up against me.
Deliver me from evildoers
And save me from bloodthirsty men.

I have done no wrong, yet they are ready to attack me.
Arise to help me; look on my plight!

But I will sing of your strength,
In the morning I will sing of your love;
You are my fortress,
My refuge in times of trouble.

O my Strength, I sing praise to you;
You, O God, are my fortress,
My loving God.

Psalm 59: 1-2, 4, 16-17 (NIV)

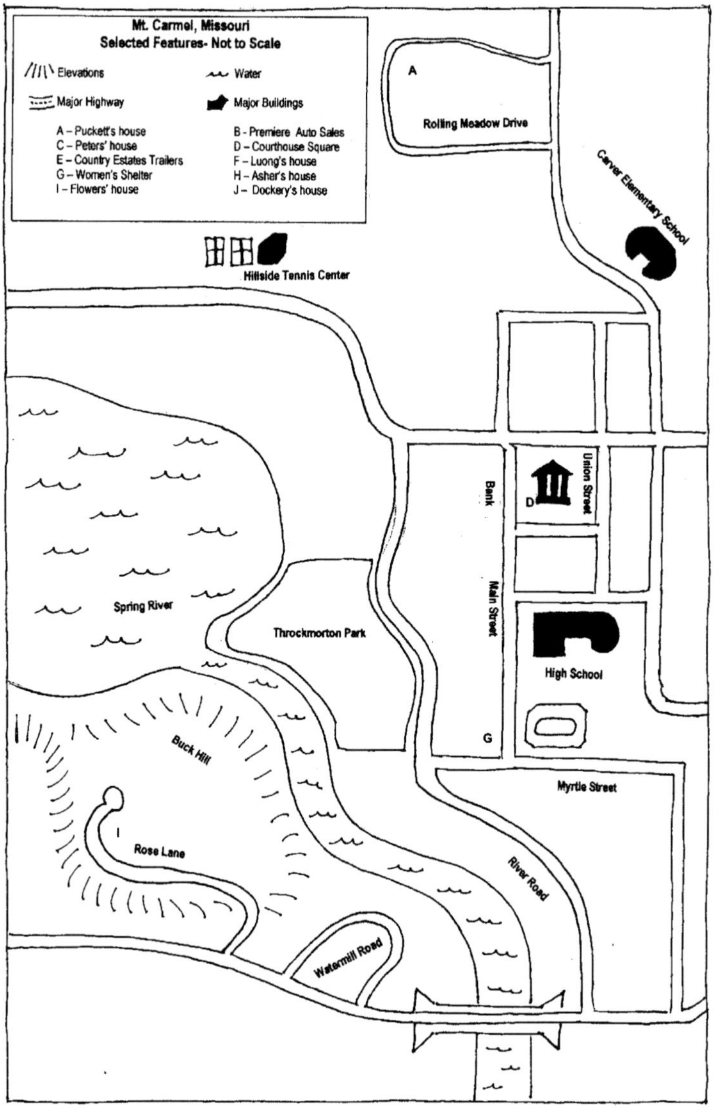

Mt. Carmel, Missouri
Selected Features- Not to Scale
Elevations
Water
Major Highway
Major Buildings
A – Puckett's house
C – Peters' house
E – Country Estates Trailers
G – Women's Shelter
I – Flowers' house
B - Premiere Auto Sales
D – Courthouse Square
F – Luong's house
H – Asher's house
J – Dockery's house
A
Rolling Meadow Drive
Carver Elementary School
Hillside Tennis Center
Bank
Union Street
D
Main Street
High School
G
Spring River
Throckmorton Park
Buck Hill
I
Rose Lane
Myrtle Street
River Road
Watermill Road

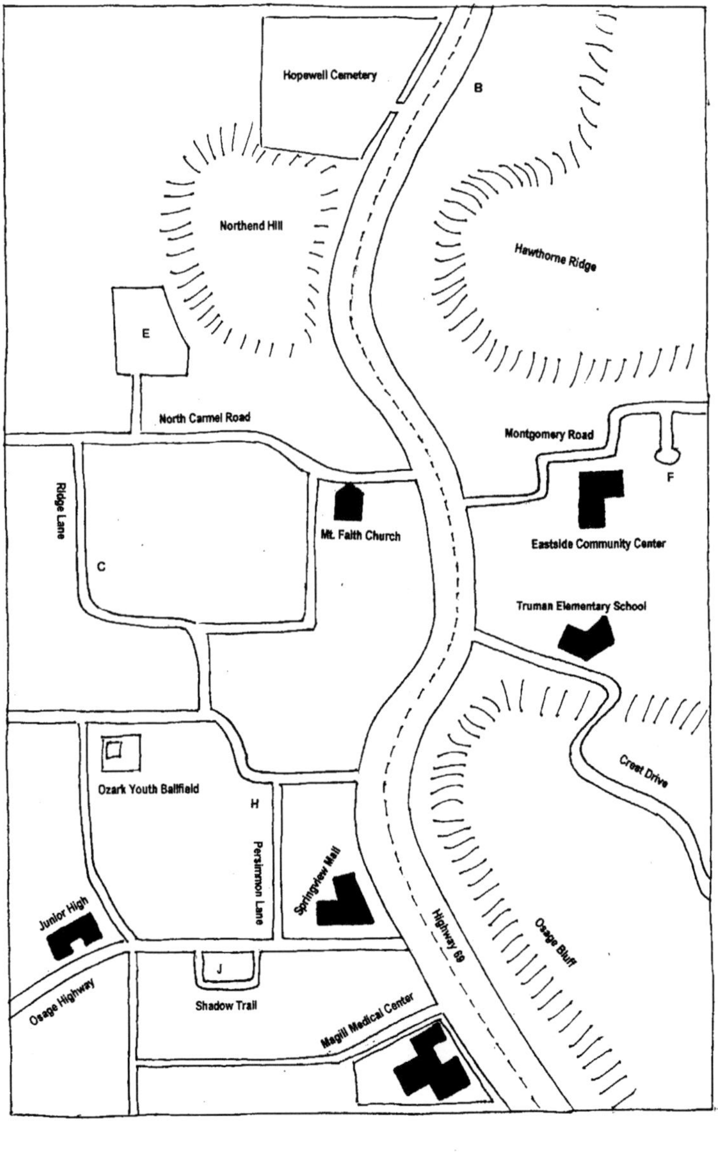
Hopewell Cemetery
B
Northend Hill
Hawthorne Ridge
E
North Carmel Road
Montgomery Road
F
Ridge Lane
Mt. Faith Church
Eastside Community Center
C
Truman Elementary School
Crest Drive
Ozark Youth Ballfield
H
Persimmon Lane
Springview Mall
Junior High
Highway 69
Osage Bluff
J
Osage Highway
Shadow Trail
Magill Medical Center

Chapter 1
Sunday

An irresistible urge, like the gnawing hunger of a starving man, had thrust him across the gentle Ozark hills. He longed to see her. The compulsion had pushed the black sports car with abandon down the two-lane roads and through the one stop-light villages. He must see her, no matter how long he now had to park and wait in the sultry August heat. A bead of sweat rolled between his shoulder blades, yet his deep brown eyes peered unwavering toward the Peters' house.

What's taking her so long?

His fingers traced again the leather stitching of the steering wheel. Shimmering shadows from the silver poplars, towering over the well-tended suburban yards, danced across the car in a mesmerizing cadence. He glanced along the sidewalk, concerned that even on a drowsy, Sunday afternoon, someone in the small Missouri city might grow suspicious if he sat here too long.

As though answering his demand, a glimmer of light reflected from a car cresting the hill. He fumbled to hit the 'Record' button on a palm-sized silver machine. The SUV pulled into the driveway of 423 Highview Drive.

"Four ten p.m. Keri home."

"Can he really set a record, Dad?"

Barry's sleeping eyes popped open at Jason's outburst. He felt dryness cling in his mouth like cotton.

"Who? What record?"

"Carmichael is coming up." The twelve-year-old perched on the front edge of the overstuffed, green couch, eyes locked on the final innings of the televised baseball game. "He's already had a single, a double, and a home run in this game. The announcer said he just needs a triple to 'hit for the cycle.'"

The pastor of Mt. Carmel's Mt. Faith Church brought the footrest of the comfortable, brown leather recliner down with a thud.

"What does 'hit for the cycle' mean, Dad?"

"It's when a player gets four hits in one game, one to every base: a single, a double, a triple, and a home run. I think it's only happened a couple of hundred times through all of baseball's professional history."

The ring of the telephone interrupted their attention. Keri Peters peered around the corner of the kitchen where she had been putting up the groceries. "I'll get the phone," she said, putting a box of cake mix on the kitchen counter.

"Let me know when Carmichael comes up again." Barry tucked the newspaper under his arm and sauntered toward the kitchen.

Keri hung up the phone as he entered. An impish smile danced on her face. "Are you reliving the glory days? I can still remember watching a game when you slid into home plate with the winning run against Tech. I jumped up to cheer, lost my balance, and nearly fell out of the bleachers."

"Hmm. The glory days. I just wish this middle-aged body could still sprint around those bases like that."

"You and me both, lover boy." She pinched his trim side just above the belt. At forty-three, though his dark hair had begun to gray at the temples, his piercing black eyes could still

2

melt her heart.

"Watch it, now," he said, winking. "Those glory days faded twenty years ago!"

"I know. Where did the time go? We moved to Mt. Carmel six years ago last month, but it seems like just yesterday."

"The way I see it, you haven't aged a day since the moving van dropped us here." He circled his arms around her lithe waist and returned the pinch.

"You know just what to say." She pulled a strand of burnished gold hair back from her face to peck his cheek.

The tall stool at the breakfast bar creaked as he settled on it to open the Sports section of the newspaper.

"Who called?"

"Lisa Burns, a young mom who visited my class this morning. She wanted to know if we could visit with her after the home fellowship tonight."

"I wanted to come home and watch the exhibition football game."

She opened the kitchen cabinet to gather ingredients for a dessert. "I think she's got a lot of problems. I told her we would come as soon as we could."

"You know that I don't feel good about marriage counseling. You can read people like a book. I never know what's really happening with them."

"I'm sure just listening will help her."

He rustled through the paper, unconvinced. "Lately people have acted like I'm a magic answer ball—just shake me and get an answer from God."

"They're just looking for some help and sympathy." She added water to the mixing bowl. "Surely you can give that."

"Maybe that's why I feel so worn out. I could hardly drag myself through the service this morning. It seems like I never get a rest from …."

The ring of the phone cut short his lament.

She laid the measuring cup down. "Hello? Hi, stranger!" She covered the mouthpiece with her hand. "It's David," she mouthed, turning quickly to carry the cordless phone to the wingback chair near the living room window.

He let her go and returned to the box scores, the interrupted complaint reverberating through his mind. She didn't understand the weariness that had dogged him, morning and evening, for weeks. Attending the home prayer meeting tonight seemed enough of a challenge without adding another stress-filled encounter.

Jason called from the family room, "Dad, look at this homerun!"

"I'll be right there." No one wants to listen to a tired preacher anyway. He folded the paper and ambled into the family room.

One block west of Highview Avenue, trim and stylish Daemon Asher steered his dark-green Lincoln around the corner of Willow Street. His well-controlled demeanor normally conveyed a commanding presence. But just now his wife, Nadine, could see his thin lips set in a harsh line of displeasure.

"I don't like these home meetings on Sunday evenings. When Brother Bob led the church, the auditorium filled for every Sunday night service. Remember when Jack sang in the youth choir at that service nearly every week?"

Through their forty-nine years of marriage she had heard his complaints about the church programs countless times. "I'm looking forward to seeing the Simpson's home since they added the extra room."

"I don't understand why we go to houses all over town

when we've got a nice church building to meet in."

The Lincoln eased to a stop in front of a beige brick, ranch-style house where Sid and Claire Simpson lived. "I love the oak trees around this house," Nadine said. "Years ago, Claire and I would sit on the porch and watch Jack and Mitch swing from the branches."

"Those good times seem lost now." He took her arm to walk up the sweeping drive toward the front door.

"Come in! Come in!"

Sid's boisterous welcome boomed when he opened the screen door. He hugged Nadine's oversized frame with a hearty laugh, squeezing her against his rotund midsection, then pulled them into the brightly decorated entry.

Red-haired Claire hurried from the kitchen, wiping her hands on a dish towel and leaned close to Daemon. "I thought you'd never get here!"

"Don't be nervous. The plan will go just fine," he whispered.

Soon more people arrived, prompting the talk and laughter to grow louder. The women gathered in the brightly decorated, yellow kitchen, while the men settled in the new patio room. Several followed Sid around the massive new addition, quizzing him on construction details and contractors. The booming economy provided incentive for remodeling older houses to market to the new families moving to the area. What Sid said about his recent adventures with contractors and code inspectors caught their attention.

Another group of men sat with Daemon in the family room. Like him, they had grown up when bustling farms, not shopping centers and video stores, sat at the city limits of Mt. Carmel. Their conversation drifted to the escalating pace of change sweeping across the forested hills of the Ozark city.

"Did you see that they tore down the old rock house

down on Black Cat Road last week?" The question came from a slightly-built, balding man named Fred. "It's where the Cleere family lived when I was young. Nice family. I think they moved to Little Rock. I remember once when their little girl got tangled up in some barb wire. A bunch of us boys were there on our bikes when the doctor got there. I wonder what they'll build there now."

"It's another out-of-town restaurant coming in," Daemon said. "Probably won't take long until another one of the family-owned restaurants we grew up with goes out of business!"

Soon Claire's voice called from the new room to gather for the devotional. The group of twenty friends slowly complied, pulling their chairs into a loose circle around the perimeter of the wood-trimmed room.

Sid took the lead. "We've looked forward to having everyone here since Brother Barry announced the home meetings. We never get time to visit enough on Sunday morning. Claire, come help us with our prayer time now."

Claire perched stiffly on a straight back chair, her small, narrow face intent on the task. "I'd like for each couple to share a request, if you would. Minnie, will you write down what people say?"

Soon, the simple needs found expression: health for a new grandchild, concern over a pregnant and unmarried granddaughter, a mention of someone who hadn't come to church in many months, and a brief mention of the ministers who served at Mt. Faith Church. The group listened patiently, then bowed heads as Burt, a tall man with a raspy voice, prayed.

Then came Sid's turn. After reading the Bible passage on the crossing of the Red Sea by the Hebrew people, he spoke energetically about the power of God to handle the problems of life.

After some minutes, Daemon shifted uneasily in his

chair. The attention of the group was drifting toward the smell of coffee and desserts covering the kitchen table. Most seemed more than ready to finish the serious part of the evening. He caught Claire's eye, checking on her readiness to follow the plan. Finally, Sid finished and placed his Bible on his lap.

Daemon's voice shattered the comfortable atmosphere.

"Sid, I don't know if I should interrupt now or not, but there's another matter we need to discuss."

Every eye turned his way.

Claire quickly supported the comment. "I think we have time before the desserts are served."

Daemon surveyed the curious faces. Slowing his words for maximum effect, he said, "A very serious problem threatens our church. We must talk about it tonight."

"I'm so pleased to hear from you. How are you?"

"I'm doing fine! What's going on at the preacher's house today?"

Keri had known David since the early days of ministry in Mt. Carmel. His intense energy always kept some project going, many times entangling his wife, Morgan, in the adventure. Frequently, Morgan would call her best friend, Keri, to help her tackle the new endeavor.

"Oh, Barry and I were talking about the home meetings tonight. Do you know that church services are dismissed for people to meet in homes? We're planning to go to Kent and Beth Puckett's house. You should go with us."

"I'd like to, but the weekend at my parents wore me out. Too many relatives and too many memories."

"I can believe that. The memories tug at me, too. I just try not to let them get me down."

"Yeah, but it happens anyway. The car felt empty on the way home from Springfield."

"I'm sorry."

"I'm trying to adjust to those feelings being part of life now, you know."

The pain in his voice brought a flood of memories to Keri's mind. She glimpsed flashing police lights mirrored on rain-slick pavement. The smell of a spring thunderstorm filled her lungs. Rain dripped from the young leaves and flooded across the streets, leaving the intersection awash. She remembered slowing her car to look past the police cars parked askew at the accident scene. The wrecked auto sat twisted, a grotesque sculpture of tangled metal and shattered glass. Then her eyes had fallen on David, hunched under a yellow police poncho. Trembling and bloody from the collision, he looked up at her when she darted past the startled bystanders to kneel by his side. Together, they watched the jaws of life ripping the crushed Blazer apart to free the woman trapped inside. Morgan!

On that terrible day, Keri had fallen in behind the speeding ambulance that carried her friends toward the hospital. After Barry arrived, they huddled together, clinging to hope, praying as the hours in the crowded waiting room crawled across the clock face. Finally, a tall doctor emerged from surgery, shoulders slumped with weariness. The scrub mask hung under his chin like a deflated green balloon. He laid a heavy hand on David's shoulder. "We couldn't save her," he confessed. The color of David's face drained to the hue of the gray skies outside. Morgan was gone.

"Were your parents not doing well this weekend?" Keri pushed the memories back so she could help David with his needs now.

"Oh, all of us struggled." Agitation leaked into his voice. "Even when Dad and I played golf we had trouble talking. We felt the holes in the conversation-- then I figured out we were waiting for Morgan to jump in with something interesting, like she always did. You know, yesterday marked six months since the accident. They're hurting too, I guess. They didn't want me to leave, but I honestly felt glad to get on the road."

"I know they miss Morgan like the rest of us."

Moments passed in silence before his voice lowered. "Can I tell you something?"

"Of course."

"You're going to think I'm crazy."

"No, I won't. What is it?" She squirmed in the chair.

"When I got home a little while ago, I came in the house and put my suitcase in the entryway. I turned to go back to the car when... I thought I heard her."

"You thought you heard Morgan?"

"Yeah. Lots of times she would be working in the utility room when I came in. She would call, 'I'm back here.' I'm not kidding you, Keri. I thought I heard a voice... her voice... again." His words trailed off until he mumbled, "Do you think I'm crazy?"

"No, not at all. You loved her. You can't leave all those memories behind, David. I can't either. We all loved her. I've picked up the phone to call lots of times, then realized I wouldn't ever talk to her again."

"You know how the imagination can play tricks on you. I'll be O.K. when I've had a good night's sleep. I appreciate you listening and not calling the men in white coats."

"You know I don't mind. It's the least I can do for all the good times Morgan and I had together. She accepted me for who I was and never demanded I fit her requirements. That's a pattern I want to repeat with others, especially you."

"It feels good just to know you understand."

Keri glanced at the living room clock. She still needed to finish that cake. But caring for this grieving friend came first.

"Carmichael could do it this time."

"He needs a triple to hit for the cycle, right?"

"Uh-huh. The count is 2-1."

The third base coach brushed his arm with a signal. Carmichael nodded, stepped in the box, and locked his eyes on the mound. The pitcher delivered a slider and he snapped the bat, sending a pop foul into the first base seats. The count fell to 2-2.

The next pitch broke slowly, hanging over the plate. The crack of the bat sent the ball sizzling down the first base line in a white arc. Hitting the turf just inside the foul line, the ball bounced to the wall, sending the right fielder sprinting in futile pursuit.

"Go!" Jason pumped his arm while Carmichael streaked around the base path, rounding second with his head down. Every eye focused on the slide at third, the tag, and the signal of the ump. Safe!

"A triple! He hit for the cycle!"

Barry stood to return his son's high five. "I've never seen that before!"

Keri stepped in from the kitchen. "What happened?"

"Mom, Carmichael just hit for the cycle!"

"What does that mean?"

"It means hitting a single, double, triple, and home run, all in one game. It doesn't happen very often."

"Really? I'm glad you saw it." She rubbed his light brown hair. "During work on Friday, I heard the bank officers talking about a website on the internet filled with all kinds of baseball statistics. Why don't you get online and look it up? Let me know how many players have 'hit for the cycle' this year."

"O.K., but after the game. I want to tell the guys at baseball camp tomorrow about this."

Lisa Burns nursed the battered Ford Escort eastward

along Mt. Faith Road, the four-lane street connecting downtown Mt. Carmel with HW 69. On her right, the south side of the thoroughfare passed well-kept neighborhoods nestling young, upward-bound families behind tall wood fences. To her left, wood frame farm homes stood proudly on wooded, ten-acre plots. Her destination lay further up the road, where the glaring afternoon sun shimmered on the rectangular steel roofs of a nondescript mobile home park nestled on the gentle slope of Northend Hill.

At the corner of Mt. Faith Road and Northend Drive the dark-haired, twenty-four-year-old turned from the pavement to the rutted, gravel road. A white cloud of dust boiled from beneath the wheels. The open windows gulped the swirling grit and brought a cough of protest from her daughter, Courtney, strapped in the car seat.

Lisa spoke in baby-talk to the black-haired one-year-old, "We'll be home in a minute, sweetie-pie. I'm glad you helped me get some groceries. We'll make something good from these damaged cans. The stuff inside is still good for my babies."

The Escort stopped with a cough of blue smoke. Though Trailer #6 in the Country Estates Village offered a small two-bedroom, furnished address for the young family, Lisa hated the blue-green tin can from day one.

"Hi, Momma! Need some help?" Kendra called from the porch of the neighboring trailer. She waved good-bye to the older woman who had been watching her while Lisa ran errands and scampered across the bare, weed-filled yard, skipping with all the enthusiasm of an eight-year-old. She grabbed a grocery bag while Lisa lifted the baby from the car seat. "Did you find me a new lunch box?"

"No, honey. I didn't even look. We just can't afford one right now. But when Dad sells a bunch of cars we'll have money to let you pick out any one you want. Besides, it's still three weeks before school starts. We've got a lot of time to buy school supplies."

Together they walked into the house and closed the door against the blistering heat. Lisa dabbed the sweat from her neck, then stored the groceries. Occasionally, she glanced out the front window to look for Cody. He had left her asleep long before dawn to fish with his uncle. When he came back, she wanted to finally tell him about the church.

She first ventured into the worship service three weeks ago. With a dry, nervous mouth she had driven the aging Ford to the big church on Mt. Faith Drive. Everything felt strange, like suddenly stepping into the climate of a foreign land. Yet, she ventured back the next Sunday, moved by a longing that welled up in her anxious heart each time she looked across the table at the bouncing girls she had borne. She grew more comfortable when the workers in the nursery commented on Courtney's bright smile.

This morning she had gained enough courage to attend the women's Sunday School class. The longing inside propelled her across the room after the final prayer. Gripping the old Bible, she stretched her petite frame tall and boldly extended her words of invitation to the pastor's wife.

Kendra interrupted her thoughts. "When is the lady from church coming?"

Lisa looked at the clock. "She and her husband had to attend a meeting tonight. Her husband is the preacher, you know. I need you to help me do some straightening up around here before they come."

"Can I show her the sun catcher we made in Sunday School today?"

"I'm sure she'd be glad to see it."

The curly-haired child skipped back to the small bedroom she shared with Courtney. Lisa retrieved a stained rag to dust the furniture. The old air conditioner whined in protest of the afternoon heat.

"With a little work, maybe our guests won't even notice this old rattletrap trailer."

After taking Jason to the youth meeting, the Peters hurried toward the downtown business district, then turned north from the courthouse square to find the address of Kent and Beth Puckett. The winding, black asphalt of Rolling Meadow Road followed the wide Spring Creek valley north from Mt. Carmel. Three miles from town, a new subdivision of solid brick homes, with soaring gables and spacious windows, nestled among the towering, straight hickory trees on the east side of Spring Creek. The pretty homes along the road caught their attention.

"We've seen lots of changes, haven't we? I guess you can't stop progress," Barry said. "Five years ago only a few Holsteins lived in the pasture at the Green's old place."

"You said on your first Sunday as pastor that big things would happen. Two weeks later the announcement about Nokuma Electronics new plant hit the news."

"Five hundred new jobs changed everything around here."

"I thought about Mr. Green just the other day." She checked her makeup in the visor mirror. "Do you remember him crying when he told you about the plant being built on the land where he and Mabel first farmed?"

"Sure. I went out with him to watch the groundbreaking. That big hoopla didn't mean progress to him."

The huge, roaring machines uprooted the majestic oak trees and tore the yellow clay while the men watched. Even as the new factory took shape, Mt. Carmel itself changed with the clang of construction. Grass-covered pastures became subdivision lawns. Franchise stores hung flashing signs next to the worn paint of family businesses. Cars with out-of-state plates and strangers with Yankee accents appeared on the streets. Civic leaders heralded the quickening pace of the small, county-seat city. In the conversations of longtime residents, however, questions quietly surfaced about the real price of change.

Barry slowed the car. A dark, red brick house with cream trim matched the address on the invitation. He parked at the curb and opened the door for Keri, taking her hand to walk across the fresh-cut yard. The evening sun glimmered on the leaded-glass front door, making small rainbows on her bright yellow cotton blouse and skirt.

"Hi, Pastor! How are you, Keri?" Kent, a tall man whose salt and pepper beard gave a professorial appearance, shook Barry's hand vigorously. He led them quickly across the tile-floored entry. "The Peters are here."

Beth, a tall, dark-haired woman of Italian descent, waved from the kitchen. "Come on in, Keri. You can help me with the ice for the drinks."

Several ladies stood in the commodious kitchen and breakfast nook, chatting and sampling the snacks. Though Beth and Kent had only been members for a year, they had become friends with many of the middle-aged couples. Keri placed her cake on the marble counter and greeted the circle of women.

Beth handed her a bucket of crushed ice. "How did your afternoon go?"

"I got a short nap, then chatted with a friend on the phone. What about you?"

"Busy! Kent inspected the house ten times to make sure everything looked just right. That's an engineer for you. I don't know why he feels so nervous. But at least he helped. You know how men can be."

In the wood-floored great room, a dozen men gathered near the towering rock fireplace. Their stiff, guarded conversation gladly welcomed a distraction when Kent escorted Barry into the room.

"Pastor, you've got a night off!" The good-natured remark burst from Lance Adkins before Kent could say a word of introduction. The stocky, heavy-bearded man wrapped the Pastor in a ferocious bear hug. A new Christian, Lance professed faith only a year ago, after months of personal struggle and counseling.

"And now I have to spend it with the worst sinners in town!" The pastor raised a hoot of laughter from the men. "I'm going to talk to the Personnel Committee about combat pay." He stepped around the wide room, shaking hands. Slowly the men relaxed, finding common ground to explore in their conversations.

Kent eventually glanced at his watch. "Guys, if we don't have some prayer time, we'll never get to eat the goodies the ladies stirred up for tonight."

After gathering chairs from the dining room, Kent gathered the entire group in a large circle around the family room. Lance sat with his wife, Jean, near the patio windows. Five years ago the energetic couple took a risk, purchased a failing retail store, filled it with innovative products, and watched sales skyrocket. Their schedule bulged with events, but somehow they always squeezed out a few minutes to help when church needs arose.

Across the room sat Joan Ensign, in her 30's, divorced for about a year. Her lined face and the sadness in her dark brown eyes revealed more pain than she would ever admit. Only Beth's insistent invitation coaxed her into joining the gathering tonight.

Brian and Julie Lowe occupied the chairs to Joan's right.

They had joined Mt. Faith Church more than thirty years ago. In his 50's now, Brian ran Central Middle School like a business and used the same skills in the programs at the church. Julie, a petite woman with wire glasses, had a community-wide reputation for her strong soprano voice.

Next to the Lowes sat Phil and Paulette Powell. Phil sat with his arms crossed tightly across his chest, hoping the beeper on his belt would deliver him back to the hospital pharmacy. His Sunday workload provided a perennial excuse for not attending church. Paulette wanted desperately to make this second marriage work. Her daughter, Mandy, would be married this next weekend by Brother Barry. She hoped Mandy would find a happier marriage than her own had been.

Liz Emory gripped a glass of ice tea while she waited for the meeting to begin. She started working at the church office only ten months ago. Middle-aged and reserved, with large glasses that gave an owlish appearance, she remained a bit of an outsider at the office in spite of her impressive skills in data processing. The church staff knew little more about her past, except that she had never married. Her reluctant participation in the banter among the ladies in the kitchen conveyed the distinct impression she wanted desperately to keep to herself during the sharing tonight.

"I'm pleased that you've come and hope you can meet a new friend tonight." Kent's words garnered the attention of the group. After sharing a reading from the Gospel of John, he rehearsed the instructions provided for each home prayer group meeting. "Getting to know one another assumes a high priority on our agenda this evening, but we also know prayer is at the heart of Mt. Faith Church." He gestured toward Barry. "The pastor has taught us that our experience with God should be intimate, like knowing a best friend. We don't want to pray in fancy words or long-winded speech, but in a personal conversation. Everyone should feel free to join in–whenever you want to–or just listen to others."

Heads bowed around the circle. Joan spoke first, then Lance. Julie mentioned a brother in the middle of a messy divorce. Beth quoted a Scripture. Then silence fell. Their prayers seemed stuck in quicksand. The silence stretched on and on.

Only Kent plunged toward spiritual depths. His first prayer lasted only a few moments, yet overflowed with a passion for God. A few minutes later, after Brian and Paulette had taken a turn, Kent began to pray again. For a moment his voice sounded normal. Then his tone changed, marked with inner pain. "Oh, Father," he groaned. The emotional tone of the room grew more intense, with every heart curious about the powerful disturbance in the soul of their host. Beth snuggled closer to her struggling husband.

"Deliver me from my enemies, O God! Protect me from those who rise up against me. Deliver me from evildoers and save me from bloodthirsty men!"

The praying circle waited, hardly drawing a breath. Barry wondered if the words came from the Psalms. He tried to remember whether Kent had mentioned anything about problems at work. Since he had recently received a promotion, perhaps his anguish stemmed from the threat of some jealous associate.

Kent's voice sounded once more, detached and impersonal.

"See how they lie in wait for me! Fierce men conspire against me for no offense or sin of mine, O Lord! O my God, I watch for you. You are my fortress, my loving God."

Beth's hand stroked his back, trying to calm the shivering muscles. The chairs rustled as Lance slipped across the room to kneel in front of the anguished man. Placing his hands on Kent's shoulders, he prayed, "Lord, I want to pray for my brother as he struggles tonight. It's hard when we face enemies. We don't understand why these attackers come against us. Just help him, Lord, and keep . . . "

"Lance, wait. Wait just a minute." Kent held up a shaky hand in correction. "Those words weren't for me."

Every eye riveted on the bearded man. A dark shadow of concern crossed his face.

"As I prayed, I could see a man under attack. I saw vicious-looking men, several of them, all in black, closing in around this guy. He seemed unaware of the danger I could see so clearly. They stalked him, then leapt to attack. I shouted to warn him. I guess that's when I blurted out what you heard."

"You must have been terrified when they attacked you," Lance said.

"No. You don't understand. I wasn't the one assaulted." He hesitated, struggling for words. He looked down, then at Beth, then down again. Finally he gazed around the silent room. His hand lifted slowly to point at the pastor.

"Barry, you were the target of the attack. The Lord intends my words of warning for you!"

Daemon stood in the busy entryway, alert to each farewell handshake and hug of the departing guests. They had lingered long to discuss the unexpected topic of the evening. From their words, he could tell his surprise announcement had struck a responsive chord. A thin smile of success brightened his face.

The towering frame of Ed Loomis paused in the doorway. "You know, I've invested years in this church," he said to Daemon. "Doris and I stood at the site when the church broke ground for the sanctuary years ago. Now we enjoy sitting with

Jim and Sandi and Jenni," he added, naming his son, daughter-in-law, and granddaughter. "I sure don't want anything to disrupt God's work."

"That's my concern, too, Ed."

"I've never opposed growth and change. Couldn't have made the furniture store successful with that attitude, you know? But what you've said piques my interest. When you have some time this week, come by the office. I want to ask you a few things."

Daemon nodded and reached out to shake his hand. "I'll give you a call."

Harvey and Edith Flowers made their way to the door. Edith spoke to Sid and Claire about the nice arrangements for the evening, giving the stooped, white-haired, retired carpenter a moment to pull Daemon close.

"Daemon, your report tonight bothered me. The way I see it, no one is perfect. I'm certainly not. And after all my years on the church board, I don't expect the preacher to be perfect, either."

Daemon frowned. Harvey's gentle presence still influenced even the young families of the church. He measured his words. "I only wanted people to understand some of the disturbing events happening at our church, Harvey. We've had a lot of people come and go over the years. It's up to the older members to see things that the new ones miss. I'm not bragging, but you and I have served at Mt. Faith for nearly more years than Barry has been alive. That's important."

"But what you described tonight involved much more than a church program. The things you said about Pastor Barry and Keri, well, I'd call it character assassination. I don't like that. We need to respect the pastor God called to serve His church."

"I merely told the truth. Some people may want to sweep it under the carpet. But we can't ignore the facts. I figured out long ago that the best way to solve a problem is to bring it out in the open."

The men fell silent when Edith approached. Harvey pushed open the door to let her step out, then turned around. The warm evening breeze filled the entry hall. He locked his eyes on the slender man.

"I've learned something over the years, too, Daemon. Don't try to harm God's anointed."

The door closed behind in Daemon's face before he could reply. Stupid old man. He turned on his heel and marched to the kitchen.

Claire stood at the counter, pulling plastic wrap around a plate of cheese. "I thought the evening went well, didn't you, Daemon?"

"Just like I'd hoped. The truth shocks some people. But we cannot stand still. I feel the eyes of the church must be opened, no matter the cost. This evening will plant an idea we can reap later."

"But what about Harvey?" Sid sat down at the counter. "What did he mean by that last comment, 'Don't harm God's anointed?'"

"I think there's a story in the Old Testament about a prophet that says something like that," Nadine said.

Daemon shrugged. "I'll need to look up the quote. Frankly, it seems a trivial thought. The future of the church rests on what we do in the next few weeks."

Sid sneered. "I don't know how much anointing our pastor has anyway!"

Claire's small hand held up a yellow, letter size envelope. "Should I get this ready for tomorrow?"

Daemon's thin smile returned. "Yes, indeed. We can't stop now."

"For me?" Barry's heart pounded with the question.

Every head turned toward him. He tried to smile, but his lips would not obey the impulse. He felt Keri's hand on his, and the grip steadied him. He exhaled slowly.

"What do you think it means?" Phil's eyes stretched wide with excitement.

Kent shook his head. "I'm not sure. I didn't recognize any specific faces. Sometimes these visions are, well, sort of vague."

"I've got chills. This feels too spooky for me," Jill said, rubbing her arms.

"But we can't ignore it," Phil said.

"I agree with Phil." Lance drummed his fingers on his leg in double time. "We may not understand it, but I think we're stupid if we don't pay attention."

Brian pulled a pen from his pocket. "I think we should keep our eyes and ears open to anything suspicious. If we notice something out of order, we can immediately call Barry. Maybe we should meet again next Sunday to follow up with prayer."

"I especially like the part about further prayer," Kent said.

"You think this is for real, then?"

Lance set his mouth in a firm line. "Phil, I think all of us hope nothing happens. But I know Kent, and I think the Lord has worked tonight in this mysterious way to help Barry. Yes, it's real."

Barry felt a quiver inside, a tremor of fear that threatened to bring a shiver down his back that everyone could see. He took a deep breath again to steady his nerves.

"I appreciate the comments each of you shared. Believe me, I take this seriously. Let's all keep our eyes open. But let's also keep this to ourselves for now. There's no need to stir up the church over something we don't fully understand."

Heads nodded around the circle. Kent fixed his gray eyes on Barry. "Let's close by praying for the Lord's protection, Pastor. You and Keri come kneel here in the middle of the circle.

Each of us can touch you and pray for you."

"I appreciate that." He stood and helped Keri to the middle of the room. They knelt side by side, leaning on a chair, while the others crowded near to pray once again.

One hour later, the Peters arrived at trailer #6. During the quiet ride across town, Barry reflected on the perplexing vision. Keri rode in silence, too, only once venturing a quiet "I love you," when Barry squeezed her hand.

"This looks like the place," he said, eyeing the old trailer. The lengthening shadows of the twilight magnified its poor state of repair.

They mounted the creaking wood steps without enthusiasm. Keri forced the troubling prayer time from her mind and pasted on a smile.

Lisa answered the door. "Hi, Keri. Won't you come in?" Her long black hair hung in a single pony tail. A plain, red t-shirt and jean shorts complemented her pale skin. Kendra stood nearby, back from the door, holding the baby on one hip.

"Thank you. I guess you recognize Barry."

Barry shook her hand. "It's good to meet you. Thanks for the invitation to come by."

"These must be your children," Keri said. She stepped close to Kendra while Lisa introduced the girls. Courtney wriggled in Kendra's arms, grasping her sister's blouse, unsure about the strangers.

"Let's sit around the kitchen table." Lisa pulled the chrome and yellow vinyl kitchen chairs near the table and gestured for them to sit down. "Could I get you some iced tea to drink? The old air conditioner doesn't keep it cool enough in here without something cold in your hand."

With their agreement, she cracked some ice from the freezer trays and poured large glasses of tea. "This broken-down trailer isn't much of a place to have guests. We lived in a pretty, brown frame house on Hickory Street when Cody lost his job. Now that he's working again, I hope we'll be back on our feet in a few months."

Keri glanced around the trailer. The worn counter top, the cracked window in the living room, and the stained carpet gave signs of too many renters and too little maintenance across the decades. "I'm glad you came to my class, Lisa."

"You're a good teacher. I need to let you know that Cody and I haven't gone to church much. He's not interested at all. But I know the girls need to learn something about God."

"That's important," Barry said.

"Pastor, that's one reason I invited you over tonight. I wanted you to speak with Kendra. My aunt in Pine City attends church all the time. She talked to Kendra about being baptized. Now that we've started attending your church, I think she might be ready to do just that."

Barry winced inside. He loved kids and liked to talk with them about faith. But the work became harder when Mom put them on the spot. He looked at the smiling youngster. "Would you like to talk?"

Seeing her eager nod and bright eyes, he turned back to Lisa. "Why don't you and Keri visit a few minutes, and I'll sit with Kendra on the couch? We can talk better that way."

"Let me hold the baby," Keri said.

Kendra handed over her wide-eyed sister and walked across the small room. Sitting down on the creaky couch, Barry looked at the slightly built eight-year-old.

"Your mom says you've been thinking about some very important things. Would you tell me what they are?"

"In Sunday School we drew a picture of Jesus on the

cross. It made me cry."

"Why?"

"Because he died."

"Do you know why He died on the cross?" From experience he made his questions open-ended, allowing Kendra to frame her own answers.

"He died because people had done bad things. Jesus loved us and didn't want us to be hurt by the bad things we did. He died to save people so they could be friends with God."

"Have you done any bad things, Kendra?"

"I've told Mommy lies. But I told Jesus I was sorry. And I asked him to help me."

Her youthful understanding took him by surprise. He set aside his earlier concerns and opened the pages of a small New Testament. Finally, he took her hand and listened to her whispered prayer—the quiet, precious words of a child talking to someone who loved her. He had always possessed the conviction that God had no interest in making religion a conundrum for the intellectual. Instead, the Bible made clear that simple trust in Christ opens a new relationship to God. Even a child could understand this wonderful story of love.

When they finished, Barry caught Lisa's eye. She hurried to join them on the couch to hear the report.

"I think something real happened with Kendra. You want to tell your Mom about it, honey?"

Kendra jumped into her mother's lap, leaned close and whispered, "I asked Jesus into my heart."

"I'm proud of you," Lisa said, squeezing her tightly.

"Maybe you could be baptized next Sunday," the pastor said. "We like for all the family to come to the worship service when someone is baptized."

Lisa's frown showed a shadow of concern. "We can talk about it when Cody gets home. Like I said, we haven't gone to church very much."

"That will work just fine. I'll have my secretary call later this week."

"I want to, Mommy," Kendra said in a strong voice.

"O.K. We'll talk with Daddy about it."

"Why don't we have a final prayer together? Come on, let's all hold hands," Barry gestured, and they linked hands in a tight circle.

When they left the trailer, the heavy night air surrounded them. Once in the car, Keri leaned over and kissed Barry on the cheek. "Now aren't you glad that exhibition football game could wait a while?"

"I hate to say it, but you called this one right. And we didn't see a single bloodthirsty man chasing me!" He took her hand. "Talk about a weird evening. I don't understand all this stuff."

"Do you think Kent may know more about what his vision meant?"

"He might. I'll try to talk with him more this week. I need to think about it more myself." He changed the subject. "Call Jason on the cell phone, and see if he's home from the youth meeting. We might go out for some ice cream. But let's not mention this vision thing to him."

The ringing of the phone brought Daemon out of his chair. He turned the volume of the television news down.

"Hello?"

"I thought you needed to know about something unusual that happened tonight," a woman said in a quiet voice.

"What?"

"The Pastor received a strange message tonight at the

prayer meeting."

"What does that mean?"

"Do you know Kent Puckett?"

"Not really. Is he one of the new people that joined last year?"

"Yes. I guess he brought some funny ideas from the west coast." The caller continued, describing the prayer session and the mysterious warning. Barry seemed shaken, the messenger concluded.

"I've never heard of such a thing happening in our church before. Keep me informed if you hear anything more about this. Thanks for calling." He sat quietly with the phone in his hand for several minutes.

"Who called?" Nadine looked up from the newspaper when he returned to his chair in the family room.

"A spy coming in from the cold." He leaned back in the recliner and reviewed the story. "I don't think the news of such craziness will hurt our plan for this week in the slightest."

"We've worried about the strange beliefs those new families sneak into the church, haven't we?"

He picked up the newspaper, then paused and looked at her with a gleam in his eyes. "I'll tell you what that report does for me. It confirms that Barry has opened the door for big problems in our church. Maybe God brought a message of warning for all of us tonight about his dangerous ideas and attitudes. I don't think our plan has come to fruit a moment too soon."

The hills of Mt. Carmel lay under the dark velvet of the Ozark sky. Barry fluffed his pillow for the twentieth time. He listened to Keri's soft breathing and felt the warmth of her back against his arm. Sleep seemed exiled by the whirl of Sunday's events.

> " *Deliver me from my enemies, O God;*
> > *protect me from those who rise up against me.*
> *Deliver me from evildoers*
> > *and save me from bloodthirsty men!* "

What did Kent's words mean? Did the threat come from within the church, or could some terrible event be looming just ahead? He could feel the panic that had touched him during the group prayer dancing again in the pit of his stomach.

He stretched out his hand to wake Keri and talk all this over with her. *She stayed near me tonight, like a bodyguard, when the people prayed around us. She would be willing to listen now.* He hesitated. *No, let her sleep in peace. She doesn't need a restless night over my worries.*

An hour later he rolled from the bed and walked slowly through the house. Moonlight streamed through the patio windows and fell in silver waves across the darkened family room. The quiet moment promised peace, but his heart remained restless.

Six years. He marked the statistic like a cipher on a pine fence during a sandlot baseball game. *The drumbeat of change has never stopped. I've watched the longtime members clinging to the church as a refuge of constancy, while the new families follow different priorities. They want new ways of worship, more programs for the children, and intimacy with one another. I'm like a baseball coach who can't get his players to work together as a team.*

Thunk. A loud noise from Jason's room pulled him to his feet. He hurried down the hall and turned the corner to the bedroom. A baseball bat lay on the floor near the bed where it had fallen loudly against the oak flooring. Barry calmed himself at the simple explanation, replaced the bat in its corner, and backed out of the room. I'm glad bloodthirsty men didn't cause that noise.

He soundlessly opened the back door and stepped onto the patio. A gentle breeze rustled across his bare legs. The bright face of the moon filled the silent backyard with pale light. Scanning the nightscape, he could see some things clearly, yet most lay shrouded in darkness.

That's how I feel right now. I can't see it all yet.

With a sigh, he crossed his arms. It seemed that the Lord had allowed this strange vision tonight. But what could be hidden just around the next corner?

Chapter 2
"Monday"

"Mom, have you seen that arrowhead I found at the river last week?"

Jason's urgent request caught Keri hurrying through the kitchen on the way to work.

"Try looking on the table in the entryway." She ruffled his hair. "Dad will take you to camp. I love you."

Jason dropped his spoon in the bowl of breakfast cereal and bolted to follow her directions. The prize lay exactly where she predicted. Returning to the kitchen, he held the black, pointed stone in the golden rays of sunshine. The sharp edges notched in his mind images of bronze-skinned native warriors hunting in the Ozark Mountains. For a millennium, the woods and deep valleys, honeycombed with caves, had sheltered nomadic Osage Indians. With bow and arrow they had ruled a far-flung empire of verdant hills, mountain springs, and plentiful game in the southern center of the continent. In his hand he held evidence of their long-lost culture.

Barry laid the morning newspaper on the counter. He glanced at the twelve-year-old's prize. "Find something special?"

"It's an arrowhead I found when I went canoeing with Shaun. We stopped at a little rock beach near Six Mile Bridge. I found it under a bush."

"Maybe we can go to the museum in Joplin and see if

they have others like it."

"That would be cool!" He ran his finger across the sharp point. "Dad, did the Indians go to church? I asked Shaun's dad, but he didn't know."

"No. At least they didn't attend a church like ours. The Osage worshiped a nature god named Wah'Kon-Tah. They believed he ruled the sun, wind, and lightening. The warriors met in wooden lodge buildings to worship."

"When did the settlers get here?"

Barry poured cereal in a bowl. "About two hundred years ago. The Indians still lived here then, and the pioneers called the region 'Six Boils,' imitating the Indian word for river. They liked Spring River and started the town of Mt. Carmel in 1824."

Months ago, Barry researched the history of the city for an anniversary sermon. His findings brought new appreciation for the pioneers who poured into the Ozarks during the turbulent years after the Civil War. They brought steam-powered machines to rip open the rocky hills, exposing the 'jack,' and hauled the mineral, sparkling with glint and promise, to the sunshine. Miners, hard as the rock they moved, built smelters that changed the black ore to pure lead and iron. The music of their drills drew wagonloads of new residents. In those early dirt-street settlements, clapboard churches sprang up to tell the story of a new God. The Indians and their deity disappeared, swept away from the gentle Missouri hills by the flood of Christian settlers.

"Did our church start back then?"

"Mt. Faith didn't get started for many years. They held a service on January 1, 1950, the first Sunday of the second half of the twentieth century. A little group of eighteen believers met for Bible study in a house on Sycamore Street."

Between bites of cereal, Barry reflected on the stories he

had read. The church weathered the hard years of too many leaders and too little money to eventually construct a solid foundation for the future. The visionary people sacrificed in the 1960's to buy property at the bend of North Carmel Road, one-half mile from the state highway. The first small building housed days of success and setback. Finally, a burst of vision and growth blossomed under the caring hands of Pastor Earnest Wright. On Easter Sunday, 1975, the proud builders held the first service in a new sanctuary, reaching hands across the pews to symbolize their unity.

Barry glanced at his watch. "Come on, slugger. Time to get you to baseball camp."

The trip to Mt. Carmel High School passed through the Square. The city had grown around the four-story rose granite courthouse which stood in the center of the Square. Completed in 1891, the ornate building still housed county workers and judicial offices. Towering maple and oak trees encircled the broad lawn and the prominent display of artillery pieces that had defended America in three different wars. One-way streets surrounded the courthouse property, swinging the traffic in a vehicular promenade through the business district.

On all four sides of the Square, Barry saw the businesses opening their doors for the new week. The Green Door restaurant, McGinty's Men's Store, The Lux Movie Theater, and Henderson's Hardware anchored the four intersections, flanked by other retailers. Every store front was occupied, a barometer of the recent prosperity. Making the circuit around the courthouse, they headed south two blocks to the gray brick high school that hosted the week-long baseball camp. Jason waved once and jogged toward the ball field.

Ten minutes later, the pastor wheeled into his space near the entrance of the church office. The unmarred blue bowl of the sky permitted a full dose of morning sun to pour down on his shoulders. His watch read nine o'clock. Keri should be finished with her officers' meeting at the bank, and Jason should be catching fly balls. Now came Barry's turn to report for duty.

With forty-five years of ministry behind her, the substantial congregation meeting at 2047 North Carmel Road garnered the polite envy of many churches in Mt. Carmel. Each Sunday more than 400 well-dressed stalwarts from the middle and upper echelon of the city gathered for worship and socializing. The massive, three-story stone building anchoring their witness dominated the bend of the wide thoroughfare, providing a landmark for busy lives cruising to a thousand destinations.

When he opened the door, Barry stepped on a yellow extension cord snaking across the multicolored blue carpet of the atrium. Mike Mitchum stood behind the kneeling form of a custodian, watching the repair work underway on a damaged wall.

"Morning, guys. Do we have a problem?"

Mike shook his head. "Looks like one of the junior saints let one of the table racks get out of hand. The kids helped put up equipment after their home fellowship last night. The rack gouged a hole in the wall. Billy and I just started repairing it."

"Everything else O.K.?"

"Haven't had time to check on much else."

Mike carried the responsibility for Christian education and church administration. He could no more have let the defaced wall go than he could have ignored a doughnut in the break room. Short and round, his glasses perpetually low on his nose, he thrived on fixing one problem or another.

"Thanks for taking care of it." He stepped past the workers toward the open door of the church office.

"Good morning, Pastor." Mary Butler sat at the reception desk. Her slender face held a perpetual smile. "How are you this morning? I appreciated your message yesterday."

"Thank you. I'm doing fine. I've got some business for you. Would you contact Lisa Burns about arrangements to baptize her daughter next Sunday? They live in the Country Estates Mobile Home Park. Her daughter, Kendra, talked to me last night."

"Do you want her to meet the baptism hostess before the service next Sunday?"

"Yes. Also, call Donna Galloway about her Sunday School class helping the family. It looked like they could use some groceries."

"I'll get right on that. I'm glad you had such a good visit."

Barry stepped past her desk into the main office. The office suite lagged behind the growth that had lifted Mt. Faith from three hundred to four hundred in attendance since Barry took the helm. A large central area housed three secretarial cubicles, separated by gray, five-foot tall dividers. In each corner of the large room a door led to the office of a minister. While the stately stone of the sanctuary exterior created an impression of tasteful elegance, the offices conveyed a different philosophy. Mt. Faith headquarters displayed discount furniture and religious pictures chosen by a decorating committee several years ago. Functionality marked the area, signaling that luxury might offer a temptation to the flesh.

Liz Emory sat at the black metal and chrome desk in her cubicle, shuffling scattered pages of attendance reports. She looked up from the computer to offer a brief smile when Barry spoke.

"Good morning. Glad you made it to the Puckett's last night," he said, stopping at her desk.

"They have a beautiful house."

"Keri coveted their kitchen, I think. I probably need to

make her confess that sin, you know."

Liz only smiled and kept adding up the figures. As if by mutual agreement, neither commented on the strange events of the previous evening.

From one corner of the large room the repetitive thump of soft rock music boomed. Brent Burroughs, Mt. Faith's worship leader, stuck his head around the door and caught Barry's eye. "Mary signaled me that you'd come in. Do you have time later to look at this wireless intercom?"

"Sure. I'll get with you before lunch."

Brent signed on five years ago, the first minister to join the staff under Barry's administration. The two ministers forged a close bond through the crucible of change in worship style. Barry enjoyed the idiosyncrasies of the bald-headed young man, recognizing him as a great motivator with a fun-loving spirit. Church members flocked to his lively choir practices, which explained why the music program of the church always featured talented people. Barry sometimes admitted the music, not his preaching, brought the larger crowds to worship.

The pastor considered the prospect of a wireless intercom. *I'm sure that's what every preacher needs, so some sound technician can sneeze and break my train of thought at the height of the sermon! I'm not sure I would call that progress.*

In the cubicle nearest the pastor's own door, Lauren Reed looked up from her calendar preparation.

"Morning, Brother Barry," she said.

"How's everything going this morning?"

"No warning lights yet—but it's not even 9:30!" Lauren occupied the position of Pastor's Secretary. Barry knew her loyalty, combined with a sixth sense for spotting potential difficulties, made her invaluable. Her leadership skills had been honed as co-captain for the University of Western Missouri volleyball team. Now her talents brought a gentle authority to the church office. One day a furious member stormed into the office, demanding to see the preacher. Lauren simply stood near the man and stared down from her 6' 3" height until he took a seat. By the time Barry came out of the office, the subdued man had reconsidered his attitude!

"Maybe this week will bring smooth sailing for us all," Barry said.

"I hope so. Here's a calendar for the week."

"Thanks. Keep folks out of my office for a while, would you?"

"Yes, sir."

Stepping into his book-lined office, he pulled the door closed, laid the calendar page on the dark pine desk, and opened the drapes. For the next half-hour he would put the demands of the job in a higher perspective. Opening his prayer journal, a Bible, and a book of meditations, he began to read. Alternately reading, praying and writing, he sought to clear the Monday morning spiritual fog with the refreshing presence of God.

The heavy oak door pulled open easily, bringing a surge of scented air from the fifth floor conference room directly into Keri's face. She inhaled the seductive aroma, a mingling of leather from the deep chairs, varnish from the expensive wood, and cologne from well-dressed men. Sometimes it seemed powerful enough to induce dreams of great deeds and grand plans. The scent had captured her attention from the time she stepped in the room on the new employees' orientation tour five years ago.

She waved a hand in greeting to the executive team members already seated. An older man turned her way.

"Good morning, E.C. How are you today?"

The gray-suited attorney hardly smiled. "I'm afraid this

won't be a banner day at Security."

She settled in one of the twelve black leather chairs circling the table and glanced toward the expansive windows to smooth her golden hair in the reflection. What did he mean by that?

The executive leaned closer. "Wait till Ledbetter gets here."

She nodded. Since her January appointment as assistant vice-president for Community Services, he had often taken time to clue her in to the inner workings of the bank.

"How did church services go yesterday?" Sterling O'Brien, director of the mortgage department, interrupted her. His carefully cultivated red mustache bounced when he talked.

"It was a good day. We had special prayer meetings in homes last night. I think Barry felt glad to have the extra duties behind him this morning."

"He's busy every day, I'm sure."

The Peters had prayed at length over Keri's career moves. The church salary, while solidly middle class, never seemed enough to support all they wanted to do. A hidden cost, however, had surfaced with the disapproving comments of the older members. They saw the place of a pastor's wife firmly fixed in the church parlor leading mission studies, rather than in the boardroom of the bank.

"Hi, Merylene," Keri said to the president's secretary when the slender woman arrived. "What's on the agenda today?"

Before Merylene could reply, the door burst open with the entrance of Jack Ledbetter, striding toward the head of the walnut conference table. He slapped a bulging folder down on the polished surface and leaned forward, hands on the table, to confront his employees.

"I'll get right to the point," the stocky president said. "Keller confirmed to me a few minutes ago what your senior management has suspected for weeks. Today an out-of-town lawyer will go public with the accusation that our bank is neglecting the Vietnamese population in Mt. Carmel. That means only one thing, ladies and gentlemen: we've got a problem! Let's nail down a plan to handle this mess."

Concern furrowed the man's broad face. Two decades before, he had launched his banking career at the century-old Community Bank downtown, but the arena soon proved too small for a man with his dreams. After a stint with a large Kansas City institution, he seized the opportunity to return to southwest Missouri and run Security. His aggressive drive pushed every employee to the limit. Market research showed they nipped at the heels of his rival last quarter.

"Who's behind this deal?" Jim Johnson, a narrow-eyed trust division V-P, shot the question across the table.

Ledbetter gestured to the graying man who sat on his right. E. C. Keller controlled the legal department with exacting skill. He gathered his notes, pursed his lips, and answered with measured tones.

"Mr. Nha Van Dang leads the Vietnamese Citizens League."

"The group based in St. Louis?"

"That's correct. They've retained a St. Louis firm, Walpole and Smith, to work for them. Junior attorneys have been prowling around the courthouse and the east side of town for two weeks, collecting information on the situation."

"I suppose they plan to call a press conference?"

"A sucking circus is what we'll really see," Ledbetter said, leaning back in the chair. "We understand their announcement will come from the Eastside Community Center. They'll point out plenty of rundown houses and old cars for the cameras, showing how our bank has failed to help the Vietnamese community. The reporters will love every tear-jerking moment."

Keri nodded. "They've actually chosen a great time for this stunt. This weekend marks the beginning of the Marian Days Celebration in Carthage."

"What's that got to do with it?" Johnson's voice sounded sharp.

"Every August, thousands of Vietnamese hold an ethnic reunion there. The Celebration is organized by the Catholic priests who fled from Vietnam in 1975. They established a Vietnamese seminary and a church called the Church of the Mother Co-Redemptrix." Turning to level a glance at Johnson, she continued, "For years, former immigrants and their families from all over the nation have filled the city for this celebration. Last year the count hit 40,000 for the weekend."

Ledbetter gave a low whistle. "Mrs. Peters' information shows us how carefully we must treat this keg of dynamite." He walked slowly toward the table and gripped the back of his chair. Every eye followed him. "This bank has made a run for the roses in the last five years. I refuse to allow a half-baked pressure group to stop us now. We're not going to play dead while a bunch of St. Louis lawyers slaps us with a label we don't deserve."

"Mr. Ledbetter, maybe the Viets shouldn't be the only ones on the east side this afternoon," Keri said.

"What do you suggest?"

"I have some friends who might be willing to help us."

Fifteen minutes later she returned to the office, her mind rapidly hammering together the skeleton of a plan. Fran, her secretary, jotted down notes.

"I'll get right on it," Fran said. She returned to her workstation, settling her large frame in the chair and sliding the keyboard under her hands.

Keri glanced through the phone messages the secretary

had collected. David's number appeared on the list with the note "Personal business." She pursed her lips with concern. *I hope he hasn't heard Morgan's voice again or something worse.*

Before she could return any calls, the intercom buzzed. "I've got Duyen Luong on the phone," Fran said, fumbling the unfamiliar name off her tongue.

"Thank you. Put her right through." She picked up the phone and focused her attention on helping Security State Bank dodge a haymaker.

Barry pushed away from his desk with a heavy sigh. His daily habit of morning prayer usually lifted his spirit and focused his mind. Today, however, anxious thoughts manacled his soul like ropes on a hot-air balloon.

He pulled the drapes wide. The bright sunshine contrasted with the dark yoke of weariness pressing on his shoulders. Visions. Disagreements. Tragic deaths. Today the burdens of his church threatened to crush his spirit.

He looked at a fragile conch shell illuminated by golden rays on the wide windowsill. The smooth orange and white surface glistened with a beauty that drew his mind back across the years.

He had found the treasured keepsake while laboring in Puerto Rico on a mission trip. Volunteers from the University of Missouri had eagerly embraced the challenge of a week-long construction project. With enthusiastic devotion, they endured the brutally hot, backbreaking labor, making concrete blocks for simple homes. The pastor from his college church accompanied the crew. Brother Jim couldn't claim great skill as a carpenter or electrician, but with each long day, Barry's appreciation of the man grew. Like a sponge, his young soul soaked up the encouraging words and deep faith expressed by the devoted minister.

On the final day of the trip, the team drove to the glistening ocean waters of Luquillo Lagoon. With whoops of delight, Barry and his friends launched themselves into the water. Swimming and hijinks in the warm, crystal blue water washed away their weariness like a balm.

Around noon, he strolled down the beach until he finally spotted Brother Jim in the shade of towering palm trees. The pastor sat cross-legged in the sand, engaged in earnest conversation with a plump coed named Patti, who had lingered unhappily on the fringes of the group all week.

In that moment, he saw more than just two people talking. He glimpsed the heart of this leader, who had denied his own pleasure to help a needy girl. A palm-framed epiphany touched his soul, filling him with a quiet Voice. "That's what I want you to do," God directed, illuminating in a single moment the direction for his life work. He returned to the University energized, redirecting all his energy toward becoming a pastor, just like Brother Jim.

Lord, I've never doubted hearing Your call on that beautiful beach. But what about the way I feel now?

He replaced the old shell carefully on the bookcase. In contrast to the shiny shell, he felt like a billboard weathered by twenty years of stormy weather, beaten and drab under the expectations that assailed him daily.

Some members want me to shepherd each member personally, intimately acquainted with every need. But how do I do that with a thousand people on the church roll? Still others want a community giant, attending every civic club as a compass of moral guidance throughout the city. But how can that happen when so few of the business people have any connection to a personal faith? Another faction wants me to boldly denounce the ways of the world, marching in picket lines. And what about those who want an administrator who will keep the church on track like a well-oiled machine?

Reaching across his desk, he fingered a letter printed on heavy, embossed stationery. "Potter's House," the letterhead proclaimed, "A house of love for God's children. Kansas City, Missouri." More than any problem in the congregation, this letter distracted his thoughts. After six weeks of contacts and negotiations, the administrator of Potter's House had offered him a position as Director of Religious Life. His duties would require helping the children's home with fund-raising, community relations, and religious instruction—a cake walk for an experienced minister. At 5:00 p.m., he could drive home and forget the needs of that position until the next day. The weekends would be his to enjoy. Relocating in the Kansas City area promised a pleasant change from Mt. Carmel.

"Pastor, you have a call." Lauren's voice startled him. He glanced at his watch. His hour had disappeared. He reached for the phone and pushed the blinking light to hear the needs of another caller.

Claire Simpson placed the last bundle carefully in the bulging yellow envelope, licked the seal with a grimace, and sealed the flap tightly. Now, where to put it until Daemon came? She surveyed the kitchen. The small drawer by the refrigerator seemed perfect.

The ringing of the telephone drew her across the room. She recognized the nasal tones of Gloria Jenkins. Her fellow church member rushed to explain her plan to host a social next Thursday morning.

"How many people do you expect?"

"If you can come, we'll have fourteen," Gloria said. "I'd like the pastor's wife to come too, if she can. I called the bank and left a message, but she hasn't called back."

"It may be hard to get her. I've heard a lot of people say she's just too busy to return their calls. Of course, I don't know what all those people at the bank do all day anyway."

"I think she's been promoted to an officer or something," Gloria said. "So I'm sure it keeps her very busy. I did speak to her the last time I was in the bank. She looked so professional."

"Are you still banking down there?"

"Have been for thirty years. Why? You haven't heard about a run on the bank, have you?"

"No, nothing like that. But Sid and I moved our money after Keri received a promotion."

"What would Keri's promotion have to do with your banking at Security State?"

"Nothing directly, I guess. But we were just, uh, concerned, I suppose, about her being in such a position, with access to all the account balances and everything."

"You mean she looks at the bank accounts of church members?"

"She could. We just didn't want it to happen to us, too."

"Did somebody tell you such a thing happened to them?"

"I shouldn't say anything else."

"Now, Claire, I can keep a secret."

"You must promise not to repeat this. About six months ago Margie Lewis, in the other ladies' class, received a sizeable inheritance. She deposited it in her account at Security State Bank. The very next week, Keri sat down next to her at the Wednesday church dinner. Margie said Keri had never spoken ten words to her before that night. But that little blonde really turned on the charm during dinner. Margie figured she knew about the big deposit and hoped she would give a lot to the church."

"Did Keri ask her about the money?"

"No. I mean, I don't think so. But she had to know about it. Sid and I feel sure of it."

"That seems so conniving! Something ought to be done about this. Maybe the deacons need to talk about this problem."

"Daemon feels the same way. He's talked to some others who share our concern over this situation. I've never felt good about a pastor's wife who worked outside the home. She ought to be working for the good of the church, don't you think?"

"I know Mary Ellen Patrick never worked in a secular job. She attended every funeral and wedding. When my Henry died, she brought food to our house before anyone else. She helped Dr. Patrick in his ministry all the time. Keri has some good points, but I wish we still had Mary Ellen as our pastor's wife."

"Sid and I feel this new generation of pastors show more concern about keeping up their big houses than caring for people. That's why the wives work."

"I know Daemon will do what's right. He's helped the church make the right decisions for years."

Claire heard the garage door open. Sid crossed the kitchen and prowled inside the refrigerator while Claire finished with Gloria.

"Talking with another concerned church member?"

"Yes. Gloria Jenkins had a lot to say. After talking with her, I think more people may line up on our side than we thought." She opened the drawer and held up the fat envelope. "I think we're right on schedule for Daemon's special delivery."

"That's enough, Mom," Jenni Loomis said with a

grimace, her aching muscles complaining under the well-intentioned massage. She couldn't remember when her back, her feet, or her side didn't ache with the discomforts of pregnancy. Mom kept telling her the suffering would be over in just two weeks. But two short weeks to Mom sounded like 336 hours to Jenni, and that sounded like forever. She rolled over to sit on the side of the bed.

"Is that any better?" Sandi Loomis rubbed her own weary hands. The two women, one pencil-thin and the other painfully swollen, looked at each other across the rumpled bed sheets in the teenager's brightly decorated room. Blue and white Mt. Carmel High pom-poms hung over the foot board. A photo of the cheerleader squad waving from the sidelines stood on the dresser. A bulletin board above the desk held the jumbled icons of a popular teen. But the twisted bedcover thrown on the floor testified to Jenni's suffering through the long night.

"Yeah. I guess. I just hurt all the time, Mom." Jenni shook her head. "I wish I had never gotten pregnant."

Sandi chocked back the caustic words of agreement on her tongue. She wouldn't dare admit how much she shared the opinion! Jenni had no excuse for getting pregnant in this day and age. How stupid not to use something! Now the hot summer months of pregnancy had stretched long and miserable for the whole family. Her husband, Jim, and his parents, Ed and Dorothy, had retreated to the background amid the growing tension filling the home.

Jenni stood up, trying somehow to stretch her tummy larger than the active baby boy jostling within her. She waddled with unsteady steps toward the kitchen. "Do you have any juice?"

"I just made some this morning. You need to take these vitamins, too."

Jenni eased onto a bar stool while her mom silently counted out the pills and poured a glass of apple juice. She pulled the ill-fitting maternity shorts down from her abdomen to ease the pressure.

"Do you remember the last weeks of your pregnancies? Did you feel like this?" She flipped the pages of a baby magazine. The well-worn pages showed her interest, especially the crinkled section with an article entitled, "Taking care of Junior: the first seven days at home."

"I don't guess I remember very much about those last two weeks. I know I couldn't wait to deliver. But I felt nervous, too. Your Grandma came to help me a week before you were born. What a mistake! We fought every day."

"Did you ever feel afraid that something would, like, happen? You know, to the baby or something?" Jenni's words stumbled with the fresh images of a haunting dream on her mind, a nightmare bringing slow-motion visions of herself on a white-sheeted bed, weeping in anguish, holding a dead child.

"Jenni, just stop talking like that." Sandi turned from the sink to look directly at her child. "Nothing's going to happen. You've filled your head with fears that don't make sense. You're O.K. The doctor says the baby is O.K. Leave it at that!"

"You've never understood how I feel! I've tried to be good with this pregnancy, but you've never forgiven me. You're still angry, and Dad is too. Like you never made a mistake in your whole life?"

"Don't shout at me! I didn't get pregnant by a high school jock. We've tried to help you through this stupid mistake." She shook her finger in Jenni's face. "We could have thrown you out or made you get an abortion. But we didn't."

"So, I guess I'm the problem!" She heaved herself from the barstool and threw the magazine across the room. "Nobody cares about me!" Covering her face, the teen bolted toward her bedroom.

"Jenni!"

The bedroom door slammed with wall-rattling vengeance. The teen threw herself across the bed, tears rolling untended down her cheeks. When would this nightmare be over? The baby gave a swift kick to her ribs, as if to add to her misery.

"Oh God," she sobbed, "please hear me. Please!" Awash in pity, she prayed the same words again and again in a chant of lament.

"Ready?"

Brent held out a small package of wires connected to a pocket-sized, black plastic case, turning it over so Barry could inspect it. They stood together in the Sanctuary, bathed in the deep-blue light of the towering stained glass windows. The dark pews still held a few programs from yesterday's services, scattered across the seats as if by a gust of wind. The lingering scent of reverence from many years of worship, seemed to pervade the quiet room. "We actually tested this yesterday during the services."

"You did? I didn't see anything."

"That's the beauty of it, pastor. No one can even tell we've got the little mic or earpiece on. But we can communicate anytime. I'm going to put a unit on the sound tech, the usher chairman, the instrumentalists and the staff."

"Sounds interesting. I guess keeping in touch during the service would help us."

"Let me show you how to wear it."

Brent slipped the small case on Barry's belt. He placed a hook-shaped, flesh-colored plastic piece over the top of Barry's ear, with the button-like end pressed into the ear canal. Then he clipped another button-sized piece, the microphone, to Barry's shirt. The absence of wires made the small pieces nearly invisible.

Walking toward the rear of the worship center, he moved a small switch on the case he wore. "Can you hear me?"

Barry touched his ear. "Hey! You're coming through clear as a bell!"

"You have to press the belt pack for the microphone to pick up your voice. Like this." He gave the case a slight squeeze.

Barry touched his own unit. "How's that sound?"

"Perfect." Brent walked to the far wall of the worship center. "It sounds like you are standing next to me."

"I think it sounds like Star Wars." The bass voice of Drew Carter, minister to students and singles, growled across the radio frequency.

Barry's eyebrows shot up in surprise. "Hey, where are you?"

"I'm sitting in my office."

"That's halfway across the church!"

Brent chimed in. "The secret is a wireless amplifier we installed in the sound booth. It picks up the transmissions then re-broadcasts them. The signals cover the entire church property."

"So, if the staff sneaks back to the Youth Center to watch a football game while I'm preaching, I can tell them to report for duty immediately?"

"You've got it, boss," Drew said.

"But what about when I'm preaching? I don't want you guys talking about touchdowns in my right ear while I'm trying to preach about the beasts of Revelation. That takes concentration."

"No problem," Brent said. "The technician at the sound booth has an on/off switch. We'll just turn off your ear piece when you start preaching." He added with a grin, "You'll never hear our cheers—or the snide comments—about your sermon."

"O.K. I like this deal. Can I get in on the fun Sunday?"

"We'll have it powered up and ready to go. Let's take the units back to the office, and I'll label each one."

"Quite a toy, preacher," Drew said from the door of his office when they arrived. "Seriously, it's about time we started using twentieth century technology in the church. We're always at least three decades behind the times."

"I know progress comes slowly. Remember when I came? We only had one computer."

"And that happened only because Mr. Redding insisted on buying it. Dr. Patrick wouldn't even touch it! He thought computers evolved from the anti-Christ new world order."

Drew had joined the staff eight years ago. He discovered that the pastor, Dr. Hiram Patrick, a patriarchal Southern gentleman, was focused on retirement. The silver-haired minister held the respect of the community through his active service on civic boards. At the church, however, benign neglect brought stagnation. During the months following Dr. Patrick's retirement, the youth minister joined many in fervent prayer for a minister with more progressive ideas. Many felt God had answered in the person of Barry.

"Barry, line 3 is for you," Mary called from the front desk.

Lauren looked up from her computer when Barry and Brent walked by her desk. "Pastor, what did you think of Drew's toy?"

"Makes me feel like Commander Kirk on the bridge of the Enterprise." He handed the intercom to Brent. "I'm not even going to ask how much it cost."

"You don't want to know."

Lauren pulled a note from her pad. "Pastor, Ryan Thompkins called to say they're running behind for the marriage counseling appointment."

"O.K. Let me know when they come in."

The blistering, afternoon sun heated the tar on Hickam Street to a soft putty, caking sticky pieces of gravel to the shoes of reporter Dominique Greer. The tall African-American woman scraped the stones loose in the grass and glanced toward the sweat-stained television crew setting up at the brown-brick Eastside Community Center.

Butch, the crew leader for the Channel 9 mobile unit, motioned for her to join him in the shade of an aging cottonwood tree near the news van. He gestured over his shoulder when she approached. "What is this Community Center?"

"It's the gathering place for the Asian community in Mt. Carmel," Dominique said, fanning her face with her notepad in an attempt to dissipate the fierce heat. "They began to move in during the late '70's, after the Vietnam War ended. Now, they're the second largest ethnic group in town."

"So what's this assignment all about?"

"A press conference. We'll shoot a statement by the leader of a Vietnamese civil rights group. I think they want to put pressure on one of the banks."

"Cool." He pointed toward a convoy of black cars cruising toward them. "Look at that, would you."

The assignment editor at Channel 9 had told her to expect a class operation. It now appeared he may have underestimated the Vietnamese Citizens League. The reporter quickly counted five cars in the procession with list prices of more than $40,000, a cost nearly double the value of the little houses nearby. When the caravan stopped, a scowling Asian man emerged and quickly opened the trunk to retrieve a lightweight podium.

She caught him before he could close the trunk. "I'm Dominique Greer, from Channel 9. I'd like to get some background information. Are you the publicist?" Without losing his frown, the black-haired man nodded. She peppered him with questions while he carried the podium to the front door of the Center.

"Now who is Nha Van Dang?" She made an effort to roll the unfamiliar syllables off her tongue properly.

"Mr. Van Dang serves as president of the Vietnamese Citizens League. For the past ten years, he has invested his distinguished career in support of Asian immigrants in Missouri. Today he plans to address the deplorable situation here in Mt. Carmel."

Dominique's pen noted, "Pres- 10 year- struggle."

The man continued. "You will need to tape all eight minutes of Mr. Van Dang's remarks. Afterward, you may speak to him for a two minute interview. I'll have a transcript of his remarks, so you can verify the facts."

Slick. Dominique countered with a question. "Does the Citizens League plan legal action against Security State?"

Before Mr. Scowling Face could reply, their attention shifted to the last black Lexus in the caravan. Four burly men in black suits had surrounded the car, facing the crowd. One opened the door while the others scanned the small crowd of curious bystanders and reporters. A taller Asian man swung his legs from the rear seat and stood to survey the neighborhood.

"Looks like we'd better get ready," Butch said. Dominique hadn't been aware of his presence at her shoulder. "Here's a mic. I've already tested it; so as soon as Mr. Big is done with his speech, grab him, and we'll roll the camera for the interview." The cameraman scrambled to place the camera on the tripod, then zoomed in close to the dark-haired man's face. Another shoulder camera, run by an Asian man from the convoy, circled in from the side.

The advance man tapped on the microphone at the podium. "Ladies and gentleman, the Vietnamese Citizens League introduces Mr. Nha Van Dang for an important statement on justice and equality in Mt. Carmel."

The handsome man with razor sharp eyes gazed with confidence across the crowd. His voice sounded smooth and measured.

"Today the citizens of Mt. Carmel will take a large step toward justice and equality, supported by the Vietnamese Citizens League. Many months ago fair-minded residents in Mt. Carmel requested our organization look at a disturbing trend. They expressed concern at a pattern of community neglect persisting for years here in Mt. Carmel. We set out to see what an impartial and unbiased examination might reveal."

"Over the past four months, a team of investigators has worked behind the scenes to investigate the charges. We found most of the residents in this fine city fair and open-minded. But our research also uncovered some startling facts. I must present this sad news to Mt. Carmel today."

The camera's viewfinder filled with the stern face of Van Dang.

"We believe the Asian citizens of Mt. Carmel suffer from neglect and misunderstanding by the officers of Security State Bank. Not a single Asian-American is employed by the bank. No community programs help these struggling citizens. Around us the neighborhood itself gives evidence of exclusion from the power structures of Mt. Carmel. Such injustice denies them equal financial opportunities in this city and insults every fair-minded citizen in Mt. Carmel."

"Because of this, the Vietnamese Citizens League plans to call a community meeting to discuss a boycott of this bank. This pattern of neglect and bigotry cannot go unchallenged. We intend to build solidarity with the suffering families in this community until a new day of hope dawns for Asians in Mt. Carmel."

Dominique gathered her pad and moved quickly toward the podium. She could already visualize a blockbuster story for the evening news.

Ryan Thompkins and Mandy Powell exchanged wary glances before they followed Barry's welcoming gesture to sit on the plush office couch. Their wedding ceremony loomed on Saturday, only five days away. The pastor had called them in to review the results of their premarital inventory, a prospect that added even more anxiety to their fretful minds.

Barry pulled a chair close to the couch and took a seat. "Mandy, tell me about the progress of the wedding plans."

The attractive bride, a brunette with a strong chin and buxom build, eagerly took a soft drink offered by Lauren. She managed a smile with her reply. "Everything seems on track. Mom and I called the flower shop and the tuxedo rental today to double-check the details."

The pastor had watched Mandy struggle through her parent's divorce and Paulette's remarriage. During high school she had eagerly participated in youth activities, but in college her pattern of devotion had fallen to only an occasional appearance at a worship service. Her physical therapy studies, and Ryan, took most of her attention.

"No big fights over wedding cake or honeymoon?"

Ryan's anxious mind failed to catch the humor. "No, nothing like that at all. We work together on all the choices." He drummed his long, artistic fingers on the arm of the couch and looked again at Mandy.

Barry raised his hands in a reassuring gesture. "I didn't think that would be a problem. You've made good plans and have developed good communication skills in the eighteen months since you started dating. I know everything will go just fine."

For years Barry had believed that the church, more than any other institution in American culture, could help marriages grow stronger. He decided to help couples by requiring the bride and groom to meet with him three times. In the first session, he administered an inventory of beliefs and attitudes prepared by a national testing service. The questions asked on the test sometimes made the prospective bride and groom uncomfortable, probing attitudes on subjects from communication to sex. By the time the sessions concluded, however, most couples felt better equipped for the challenge of marriage.

"In the first two sessions we covered areas in which you share a great deal of common ground. We also looked at a monthly budget. Did the budget figures balance after you had time to go over them again?"

"I think we've got it worked out," Ryan said without offering further details. The slightly-built musician had tried to talk Mandy out of using her pastor, fearing he would be too pushy in the counseling.

Barry ignored the cool reply and plunged ahead. "Ryan, one of the areas of concern I have involves the area of religious faith. Mandy's answers indicate this subject is important to her. Your answers indicate that you don't share that feeling. How do you think that will affect your marriage?"

The young man shifted in his chair and looked at Mandy.

"I really respect her for what she believes. I guess I've admired how it has given stability to her life and to her parents. I've just never been interested, you know, in church per se." In reality, just last week he questioned Mandy about how she could be deluded by the confusing religious talk and strange rituals. The investigations on television had revealed to him that most preachers carried on like con artists who fleeced the flock to build palatial homes. He wanted none of it.

Barry took another tack. "Which would you say is easier, balancing on a bike or sitting on a three-legged stool?"

The groom snickered at the simple question. "Sitting on a stool. It's got better balance, you know, because of the three legs."

"I know it's a stupid question." He leaned back in his chair. "I wanted to make a point. The two of you can choose the degree of stability and strength in your marriage. You can base it just on the strength the two of you possess and it will always balance precariously, ready to tip over, like a bicycle." The pastor held up his hands to show the shaky balance. "Or you can add God to the equation. He becomes a third partner in the relationship, like the third leg on a stool. With Him, you build a firm foundation to survive the tough times."

Ryan nodded and took Mandy's hand. "I want our marriage to be strong. When my parents divorced, I swore I would only marry when I knew it would work. That's what I want."

The discussion moved on to additional areas of marital adjustment based on the inventory report. Barry told a light-hearted story about the challenges of adjustment that he and Keri had faced years ago. The young couple enjoyed hearing about the stumbling efforts of the young preacher and his bride. When the interview concluded, a more relaxed atmosphere filled the office.

Mandy took Ryan's hand when they stood to leave the office. "Thank you for talking to us. We'll make sure everyone is ready to do their part."

Barry had just settled back in his chair when Lauren stuck her head through the open doorway. "Keri is holding on line two for you."

Barry picked up the receiver. "Hi. What's going on?"

"I'm on my way to a press conference on the east side of town. You won't believe what happened today. The bank's been threatened with a boycott by a Vietnamese group. Ledbetter sent me to watch the press conference and deal with the TV people. Listen, can you pick up Jason at five? I know I won't make it there in time."

"Uh, well, I guess so. I'd planned to stop by the bookstore after my men's group."

"There's nothing I can do to change this."

His voice flattened with irritation. "O.K. Do I pick him up at Stephen's?"

"Yes."

"I'll do it. See you at home."

"Thanks, honey. I'll tell you all about it when I get home. Pray for me. Bye."

He slowly laid the handset in the cradle. *I just finished talking about adjustments in marriage. Maybe I'm not doing such a good job myself. It seems like we're traveling on different roads, our paths crossing only to share a hurried dinner or a few minutes in bed, and then we're off again. Maybe we're the ones who need counseling.*

Red-faced with anger, Cody Burns trounced the accelerator of the dented Ford, blasting gravel from beneath the wheels. The alley behind Premiere Auto Sales echoed with a savage, broken-muffler roar.

"You can shove it, man!" He shook his fist at the stooped figure in the doorway. "If you think you can treat me like that, you'd better be watchin' over your shoulder!"

Three weeks earlier, Cody had surveyed the small used car lot with high hopes. He sailed through the first days, energized by five slick deals that pleased Hank, the grizzled owner of the used car lot. At that pace, he would need only a few weeks to get on his feet. With that success he could erase the embarrassing record of short-term jobs from the past year.

Cody had mastered every secret in the book of sales techniques across his checkered career. He even added a few just for himself. He called one of his special additions "prowling." In quiet hours, with no one around, he liked to snoop through the office looking for bits of information that could give him an edge. Flipping through business records or going through someone's desk carried some risk, but it never hurt to know more about the other guy than he knew about you—until today, at least.

Speeding south on HW 69, Cody figured out what had happened. Hank must have parked in the alley instead of his usual spot under the tree near the small frame sales office. The filing cabinet stood wide open when the door chime sounded. Both men looked at each other, surprised, Hank's hand lingering on the door, Cody's big fist gripping the file of Accounts Payable. The trial and sentencing lasted only thirty seconds. Hank dismissed the burly young man's stammered lies and fired him on the spot. Only the slamming of Cody's truck door cut off the spew of insults and threats from the crusty old owner.

He slammed his hand on the steering wheel, directing a final epithet at his former employer. "You old idiot!"

What would he do for work now? He could picture Lisa's recriminating look, hair over her shoulder, chin stuck out, eyes fixed on him like a hawk, furious at his irresponsibility. Money problems squeezed their check book constantly, especially since Courtney's birth last year. Today's stupidity added to the string of lost jobs and promising opportunities cut short by his temper or too much to drink. Now, he had invented a new way to lose a job. Lisa would give him that look—a look of disgust and accusation—that branded him a dismal failure.

He couldn't stand to think of facing her yet. He ran his hand through his long, straw-colored hair. What about stopping at the bar for a few minutes?

"Maybe I can calm down some and get that fool off my mind," he growled, abruptly changing lanes to turn down Osage Highway toward Harry's Place.

The dilapidated, green-frame shack blended in behind the unkempt shrubs near the river bridge. Clyde, the unshaven bar owner, always offered a listening ear. Sometimes he even gave the rough young man a bit of fatherly advice. At this time of the afternoon, the regular crowd wouldn't be around. A cloud of gravel dust swirled when he skidded to a stop.

I'll face Lisa when I'm good and ready.

Mary looked up from her keyboard to see three men pushing their way through the door of the church office.

"Time for your appointment with Barry?"

"Wake him up and tell him the FBI is here," the tallest of the three said in an ominous tone.

"Pastor," Mary called over the intercom, trying not to laugh, "three men from the FBI want to see you."

Barry's gangster voice could be heard in the reception area. "Tell them I ain't got nothin' to hide. They can search my office themselves."

C. K. Haskins, Sam Lane, and Brad Upton grinned at the riposte. The three men had made the same journey regularly over the past two years. They weren't with the FBI, but they did pursue serious examination of spiritual matters.

Lauren stood to open Barry's door. "How are you

gentlemen today?"

"We're fine," Sam said. "Looking forward to giving your boss trouble again." The tallest of the three, in his early fifties, Sam added spiritual dynamic to the group. Three years ago at a men's conference, he heard a powerful message vividly describing the loneliness of modern men. The speaker challenged each man present to join a small group. Little interaction with the other account consultants in his office at Missouri Financial Solutions made the prospect of close relationships enticing. So, he approached men in the church about joining him in a weekly meeting. True to his hopes, his faith had blossomed from the face-to-face sharing.

"How are you, preacher?" Brad wrapped his strong firefighter's arms around the pastor's shoulders. Brad's spiritual life floundered in confusion until he moved to a new house in the same block with Sam. Soon they developed a close friendship. Convinced by his friend's enthusiasm, Brad joined the group. In their meetings, his thoughtful insights often cut to the heart of the issue.

C. K. Haskins closed the door while the other men sat down. The balding head with a fringe of white hair showed his senior status among the four men. Eight years ago Mt. Carmel became his retirement home, chosen for proximity to his children. He shook Barry's hand. "Has it been a busy day?"

"Not really—only two earth-shattering events so far!"

The men laughed as they found familiar places in the small sitting area of the office. For a while friendly banter filled the room.

Barry took the initiative after the small talk faded. "C. K., did you ever feel like you were being pressed through a meat grinder by the problems of your church?" He didn't wait for a reply. "That describes the last few weeks for me. The phone won't stop ringing. We had to come back early from vacation to do a funeral. The summer money crunch has Board members ready to cancel the youth retreat. Some nights have been long and sleepless. Even Keri's feeling frustrated, too."

The soft-spoken elder nodded. "I do know how you feel. In fact, escaping that pressure has proved to be one of the nicest things about retirement."

"You mean, you had to live with it your entire ministry?"

"In some fashion, yes. The size and background of the congregation had a lot to do with it. Some churches supported us wonderfully, but one or two ambushed us."

Sam interrupted. "How many churches did you serve in your ministry, C. K.?"

"I pastored nine churches across the Midwest, serving 38 years before I retired. I stayed seven years in my longest tenure."

"Is that a normal career track? The pastors of the larger churches in Mt. Carmel seem to stick around for years and years."

"Things have changed since I first took a pulpit in the late 1950's. Back then, some joked about the moving company coming to load a house and the foreman asking, 'Are you a coach or a preacher?' Every three years or so, the preacher would shuffle off to a new church, and another minister would move in to the parsonage. That's what everybody expected. Of course, moving that often allowed me to preach the same sermons again, and nobody knew the difference!"

After the laughter, he continued. "You know what brought the change? The churches sold the parsonages they owned. That seemed to make good sense, with the housing boom and low interest rates. Instead of the church owning the house, doing all the maintenance and paying the utilities, the churches found they could pay the preacher a little more and give him the opportunity to buy his own house. Of course, the preachers liked it because they reaped the benefits of home ownership."

Brad joined the discussion. "Barry, you own your own house, don't you?"

"We bought it within a few weeks of moving here," Barry replied.

Brad turned to C. K. "What's wrong with that?"

"Nothing at all. But home ownership changed everything about the way preachers looked at the community. Living in a parsonage seems like just renting an apartment. You simply give two weeks notice, load the boxes, and away you go to another parsonage somewhere. But a pastor who owns his house faces a different world. He must worry with the housing market and with his wife, who has spent months decorating her house just the way she likes it. The hassle of selling and buying a house made changing churches a huge decision for preachers and dramatically increased their tenure. The average tenure now exceeds five years."

"I see. And I bet that's where the tough part comes in," Brad said, his eyes bright with the flash of insight. "Pastors stay longer, and that forces everyone to a new depth of relationship. After three years, the shine disappears from both preacher and people. They must learn to solve problems and work with one another."

Sam joined in. "And some churches don't make it, do they? Either the preacher or the people leave to find another fantasy."

The group sat silent for a moment. Brad looked at his watch, "Speaking of leaving, I guess we'd better wind this up. Are we ready to pray?"

Kneeling, each of the men prayed in turn, fervently petitioning God to meet the needs of each family and the church. C. K. prayed with special earnestness for Barry.

Only Liz still remained in the office when the men made

their way toward the front door. Barry waved goodbye to her and locked the office door. Driving away from the church, he dialed the cell phone to let Jason know he was on the way.

Fifteen minutes later, the locked front door of the church office rattled loudly. Liz scurried around her desk to meet the unexpected visitor. She glimpsed Daemon's pinched face peering through the glass.

"Mr. Asher! I'm sorry," she said, pulling the door open. "We always lock the door at five. May I help you?"

"I'm sorry to be a bother, but I saw your car still in the parking lot and wondered if you might help me. I ordered some books for the Sunday School class. Do you know if they've come in the mail yet?"

"I haven't seen them, but they might be stored in the workroom. Let me look. Won't you please come in?"

"Thank you."

He stepped quickly into the office, throwing a furtive glance to see if anyone else might be working late. Only then did he place a yellow package gently on the counter.

The small workroom near Brent's office had a wide counter where Mary always deposited the mail. Liz glanced quickly through the skewed pile of brown paper packages. One marked 'Daemon Asher' lay near the bottom of the stack.

"I found it." She carried the package to the counter and laid it in front of him. "This one has your name on it. I hope it contains your order."

"Let me check to see if they sent the right books." He opened the package with a small pocket knife and slid out the volumes. "Perfect. Here's the one on the Gospel of John and the other about the Reformation. Just what I hoped to find."

He replaced the knife in his pants pocket, and then placed his hand on the large yellow mailing envelope. His eyes locked on hers.

"I brought some special material for Barry. Would now be a good time to give it to him?"

Her eyes widened. "I... yes... I think this would be a good time."

He pushed the fat envelope toward her.

The movement seemed to paralyze the gray-haired woman. She stared at the envelope, not a muscle moving.

"Hurry!"

The barked command forced her into motion. She grabbed the soft bundle and hurried to Barry's office. The key in her trembling hand missed the lock twice before the pastor's door creaked open. Without turning on the lights, she slipped across the office to his desk. Her mouth felt dry as a desert when she turned to leave.

"Thanks for finding the books for me." His voice sounded soothing this time, noting the nervous tremor of his conspirator's hands. "I'll go and let you lock up again."

She nodded with a quick bob of her head and watched him leave without speaking another word. Returning to her desk, she noticed Barry's office door standing open. Guilt welled up, accusing her like an angry judge would a brazen criminal. A rising panic urged her to get away, now. In less than a minute, she gathered her purse and fled the office.. The heat from the surface of the parking lot blazed in her face like the fires of perdition.

I know I did the right thing.

Lisa jerked awake at the metallic *whack* of a truck door slamming near the bedroom window. Her late afternoon nap, snatched after Kendra left to play with a friend and the baby fell asleep, seemed too short. In a moment, the rattle of the screen door confirmed Cody's unexpected presence in the trailer. She stood and steadied herself on the door jamb.

"Cody? Why are you...."

A spew of profanity cut off her words. His bulky body stumbled across the kitchen, flailing an angry kick that sent Courtney's stroller bouncing across the worn, yellow kitchen floor.

"Cody! What's wrong with you?"

He dropped heavily in the vinyl kitchen chair. "Hank fired me!" The slam of his hand on the table shook the trailer. With slurred, disjointed words he tried to sell an alibi about the crusty owner stealing part of his commission, then bringing down the axe when he stood up like a man to claim his rightful portion. Sitting at the bar earlier, he had harbored a faint hope he could tell the story and spin his deceit to an act of manly courage. He never dared look at her until the rambling narrative concluded.

She stuck her hands on her hips and looked him directly in the eye.

"You lost your job *again*? For the *third* time?"

Her withering stare and the beer mutated his shame into an explosion of hate. He launched himself toward her.

"You shut up!"

He shoved her backwards. "I don't need a pint-sized woman like you kickin' me about my troubles."

"If you could keep a job . . . ."

He swung backhanded, smashing his huge hand across her scornful cheek. The blow sent her sprawling across a kitchen chair to crash against the wall. The trailer shuddered as she landed in a crumpled heap on the dirty linoleum. A wedding picture crashed down beside her, jettisoning pieces of glass across the floor.

She sensed his massive body towering over her like a

primeval beast. Her spinning head couldn't make sense of his shouting.

"You ain't worth nothing to me. I don't see you out there earning any money. If I'm so bad, why don't you just get out?"

She cowered there, fighting to get the breath knocked out by the blow, while his tirade continued. Finally, he turned away from her, growling with profane fury, to dump himself in the recliner.

The floor felt cool against her stinging cheek. Her eyes couldn't focus on the wobbling room. A salty taste filled her mouth. The cries of the baby, awakened by the shouts and clatter, slowly penetrated her thoughts. The baby. Got to see what's wrong. Motherly instincts forced her up to stagger past Cody toward the little bedroom.

She found Courtney wailing, face wet with tears of fright, huddled in a corner of the rickety wooden baby bed. The dazed mother lifted her off the pink sheets and pulled her close. The curly-headed child clamped a death-hug on her mother's neck. Through the shooting pain, Lisa sat down in the old rocker and began to hum a lullaby. The gentle motion soothed the child's shuddering sobs until she lay quietly against her mother's shoulder.

Lisa sat very still, seeking to recover her own senses. Drops of blood from her mouth dripped on Courtney's curly brown hair. With the corner of a diaper she dabbed the red stain away and gingerly felt her face. The lacerated lip felt hot and tender. She listened for more of Cody's rage but could only hear the roar of the television.

I'll stay here in the bedroom until he settles down. The creaking chair seemed to ask yet another nagging question. How much longer can I take this?

Keri poured a glass of tea and placed it on the kitchen

table. Even the bustle of fixing dinner felt good after the stress-filled day at the bank. Working in the small kitchen, lined with oak cabinets and hand-painted tile, always lifted her spirit. When the family schedule whirled out of control, this cloister anchored her heart to the true center of life.

"Jason, would you put the plates and silverware on the table for us, please?" The youngster nodded, pushed a pause button on the hand-held video game, and headed for the cabinet.

Keri's search for the house of their dreams filled many long hours the first weeks after the move to Mt. Carmel. Nothing pleased her until she glimpsed the cream-colored, two-story house at the corner of Highview and Ridge Lane. She fell in love with the long veranda and towering trees. With help from church friends, they moved in a rush over a long Fourth of July weekend.

Barry entered the kitchen from the garage and kissed her on the cheek. "What's for dinner?"

"I've started some hamburgers on the grill. Do you want cheese on yours?"

"A slice of cheddar would be fine."

"Get it from the refrigerator while I check the burgers."

She opened the patio door to a blast of hot air. The brick paving stones held the heat like an oven. *We need to cover this patio so I don't cook while I'm cooking the hamburgers. Even though we've lived here five years, we've got a lot to do to improve this house.*

From the white wood bench under the huge black oak in the front yard to the little fountain near the patio, she had tried to add small items to create a haven for the family. The gentle decor of Ozark crafts filled every room with hanging quilts, paintings of farm animals and scenes of green pastures. The dinner table, a distressed walnut piece with four chairs, had been rescued from an old farm in Arkansas, anchored the hospitable kitchen.

Within minutes, the platter of sizzling burgers fresh from the grill drew the family to dinner. After Barry asked the blessing, Keri passed the plate to Jason. "What did you and Stephen do this afternoon?"

"We went to the bowling alley." He took a mammoth bite of french fries and ketchup.

"I didn't know you were a bowler."

"You bet I am! I even threw three strikes."

"I hope it didn't hurt your arm. You said last week after pitching that it felt sore."

"It doesn't hurt now."

Barry poured a soda for Keri. "Tell me about your day. Did something go wrong?"

"I had to work on that publicity project. A political pressure group of Vietnamese has moved into town. They're accusing the bank of ignoring the needs of Asians. I went to their press conference. The whole business could get ugly if we don't handle it right."

"I know you can do a great job if Jack gives you a chance." He polished off his cheeseburger and leaned back with a toothpick. "What are you planning this evening, buddy?"

"I want to see what I can find on the Internet about hitting for the cycle. Matt said he looked at a neat baseball web site called World of Baseball."

"I'd like to know what you find out. I'd never seen anyone hit for the cycle before." He took a final drink of tea. "I think your mom and I will go play tennis."

"Okay, I guess it is Monday. You guys always do the same thing every week."

Barry winked at him. "I told your mom I would keep doing it until she beat me."

"Hey, I can beat you any time I want to."

"We'll just see about that tonight. Jason may want to post the scores on the internet to let everyone know."

He stood and retrieved a Bible from a drawer near the refrigerator. "Before we go, let's take care of our Bible reading. Mrs. Tennis Pro, I think it's your turn to read."

Keri pointed a finger at him. "You're just trying to delay your fate."

"All things in their time—I think we're in John, chapter 7."

After the Bible reading Barry asked, "What do we need to pray about tonight?"

She folded her arms. "I need the Lord to help me with this bank problem. I've got an idea I hope will work, but anything can happen at that place."

"Stephen's mom looked real sad today," Jason said. "You know, his Dad moved out last month."

"I'd like us to pray for Brother Bellamy, the evangelist coming here to preach in October. The church needs a powerful meeting to draw us together. So let's hold hands and pray."

One hour later, Keri placed the cell phone on top of the sport bags. A bank of clouds in the west blocking the sun lowered the temperature enough to make playing conditions bearable at court three.

Barry volleyed some warm-up shots across the net. Joining the Hillside Tennis Center two years ago gave the family an activity they could do together. He especially liked Monday evenings and the weekly marital challenge match. He took special note that Keri's figure looked great in the teal and white tennis outfit.

Keri concentrated on improving her backhand during the warm-up. The tensions of the hectic afternoon eased with every stroke. She toed the service line. "Are you ready?"

"Give me your best shot, miss."

She lobbed the ball toward the twilight sky. *Whump!* The ball sizzled to Barry's left, stretching his backstroke to return it.

It took all three sets to decide the dinner table challenge. She took the first set. He returned the compliment in the second and kept the momentum to capture the match.

The humble champion tossed her a towel when they left the court. "Would it ease the pain if I bought you a snowcone?"

"I thought the loser had to pay."

"Tonight we'll make a special deal. I got to beat the prettiest girl in the club, so that costs me. I want to keep her happy."

She pushed a playful finger to his chest. "What's your plan, buddy? Sounds like I need to watch myself."

"Just be careful if I get some time later in a more private place." He picked up their bags and phone. "I'll even make that a giant snowcone."

Jason was sitting on the patio, immersed in a small video game player, when his parents returned.

Keri sat down next to him. "What did you discover in your baseball research?"

"I couldn't find anything. I thought I could find the statistics listed under the category of 'Hitting,' but none of those mentioned about 'hitting for the cycle.'" His bright brown eyes never moved from the tiny video screen.

She licked the bright green, lime-flavored snowcone. "Not anything?"

The preteen pulled his attention from the game. "Uh, no. Well—maybe. I decided to leave a question on the forum page. Maybe some baseball whiz will see it and give me an answer. So, I wrote my question and posted it."

"Great! Won't you feel good if you get an answer?"

The phone rang before he could respond. He grabbed the cordless extension and disappeared inside.

A few minutes later Barry came out to enjoy the star-filled evening. "Beautiful night," he said, settling beside her on the wood and canvas glider.

"I thought you might say that, Mr. Champ."

He put his arm around her shoulder. "I would say that no matter what the score, if I found myself sitting next to a girl like you in an outfit like that one. Did you put that on just to bother my concentration, or do you always wear such exciting clothes?"

She leaned against his chest and put her hand on his leg. "Sometimes it's not the clothes that make the excitement."

Yes, a beautiful evening indeed, the pastor decided. He placed his hand on hers.

"Dad!" Jason pulled open the patio door. "Telephone for you. It's Mike and he says it's urgent."

Barry pulled his hand away to take the phone.

Daemon felt a twinge of nervousness rattle his hand when he dialed the familiar number.

"Claire?"

"Hi, Daemon." She bypassed the pleasantries. "Did you get it delivered?"

"I went to the office a little after five. I found Liz alone. She put the envelope on his desk just like I asked."

"Good! I imagine quite a commotion will occur tomorrow morning around the church office."

"Perhaps we can get some details from Liz after work. I'd even pay a little to see Peters' face when he finds that envelope. But seriously, I know this is costing you and Sid quite a bit."

"We did have a place or two we could have put the

money. But we've served at the Church a long time, just like you and Nadine. We consider this a small investment to rescue the church."

"I'll let you know if I hear anything."

Daemon hung up and eased back in the faded leather office chair. *We've come a long way since the prayer meeting yesterday. Now we've taken a big gamble. How can I better the odds?*

Ed Loomis. The name hit him suddenly. *Last night at Sid's house, Ed mentioned he wanted to get together and talk about the problems of the church. There's no better time than right now.* He opened the telephone book and quickly dialed.

"Hello," a deep voice rumbled.

"Ed? Daemon Asher here. How are you?"

"Just fine. Doris and I just returned from a nice walk. What can I do for you?"

"You mentioned last night that you would like to have lunch and discuss the concerns I raised. Could you meet at lunch tomorrow?"

"Tomorrow is Tuesday. Let me look at my planner. I don't have a thing on my calendar all morning. I'd like very much to visit with you.

"Good. I need to share with you some important details that led me to speak as I did last night."

"I'd appreciate your thoughts. You may know that I've agreed to serve as chairman of the Personnel Committee starting in October. If trouble is brewing, I need to know about it before it starts to boil."

"I couldn't agree more. What about the Green Door restaurant at 11:30?"

"That will work fine. I'll put it on my calendar right now. Thanks for calling. I'll see you tomorrow."

Daemon carefully wrote in his date book, 'Loomis 11:30 @ Green Door.' He tapped the pen again and again against the desk.

There's no room for this plan to fail.

Chapter 3
Tuesday

"This is the day, this is the day that the Lord hath made, that the Lord hath made, I will rejoice and be glad in it."

The bouncy words of the familiar song stirred through Edith's heart with the melody of water filling the coffee pot. Through the kitchen window, she gazed at the clouds above the ridge of Buck Hill, towering like clusters of wispy grapes, red and purple in the dawn's first light.

She loved the quiet, summer mornings. The hushed minutes before Mt. Carmel came awake gave time to get the coffee pot perking, let out the dog, and then sit a moment in the kitchen, letting the first rays of sunshine warm her skin. A few solitary moments of reflection and prayer before Harvey stirred let her soul rise with the promise of the morning.

The warmth of the coffee cup toasted her hand. *This is a day to be glad. This afternoon the little grandkids will come by to help Harvey in the garden. I should get some meat thawing about noon.* Settling in a kitchen chair, she gave thanks for the joy of seeing their bright faces.

"OOOh!"

A deep moan burst from the bedroom, fracturing her reverie with a guttural agony. A crash of furniture and a sickening thud of heavy weight against the floor brought a rush of fear that propelled her from the chair.

"Harvey!"

Her shout reverberated through the small bedroom. His pajama-clad body lay sprawled on the hardwood floor. She jerked the overturned lamp away from his face. The stare of his vacant eyes filled her with horror.

"Harvey! What's wrong?" Shaking him hard, she called again, louder. No response. Is he breathing? She turned his face but couldn't tell.

"Oh, Jesus! Help me! What should I do?"

The phone. Call for help. She pulled the phone from the night stand and forced her shaking fingers to find the keypad. 9-1-1. The musical tones blended with her own frightened breathing.

"911 emergency services. May I have your address please?"

"Uh... Oh... It's 69 Rose Lane. 69 Rose Lane."

"What is the problem, ma'am?"

"My husband—he's fallen. His name is Harvey. He won't wake up."

"Do you need an ambulance?"

"Yes! Hurry!" Edith looked again at the ashen figure lying silently near the dresser. "I don't even know if he's breathing."

"I'll dispatch a unit right now. Do not hang up."

"I won't."

The minutes crawled by while she prayed and talked and wept with the caring woman on the phone. Her hand stroked Harvey's quiet face again and again. Finally, the sharp rap of the ambulance crew banging on the front door sent her rushing through the house.

"Come in. He's in the bedroom. Hurry!"

The tallest man rushed forward, followed by a dark-haired woman carrying a red case. Another man from the ambulance led her gently to the kitchen, assuring her they would do everything possible. She struggled to answer his questions.

Amid her confusion she could hear the measured voices of the medics checking Harvey's vital signs and the crackle of their mobile radios trading information with the ER at Ozark Regional Hospital.

"What happened, Mom?"

"It's your Dad." Edith looked up to see Roger's face, flushed with the exertion of running from the car. She stood to hug him. "He collapsed when he got out of bed. I called the ambulance when he wouldn't wake up. How did you find out?"

"Mrs. Kincaid called me. She saw the lights of the ambulance from her window. I got here as quickly as I could." Roger—everybody called him Red—lived just a mile from the little house where he had grown up helping his Dad with chores in the garden. "Did he say anything about feeling bad during the night?"

Tears spilled down her cheeks. "Nothing, nothing at all. He was sleeping peacefully when I got up. I shouldn't have gone to the kitchen...."

"Now, Mom. It wouldn't have made any difference. What was going to happen, did. You helped him the moment he fell. He's going to be O.K. You just get your clothes together, and we'll go to the hospital."

The emergency team burst from the bedroom, hustling the gurney toward the front door. Harvey lay silent and chalky-gray under the oxygen mask.

"We'll follow you to the hospital," Red said to the crew.

The whirling silver and red emergency lights of the ambulance painted a kaleidoscope on the glass front wall of the emergency receiving room when the Flowers' arrived. The automatic doors slid away, revealing a well-appointed waiting room, demarcated with rows of burgundy and blue chairs. The weary faces of a few persons scattered in the sitting area looked up to check out their arrival. High in the corner the cheery face of a morning talk show host filled the TV screen. Red looked around the room to get his bearings.

A young Asian clerk with a bright blue shirt emblazoned "Magill Medical Center" stood up behind the counter. "May I help you?"

"My Dad just got here in an ambulance. We need to see him."

"I can take you back there in just a minute. First, I need to get some information."

"I didn't bring my purse. But I think I can remember what you might need to know." Edith's voice quavered with anxiety.

"Take a seat right here. Now, has your husband been a patient here before?"

Red held his mother's hand tightly while they answered the rapid-fire questions. The young woman entered the answers in a computer. Minutes ticked by while admission papers were explained and signed.

"Can we see Dad?"

"I'm sorry this is taking so long. Let me call back to see how they are doing." After a brief conversation, she led them through heavy wooden doors to the treatment rooms.

A man in green surgical scrubs greeted them in the hall. "Are you the Flowers' family?"

"I'm Mrs. Flowers," Edith replied, holding her voice steady over the pounding of her heart.

"Your husband is right here." The nurse whisked back the blue curtain. Harvey's mouth gaped open with a large clear tube protruding from it. Nurses bustled near him, speaking arcane terms. Wires led from his chest to a machine that flashed colored numbers on a TV screen.

Red steadied her. "Speak to him, Mom."

She stepped closer to the bed. She could see his mouth open under the clear plastic mask. Gently, she stretched out her hand to caress his face, stubbled with unshaven whiskers. He made no response to her soft touch. "I love you, darling. Keep fighting. Don't give up."

"Ma'am, we need to take your husband now." A chubby, red-cheeked woman interrupted her loving gesture. "Dr. Billington believes he may have suffered a stroke. The MRI can tell us more. But we need your permission for the test. Would you sign these papers, please?" She held out a clipboard and pen for Edith's trembling hand. At the final stroke of the pen, the aides pushed the bed and the silent victim away from Red and Edith.

The man in the green scrubs saw their confusion and uncertainty. "We can find a more comfortable waiting room near the main reception area for you. Come with me, and I'll show you."

Red could feel his mother trembling as he steered her down the cold hall. Directly across the waiting room stood a door marked, "Consultation." Their helpful guide opened the door. The small room held three burgundy cloth chairs, a matching love seat, and a metal end table with a telephone and ceramic lamp. A shaft of sunlight streamed in through a tall window.

"You'll have more privacy in here. I'll tell the reception desk and Dr. Billington's nurse where you are. The tests shouldn't take long. I'm sure they will come immediately to let you know what has happened to your husband."

Red shook his hand with a grim smile. "Thanks. We'll stay right here."

Seeing the telephone, Edith said, "Call Brother Barry. Tell him to hurry."

The shrill ring of the phone caught Barry putting on his socks. "I'll get it," he said, and stepped to the bedroom phone, one foot still bare.

"Brother Barry, this is Red Flowers. I'm real sorry to call you so early."

Red held membership at Mt. Faith Church but often

failed to make the better choice between his camper and attending church. Months had passed since Barry had seen him at a worship service.

"That's all right, Red. What's wrong?"

"It's Dad. We're at the hospital now. The doctor thinks he's suffered a stroke. They've just taken him in for some kind of test."

Clamping the phone on his shoulder, Barry finished his socks and shoes while the story poured out.

"I'll get there as soon as I can, Red. Tell Edith we're praying for her. Sit tight for now. Thanks for letting me know."

Keri stopped applying her makeup and stepped to the doorway of the master bathroom. "What happened?"

"Harvey Flowers is in the emergency room with a possible stroke."

"Good heavens. That's terrible." She loved Harvey and Edith for the acts of kindness they had shown her during their ministry in Mt. Carmel. Just last month Edith brought cookies for Jason's birthday.

"Harvey hadn't really complained of heart pain. If this is a stroke, it's a bad one."

Barry filled his pockets with a set of church keys and car keys, a small New Testament, a handkerchief, and some change left over from the day before. On the way to the garage, he brushed by Keri's half-prettied face with a soft kiss.

"I'll let you know what happens. Pray for us."

"I'm leavin'."

The floor of the old mobile home creaked under Cody's heavy steps. He pulled a dirty baseball cap down on his head. "I don't know when I'll get back."

"O.K.." Lisa didn't look up from stirring the baby food.

With a grunt, he slammed the door. From the high chair, Courtney jerked her head around to see what had happened.

"Daddy's gone bye-bye," Lisa said to the baby's surprised look. "And I'm glad!"

An ice pack lay half-melted on the table. All during the night the pain in her swollen cheekbone had ebbed and flowed, bringing fitful sleep. Fearful of waking Cody, she had finally tiptoed to the bathroom and taken another dose of aspirin. The medicine at least helped her to doze a few minutes before the baby called for attention in the early light.

The roar of the Cody's old pickup rumbled out of the trailer park and down the gravel road. Where he was going? Would he look for another job? She knew she wouldn't hear from him all day—that's just how he'd always been—and today that suited her heart just fine.

"Do all men act like that?" Lisa addressed her question to the baby, who responded by rubbing her big brown eyes. "I remember your grandpa lying on the couch a few times, drunk. Momma didn't want me to see, but I did. And I hated it then, too."

Paying no attention, the toddler chased another piece of breakfast cereal across the tray of her high chair. Lisa's thoughts returned to the red-shuttered house near Spring River. Yes, her parents had struggled in their marriage. Her father never seemed to understand the needs of his shy, quiet daughter, but Mom always surrounded her with love. Mom gave laughter and hope and protection with a hug big enough to swallow the fears of her petite child. Lisa could almost feel her squeeze again now. No matter how rough the world treated her, Mom provided a haven.

At least, until the cancer came.

No fifteen-year old should lose a mom. She often thought of the good times stolen by the voracious disease. They could have talked about boys and love and grades and her music.

Those years might have been the best ones of her life. But how could she talk to a gravestone? The cancer ate away her mother's life in just eight, brief months. All the answers she needed to hear about growing up died on that blustery November day when they lowered her mother's body into the cold grave.

"Ready to get down?" Courtney held up her hands for a quick swipe with the wash cloth. Lisa removed the tray and put the little one down with a kiss on the forehead.

Maybe Mom would have warned her about husbands who drink, or about how beer makes you do things you wouldn't even think of doing—like dancing naked with Cody, or feeling the power of his body pressing her down. After that, she didn't want to date anyone else. She'd moved in with him after graduation, hoping to keep his love and to fill some of the emptiness in her own wounded heart. She had just turned seventeen when Kendra entered the struggling family.

She stepped into the bathroom to examine the aching wound. The cracked mirror revealed a dark blue patch spreading across her cheek and around her eye like a Halloween mask. Her shoulder ached so much she could barely lift her arm to comb her long strands of dark hair. The haggard face staring back at her in the stark light pondered only one question.

Had the time finally come?

"Come on. I can't sit here all morning." Lauren Reed tapped her fingers on the steering wheel, the fourth car idling at the drive-through window of the Donut Delight. She checked her watch, then slipped a small spiral notebook from her purse. Her eyes ran down the list of reminders for her work week. Lots to do today, but the tradition of treats on Tuesday had a certain priority. Finally, she placed her order for a dozen, mixed. The sweet aroma of the baker's goodies brought a smile as she turned from the lot to make the short drive to the church.

Most of the staff had already arrived for work by the time she pushed through the office door with the white pastry box. "Donut alert in the workroom for anyone who's hungry."

Her distinctive, high-pitched voice attracted immediate attention. Liz and Mary joined her in the small, crowded workroom. "Girls, I had the bakery remove every calorie from these treats."

"Oh, my diet doesn't count calories from any food forced on you at work," Mary said.

Lauren watched Liz smile slightly and, without comment, take a donut. The newest member of the secretarial staff always kept her thoughts to herself. Lauren had often looked into the eyes of the gray-haired woman. She sensed a shadow of sadness hidden behind them. What secret could Liz be hiding?

A similar grief appeared in her own mirror five years ago, betraying a wound at the center of her soul. When Lauren graduated from college, two dreams filled her mind: making the Olympic team and marrying Rich. On the former, Coach Engels had encouraged her to attend the tryouts in Colorado Springs. He lobbied to get his promising star an invitation to the tryout camp, even finding a sponsor to pay for the plane tickets. She thrilled at the beginning of an athlete's dream come true.

But all her shining hopes died one hot, July afternoon in the green-brown water of Grand Lake. Her steady boyfriend, tall, easy-going Rich, wanted to spend the afternoon on the jet-ski. Even now, she remembered each detail of the cobalt-blue, summer sky, the touch of the cool, deep water of the northeastern Oklahoma reservoir, and the roar of the wave runner in her ears. When they pulled away from the marina, she wrapped her arms around his life jacket and whooped with delight at the bouncing, high speed zigzag across the white caps.

The accident happened so fast. She felt her body fly

weightless from the machine. The sharp slap of the concrete-hard water flipped her into a sickening roll, limbs flopping like a rag doll. Disoriented, she bobbed to the surface, choking and gasping for air. Her life jacket held her afloat while white-hot flashes of pain surged up her legs.

Rich struggled for endless minutes to pull her onto the unsteady watercraft. The waves of agony pounded while he motored slowly to the dock, whispering to her, "I'm sorry, I'm sorry." The pickup ride to the hospital in Grove brought moans with every bump of the rough road. Soon the doctor's exam confirmed her fear—severely torn muscles in her left knee. Surgery and twelve weeks of rehabilitation lay ahead. The Olympics could be hers only to watch on television, mocking her lofty dreams.

For the first two weeks of her rehabilitation, Rich stayed at her side. His daily visits brought laughter amid the pain. They had dated for a year and talked about marriage after she finished the Olympics. But during the third week of her life on crutches she noticed a change. Her boyfriend seemed distracted, preoccupied, in a hurry. Three days went by with no contact. Hurt, she questioned his excuses until they blew up at each other. When he called two days later, the truth came pouring out. He wanted to go to grad school in Boston—alone. The pain she felt when he left that final night tormented her worse than the knee twisted in the foaming wake of the jet-ski.

Brent popped through the workroom doorway. "Looks like another healthy breakfast to me."

"We saved the creme ones just for you," Mary said, holding out the box for him to examine.

Within a few months of the accident, Lauren found herself out of college, out of love, and out of her dreams. Life itself seemed deflated, like air from a volleyball. The pitch black loneliness surrounding her felt like the despair after a loss at matchpoint—but it continued day after day.

That's when her drinking began. The fragrant wine promised a blurry escape that eased her pain for awhile. During the day she worked at her department store job, capably selling women's clothes. When night fell over the dreary apartment, however, she sat alone with the TV and a zinfandel. Night after night she made the pain disappear. No one knew—and no one cared.

In the fourth month of that sad, dark winter, something strange occurred. She awoke one Sunday morning, showered, and pulled on a dress. From deep in her soul a hidden energy pushed her to leave the apartment. She followed the unbidden, powerful compulsion and found herself parked at Mt. Faith Church. The open glass doors bid welcome her questing heart.

She tried to hide on the back pew. The unfamiliar words mumbled from her tongue. She fumbled with the thick, black Bible that others leafed through with ease. In spite of the strange surroundings, an unusual stirring gripped her soul. Love—warming, nourishing—touched her. At the close of the service, the man who preached stood at the door. When she came by to shake his hand, he made her pause. He looked directly in her eyes.

"You seem sad. Please call me this week if I can do anything for you."

She nodded and found her car. Her heart pounded like at match point of a championship game. Driving away, she told herself 'No' a dozen times. Yet, Monday found her seated in this very office, waiting for an appointment with Pastor Barry Peters.

Her visit that day brought no booming voice of revelation, no visions or angelic choirs. That night, she talked to God for the first time, just as Pastor Barry had prayed so simply in his office that afternoon. The wine stayed in the refrigerator. The same Encounter took place the next day, and the next. From that day a fresh, new spring warmed her soul, melting away the cold winter of grief and disappointment.

One year later she started working at the church. Now, the job meant everything to her. To help Barry, to help others, to make a difference in the life of someone—these desires formed the reasons Lauren worked with fierce loyalty at Mt. Faith Church.

"Thanks for the treat," Brent said with a thumbs up sign.

"Next Tuesday it's your turn," Lauren said, pointing back at him.

"I'd better get back to my records." Liz dropped her folded napkin in the trash and turned away from the others.

I must talk to her, Lauren thought. *She's hurting. Maybe I can help.*

The automatic door sprang open before Barry's hurried steps. The recently-renovated waiting room in the Emergency Department of Magill Medical Center showcased an modernizing effort aimed at retaining customers in the ever-competitive region. While the huge medical establishments in Joplin, Springfield and Tulsa spent millions every year, the local hospital struggled for funds and personnel. A few months ago, rumors of a buyout by a national hospital conglomerate sparked a flurry of community debate. Administrators battled the negative press with a remodeling project. When Morgan lost her life, the remodeled emergency center had only been in operation for two weeks. Now, another tragedy fueled Barry's urgency.

"I'm Pastor Peters. I'm looking for the Flowers' family."

The dark-haired Asian woman nodded, grim-faced. "Let me take you to the family consultation room. It's right next to the reception area. I can tell you, pastor, they've just had some bad news."

His stomach tightened at the ominous words. "Oh, no. I

was afraid of that from what Red told me on the phone."

They stepped quickly across the waiting room. A door opened at her knock to reveal Edith, Red and Red's wife, Verna, seated in the small, sparsely-furnished consultation room.

Edith's face looked drawn and pale. Verna perched on the next cushion, a thin woman with gray hair, her right arm wrapped around Edith's shoulders. Red stood stiffly nearby. Edith did not stand but stretched out her hand when she saw Barry.

He bent over to share a gentle hug, then knelt down in front of the trio.

"I'm so sorry about what's happened. Have you heard anything on Harvey's condition?"

Edith and Verna looked at each other, eyes filling with tears. Red stepped closer and laid his hand on Barry's shoulder.

"Dr. Billington came by a few minutes ago, preacher," he said, voice quivering with shock. "Dad's gone."

"Oh, no!" He stood and turned to Red. "What happened?"

"He said Dad never regained consciousness after the stroke. He stopped breathing in the ambulance. They revived him, but when his heart stopped again, they couldn't do anymore."

Edith sobbed into a white handkerchief. Verna hugged her close.

"I can't believe it," Barry said, kneeling down once again to take Edith's hand. "I just talked to him Sunday morning! He told me all about the roses he wanted to take to the county fair. I'm so sorry, Edith."

Verna patted her mother-in-law's shoulder. "I know the doctors did everything they could to pull him through."

Edith nodded, wiping away the flood of tears. "I know. I know they did."

A knock on the door brought the nurse again, escorting

an older couple. Red stepped forward to greet them.

"This is Dad's sister, Bernice, and Don, her husband," Verna said to Barry.

The pastor stepped back to let the family members comfort one another. His knees felt like rubber from the shocking announcement. Harvey hadn't complained of ill health. And Edith—how would she deal with the sudden blow?

In another moment, more friends appeared. The bad news must have spread quickly. Each visitor hugged Edith, taking a moment to murmur words of comfort. Ruth Clemons, teacher of the senior ladies class, approached Barry. "I'll contact the entire class about helping with a lunch. Just let me know when the service is going to be held."

Time after time he had watched the senior adults deal masterfully with the grieving moments of life. Within a few hours, the widows of the church would be at Edith's side, smoothing the rough road that lay ahead. He nodded to Ruth. "I'll call as soon as I find out what the family wants to do."

He scanned the crowded room. Turning stricken hearts to God appeared the most important need of the hour. Without asking, he felt sure Edith would approve.

"If I could interrupt for a moment, I'd like to lead a prayer for Edith and all the rest of us. This tragedy is too much to bear without the Lord's help. Let's all join hands." The murmur of conversation died as everyone drew together, linking hands to form a circle.

"Holy Father, our hearts are broken right now. Help us today to see your light shining above the dark shadow of death." With gentle words, he focused their attention on the comfort of God's tender compassion.

When his petition ended, the circle of friends converged to take care of Edith. Ahead lay an endless stream of papers to be signed, decisions made, and visitors received. Red assured him that he and Verna would stay at her side all day. With hugs for all, Barry headed back to his car.

Driving away from the hospital parking lot, he powered the cell phone and dialed Keri's number. She would want to know.

"This is Keri."

"Hi, babe. I'm just leaving the hospital."

"What happened?"

"They couldn't save him."

"He's gone?"

"He had a stroke, then his heart failed before I got there." He repeated the details of his conversations. "I don't think there's anything you can do now. Let's plan to go over there this evening. I'll talk with her about the funeral arrangements, and you can encourage her, too."

"Oh, poor Edith. They loved each other so much." Her voice hung heavy with hurt at the pain of her elder friend. "I'll let Jason know that we'll need to make a visit tonight."

"Seeing Edith so devastated made me think how much I love you. I'll see you soon."

He parked at the church and walked slowly toward the tall front doors. His hand paused on the handle. *My last conversation with Harvey took place right here just 48 hours ago. Sometimes life changes so quickly, never to be the same.*

Mary sat at the front desk. "What happened to Harvey?"

"It's bad. His heart stopped, and they couldn't revive him."

"Oh, no!"

Lauren and Liz hurried across the office to hear the details. He relayed the story once more. By the time he finished, Mary had already written a notice on the "Member Needs" bulletin board in the hallway near the office. The work of caring for a broken heart demanded the church take action.

Keri saw the line of cars snaking from the new parking lot down Jefferson Street, red tail light following red tail light. The grand opening for the new location of Doogie's Deli had apparently caught everyone's attention. She knew the old diner well, having traveled many times to the weather-beaten storefront near the river to enjoy the famed Ozark Garden Delight sub sandwich. When Doug Douglas, known to everyone as Doogie, had signed the loan papers for the new endeavor, Keri promised him she would bring the whole bank to celebrate the new location. Now, it looked like half the town had the same idea.

She perked up. The traffic jam included the Channel 9 news crew, who piloted the white van to a parking place just as Keri turned the corner. This could provide a perfect opportunity for the plan she had been working on all morning! She swung the Accord around in a quick U-turn and drove back toward the van with the prominent 'Channel 9 News' emblazoned on the side.

"Hi, Keri." Dominique rolled down the window of the news van. "I saw you at the press conference yesterday. Pretty tough talk for our little city."

"Our Prez is bent out of shape about it. That's why I stopped you. Can we talk for a minute?"

"Sure." The reporter turned to speak to Butch, the driver and cameraman. "You guys go ahead and get in line. Order me a combo plate."

Keri knew the statuesque black reporter from tennis tournaments at the Hillside Tennis Center. Last summer they had shared a hastily-arranged, Saturday morning doubles match against a set of high school girls and won in a tie-breaker.

She led her a few steps away to a welcome patch of shade near the bright red brick restaurant.

"We need a fair chance to counter Van Dang's accusations. I've got a person who can give another side to this business. Would you be willing to interview her?"

Dominique shrugged. "I guess anything is possible. We aired the story at the top of the news cast last night. But, I can't promise anything."

"I don't expect you to do that. Just promise me you'll give us time for an interview tomorrow."

"I have to get approval from the news director. What do you have in mind?"

She cranked up the charm. "I don't have all the details yet, but I know it will be worth your time. Bring your crew at 10:00 Thursday morning to the Community Center."

"Over at Eastside? I figured you'd want to shoot the segment at the bank."

"No, I've got something different in mind. And listen— you'll be glad you've made the effort."

"Come on, Dominique," Butch called from the door of the restaurant, tapping his watch.

"O.K." The reporter turned to Keri. "Unless my boss throws a fit, we'll see you on Thursday. I hope you've got something good."

"I'll make you a winner, just like at the doubles' tournament last summer." She made a quick motion to imitate a forehand smash. "See you then."

The clock showed nearly 10:00 a.m. when Barry carried the mail back from Lauren's desk to his office. His spirit felt lacerated by the sudden slap of tragedy. The anguish on Edith's face replayed with technicolor vividness. Thankfully, she wouldn't have to face the grief without family and friends.

He tossed the mail on the corner of his desk. A thick, yellow mailing envelope lay across the writing pad. What could this be? He raised the parcel, turning it from one side to another. No marks of any kind betrayed its origin but the contents seemed bulky and heavy, and shifted slightly as he turned it curiously from side to side.

Taking the letter opener, he sliced open the sealed flap.

A peculiar odor wafted from the envelope. He stretched the opening wider, letting light illuminate the jumbled contents. His dark eyebrows raised in a reaction of disbelief. On impulse, he upended the package and shook out the cargo.

A cascade of $100 bills flowed like a green landslide across his desk.

He slumped down into the chair, breath suspended at the sight. Crisp, clean, green bills covered the dark, wooden desktop. He looked again at the empty envelope, front and back. No writing at all. Just a yellow 8.5 by 11 inch envelope—and a mountain of green money like he had never seen in his life.

How much? His shaking hands began to flip through the pile. One, two, three hundred. Two stacks of 10 bills, then three, then five stacks.

$5,000!

Where in the world did this come from?

The church had not issued any special appeals or promoted a special offering. Summer months usually brought smaller receipts, with family vacations eating up disposable dollars that might ordinarily land in the offering plate. The Peters never had that kind of extra money to loan anyone, so it couldn't be intended to pay back a debt.

He fingered one of the crisp bills, holding it up to the

light. It looked legitimate. But why would a fortune be left for him to find in an unmarked envelope?

I can't just leave this here.

He jumped into action, gathering the five stacks and stuffing them quickly back in the yellow envelope. He jerked open the lower left hand drawer of his desk, finding the space only half-full of stationary, envelopes, and memo pads. He shoved the envelope as far back as it would go. Looking up, he noted that his door had remained closed for the entire five minute episode of discovery.

Now what do I do with it?

Church policies divided all receipts between two categories. Money for the General Fund paid for all the church operations as the annual budget dictated. The other type of receipts fell in the category of Designated Gifts. These gifts had specific instructions attached: 'For the building fund,' or 'For the youth trip to Jefferson City.' Thousands of dollars came to this category every year. IRS regulations required the funds to be spent for only those purposes. Just a few years ago, a prominent televangelist went to prison because he misused money that had been designated for a special purpose.

Did those regulations cover a treasure of unbidden cash in an unmarked envelope?

The leather recliner squeaked loudly as he leaned back and put his hands behind his head. Across the years, he had received small amounts of money as love gifts, usually letters that arrived with a note of appreciation and a check for $20, or even $50. Sometimes the sender preferred anonymity. He remembered the Sunday after Keri gave birth to Jason. When he had finished visiting with the parishioners, he went back to the pulpit to get his Bible and notes. Resting on the pulpit he found an envelope containing a ragged $20 bill and a note scrawled in the writing of an older person. "For Keri and the baby's first dinner out," it read. The young parents kept the note and enjoyed the dinner, just as the instructions dictated. The pleasant memory brought a smile.

But a love gift of $5,000 in cash? That seemed unbelievable.

He glanced toward the closed door, then quietly slid the drawer open to look at the treasure trove again. He removed the envelope. This time, he looked carefully around the bills, seeking perhaps a small note, or some instructions hidden from view. Then he surveyed every item on the top of this desk. Not a single clue could be found to reveal why this money bag had appeared from nowhere on his desk.

Is it church money or my money?

His imagination soared with the possibilities. What had he and Keri talked about buying? A big screen TV. Taking a vacation to Cancun, just the two of them. Or an investment that could really pay back big. Five grand could go a long way.

He would have to set aside 20% for taxes, of course, and report it on his income for the year.

Of course. Report it to the church, and to the IRS. That's what he should do.

But cash left no records. He fingered the stiff bills, rubbing them between his fingers, feeling the texture of the unique government paper. How could it ever be proved he even had the money, if he didn't deposit it? What if he didn't even tell Keri about it? He could keep it in this drawer and just use the cash slowly for special things.

This could be my own quiet stash for just what I want.

Once again, he stuffed the cash in the envelope, then slid it back into the far end of the drawer. Someone knows the answer. Nothing could be settled until he uncovered that mystery.

"I understand. Let me give you a call next week, and

we'll reschedule lunch to review your medical policy. I appreciate your business. Bye, now."

David glanced at his watch. Zack's call to cancel lunch meant more than a delay in closing a deal. Without someone to eat with, he would face another lonely meal in an empty house. He usually avoided the problem by making lunch a time to do business. But not today. Perhaps mingling with the crowd at Sandy's Burger Treat, the small restaurant near his office, would fill the emptiness. He stuck a copy of "Newsworld" under his arm, closed the door of his insurance agency, then drove down 33rd street.

During his thirty-nine years, David had faced his share of challenges. Most had fallen quickly to his energetic, take-no-prisoners lifestyle. The grief over Morgan hadn't disappeared so easily. He worked everyday to push his mind past it. Three weeks after the funeral he had said to a friend, 'I just can't sit down and give up.' The words now formed his mantra. Occasionally, he felt very strong and positive. Other days came like heavy rain clouds, dampening his initiative and flooding him with dark waves of grief. Most days he just kept his schedule tight, taking care of clients and keeping in touch with friends.

"What can I get you today?" The blond waitress wore a red t-shirt emblazoned with 'Sandy's Burger Treat.' She poised a stubby pencil above her pad.

"Just a cheeseburger today."

"What about a drink?"

He handed back the menu. "A Dr. Pepper, please."

"I'll have your drink right out." She turned and headed toward the kitchen. His eyes followed her wide frame. No comparison to Morgan's shapely figure there. He opened the magazine to keep his mind occupied before the sandwich arrived.

The Dockerys had married eight years ago on a spring afternoon filled with blooming flowers and bright hopes. People all across town noted David's skills in the new insurance agency and Morgan's personable enthusiasm. Soon, the firm began to prosper. The bride busied herself in volunteer work and an occasional business venture. Friends still laughed at the October when she and Keri Peters decided they would paint faces on pumpkins and sell them at Phillip's Grocery. It occupied countless hours and produced a grand mess that netted a profit of $15.53 each—plus a hundred priceless memories.

"Here's that Dr. Pepper." The blond sat the drink on the table with a perfunctory smile. "The cheeseburger should be out in just a minute or two."

He took a deep drink. So much of that happiness still lingered in his memory. Maybe that made the grief just as vivid, too. Sometimes the heartache frightened him with its intensity. He had pumped up enough courage on Sunday to tell Keri about hearing Morgan's voice. Even now, sitting in the daylight amid the busy atmosphere of the restaurant, the experience sounded crazy. He knew his mind had just played a trick on him. But the haunting moment even now made his heart beat a little faster.

"Here you go," the waitress said as she slid the plate down in front of him. "Can I get you anything else?"

"Just a refill on this drink, I guess."

"I'll be right back with a fresh glass."

He took a bite of the sandwich and raised the magazine to find the cover story. One page contained a perfume ad, printed on heavy paper. When he thumbed the page, the microcapsules on the specially printed advertisement released their fragrance. In the next moment, the provocative aroma of Morgan's favorite perfume surrounded him.

He fanned the page again, breathing in deeply. His wide eyes focused on the picture in the ad. A bikini-clad model reclined seductively on a hunter green sofa, Morgan's favorite color—and the color of her mangled, blood-stained sweater returned by the hospital the night of the accident.

Oh, God, he thought. Am I losing it, or what?

He closed the pages to escape the alarming ad. *I am crazy, just like that dream last night showed.* He had managed to work through the entire morning without reviewing his bizarre dream. Now, the scenes played again, carrying him far away from the clatter of the restaurant.

He saw himself sitting with Morgan in the worship center at Mt. Faith Church, just as they had done nearly every Sunday of their married life. The familiar pews bulged with people. Morgan sat close, snuggled under his left arm, as usual. He felt her lay her head on his shoulder in a tender gesture. Then, the dream turned strange. With the preacher thundering the Bible message, David began to caress her cheek. She snuggled closer, inviting more. He grew more aggressive, brushing aside her dark hair to kiss her neck. No one in the fantasy congregation paid any attention. Gently, he took her chin, lifting her lovely face toward his lips.

The woman had Keri's face.

The blow of seeing those fresh blue eyes jerked him awake, heart pounding, early this morning. Feelings about Morgan, Keri, the church, his loneliness jumbled upon each other. *Do crazy dreams mean a mental breakdown?*

His attention returned to the restaurant and the hamburger growing cold in his hand. The scent of the perfume had dissipated amid the smell of french fries and burgers. He glanced across the busy crowd at Sandy's, wondering if anyone had observed his momentary trance.

The waitress stood at his elbow, looking at him with her brows knit. "Can I get you anything else?" Her voice sounded concerned about more than just offering him a dessert.

"Uh, no. That's fine." He grabbed up his drink. "Good stuff."

"Glad you liked it. I'll leave the tab here. I'll be your cashier when you're ready."

She had hardly made it back to the serving counter

when a chair scraped loudly across the floor. She turned to see the man throw down his money across the half-eaten sandwich and march out the door.

He didn't look back. *I must keep my mind clear. If I lose my marbles, I'll never finish the plan.*

"Daemon, you know I've never liked beating around the bush. I prefer things out in the open so everyone can see them. That's why I wanted to visit with you privately."

Ed Loomis' 6' 6" frame sat wedged in a quiet booth of Mt. Carmel's best steakhouse, the Green Door. The large window beside them looked out on the Square, bordered with tall cottonwood trees guarding the courthouse lawn.

"I appreciate your willingness to listen." His slender hands rearranged the silverware and napkin on the table. "Some people aren't so kind. After the meeting Sunday, one man even tried to quote the Bible and scare me away from discussing these issues. I suppose some people never want to face the facts."

Ed looked across the polished table at the man he had known for years. "You know I'm serving as chairman of the Personnel Committee this year. That makes me doubly interested in anything said about the Pastor. I have one question—do you have any facts to back up what you're saying?"

"The truth stands out to anyone who cares to look. I don't particularly like to blow the whistle but consider our situation today." His voice dropped in volume. "Brother Peters' leadership is crippling the church. The people who made this church great refuse to follow him. Have you noticed how few folks our age attend the services? For the last few months I've made it my duty to talk to them and listen to their opinions. I'm telling you, they feel left out, with all the young families joining now."

"Don't we want new families to join?"

"Perhaps." He shrugged his shoulders. "I'm sure we need more families of all ages. But, some of these young families are actively seeking control of the church! They're making changes in everything." He drove his index finger on the table top. "Barry encourages these outlandish innovations. He has no interest at all in the people who have stayed faithful for a long time, like you and me."

"The facts show the church has grown, Daemon."

"But, what kind of people are joining? When I see the new members introduced each week, I wonder if any of them believe the great truths that anchor our faith. Just this morning Dale Galloway called to let me know about a poor family his wife visited yesterday. The pastor made one visit to them and now is rushing ahead to get the eight-year old baptized! I think Barry's just interested in pumping up the numbers so the denominational executives in Jeff City will pay attention!"

A tall waiter appeared, bearing the entrees ordered earlier. Daemon rearranged the plates to his preferred order.

"I like to see children come to our church," Ed said when the server stepped away. "And remember, those new people give to help pay the bills."

Daemon swallowed a bite quickly. "There's something else that troubles me. Here's a fact for you—he's got his wife working at the bank where most of our people have their accounts. They drive two brand new cars. I think Barry wants to build his nest egg with all those new people, more than he wants to talk about doctrine."

"Are you trying to say we're overpaying him? As chairman of the Personnel Committee, I've tried very hard to keep...."

He lifted a hand to defuse Ed's protests. "No, no, not at all. You're the lone voice of sanity and experience in the church leadership right now." A pause for a drink let his compliment sink in. "The problem does not lie in what he's being paid legally. The real problem lies in what may take place somewhere else." His quiet voice seemed to hold a secret.

"What do you mean, 'somewhere else?'"

He glanced at the tables to their left and right before leaning forward. "Ed, I'm really not at liberty to reveal right now everything my research has uncovered. But let me assure you, I know of something brewing right now that could blow Peters' ministry sky high and ruin our church." His face tightened. "It's money, Ed, pure and simple money. Barry has let greed take control of him. His wife neglects her work at the church to hold a high-paying job at the bank. I've heard from someone in a position to know that irregularities exist. We'd better keep our eyes open, or the flock of Mt. Faith Church will look like sheep after shearing—and more will be missing that just a wool coat!"

The waiter stopped by the table to pour more tea. The conversation paused while Ed took a bite to collect his thoughts. Putting down the fork, he jabbed a finger toward Daemon's chest. "I said I don't like to beat around the bush. Give me a straight answer. Do I hear you accusing the Pastor of embezzling church money?"

The moments ticked by like seconds on a detonator. Ed's eyes never left Daemon's proud face.

"We could know an answer to that question in just a few days," the little man said, his lips twisted with a quizzical smile.

"46 Mt. Carmel," Corporal Josh Allen called to the dispatcher at the Mt. Carmel Police Department. "I'll be 10-6 for lunch at Mt. Faith Church."

"10-4, MCPD," the dispatcher's voice crackled from the speaker.

Locking the doors of the patrol car, the lean, well-muscled officer adjusted the 9mm Sig Sauer pistol hanging on his hip, and headed across the parking lot of Mt. Faith Church. The strong midday sun cooked his shoulders through the dark blue uniform.

Mike Mitchum burst out the front door of the church a moment before the officer arrived.

"What's the hurry, Mike? It's too hot to go out for lunch. You'd better stay here and enjoy the air conditioning."

"I'd like to." The stocky minister already showed a ring of sweat beads across his forehead. "But, Beverly called. The car overheated. She's stuck at the grocery store."

"Oh, man! She'll be overheated, too, I bet. If you need any help, call me here."

"Thanks."

He crossed the empty atrium and pulled open the office door.

"Hi Liz. Is Lauren in here?"

Liz had moved to Mary's desk to work as receptionist for the lunch hour. She nodded, "I'm sure she's at her desk. I think she's waiting for you."

During the last four months the handsome, brown-haired officer had become a fixture around the Mt. Faith office. Mentioning his name to Lauren brought a distinct glow to her face. This prompted the staff to diagnose an acute case of love sickness.

"Hi!" Lauren beamed when Josh stepped around the corner of her cubicle. "Ready for some lunch?"

"Only if we can eat here at the church! It's broiling outside."

"That's why I made a double brown bag lunch today. We can go over to Baxter Hall and eat there."

Few activities tied up Baxter Hall, the church dining

and activity center, at noon during the week. Occasionally, staff would bring their lunch to eat there, just to save time and money. Today, the spacious room promised a good spot for a couple who wanted privacy.

Josh slipped his hand around hers as they walked toward the dining room. These very halls provided the setting a year ago when he first met the tall beauty. At that time, he had just moved from Springfield to the smaller Mt. Carmel police force with the hope of advancing faster through the ranks. That goal still held his attention, but these days his mind seemed to be on something other than his career.

They chose a table near the kitchen of the empty hall. She opened the bag and unwrapped two roast beef sandwiches. "Have you had a busy morning?"

"I pulled an assignment at the East Side Day Care Center this morning. I talked to the little guys about safety and gave them some tips on what to say if they have to call 9-1-1. Pretty lively group of kids. All one kid wanted to talk about was my gun. I didn't think much about it until the teacher told me later that the boy's Dad had been shot last year."

"How sad! Did you let him hold it?"

"No, that's not a good idea, because the little kids can't tell the difference between a gun being a toy and it being real."

"I can understand that." She liked it when he sounded so professional.

Josh popped the top of a soda. "The East Side has a tough reputation. One of the day care workers mentioned the Security State Bank controversy. You know, I can see why people are suspicious. Gangs rule the place. That's why the little guy's Dad took a bullet.

Lauren's hand-made, double-meat sandwich tasted even better than he had hoped. He finished it and drained the soda. Glancing across the table, he also drank in the shine of her auburn hair laying across the sleeveless navy top.

"On the way over here, I heard an ad on the radio from one of the TV stations about a follow-up news report tonight about that bank story. I thought about Keri Peters. Isn't that the bank where she works?"

"Yes, it is. In fact, she works in community relations."

"What's Keri like, anyway? I hardly know her, though I see her sitting in church every week."

She cut an apple and handed him a slice. "Keri's a neat person. She really thinks about other people. That's probably why she advanced so fast at the bank. Anytime I do something special to help her, I get a thank you note from her. Not many people take time to write those anymore."

He finished a first slice of the tart, green-skinned apple. "What's your morning been like?"

She dropped her voice, even though the hall stood empty. "Brother Barry asked about an envelope he found on his desk. I didn't know anything about it. Of course, nearly every week someone losses something around the church and asks us to track it down."

"So why the big mystery?"

"He wouldn't tell us what the envelope had in it. I'm guessing it had a complaint letter."

"You know, anonymous mail would get my blood boiling fast. At least on the police force, when someone has a complaint, the supervisor calls you in and talks about it right up front. At the church, people whisper behind your back way too much. I think the pastor needs all the support he can get, not anonymous letters."

She looked in his dark brown eyes. The way he thought—direct, open and honest—enchanted her. In the four months they had dated seriously, she had never heard him say anything angry or derogatory towards anyone. Talking with him made every day brighter. This one hour lunch just wouldn't last long enough.

Keri sat straight-backed in the plush, gray chair near the inlaid mahogany desk of the bank president. She watched his stubby, black shoes make deep indentations on the thick carpet in his second nervous circuit of the fifth floor office.

"Do you really think the interview with your Vietnamese friend can stop this smear campaign?"

"As you know, sir, public perception is public reality. I...."

"Yes, I know it quite well. Not two hours ago the school district CFO called to express his concern. He just wanted to reassure himself we were clean from these accusations. And he pointedly reminded me of the $5 million they have in our bank!"

"I have a gut feeling people in the community will identify far more with a Mt. Carmel assistant principal than with a lawyer from St. Louis."

He stood near the window, gazing at the pedestrians on the street five stories below. "It just makes me nervous that we are depending on the news media to reach those people down there with our message."

She shifted in her chair. "I understand your concern. No one has a guarantee when a news director gets his hands on a story. But the reporter, Dominique Greer, is a friend of mine. I think after talking with her this morning she is willing to give us a fair hearing."

He stood silent for several seconds, hands clasped together behind his back, rocking back and forth. "I've been in this business for more than two decades, Keri. I know how the word-of-mouth on the street can make or break a bank like ours.

Every day of success is dependent upon what those people believe. We can have the best advertising campaign and give away toasters until we are blue in the face, but when the community loses trust in you, the game is over."

The president slowly turned and sat down in the high-back leather chair. His eyes locked on hers.

"I know you're trying hard. Give it your best—and say a few extra prayers."

"Yes, sir. I will."

"Let me know immediately after the interview how it went. I want to know every word the lady says."

She stood. "I'll call you immediately. I know Duyen believes in our bank. No news director can edit that out of a video tape."

The telephone rang. "I hope you're right," he said, scooping up the receiver.

"Thank you, sir." She waved and retreated from his office, her mouth as dry as sandpaper.

Merylene sat at the receptionist desk outside the office. She looked up when Keri closed the president's door. "Are you O.K.?"

"I'll know a lot more by this time tomorrow. Keep watching him for me. And run the other way if you see any Vietnamese lawyers."

"Would you keep the peasants from storming the Bastille? I'm going to work on Sunday's sermon for an hour or so." Barry twisted a paper clip into a stick figure with a broken leg and handed the impromptu sculpture to Lauren. "This is what they do to pastors who don't preach very well."

She laughed and dropped the twisted wire to her desk. "Looks pretty brutal. I'll do my best."

The click of the door closing gave hope that his scattered thoughts could be tamed. Sermon preparation usually marked a highlight in his week, but today the squeeze of events threatened to push his mind in other directions.

Once again, he opened the lower drawer to check on the yellow envelope. The mysterious package lay undisturbed.

What should I do? The question hung in his mind, unresolved. He slid the drawer closed as gently as a father tiptoeing around a sleeping baby. Can't worry with that now. The time had come to focus on a sermon. The money could wait—for now.

Since his first sermon at Lake Jefferson years ago, Barry had enjoyed the title, 'Preacher.' The colloquial designation reflected his most public activity. His experience through the years confirmed that a minister might carry expertise in management, human relations, teaching, or crisis counseling, but always and forever the central duty in the mind of members remained preaching. Other duties of the job could be handled poorly, but if his pulpit skills shined, most parishioners stayed happy.

The buzz of the telephone intercom interrupted his thoughts. "Before you get started, let me bring in a couple of messages that came during lunch, Pastor," Lauren said.

He looked up when she dropped the pink forms with her notes on his desk. "Did you have a nice lunch today?"

Her face reddened at his playful question. "Well, yes, I enjoyed it. Josh came by. We just stayed here to eat since it's so hot."

"He seems like a nice guy. I'd like to have lunch with him one of these days and get to know him more. Maybe he would even give Jason and me a ride in the patrol car."

"I'm sure he would. He speaks very highly of you so I haven't told him all the stories I know about the real you."

"Well, make sure you don't! I've managed to hide my

secrets for years, and I don't want them out now."

"They're safe with me," she said with a grin. "By the way, Drew wants to meet with you about something he said was important."

"Is he in his office now?"

"Yes."

"O.K. I'll take care of it. But I may have to preach last Sunday's sermon again, at this rate."

He followed her out the door and crossed the suite to the cluttered office of the Minister of Students and Singles. Drew waved across his desk, an edifice piled high with magazines, literature that needed to go to the lay volunteers who taught the students each Sunday, and assorted paraphernalia from the singles' party last Friday.

"Lauren said you called while I was on the phone. What's up?" Barry moved a backpack off a chair to sit down.

"I talked to Jean Adkins this morning about helping with the back-to-school retreat. She mentioned being in the home prayer meeting Sunday night at the Puckett's house. What's the deal about this prophecy Kent made?"

He shrugged his shoulders. "I don't understand it all. I think Kent was quoting a Psalm, though I haven't taken time to look it up. But, the truly weird part came when he described me getting mugged!" He related the disturbing scene Kent pictured for the group.

"How do you feel about it? Was he trying to scare you or something?"

"No, I don't think so. Kent and Beth have always supported the church and my ministry." He hesitated, searching for words to name the way he felt after the strange incident. "It felt spooky. Honestly, I could hardly get to sleep that night. I don't know what kind of problems I could be facing—or if Kent just had a case of indigestion!"

Drew smiled. "We may have to hire Josh Allen as your

body guard. At least, he'd enjoy sitting near your office, if you know what I mean!"

Mary leaned around the doorpost. "Sorry to interrupt. Mrs. Flowers wants to know about tonight's visit. What time are you and Keri planning to come?"

"7:30, if that's convenient for her. That'll give us time to finish with dinner."

She headed back to her desk with the message.

The youth minister had a somber expression on his face. "It's terrible to think about Harvey not being with us anymore. The church will miss him."

"I'll always remember him as a great friend. He stood by me when lots of people wanted to send me packing. He had more vision for the future than most people half his age."

"I bet a huge crowd shows up. Mike may blow a gasket making sure the building looks just right. I guess we'll feed the family a lunch?"

Barry twirled the straps of the backpack in his hand. "The older folks wouldn't have it any other way. The meal gives the family a good gathering place to ease the stress of the funeral."

The intercom on Drew's desk buzzed. "Pastor, Keri is on line three for you," Liz reported.

"Thanks, Liz. I'll take it in my office." He stood to leave. "I appreciate your concern over the vision thing."

Drew's big hand flashed the O.K. sign. "Let me know if you find out anything more."

In his office, Barry pushed the red light for line three. "Hi, babe. How is it going?"

Keri's voice sounded tight. "Nerve-wracking. Ledbetter seems really uptight over the way I want to handle this Vietnamese deal." She filled in the details of the interview. "But I really called to find out about tonight. What's our schedule?"

"We're due at the Flowers at 7:30. You want me to pick

up some pizza on the way home?"

"Great idea. I'll pick up Jason."

"Hey, let me tell you one more thing."

"What?"

"I love you, and you're the best V-P at that goofy bank."

"Tell the boss," she said with a rueful tone.

"I'll do that one of these days. See you in a little while."

Nadine stood in front of the mirror in the master bedroom, patting a stray lock of her reddish-brown beehive into place. She heard the distinctive creak of the door opening from the garage to the kitchen. "Is that you?"

"I'm here," Daemon said, "and glad of it, the way things smell. Someone coming for dinner tonight?"

She met him in the kitchen. "No. I thought you might like that lasagna we ate at the Burton's a few weeks ago. I called her this afternoon to get the recipe."

Daemon laid his papers on the kitchen bar. "Let me wash up and I'll be ready." He headed toward the master bath, humming "A Mighty Fortress." The strong melody of his favorite hymn reflected his confidence that his lunch with Ed had strengthened the plans to change the deteriorating church situation. "A bulwark never fail-l-ling," he voiced, drawing out the syllables with a flourish.

Nadine had poured tea and taken a chair at the breakfast bar when he returned. The aroma of cheese and spice filled the kitchen. After he said a prayer, he held up his plate to receive a heaping portion. "What happened around here this afternoon?"

"Not much beyond my lasagna project. I did start cleaning out the closet in the hall. I still had a dozen boxes from Mom's house that I haven't sorted out.... Oh, wait. Did you hear the news from church?"

"Nothing major, I guess. What news?"

"Harvey Flowers died this morning."

His fork froze in midair. "Good Lord! What happened?"

Between bites of lasagna she recapped the tragic events. "He never even got to say good-bye to Edith. It happened so suddenly."

"Did he know of a medical problem? High blood pressure, or anything?"

She shook her head. "Edith told Gloria he didn't even take any medicine regularly. They made such a happy couple. The funeral will be on Saturday. I've already said I would take a dessert for the meal at church."

"Remember Harvey's comment Sunday night? I still don't know what to make of it."

"I thought of that very thing after talking to Gloria."

They finished the meal lost in their own thoughts. After clearing the dishes, Daemon settled in his gold print recliner in the family room. Nadine followed shortly, bringing a large print crossword puzzle book.

"I'm going to finish this puzzle. It uses names of Bible characters. Problem is, I've never heard of most of them."

"I guess I'll catch up on this magazine." He pulled the handle of the recliner to elevate the footrest, opened the new copy of "Finance," then located a television news program. His interest focused primarily on the magazine until the camera zoomed in on an old brick building in downtown Charleston.

A young reporter stood in the bare group therapy room of the drug rehabilitation center. Behind him a few young men, shabbily dressed, slouched in plastic chairs. The newsman nodded toward them. "The work here seems painstaking and often frustrating, but one-by-one, the lives of these young clients find new hope. I'm standing here with the director, Ben Stanford..."

Daemon threw down the magazine and punched the television remote control repeatedly. The channels flipped in a rapid blur of confused images.

"What's the matter?"

"Those stupid social workers don't know anything," he snapped. "Drug addicts can't be helped by sitting around whining about their problems to each other. Those centers ought to be shut down. They do nothing but suck up government money!"

"Daemon. Don't talk like that."

"It's my house, and I'll talk the way I want to talk. Maybe I didn't talk the way I should have ten years ago."

She penciled in another answer on the puzzle without a response. Nothing could stop his anger now.

"The potheads started taking over the world just about then. If we'd have stood up and tossed them all in jail, the whole mess would never have gotten started." His cheeks grew red. "But no! We just sat around scratching our heads. Marijuana, then LSD. It got worse by the year. The cops ignored it, and the bureaucrats wouldn't deal with it. Even the churches clammed up."

The TV clicked off. Nadine gazed at her puzzle, hoping that silence would quell the building storm. Her strategy failed. With a bang, the footrest slammed down. He stood up, pacing the room, his words growing louder with each step.

"Jack listened to it all. When he joined that fraternity they crammed it down his throat. He was hip! They brainwashed him. And who knows how many of those liberal professors smoked the stuff themselves? Barry could have helped Jack when we finally got him home. We had that one time when we took him to church. He said he wouldn't mind hearing the new pastor. Do you remember going? We all sat together. I had prayed so hard for that day. I just knew if Jack would listen to a good gospel sermon he could change. But do you know what happened?"

She knew so well. She had perched on the pew that spring morning, hardly daring to breathe, praying that somehow the family could be whole again.

"He preached on finding yourself! On how God accepts us! He never mentioned sin, never mentioned Hell. Jack didn't hear what he needed to hear."

"But Barry didn't know the situation. We didn't tell him...."

"Shut up! He didn't preach the gospel!" His finger punctuated every point. "Jack needed someone to look him in the eye and tell him right from wrong. He needed a kick in the backside from God to come clean. Barry messed up, Nadine, he messed up big time. And I intend for him to pay. He helped destroy my family. And I'm going to make him pay for it!"

He marched to the kitchen, hands trembling with rage. Jerking the upper cabinet open, he reached for help to cool his rampage.

She tossed her puzzle to the floor. "I'm going to take a bath and go to bed."

He brought a vodka bottle down on the counter with a bang. His unsteady hands filled a shot glass with alcohol and a squirt of orange juice. He sat down heavily at the table near the window. "I'm going to get him for what he did to my son," he shouted to the empty room.

The humid, evening air hung like a warm, wet sheet when the Peters closed their front door and walked to the car.

"Looks like rain." Barry surveyed the dark clouds above the western hills of Mt. Carmel.

"I just hope it doesn't storm." Keri leaned her head back against the leather seat and closed her eyes. The emotions of the work day had sapped her strength. Now, she faced a visit with a grieving friend. Her heart darkened with dread.

The Toyota merged into the traffic on Osage Highway, heading toward the Spring River bridge. Barry glanced at his wife's quiet face and kept his silence. During dinner, his thoughts had strayed back to the strange envelope in his office. He didn't want to mention it yet. No use getting her stirred up, and he really didn't have any answers about the mystery.

Rose Lane wound back and forth up the side of Buck Hill, the forested rise that formed the west bank of Spring River. The Flowers' home stood half way to the crest, a small frame house painted dull gold. The roses Harvey so carefully tended stood under the front window to the right of the high porch, aglow with a silent tribute of red, yellow, and cream blooms.

Barry took Keri's arm as they climbed the porch stairs.

Across years of ministry they had made this burdened journey many times, taking their places in living rooms where grief cast a dark shadow. They noticed that at such times, family members assumed new roles. The person who throbbed with life might become a recluse, quiet and introspective. The daughter-in-law who felt on the outside of the family circle might become the organizer, helping every detail fall into place. Usually, a curious quietness pervaded the house, reflecting the struggle of the soul at the specter of death looming so close.

Verna opened the aluminum screen door to greet them. "Come on in, please. Everyone but Mom is here in the living room." She grabbed Keri's hand, pulling her through the door to the small front room, announcing, "The pastor and his wife are here."

Barry started around the room, shaking hands. He didn't know most of the guests. A short, rotund daughter and son-in-law from Little Rock stood up to meet him. The brother he had seen in the emergency room waiting area this morning stood next to the kitchen door. The crowd provided a testimony of family love for the man who had always given so much of himself.

"Oh, my pastor's here." Edith's voice interrupted the conversations. She entered the crowded room and embraced Barry. Her eyes drooped dark from the tears of the day. The hug for Keri lingered until she noticed the tears of the sensitive pastor's wife.

"Now, Hon, don't cry," she said, patting Keri's shoulder. "Harvey's left us, but he's with the Lord. We can't be sad for that."

"Edith, we're so sorry this happened." Barry said. "Harvey appeared in rare form Sunday, so full of energy. He seemed to be in fine health."

"He never complained about health problems. The stroke hit so suddenly. But God has His reasons."

Keri spoke up. "Edith, your faith amazes me."

The silver-haired woman grasped Keri's hand. "Harvey and I shared that faith, hon. We loved the Lord together. And we'll be together again someday soon."

She led them to the little oak kitchen table and invited them to take a seat. Verna brought large, blue glasses filled with iced tea. For the next few minutes Barry took notes about the family's desires for the funeral service.

"We want the service on Saturday morning, so the oldest grandson can arrive from South Korea," Verna insisted.

A red flag waved in Barry's mind about the Saturday schedule. *That means the Powell wedding decorations can't be placed in the sanctuary until Saturday at noon. I'll need to talk to them, and I hope they agree.* His mind whirled with arrangements. *The lunch, provided by the church, needs to take place here at the Flowers, because the decorations for the wedding reception that evening will already be in place.* While the women talked, he dashed off a list of necessary calls to make immediately.

With the details finally in hand, Verna helped gather

everyone so Barry could lead a family prayer.

"Let's hold hands," he said to the grieving family circle. "We can count on God to know what we need before we can even ask. We need to remind ourselves that He really does care. Let's pray." With hands held tightly, the wounded family listened to the pastor's prayer for them, the service on Saturday, and the church.

On the drive down the steep slopes of Buck Hill, Keri glanced at her watch. "We need to pick up Jason from the Jenkins."

"Give him a call so he'll be ready. I'm tired."

Keri dialed the call, only to hear her son offer a different idea. Could he please stay one more hour? Keri granted permission and settled back in the seat.

Osage Highway east of the bridge took a sharp twist. Older stores crowded together along the road. The dull brick of the storefront buildings had seen many days come and go. The flecked paint seemed tired from the weary passage of time.

Keri watched the storefronts go by. "I hate to drive down this street."

Barry's brow furrowed. "Why?"

"Because of what happened here."

Silence filled the car.

"Don't you know what happened here six months ago?"

"At this intersection? I don't guess so."

"You can't remember?"

"You know I can't even remember our own anniversary. What are you talking about?"

"Is that how quickly you forget people?"

"Forget who?" After the strain of the conversation with the Flowers family, he had no interest in guessing games. "Did somebody live on this street, or something?"

"Someone *died* on this street! Someone *I* cared about very much."

"Are you talking about Morgan?"

She crossed her arms with a huff of irritation.

"Give me a break, would you? My mind is stuck on that funeral. Besides, I wasn't even here after the accident like you were. And I cared about her, too, believe it or not!"

She wiped a sudden tear from her cheek. *I lost my best friend, and he has forgotten it like last week's baseball scores.*

He pulled in the driveway and rammed the shift lever into park. "You seem to forget that I have to worry about two hundred families who call me pastor. No, I can't remember everything. I've worked with a hundred family problems since then."

The slamming car door cut off his words. She marched into the house, her heart raw at his callous attitude.

His sharp words sliced down the hall behind her.

"Maybe it's time for you, David, and everyone else to get over this and realize life goes on—even without Morgan!"

She whirled toward him from the bedroom doorway, eyes blazing. "I loved Morgan! I'll never forget her!"

She slammed the bedroom door closed hard enough to shake the house. No further words came from the other side of the closed door. Her sobs of sorrow flowed from wounds as fresh now as the moment Morgan's life ended. Lying across the bed in the dark room, she wept from the pain. *Why can't anyone understand how I feel?*

The evening sun, blistering the west windows of the Big Hits Video store, radiated heat across Francie's arm. With a grateful sigh, she eased her ample frame down on the stool near the front register. Only one teenager meandered through the store, providing a lull from the after-work rush and relief for her aching feet.

She glanced up when the entrance buzzer. Recognizing the customer, she gave a standard welcome-to-the-store smile. The burly young man headed toward the back of the store without speaking.

What is his name? Sometimes he brought his little wife and girls. When they came together, they usually rented a comedy. She remembered the short, dark-haired woman always checked out, paying with cash. Buster usually stood behind, mostly expressionless. Then they would leave, with her carrying the baby, the movie, her purse—and his hands empty. Francie crinkled her nose in disdain for a man who acted that way.

Today the big guy came alone. She had seen that quite a few times in the last couple of months, too. Never staying long, he always headed to the adult section to make a quick choice. His taste favored plenty of skin on the video jacket. She once imagined him and the smiling woman watching those videos. It made her skin crawl.

The clatter of the plastic video box on the checkout counter interrupted her rest. "That'll be all for you today?"

He nodded and handed over his laminated ID card.

Francie swiped the card, bringing his name to the screen. Cody Burns. She scanned the movie. "Hot Nights in Rio." That's obviously educational. "That will be $3.29."

He tossed out the cash without a word.

"It's due back Thursday by 11:00. Thanks for coming in." She stopped herself before she wished him a good evening.

At the mobile home, Lisa adjusted a fan to cool the sweltering family room. Cody had finally called about 3:00 p.m. to let her know his plans. His idea was to make the rounds of the used car lots in Neosho to check for job openings, then get a movie on the way home. At least he planned something positive, and the thought of that lifted her spirit for the first time in days.

The last forty-eight hours had scarred her with pain in mind and body. Her cheek remained blue and yellow, discolored from the blow Sunday night. The shame of her appearance kept her from venturing out, except to use the drive-through window at the convenience store. Fortunately, Kendra had left after lunch yesterday for a two-day visit to the grandparents of a friend, sparing Lisa the pain of answering questions. Behind all her hurt loomed Cody's anger, like a stick of dynamite, ready to explode at the slightest provocation.

If only I hadn't said what I did. But, what will we do if he stays out of work and we can't pay the bills? Fretful thoughts filled her mind, allowing Cody to drive up and enter the trailer unnoticed. She had just laid Courtney on the counter for a diaper change when his voice at the door made her jump.

"God, it's hot out there," he said, coming behind her and placing his hands on her waist. "You O.K.?"

"Just hot. I haven't even put a shirt on Courtney all day, so she would be cooler."

His hands came around to the front on her blouse. "Let me take yours off so you'll be cooler, too." He laughed, his breath thick with the smell of beer. She fended him off gracefully and wiggled free.

"How 'bout some dinner?" She gathered Courtney in her arms. "I laid out some meat. Do you want a hamburger or a meat patty with steak sauce?"

Soon the dinner plates lay on the table. Cody actually talked during dinner, describing an interview at a dealership south of Neosho. After dinner, they watched a movie on one of the two stations the old television could receive. The summer sky had turned to a deep red over the ridge when Lisa finally got Courtney settled for the night.

Cody slid a cassette in the VCR when she returned from the baby's room. "I got a movie for us to watch together."

"Again?" Lisa put together the remark about the blouse,

the unusual good humor, the beer on the way home, and the video. Here it comes again. The routine never varied. When the action on the screen heated up, he always pulled her close. At least I won't have to watch all the crummy acting.

He had her clothes off when the baby cried. Lisa froze, distracted, waiting to see if more cries would follow. They did, loudly. Cody began to cuss, then sprang to his feet, stepping angrily toward the bedroom. She followed on his heels. They found Courtney wailing in her crib.

"Shut up, stupid!"

Lisa grabbed his arm. "Don't yell at her!"

Her action doubled his rage. He swung his meaty forearm to push Lisa away. Their struggle brought more screams from the baby.

"You stupid brat!" His huge hand covered Courtney's face and shoved her backwards. "Lay down!"

The little girl tumbled hard against the side of the crib, whacking her head viciously against the wood rail.

"Stop it!" Lisa rushed forward to grapple with him in the dim bedroom. After long moments of struggle, the baby's piercing screams rattled the walls. With a final loud curse, Cody pushed past her to stomp from the room.

Lisa lifted the screaming child from the bed. Turning on the light of the bathroom, she saw an egg-sized hunk of scraped skin, riven with a gash, hiding beneath the baby's dark locks. She balanced the struggling infant in one hand, ran cold water on a rag, then gently covered the injury. Gradually, Courtney's shrill screaming subsided into heavy sobs, the pain and fear chased away by her mother's tenderness.

"I'll get you a warm bottle to help you settle down, sweetie." Pulling on a night shirt, she made her way to the kitchen. The cavorting bodies on the forgotten television screen cast a cold light in the room. She snapped off the power switch, relieved to escape the sordid performance.

Soon, Courtney settled in her arms, nursing the bottle, quiet at last.

The silence of the trailer seemed strange.

"Cody?"

No answer. She guessed he lay asleep in the bedroom and didn't call again. Why did he blow up at Courtney? Sure, their intimacy got interrupted. But, that's no reason to shove a baby. That's wrong. Her anger boiled up again and she pulled the sleeping infant closer.

How many times would it happen? The rocker squeaked in rhythm, calling to mind the record of abuse from his violent outbursts. A black eye, a swollen jaw, a long walk home in the rain from a dance. Then the time, three summers ago, when Kendra wore long pants for days to cover the bruises on the back of her legs. The shame lay cold on her soul.

Much later, she quietly laid the baby in the crib. Now where had Cody gone? She stepped into their bedroom, expecting to find him asleep. The bed lay empty. She pulled back the curtain of the window to look for the truck.

The parking space sat empty.

He had left again! His flight grated across her heart like a rasp.

"I hate you!" She screamed the angry words through the window to the vacant driveway. The cheap window curtain fluttered in the moist, night wind.

Steeled with determination, she marched across the little room and jerked open the closet door.

"That does it, you loser."

The warm darkness that hid Cody's disappearance could also hide others.

Chapter 4
Wednesday

Thunder exploded like cannon fire over the darkened, split-level house on Persimmon Lane, shaking the rafters with long, rolling concussions. Daemon snapped awake at the roar. Near his bed, the windswept rain furiously pelted the tall window. He rolled over with a groan to squint at the digital numbers of the alarm clock. The figures read 7:48, yet the bedroom still lay shrouded in darkness from the heavy clouds of the morning storm. He slowly swung his feet toward the floor and sat, groggy, on the edge of the bed. Another flash of lightning slammed into his eyes, followed instantly by thunder that hit his aching brain like a hammer.

With an act of monumental willpower he stood and donned a velour robe, slung askance the night before across the Kennedy rocker. The smell of coffee penetrated his dull thoughts and drew him toward the kitchen to seek relief from the pounding hangover.

Nadine nodded when he sat down beside her at the breakfast bar. "Thought you might need this," she said, pouring the cup before he could even ask. Taking up the newspaper, she scanned the front page while he sipped the steaming coffee, content to let the black elixir work in silence.

He realized the empty vodka bottle had disappeared

from the table, leaving no visible reminder of the angry eruption last night. He knew she wouldn't talk about Jack's addiction, nor respond to the outbursts that periodically shattered the taboo. Their only son's last visit had taken place five years ago, the weekend he attended church to hear Barry preach. By Sunday evening the visit had deteriorated into a shouting match pitting father against son, prompting Jack to load his car and blast away with no good-bye. The years drifted past with only sporadic contacts, stilted words etched with private pain that haunted both generations.

"I need to get cleaned up." He upended the third cup of coffee. "Have you talked to Claire today?"

"Not this morning. Why?"

"I'm anxious to know about our special delivery envelope. I may call the office myself in a few minutes."

By 9:00 o'clock, helped by a hot shower and the strong coffee, his headache seemed under control. He sat down at the desk in his study and dialed the church number.

"Mt. Faith Church. This is Mary."

"Mary, this is Daemon Asher. How are you today?"

"Fine, Mr. Asher. May I help you with something?"

"You can indeed." He started his carefully planned story. "I need to know if anyone in the church office found a large white envelope. I thought I had it with me when I stopped by the church Monday afternoon but now I can't locate it anywhere. Has anyone turned in an envelope like that?"

"I haven't seen it, Mr. Asher," Mary replied. "But let me ask Lauren. Most of the lost and found items come to her desk. Can you hold just a minute?"

"Be glad to." He drummed his fingers impatiently on the ebony desktop. After a full two minutes, Mary came back on the line.

The conscientious secretary had discovered nothing. But

she had a further question. "Are you sure you lost a white envelope? Yesterday, the Pastor asked everybody about a large yellow envelope he found somewhere. Could that be the one you lost?"

"No, mine was white. Did Pastor Peters describe the contents of his envelope?"

Mary laughed. "He wouldn't tell us a thing. His little mystery had everyone puzzled."

"Well, thanks for checking. Bye."

A thin smile played across his face. His ruse had worked perfectly. Now he knew Barry had not only found the envelope but also disguised the true nature of the contents. Nothing could stop the plan to insure the future of Mt. Faith Church now.

Water sprayed from beneath the speeding Honda when Keri crossed Main Street and turned toward Security State Bank. She glanced at the heavy gray clouds hanging low over Osage Bluff. Their dark shadows mimicked the misery weighing down her soul.

Earlier, in the darkness of the still house, she had pushed herself through the shower and a small breakfast like a programmed machine. Tension from the angry exchange with Barry still seemed to fill the air. He stayed in bed while she put on her makeup. Neither offered a good-bye before she slipped out the door.

Fran's empty chair offered further reprieve when she approached her office. Her efforts at applying her makeup failed to fully disguise her puffy eyes, still suffering from her outburst of grief and anger. She drew back the thin curtains to lighten the small office. One story below, the rain-drenched downtown street glistened with the dreary rain.

Maybe I can get my mind on the work and forget about my troubles for awhile.

She pulled a handful of manila folders from the 'Current' section of her desktop stacker, laying each one methodically on the left edge of the uncluttered mahogany desk. The top folder held plans for the luncheon the bank sponsored each quarter for senior account holders. She flipped it open to scan the Gantt chart that detailed the plans. Instead, her mind filled with the broad, kind face of Harvey Flowers. He and Edith regularly attended the luncheons. To think of him not being a part of the laughter and stories added to the sadness darkening her spirit.

I've lost another friend.

A tear leaked across her cheek. Her heart filled once again with the ache of the visit with Edith, the traumatic flashback of the crash scene, and Barry's cold remarks. *If I only had someone who understood, a friend who would help bear the pain.* Shuffling the planning sheets, she let her thoughts drift back to the friends who had helped her in happier times.

Eighteen years ago, she and Barry had moved from seminary to the peaceful, central Missouri town of Lake Jefferson. Their meager possessions contrasted to their abundant hopes during the inaugural months of pastoral ministry.

The precious women of the church made a place for me. How I grew in those four years! I changed from talking about boyfriends and college football games and parties to a woman involved in real life. We shared everything: real death, real love, and real pain, all wrapped in the bonds of friendship.

On a sunny Fall afternoon she and Cindy, a co-worker at the credit union, had picnicked in the park. The hours stretched long while Cindy revealed the shame of her abuse at the hands of a visiting uncle. Through angry tears, the two women wrestled the emotional demon. The memory of hearts once knit together now warmed her again. Similar experiences had occurred at the church in Keystone and in Hannibal.

She stood, awash in a wave of loneliness, staring at the rain swept streets. The joy of friendship seemed like a glittering jewel lost long ago in the bleak days of stressful ministry.

I don't know if anyone really cares about me. I'm just expected to play my roles: a wife with wifely duties, a mom who has to be on time, and a banker reporting for duty. Perform. Produce. Now. The tears of hurt brimmed her eyes again. *Who cares anyway?*

The rain danced in wind-whipped sheets across the black asphalt pavement of Henry's Fuel and Food. Cody lumbered from the front door to the side of the pickup, jerked open the door, and fell into the worn seat. Panting, he popped the clutch and lurched the rattling truck into the traffic on HW 69. He had a new idea about where Lisa might be hiding.

The burly salesman had awakened two hours earlier from a fitful sleep. The trailer lay ominously silent. Rolling from the stained couch, he had looked out to see the Escort missing. Maybe she's gone to the grocery store, he had thought. He couldn't remember even seeing her when he had stumbled in drunk at 2:30 a.m.

Nearly an hour later, showered and thinking more clearly, Cody opened the folding closet door in the little bedroom he and Lisa shared. He saw one side standing empty, not a dress or blouse in sight. Shocked, he jerked open the dresser drawer. Empty. Stepping across the hall, he looked in the girl's room to find a similar scene. His glance fell on the vacant crib that had rocked with the baby's screams the night before.

Lisa had left with the girls.

It took a few seconds for the stunning news to

penetrate. Then the anger boiled in his soul again.

"I'll find you!" He roared the declaration like a lion warning the jungle. Seizing the handle of a mop, his rage exploded against the crib, sending blow after blow crashing against the rail. The handle splintered and he hurled it against the wall in a last spasm of fury.

Now, more than two hours later, he had to admit the zigzag route of his search across town had been fruitless. He had not discovered her car at Melanie's apartment, even in the back alley or the garage. The driveway at Becky's house, Lisa's sister, stood empty as well.

Where else could she have gone? While pumping gas, one additional hiding spot had come to mind. I can be there in five minutes, he had decided. He eagerly launched the pickup onto the rain-slick highway.

The wail of the police siren jerked his eyes toward the rearview mirror. Cursing, he pulled the pickup to the shoulder of the road. The black and white cruiser rolled to a stop behind him, strobe lights reflecting white and red on the rain-slick pavement. He saw the officer talking on his radio. "I didn't do anything," he spat through clenched teeth.

Officer Allen closed the door of the patrol car, pulled the yellow poncho tighter, and walked slowly toward the battered pickup. "Sir, I need to see your driver's license." The officer's voice sounded flat and coolly professional.

Cody leaned out the window. "What'd I do?" He fumbled to find his billfold and thrust the license toward the policeman. "Was I going too fast, or something?"

The officer made no immediate reply. He inserted the card under the clip of the small clipboard, then ducked down to survey the interior of the truck.

"Mr. Burns, I need you to step out of your vehicle. I have a few questions I need to ask you. Please take a seat in the patrol car."

The no-nonsense tone of the policeman's voice convinced Cody to open the door and follow orders. The rain blew in his face. With a huff, he settled in the cool leather passenger seat of the cruiser. He ran his fingers through his hair and wiped his wet hands on his jeans.

"Mr. Burns, we had a complaint about a vehicle matching the description of your truck driving in a suspicious manner. Were you in the vicinity of the Suncrest apartments this morning?"

"Yes, sir. I drove through there about an hour ago, I guess. I didn't know I was botherin' anybody."

The pen scratched against the paper on the clipboard. "Why did you go to the apartment complex?"

"I was looking for my wife and kids. We had a fight last night and when I got home this morning they were gone. She has a friend who lives in those apartments, so I thought she might be hiding with her."

"So you have no idea where your wife and children are. Is that right?"

He gazed at the cruiser's lights reflecting on the back windows of his truck. "She just left in the middle of the night. She took their clothes, the kid's diapers, everything."

Officer Allen continued his questioning, focusing on the dispute and Cody's intentions. Finally satisfied, he closed the notebook.

Cody interjected his own question for the brown-haired, young policeman. "Have you heard any reports of a woman and two kids in an accident or anything?

"No. We haven't had any wrecks this morning, in spite of the rain."

"I guess I'll just keep looking."

"Mr. Burns, I'm certainly not here to tell you your own

business, but surely there is a better way to find your wife than by driving around town hoping you'll see her. I'd suggest you communicate with her family and express your concern. Maybe she'll even be trying to get in touch today." He put down the clipboard. "I'm sorry for your family problems. As far as I'm concerned you are free to go. Good luck."

"Sure. Thanks."

He ducked his head and ran through the misty rain to his truck. Murmuring his hatred for small town cops, he slammed the door hard enough to rock the truck.

The officer watched the old Ford pull back into traffic. He flipped a switch to kill the flashing warning lights. The tip of his pen drummed against the steering wheel. Down deep, something didn't sound right about the kid's story.

Brent Burroughs adjusted the headphones connected to the electronic keyboard in his office. The march of church events had scattered debris around his office, evidenced now by the extension cord rolled up under the chair and the portable sound system spread awkwardly in the corner. For now, however, the chaos could be ignored. The time had come to put some thoughts down on paper for Sunday morning's service. He fingered the opening bars of the old hymn, "What Can Wash Away My Sin?"

He had just decided on the opening song when a motion in the doorway caught his attention. Brent glanced over to see pint-sized Julie Lowe leaning around the door post.

"What are you doing? Writing the first great Christian opera?"

He pulled off the headphones. "That's right, and you're the prima donna I need. Would you like to audition?"

"Sure," she giggled. "But maybe I'd better check first and

see if you still need me to sing this Sunday."

"I think so. That's what I'm working on now." He gestured toward the open hymn book. "The theme this Sunday is forgiveness."

Julie moved a folio of music and sat down in the frayed office chair next to his desk. "I heard a great new song about forgiveness the other day. Not that church people need to hear about the subject, you know. Like over at Grace Baptist—I heard some members left because they didn't like the music."

"From what I understand, the pianist led the exodus. I've noticed a trend in the last few years that more people are choosing their church based on the style of the worship service. Rather than the denomination or the preaching, they focus on the music and the emotions of the service."

"Each church has its own style, doesn't it? We noticed a difference when we attended my sister's church in Dallas. She attends a big downtown church, and the music sounded like a symphony recital."

"I'm not surprised. The older congregations keep using traditional hymns accompanied by piano and organ, while the new suburban parishes spice up the service with a jazz band and contemporary music."

"Are we in the middle?"

"Yes, and that's really what I'm striving for," Brent said in a mock stage whisper. "Don't tell a soul! I'm trying to blend styles, hoping to appeal to a broad audience. Last Sunday I started with a spiritual, you know, like the music of slaves in the south two hundred years ago. Then we used the organ and a classic hymn. The anthem was an up-tempo contemporary piece. I really believe this blended style helps us grow by appealing to most people."

"I like what we do. I guess preparing the music for the worship service is kind of risky, isn't it?"

"You bet! Don't you remember the storm clouds that blew when we changed the instrumentation? Some of the older folks objected when we added electric guitar, bass guitar, and drums. I started using them on Sunday night, and it went over fine with the younger members. But, the change in the morning service kicked up some turbulence. The preacher told me one man said the service sounded like a 'honky-tonk bar.'"

Both laughed at the mental image of the robe-clad choir jamming in a smoky bar. "The preacher tried to be patient with the objections. Sure enough, the gripes died down after a few weeks. Other families came forward to express how much the change helped their teenagers, and a few new faces even began to appear."

Julie glanced at the clock. "I'd better run. Let me know tonight what you need me to do."

After the door closed, the minister returned to his work. Using the forgiveness theme in the music for the morning worship service would create continuity. During his devotional time this morning an older hymn had popped in his mind. Now his talented fingers began to play the melody, filling the earphones with the tune.

"Jesus paid it all,
All to him I owe,
Sin had left a crimson stain,
He washed it white as snow."

Across the office suite, a much darker sentiment troubled Barry's mind. He and Keri had parted in icy silence this morning, leaving the raw edge of their misunderstanding intruding in every thought. His melancholy mood only felt magnified with the rain pouring outside.

Rubbing his tired eyes, he focused on the pages of his diary. Every line of the calendar listed an event. No time to whine with a schedule this full: meet with Brent, visit people in the hospital, prepare for his devotional tonight and a sermon for Sunday, of course. The parishioners might object if he announced Sunday he had no sermon this week because the parsonage had been declared a war zone!

I don't even know what we fought about. The visit with Mrs. Flowers had gone so well. Then, Keri came unglued when we drove past the intersection where Morgan's wreck took place. Why can't she get her grief under control?

Spreading his pages of sermon preparation, he took a deep breath to consciously relax and refocus his mind. *I can't solve any of this right now. But tonight I'm going to get to the bottom of it.*

David held his umbrella high to dart up the wide, stone, front steps of his home. Taking cover under the veranda, he tossed aside the sodden raingear in frustration. The reflection of his stocky frame looked distorted in the leaded glass of the elegant front door as he pushed his way out of the damp weather. Pausing in the entry hall, he jerked off his shoes, covered with grass from the newly-mown cemetery.

"I wasted my time today," he muttered.

Nearly every morning of this lonely summer he had driven to the quiet refuge of Hopewell Cemetery. The routine seldom varied. Parking near Morgan's grave, he walked up the small hill and placed a fresh-cut flower near the marble headstone. He often strolled an extra twenty yards over the little rise to take a seat on the granite bench under a spreading sweetgum tree. Sometimes the birds filled the air with music, soothing the wound inside his heart.

Today's visit failed to provide the daily dose of solace. The rain kept falling steadily, and he cursed it, remembering the day she died. Rain had soaked him then, sitting near the twisted wreck. A similar downpour now dampened his spirit again.

I don't want to go to the office today. Surely missing one morning won't make a huge difference in my monthly report.

Taking the phone, he dialed the office number, punched in the answering machine code, and placed a new message on the automated machine.

"Hi. This is David Dockery. I'll not be in the office Wednesday morning, but I want to help with your needs. Please leave a message, and I'll return your call this afternoon. Thanks, and have a good day."

He stepped into the bedroom to get another pair of shoes. An envelope from the Mt. Carmel school district lay on the bookcase. *What about that scholarship idea? There's a project I should work on.* He gathered the correspondence and walked to the kitchen table, gladdening at the prospect of a positive goal for the morning.

The scholarship idea had come to his mind moments after the graveside service concluded. Returning from the cemetery in the limousine, he thought of how soon the community would forget the loving labors of his wife. Then the idea came. Why not establish a Morgan Dockery Scholarship, providing money for college to a graduating senior girl at Mt. Carmel High School? Morgan had been chosen homecoming queen her junior year. The gift would provide a fitting memorial to help some young woman achieve her dreams. In the weeks after the tragedy, he phoned the school district superintendent about the project. The contact produced a nice letter from the district's attorney detailing how to set up the endowment fund from the proceeds of Morgan's life insurance settlement.

A rumble of thunder shook the kitchen. He poured a cup of coffee and read again the attorney's letter. According to the instructions, he needed to choose a bank to administer the endowment. Security State seemed the logical choice. Then Keri could help in the complicated process.

No better time than the present.

He put down the coffee cup and dialed the bank number.

"This is Keri. May I help you?"

"This is David. I'm working on a project and wonder if you could give me a hand?"

"I'd be glad to try."

"Do you remember the scholarship idea I mentioned months ago? I've been lazy but now I'm ready to get something accomplished." His enthusiasm grew in describing the possibilities. "I could bring all this paperwork down to the bank, or you could stop by the house. Whatever is convenient for you."

"Let me look at my schedule. How about tomorrow? I'll stop by on the way home for lunch tomorrow and bring information from the trust officer."

"I like that idea."

"David, I'm proud of you for thinking of this project. Some special student will benefit every year."

"That's what I hope. So you'll come by about 11:30 tomorrow?"

"Unless something else blows up down here, I'll be there then."

"O.K. Thanks for your help. See you tomorrow."

David clicked off the phone, his spirit buoyed by the action. With a brighter step, he walked to the small desk where he stored important papers. "It's a big help to know someone who's smart," he said out loud. Then, glancing at the framed snapshot of three people at the lake, he added, "And who's pretty, too."

The picture captured the fun two years ago when the Peters and the Dockerys traveled to Table Rock Lake for an overnight camping and water-skiing trip. The clear Missouri waters offered delightful relaxation to the quartet of friends. They shared turns skiing, with David and Morgan working to improve beginning skills, while Barry and Keri whooshed across the placid water like experts. Their laughter across the blue water signaled a great time.

    He slid open the desk drawer. A small tape recorder, no bigger than a pack of playing cards, lay next to a box of mini-cassette tapes. A carefully printed index, describing the content of each tape, lay on top. Of course, he knew the tape number by heart. Thirty-six. In moments the small wheels of the machine began to turn, emitting the sounds of an outboard engine, a whoop of laugher and the banter of friends. He focused his attention on Keri's bright tones. Her laugh evoked a vivid memory.

    Late in the afternoon he had watched Keri work a long ski run, leaning effortlessly right and left, throwing up sheets of spray. David couldn't help notice how stunning she looked in the two-piece blue and white swimsuit, her golden hair flying in the wind. Finally tiring, she dropped the rope with a whoop and settled in the water to wait for the boat. Barry guided the craft in a graceful circle and cut the powerful motor so she could come up the ladder on the stern.

    That's when he saw her in a new way. He stood when she climbed the ladder, providing a friendly hand to help her navigate the unsteady motion. Stepping lightly from the top rung to the deck, she reached toward him with both arms. He caught her with both hands at the small of her waist. She landed inches from his face and the momentary panorama of her bikini top filled his vision, a startling image frozen forever in his memory like an erotic postcard.

    He looked at Barry's rugged face in the picture. Once he had considered Barry a close friend. Maybe that's why the bitterness against him now ran so deep. His message at Morgan's funeral had been so mangled, so confused, David wondered if the pastor had been drinking. For days he had seethed inside at the flippant spirit that had seemed to pervade the service. Across the months his anger had hardened into a clear plan.

He shoved the letter in the desk drawer and slammed it shut. *I can't wait to see the pastor's wife for lunch tomorrow.*

"Mrs. Luong is here." Fran held open the door to Keri's office for the energetic, Vietnamese woman to enter. Keri greeted her with a warm hug.

"You look wonderful," Keri said, motioning for Duyen to sit down.

"So do you!"

"I read about your new assistant principal position. Congratulations! Are you ready for school to start?"

"I'm trying to get my office set up and it still looks like a shipwreck." Her black eyes twinkled. "But I enjoy middle school kids, so this year should really be fun."

"It's hard to believe a year has passed since I last saw you! I can still remember when I first came to work here. You seemed so excited about leaving the bank for your new career in education!"

On that blustery, fall afternoon nearly five years ago, Duyen had greeted Keri with the same warm hug. The pastor's wife mentioned a friend who served as a missionary to Vietnam before the fall of the government, and from that moment a common love of life drew them together. The succeeding years brought them together several times. One day Keri encountered Duyen while shopping in the mall. The Asian woman spoke with pride about her new home, purchased with a loan from Security

Bank. On the spur of the moment, she invited Keri to visit. An hour later, sitting in Duyen's modest eastside home, the two women enjoyed the rich taste of ginseng tea.

Suddenly, Duyen had put her tea cup down on the low table and murmured in a weak voice, "I'm sorry. I'm not feeling very well right now."

Keri watched with horror as Duyen slumped forward and tumbled to the floor. Fumbling with the phone, Keri called an ambulance. She stayed with her stricken friend until the ambulance arrived, then notified Duyen's children of the sudden emergency. Barry came to help, and together they waited with the family through the anxious hours of the bypass surgery.

With her natural energy, Duyen recovered from the surgery quickly. Keri continued to visit, and the recovering patient never tired of telling others about the providential presence of her friend from the bank. Her gratitude became a growing interest in knowing more about the faith that motivated Keri's life. On a beautiful morning last summer, Duyen knelt with Keri in the Peter's family room to receive Jesus as her Savior.

"Did Fran tell you why I wanted to see you today?"

"Yes, she did. I'll be happy to help you. I'll gladly tell about what the attitude of this bank and the financing of my house meant to me. The people here have always bent over backward to help my community."

"Thanks for your willingness to help." She looked across the desk. "Contrary to what Van Dang and the Citizen's League people claim, we have worked hard to develop the east side of Mt. Carmel. I could have called a number of people but instantly thought of you. Your willingness can help even more people on the east side. Could we meet at the Community Center tomorrow morning?"

"I have an appointment with the PTA officers tomorrow afternoon, but my morning is free. What do you want me to do?"

"Channel 9 is willing to tape an interview to hear your side of this story. It shouldn't take long."

"I don't know how well I can do on television."

"The reporter is a friend of mine. Just tell your story and everything will work out fine."

"I'll do it, but only if you go with me."

"Great!" Within a few minutes, they made all the arrangements. Watching her diminutive friend leave the office, Keri breathed a prayer of thankfulness for something going right in this dreary day.

Lauren jogged with long, loping strides across the parking lot, pulled open the car door, and flopped down in the driver's seat. "I don't think we've seen a downpour like this all summer!"

"I'm enjoying it after the heat we had last week," Liz said. She folded her umbrella and put it at her feet. "Getting in my car yesterday afternoon felt like stepping into an oven."

"I haven't eaten at Pasta Station in weeks. How does that sound for you?"

"I've only eaten there twice. It's a nice place."

The secretaries at Mt. Faith Church rotated their lunch hours through the week. On Wednesdays, Lauren and Liz shared the same hour. Lauren's idea for a meal together today had actually been received with a smile. Most days, Liz ate by herself, quietly reading a magazine to pass the lunch hour.

The windshield wipers labored to keep pace with the rain. Lauren drove slowly. She felt pleased at her co-worker's animated conversation. Apparently, the prospect of a lunch companion pleased her shy associate, too.

"Where's Josh today?"

"He had a meeting this morning, then planned to go shooting at the indoor firing range. The department holds a qualifying match in two weeks, so he wanted some extra time to practice."

"He really seems like a nice man."

"When I first met him, I never even thought about a relationship developing. But the more time I spent with him, the more exciting that prospect became. I think he's pretty special, all right."

Pasta Station occupied a corner lot in the newer section of downtown Mt. Carmel. The local owner, the wife of an attorney who traveled constantly, built the stylish, sandstone restaurant for her own pleasure, not for the income. The eye-catching interior featured huge potted plants, artistically decorated dividers, and elegant pieces of art. The hefty lunch selections brought people back time after time. With the rainstorm, however, the crowd looked thin. A hostess immediately seated the co-workers at a small table near the front window.

"Liz, what about your social life? I've never heard you talk about family or dating."

"Nothing happening in that department with me." She adjusted the napkin next to her plate. "Romance has been a scarce commodity most of my life."

Lauren started to reply but caught herself. *Let her talk. That's what you're here for.* After a few moments, Liz continued.

"You know, I guess it's really weird for me to work in a church office. After what happened, that's the last place I thought I'd ever want to get a job."

"Why's that?"

"You wouldn't believe such a crazy story. I've tried to put it behind me. In fact, I moved to Mt. Carmel to get away from it." She looked out the window at the rainy parking lot.

"Sometimes people aren't what they seem to be. Three years ago I lived in Maryville, north of Kansas City. I started dating a really wonderful man. In fact, he served as associate pastor at the church. I had been attending there about six months when he asked me out. I felt flattered. Since he was four years younger than me, I couldn't imagine what drew him my way. But that didn't stop me from accepting his invitation."

The waiter interrupted to refill their glasses. When he moved away, Lauren interjected, "Sounds like a promising beginning."

"That's what I thought. We dated quite a bit during that fall and into the spring. Honestly, I couldn't help falling in love. Richard sparkled with charm and loved to have fun. He brought out the best in me—I've always been pretty quiet, you know. We never talked about marriage, but you could feel it coming. I thought I had come to know him pretty well."

She paused to sip her tea. Her eyes grew distant with the memory. "Then one afternoon I got a call from the pastor of the church. He and an elder came to my apartment that evening." She stirred the tea, her hand trembling slightly. "I knew something had happened, of course. Their conversation tap-danced around the truth. To make a long story short, I finally forced them to tell me what took place. Richard had been arrested in Kansas City when he propositioned a police officer posing as a prostitute. The pastor and elder weren't concerned at all about my feelings. Instead, they tried to find out if I knew anything about Richard's past. I couldn't even talk to them. I just sat and cried. Of course I didn't have a clue about his terrible secrets. When they finished pumping me, they left without even saying a prayer."

"That's unbelievable! What happened then?"

"The next Sunday the pastor announced his associate's resignation. Somehow Richard managed to get out of the criminal charge, but I never saw him again. Never even heard from him. Even worse, the people at the church treated me like I had committed the crime. They shunned me. Two months later, I resigned my job and moved here."

Liz closed her eyes as if to shut off the painful memory. They ate in silence for more than a minute. Finally, she spoke again.

"That's what I mean. Sometimes people aren't what they seem to be. You won't believe how I debated about working in a church office, but I didn't have many choices. I guess I wonder now if every minister lives like a hypocrite. The one who broke my heart had everyone fooled."

"They've got their failings, for sure," Lauren said. "I've seen my share of that since working at Mt. Faith. Of course, the members have just as many problems, too."

"Would you keep this story under your hat?" She glanced at the tables nearby. "I'm not ready to publicize my heartbreak quite yet."

Lauren reached across the table to touch her co-workers hand. "I won't say anything. But I will pray for you to get past the trauma. You've got a lot to offer people. I'd hate to think this would hold you back."

"I need that."

Another bank of dark storm clouds hung above the tall oak trees when the two women returned to the church. They shared the umbrella on the way across the parking lot.

Liz pulled open the door. "Thanks for asking me today. It's a shame we have to spoil a good lunch by going back to work!

" Mary turned from the computer when the women opened the office door. "Did you enjoy your lunch?"

"Yes, we did. Pasta Station makes great lasagna," Lauren replied.

"I'm going to take my turn now. I've got to run by the

store for some camping supplies. Hank wants to go to the lake this weekend."

"I hope the rain stops. Sitting in a camper watching the rain wouldn't be much fun!"

Liz sat down at her desk. "Are the men back from lunch yet?"

Mary gestured toward the closed door. "Barry never went to lunch. C. K. Haskins is with him."

Behind the closed door, C. K. sat on the small couch. For the past half-hour he had been describing his morning meeting with Ed Loomis. "I don't feel good about what I learned," he said, rubbing his hands together in agitation.

Early that morning Ed had surprised the retired minister with an invitation to meet for coffee. He always enjoyed Ed. The big man had a way of telling a story that made it come alive. During thirty years of business, Loomis Furniture had built a solid reputation in Mt. Carmel. The business held firm even against the national chain that had opened at Springview Mall. Ed and his family had done very well indeed, as evidenced by the tastefully appointed office where the two met.

"C. K., I've always valued your opinion, so that's why I wanted you to come by this morning. What I've heard recently disturbs me. I want to know what you think." Ed began to pace like a tiger behind the bars of a cage. "To be blunt, some people in our church think Brother Barry should be relieved of his duties as pastor. I don't know whether they're right or not, but I do know their accusations may cause a major rift. I've got friends in other churches who have been through a mess like this. It's always ugly." He leaned on the massive pine desk, fixing the white-haired minister in his gaze. "I tell you, we're headed for big trouble."

C. K. cocked his head to the side. "What kinds of problems are you talking about, Ed? I've not heard anything."

"I don't want to play games with you, but I'm not at liberty to tell everything I've heard." Loomis paused near the coffee bar to refill his cup. "You know as well as I do that some people feel upset about things that have happened in recent years. They pin the blame squarely on Brother Barry."

"I've never been in a church where everyone felt happy. And that includes the ones I served." He smiled. "Some folks like to harbor a gripe or two. Most of the time it blows over in a few months, and the people get on about their business."

"I wish that would be true this time. But my gut feeling says this storm may hit like a tornado rather than a thunderstorm." He sat down behind the desk and leaned across to look directly at his friend. "Let me ask your opinion. I know you have talked with the preacher quite a bit. Be honest. Have you seen anything that concerned you about Barry's actions or motives?"

C. K. returned the gaze, trying to probe the big man's intentions. He measured his answer in careful words.

"Ed, all I've seen is a normal human being trying to do one of the most difficult jobs on God's green earth. I've seen him up and down, good and bad. But I've never seen anything that would dishonor the Lord's name. Period."

"What about money? I'm asking for your honest appraisal. Sometimes a young man—whether he is a preacher or a plumber—can get carried away by the love of money. Maybe they get in over their head, owing people all over town. Do you remember several years ago when that preacher at the little Gospel Lighthouse church disappeared? He left unpaid bills at every business in Mt. Carmel, including this one. I'm asking you honestly: Have you noticed anything funny about the preacher's finances?"

"Oh, I'm sure Barry has a little taste for luxury—he buys his suits from a tailor in Springfield, not from Penney's like you and I do. But there's nothing to indicate that he has unpaid bills. Actually, I don't think his wife could work at the bank if such credit irregularities existed."

Ed leaned back in the executive chair. "All right, that's good," he nodded. "I think you certainly know how Barry thinks. I have to admit, though, that not everyone sees Keri's employment at the bank in such a positive light." The big man leaned forward again. "I've heard from a good source that Keri sometimes uses bank information to court the well-to-do. As a bank officer, she is in the place to know everything about every dollar you or I have in there. Maybe the problems come from there."

In the church office, Barry had listened to the retired minister's account of the conversation to this point with a detached professionalism. Years ago, he learned that, at any given moment, gossip about his actions could emerge, make waves for a few days, then be gone. But the intrusion of Keri's name in the conversation broke the ice of his composure. His face reddened.

"I can't believe that! If Loomis thinks he can drag my wife through the mud, he'd better think again! Of all the stupid accusations I have ever heard...."

C. K. raised his hand to stem the pastor's anger.

"I know it, I know it. Whoever filled his mind with those ideas has really cooked up a wild tale. I couldn't take it either. You know what I did? I just stood up and said, 'Ed, I can't sit here and listen to anymore of this back-stabbing. I don't want to play the game of run-off-the-pastor.' Then I turned and walked out. Didn't say another word."

Barry's anger catapulted him from his chair, knocking a small wooden sculpture from the desk.

"I won't stand for this, C.K. Not when Keri is involved. I can't sit back and let this accusation be peddled around the congregation. I'm going public with it. If somebody thinks I'm just going to sit still and let them ruin Keri's career and my ministry, they're in for a rude awakening." His finger stabbed the air. "Mark my words. Sunday morning I'm coming out of my corner fighting!"

The buzz of the intercom interrupted the angry declaration. Lauren had a message.

"Brother Barry? I'm sorry to interrupt. Gina Spencer is on line four about her mom's cancer treatment."

"Tell her I'll speak with her in just a moment."

C. K. stood and drew close to his fellow minister. "We've got a lot to pray about. I want to talk with you again before Sunday." He put his hand on Barry's shoulder. "You need to be cautious in handling this, pastor."

With a sigh, Barry looked toward the ground. After a long moment, he nodded. "Thanks for letting me know about this. I'm not angry with you. But I am serious about what I said. I won't stand by and let some misguided zealots attack my wife."

"Just be careful. The wrong words at the wrong time could make it worse, not better."

"O.K. I'll try to think it through."

C. K. headed towards the door. "I'll call you tomorrow."

Barry scooped up the fallen figurine and replaced it on his desk. *If a handful of mutineers want to try and hijack my parish, I'm going to fight until the last musket ball is gone.*

Home. What a strange place to be at two o'clock. Keri dropped an armful of dirty clothes in the washing machine. The water poured into the tub. She pulled the utility room door closed behind her to dampen the sound.

What can I do with the gift of a free afternoon and evening?

Her plans for the day had changed when the baseball camp director called the bank. Jason had complained of a stomach ache during the morning, he told Keri. Now another camper had reported Jason sick in the bathroom with cramps and vomiting. Within a few minutes, Keri arrived at the school and loaded her pale, nauseous son in the car. Once at the house, she administered a dose of medicine and maternal love, then helped him settle in his bedroom.

Alone in the master bedroom, she pulled off the tan skirt and blazer, recalling how unhappy she felt while dressing that morning. Barry had lain silently in bed while she readied for work. Once again, her anger and wounded feelings simmered. Pulling on a pair of jean shorts and a favorite loose-fitting, blue t-shirt, she felt the tension ease.

Maybe I need the afternoon off more than Jason. The house lay quiet except for the rainwater trickling down the spouts outside. Jason is resting, so this is my afternoon now. How long has it been since I've spent some quiet time for just myself?

The old recliner in the master bedroom, her favorite reading place, beckoned her to enjoy the serendipitous moment. Moving the magazines on the end table, she lifted Barry's devotional Bible. The pages lay open to the Psalms.

"Deliver me from my enemies, O God;
protect me from those who rise up against me.
Deliver me from evildoers
and save me from bloodthirsty men!"

The echo of Kent's warning from Sunday night jolted her afresh. She saw once again the shock that had filled Barry's face when Kent revealed the object of his vision. The open Bible gave evidence he worried about all this again before he went to work this morning.

I should be more understanding of the pressure he's

under.

But why doesn't he try to understand more of the pressure I'm under, another voice insisted. He doesn't work any more hours than I do. He sure doesn't have an egomaniac boss breathing down his neck every day. Her jaw tightened with renewed frustration. It shouldn't always be my job to understand.

So, now you're going to join the pack of accusing people that 'rise up against' him came the first voice, continuing the debate in the silent house. He needs you to be his helper just like it says in Genesis, when God created Eve.

A growl of thunder rolled across the house and echoed off the bluff above the river.

What voice should I listen to?

The aroma of hot, black coffee promised a calming reprieve from the frustration twisting his emotions. President Ledbetter drank deeply and slowly. He turned toward Johnson, who stood with his back against the cool glass window of the spacious office. For fifteen years, the two men had worked together, creating a chemistry for success. Ledbetter acted the part of the visionary while Johnson brought cold analytical skills to the team.

"So what did Van Dang say?" Johnson pulled a cigarette from his pocket.

Ledbetter set the coffee on his desk. "He called—quite cordial, I assure you—to start twisting the thumbscrews. They're not interested in hurting the bank, he said first."

"Yeah, right."

"Oh, he's smooth, for sure. He suggested that a compromise might be worked out. They would not set up picket lines or pursue legal action if certain arrangements could be made."

"Like what?"

The president ticked off the list on his fingers. "They want a loan officer who speaks Vietnamese. They want a branch on the east side of town. And they have certain qualified individuals who would serve as excellent members of our board."

"They're demanding to put their own refugee buddies on the board of directors? That's blackmail! What did you say?"

The president's face reddened. "I hung up on him. I don't care if they start picketing the bank. We don't have to listen to that kind of threat."

"Just what that slick lawyer deserved." The lanky vice-president flicked ashes in the black marble ashtray and sat down on the sofa. "Did you talk to Peters today about what she's doing with the media?"

"No. Her kid got sick and she took off about 1:30. I don't know what she's done today."

"That's the trouble with women at work. When the kid gets sick, she's the one who has to go. Just leaves the work hanging and takes off. Burns me up."

"Yeah, but you'd better keep that idea to yourself. The feminists will eat you alive."

"But I'm right. And I'm especially uncomfortable with Peters. I've never liked religious types anyway. Even worse, she's a preacher's wife! I think that's dangerous, Jack. Who knows when she might turn fanatic and start driving customers away."

"I know how you feel, but we've not had any problems. The little ladies with the CD's love her. Her image in the community helps us."

Johnson stubbed out the smoke. "But is she carrying the load on this Viet issue? We've got to have somebody tougher than the Viet Cong types from St. Louis. A preacher's wife won't cut it, I tell you."

Ledbetter drained the coffee cup and sat down behind his desk. He never won when he argued with Johnson. This conflict gave him cold chills. The city's big wheels could freeze him out if he gave a black eye to the community. One wrong step with this bomb and it would blow up in his face. He needed total concentration from everyone. And Peters is at home wiping the nose of her kid. "I'm not sure how fast I can move on this. She's got her supporters on the board. They'll raise a stink if I'm not careful."

"But what's more important, a woman's job or the bank?"

The question hung in the air, unanswered.

Johnson headed toward the door. "I've got to get to an appointment on the Fisher estate. See you tomorrow. But think about what I said."

Barry glanced at his watch. Where had the afternoon gone? Gathering up his cell phone and business cards, he walked from the office.

Lauren turned from her computer screen. "Going to the hospital? Better take this list with you."

He glanced across the names. Just three patients. Good. That may leave time to work on the worship service planning I promised Brent three hours ago.

"Tell Brent I'll be back as soon as I can."

Where had Ed Loomis come up with those accusations? Barry mulled the question with the splashing of his car wheels through the puddles of HW 69. He started a rogue's list of arsonists behind the flare of trouble, listing two prime suspects by the time he pulled in the clergy parking space on the second row of the Medical Center lot.

I need to find who started this and smother the rumors before they get out of hand. He ducked his head against the drizzle and walked quickly toward the lobby entrance.

"Hi, pastor." The soft voice of the young mother greeted him on his first visit. Her daughter lay sleeping under the moist air of a humidifier. Taking a seat, Barry focused his attention on her anxious story. She needed a pastor's heart, not a rehearsal of his problems.

One hour later, Barry stood up from the vinyl chair in Room 224. He reached out to grasp the shrunken hand of cancer patient Betty Spencer.

"Betty, I could stay with you all day. But I've got to get ready for church tonight."

The shrunken woman nodded. "Pastor, it means a lot to know that the church hasn't forgotten me."

"Don't worry! We need you back in choir for the Christmas cantata. I'll let the people tonight at prayer meeting know about your treatments," he reassured. "Let's have prayer."

The crowded elevator carried the quiet minister to the busy lobby. The afternoon visits had run the gamut of age. First, a mother and a young daughter, then a middle-aged man recovering from back surgery, and finally a senior adult undergoing cancer treatment. Young and old, death and life, each one of them eager for a word about God and hope. He stopped to hold the elevator door open for those entering, then walked with a more buoyant step through the main lobby.

The glass of the two-story wall shone with a single ray of sunshine that pierced through the lingering rain clouds. He had touched the lives of his people, but they had given him back something. Their separate needs combined to portray the unfolding cycle of life. Throughout that cycle God used him to touch the needy with encouragement. A feeling of satisfaction warmed him with new energy on the walk across the wet parking lot.

The shrill ring of the phone lifted Keri from her nap. She climbed out of the recliner and crossed the bedroom to answer.

"Keri?" The young female voice whispered her greeting. "This is Lisa Burns."

"Oh, Lisa." Keri's sleepy mind slowly put the name in the proper place. "How are you?"

"O.K. Well, maybe not so good. Do you have a minute?"

"Yes. I'm home from work because my son is sick. What's wrong?"

"I left Cody Tuesday night. I'm staying at the New Dawn Shelter."

"What happened?"

"We had a fight, or well, actually, he hurt me and then Courtney." Lisa couldn't hold back the pain. Amid sobs, she recounted the violent encounter with Cody. "That night I didn't know what else to do. We had to get away. I knew Cody would be furious, so I didn't dare go to Dad's or anyplace where he could find me."

"Are you O.K. at the shelter?"

"Yeah, I'm fine so far. They are treating us real nice. We can stay as long as three weeks if we need to. My talks with Mrs. Jordan, the director, have helped, too."

"What more can I do for you?"

"Just pray for me. But please don't tell anybody where I am! If Cody found out, he might tear the place down. He gets violent when he's angry."

"I will pray for you, Lisa. Try to believe God is working even in this mess. We just need faith to keep following Him."

"I'll try."

"Please call me again."

"I will. Bye."

Keri replaced the receiver and stretched her drowsy muscles. What a courageous young woman. An alcoholic father, traumatic grief, an early marriage, an abusive husband, trapped in poverty—Keri listed the problems that had scarred Lisa's life. Yet she's still fighting to take care of herself and the kids. She's a strong woman. I hope I can help her some way.

The buzzer on the dryer drew her to the utility room. Pulling the warm clothes from the machine for folding, her mind drifted from Lisa's secret wounds to her own childhood.

Keri never doubted that her mother, Alice Edwards, liked her blond-haired first-born. But she could see that the tall, anxious woman adored her son, Anton, born two years later, even more. Even though Keri's diligent efforts in class produced 'A's,' her mother's attention focused more on Anton's latest victory on the cross-country course. The day during her senior year when she received her acceptance letter to the University produced the most painful memory of all. Beaming with the news about her future, she had floated to the dinner table, waiting until just the right moment to produce the piece of mail that proved her capability to succeed. With a flourish she laid it on the table, next to the roast beef, and looked expectantly for her mother's eyes to light up with commendation.

"I just wish one of the major universities had accepted you," Mother said with a shallow smile, "like Anton plans to attend."

Keri felt her stomach sour with the disdainful comment. That night the anger boiled for hours. She would show her mother and the whole world once and for all what one smart girl could accomplish.

That Fall at Drury University she devoted all her

passion toward a career in finance. Her determination steeled her against the putdowns and resistance by the men who dominated the banks where she worked during college. Her eventual success raised the shout of 'Look at me!' for her mother to notice and approve. But her success had come too late. The unrelenting grip of Alzheimer's had robbed her mother of the capacity to communicate. The words of affirmation lay locked forever in the silence of her mother's mind.

"Mom?" Jason's plaintive voice called from his bedroom.

She laid down the towels and put aside the memories to move toward his room. *I told Lisa that faith could discover God's purpose. With the problems I'm in now, maybe I should listen to that advice myself.*

"Pastor, this is Paulette Powell." Her words ran together in a nervous rush so that Barry placed the cell phone to his ear to hear over the car noise. "Mandy told me when I got home from running some errands that there's a problem with the church schedule. We've got everything already planned and the times set for people to come."

Barry smoothed the tone of his voice. "Paulette, I know we can iron this little problem out just fine. Let me tell you what happened. Do you know Harvey and Edith Flowers? Yesterday morning Harvey suffered a stroke and died in the emergency room. Ordinarily, the funeral would take place tomorrow or Friday. But some of the family members who live overseas can't make the trip that quickly. So, we had no choice but to schedule the service for Saturday morning."

"But we've got to decorate on Friday! How can we do that and have the funeral the next day?"

"I think the best plan would be for you to decorate on

Friday, just as you'd planned. But instead of putting the equipment in place in the worship center, just put it in the storage room. After the funeral it will only take a few minutes to bring those items out and place them properly."

"But all that takes time and we've got so much to do on Saturday. Remember, we reserved the worship center for this wedding six months ago." Paulette's voice carried a sharper edge. "That ought to give us the right to use it without somebody else bothering us! I don't understand why that funeral can't be in the funeral home, or something."

"I know you've planned ahead very carefully. But we can't reschedule the funeral and the funeral home chapel is too small to handle a big crowd. The funeral director has assured me he will clear everything by 11:00 o'clock. Your family and the church hostess can move right in and get to work. Everything will be done before lunch."

"It deeply disappoints me that the church can't keep its contracts. Our whole schedule for Saturday is completely destroyed."

"I'm sorry this disruption came up so suddenly." He ignored the barbed comment. "If we can all work together, then both families will benefit. Honestly, we've never had this type of conflict before. I'm sure we can make the wedding just as beautiful as you and Mandy have dreamed."

"If that's the way it has to be, then we will work around it. It's not like we can go anywhere else at this late date."

Barry jumped to accept her half-hearted willingness. "I do appreciate your understanding. I've already spoken to Mike to have extra workers here to clean up after the funeral so your people can move right in. With your understanding this unfortunate conflict will work out fine."

"I certainly hope so."

"Thanks for calling. Bye."

His stomach had twisted into a knot of anger. *I should just plan to make an announcement Sunday that everyone planning to have a stroke and die should give the church six months notice. Good Lord, what an attitude!*

Slamming the car door, he stalked toward the church. Inside, he saw Kent Puckett standing at Mary's desk. The bearded man greeted him with a frown.

"Got a minute?" Kent shook hands with a quick, business-like pump.

"Sure," Barry lied, knowing he had at least three other major jobs to complete before heading to the weekly church dinner. "Come in my office."

Kent found a seat on the couch. "Pastor, I know you're busy getting ready for tonight. But I've thought all week about what I said during our prayer meeting Sunday. You know, that vision thing."

Barry listened, anticipating a retraction. *Mark it down as just a weird experience. He's had second thoughts, and now I won't have to worry about the crazy incident again.*

Kent looked straight at his pastor. "Every morning when I pray, my vision becomes clearer and more foreboding. How do you feel about all this?"

Barry's heart missed a beat.

"What do you mean, Kent, by 'clearer'?"

"I just can't get it out of my mind. I know that someone wants to attack you. I don't know the person's identity or how they plan to carry it out, but I know the danger is real. Do you know anything about it?"

Barry stretched back in the soft leather chair. *What did Kent know about the situation with Loomis?*

"Kent, you've served in the church long enough to know that not everyone loves the preacher all the time."

Kent didn't hesitate. "Pastor, I feel this warning

concerns more than just a disgruntled member or two. I sense real danger somewhere, for both you and Keri."

Barry felt trapped by the insistent stare of his friend. He wanted to know more but didn't want to appear too concerned. "Sounds like I need to have a bomb-sniffing dog check my car each morning!"

Kent stroked his beard, too lost in thought to catch the humor. "I can't get the phrase 'blood-thirsty men' out of my mind. Do you remember me saying that Sunday? I sat down last night and looked it up in the Bible." He picked up a Bible from the table next to the couch. "Have you ever studied Psalm 59?"

"Not in depth. Is that where you found the words you said during the prayer? Had you read that Psalm recently, or something?"

"Pastor, I can't remember ever reading that Psalm. I think God gave the quote to me as a sign for you." He leaned forward. "I know how strange this whole thing may seem, but please don't ignore it."

Daemon Asher! The name exploded in Barry's mind like someone had shouted it in his ear. He stood and moved to the side of the desk. Hiking one leg and hip partially over the edge, half sitting and half standing, he nodded at his friend.

"You know, you might be on to something with that warning, Kent. I can't go into details, but some information has come to me that might indicate where some, let's say, misunderstandings do exist in the church."

"I knew it!" He pounded his fist into his palm. "God would not let me rest with this." "I don't want to know all the details, pastor. You can handle the issues. I just feel better knowing that I might not be crazy after all." He looked directly at Barry. "Read the rest of that Psalm carefully. I think it provides more of the answer you need."

"I will."

For the first time in the conversation, the face behind the flecked beard smiled. He stood up. "Let me know what I can do to help. You can count on me to stand with you through this."

"Thanks for coming by. Keep us in your prayers." Barry opened the door of the study. "I'll see you later this evening."

After Kent passed by, Lauren looked up from her desk and poked a note in Barry's direction. "Keri called. She can't come to church tonight. Jason came home sick from baseball camp and they've been home all afternoon."

"I'll give her a call in a minute."

Returning to his desk, he sat down heavily, leaning back to interlace his fingers behind his head, elbows flared. His thoughts whirled with Kent's insistent warning. Up to now, he had almost managed to dismiss the disturbing words spoken Sunday as simply a passing comment that would be forgotten. Now the uneasiness which had kept his mind racing into the early hours of Monday morning returned.

Daemon Asher. If there is any truth to this warning, that man could be the motivation behind it. Barry pictured the retired accountant's small face, framed by graying hair. He met Daemon six years ago. The man seemed oily smooth and icy cold. Across the ensuing years, he had tangled with Barry on several issues, reducing their relationship to only a nod in the hall. *I know he's schemed to gain control of the church board. What has he cooked up now? Perhaps C. K. could find out more, especially from Loomis.* He sighed and swiveled the high-backed chair to face the window. The slate gray clouds had once again shut the sunshine out of the afternoon sky.

The sight of the green guacamole sauce on her mother's plate made Jenni's stomach turn upside-down. She quickly diverted her eyes and pushed her shoulders to the back of the chair to take a deeper breath. The expectant teen desperately wished the family gathering at Mt. Carmel's best Mexican food restaurant, Border Red's, would end so she could go home. But her older brother, Chris, had driven in from Washington University in St. Louis, and granddad Ed wanted to know every detail of his last semester. An observer might appreciate the prestige of the men seated at the table: a furniture store owner, a prominent attorney, and a bright young college student. Jenni, however, summarized her thoughts as she listened to Chris brag about his grades with one word: boring.

"Are you O.K.?" Doris leaned close to look at her granddaughter's disgruntled face.

"It's just my stomach." The huge lump in her womb pushed away her appetite. She shifted again, this time swaying to the right to provide a few more millimeters accommodation for the tiny elbow jammed under her rib cage. The movement brought to mind her reflection in the mirror this morning. She had stood naked in the tiny mauve-colored bathroom, appalled at her swollen abdomen, marked by a grotesquely protruding navel and angry red stretch marks radiating downward.

Doris caught Jenni's eye and winked, as if to say she understood.

She forced a tiny smile. Gram always made life better. They sat together in church whenever Jenni attended. Sitting near the white-haired matriarch, she felt protected from the trash talk of the other youth. Nothing felt better than her long hugs after church.

About a month ago, while they ate lunch in Doris' kitchen, the teen had a question. "Gram, did I tell you about the nightmare I had?"

"I don't think you did."

"I saw myself sitting on a bed bawling my eyes out.

When I looked closer, I saw a..." Jenni's voice choked, prompting Doris to sit down beside her. "I had a dead baby in my arms!"

Doris gathered her up as if to chase away the dreadful sight. "It's O.K., honey. You just had a silly nightmare. You shouldn't worry about it so."

Then all the other fears and pains had poured out, covered with hot tears. She felt relieved to talk to someone who didn't lecture or grow tired of her whining. The catharsis calmed her, at least until the dream came again a few nights later.

Her attention returned to the restaurant when the tall waiter refilled her tea glass. The conversation had taken a different turn. Granddad Ed felt concerned about the problems at Mt. Faith Church. Jenni listened to him describing some people who didn't like Pastor Barry, his wife, or the changes the church had experienced.

"I'm afraid we could see a big fight," Ed concluded, wrapping his big hands around a tall glass of tea.

Gram's voice caught them all by surprise. "I've never known any good to come from running off the preacher," she said. "Jim, you probably don't remember it, but the man who baptized you years ago had come from a bad church situation. Not long after he left that church, the building burned."

"Are you saying that fire could have been a judgment from God or something, mother? We live in the twentieth century, you know, not ancient Egypt."

"Same God in Heaven, though. And maybe the same stiff-necks for Him to deal with on earth."

Sandi wrinkled her thin face, the unpaid bills at the bottom of their file on her mind. "I sure wouldn't want the pastor's wife nosing around my finances."

Ed's big hand lifted in rebuttal. "Remember that no one has proved anything about these accusations. I'm just concerned that more problems may spring up."

The strength of her grandmother amazed Jenni, contrasting the weakness and fear that wrenched her own heart. Her feelings did not come from church politics but on the looming state of motherhood. Me? A mother? The word reverberated in her mind. Mother? Her breath caught suddenly. I don't know what to do with a baby. How do I know what's wrong when it cries? What if it stops breathing? She felt ready to bolt from the restaurant, to somehow shed this appendage that had changed everything about her life.

Jenni grasped her Gram's strong hand. "I'm ready to go home."

The clock in the paneled hallway that led to the church dining hall read 5:20. Lauren checked her make-up and stepped from the ladies room. Her work day had stretched long but felt satisfying, especially the lunch with Liz. The crack in her co-worker's stony exterior promised a more positive relationship. Liz would probably never tell it all on a talk show, but she just might thaw out enough to make relations around the office a few degrees warmer.

A buzz of conversation from hungry church members filled Baxter Hall as she pushed through the tall doors to the well-furnished meeting room. Mrs. Baxter, the generous donor, had insisted on the best to honor her husband. A charter member, Bud Baxter made his fortune in the shipping business. Trucks bearing his name still ran their routes across the heart of the nation. His sudden death brought family tragedy, but Mrs. Baxter's donation of the beautifully furnished hall enhanced the work of the church he loved. Nearly 300 people could enjoy a dinner, or the room could be divided for smaller events by large moveable panels pulled along tracks in the ceiling. A well-equipped kitchen, gleaming with stainless steel, made the meal preparation easy. Each Wednesday church members filled the room to enjoy a low-cost meal. After the dinner, various classes, activities and music events made the halls hum with people. Walking through the crowd, Lauren picked up the scent of brisket when she approached the serving line.

"You look happy tonight," Joan Ensign said from her seat behind the cashier's table.

"I guess it's that great smell." Lauren tucked her auburn hair behind her ear to lean over and write a check.

"Is Josh coming to eat with you?"

"He can't attend tonight. He has some paper work to catch up on. But we may get some ice cream later."

After filling her plate, she found an empty table and claimed a seat. Within minutes she caught the eye of Danae Upton and motioned for her friend to sit down.

"How are you?" Danae deposited her infant carrier on the table, laid the diaper bag on the floor, and dropped her large frame down in the adjoining chair. Tyler, her five month old, sucked contentedly on a pacifier.

"I'm fine," Lauren said, reaching over to take Tyler's hand for a playful tug. "You look tired."

"I've run through the rain with the baby and all his stuff at least ten times today. The downpour finally let up for me to dash in here. I'm glad to sit down for a few minutes."

"The rain didn't keep very many people away, apparently. This crowd seems like the biggest I've seen in weeks. Must be the brisket."

"Or the rumors about visions. What do you know about this prayer meeting last Sunday night?"

The brash question caught Lauren off guard.

"Uh, hardly anything. I heard that Kent warned the Pastor about a danger he might be facing."

"Has Barry told you any more details?"

"No, I haven't heard anything definitive."

Danae had already formed her own conclusions. "Barry didn't say anything about the vision to Brad during the men's meeting yesterday. But I think God is trying to speak to Barry about problems in the church. Mrs. Frazier told Brad that some senior adults had really complained about Barry and Keri. Where there is smoke, there is fire. I hope Barry will pay attention."

Lauren's fork froze in mid air. She struggled to absorb Danae's startling assertions. After some moments, she offered weakly, "I'm sure Barry must be aware of the problems."

Tyler's sudden demand for some dinner interrupted further comments. Danae shoveled tiny bites to the black-haired baby until he would take no more. When they stood to go, Lauren shouldered the diaper bag. "I'll help you get this big guy to the nursery."

The main doors of Baxter Hall opened to a large vestibule that formed the center of the church facility. Straight across the room stood three tall doors opening to the Sanctuary. Left of the Sanctuary entrances double glass doors led to the west parking lot, adjoined by a double-width hall leading to the classrooms for adults. On the east side of the vestibule another set of glass doors led to the east lot, while the hall led to the church offices, the old chapel, and preschool classrooms.

The vestibule provided a good place for casual conversation. Years ago, the ladies of the Decorating Circle placed attractive chairs around the perimeter of the two story wood-paneled room. Claw-footed display tables stood against the walls at either end. Bulletin boards above the tables portrayed information on future events. High on the south wall windows let beams of light cascade across the comfortable crossroad of church life.

"It's always so busy just before 7:00," Lauren said when

they returned to the vestibule after depositing Tyler and his paraphernalia.

"A lot of these people need to get to their class and not stand around talking."

Lauren's height enabled her to easily see over the crowd. She saw Barry enter from the opposite side of the vestibule and head toward the Sanctuary. At the same moment, the entrance of four men through the doors from the west parking lot caught her eye. Daemon Asher, grim-faced, led the procession. Behind him marched portly Sid Simpson, a tall elder named Franklin Blue, and a slightly-built, young lawyer, Dale Galloway.

The parties met in the center of the vestibule. Daemon stopped directly in front of Barry. Surprised, the pastor hesitated, then reached for a handshake with a quizzical smile.

"Good evening, Daemon."

Daemon's arms didn't move. In a loud voice, tight with tension, he addressed Barry. "Pastor, I want to know the real reason behind your plan to baptize Kendra Burns." His voice could be heard throughout the large room.

Barry's black eyebrows wrinkled with confusion. "What do you mean?"

"Isn't it true that this Sunday you plan to baptize an eight-year-old girl who has only attended the church two times? I think the church deserves to know why."

Barry crossed his arms, unconsciously swinging his Bible up in front of his chest like a shield. The two quick verbal parries caught him unprepared. He struggled to sort out the meaning of Daemon's emotionally-charged questions. Holding his voice level, he replied, "I do plan to baptize Kendra this Sunday. She made a profession of faith in her home when Keri and I visited her Sunday evening."

By now the crowd, passing through the central hub of the building, had stopped to listen to the confrontation. Lauren and Danae stood frozen.

Daemon pressed on with his attack.

"Would your rush to baptize such a young girl have anything to do with your desire to inflate the membership of the church?"

"I don't have any idea what you're talking about."

"We think you do, preacher." Franklin jumped in the fray. His eyes didn't focus on Barry but instead gazed around at the crowd in the vestibule. "A membership roll inflated with young Christians makes the church easy to control, doesn't it? And the pastors of those fast growing churches really get noticed by the denomination, don't they?"

Barry attempted again to calm the situation. He looked at his watch. "I need to get to the Sanctuary to start the meeting tonight. Let's make an appointment for tomorrow...."

"More members mean more dollars, right? Then comes a bigger paycheck!" Daemon's harsh words cut short Barry's reply.

"We think you're trying to pack people in this church to feather your nest. You don't care about the soul of that girl. Just more members, more control and more money, that's all you want!"

Barry's eyes flashed with anger. "That's the craziest thing I've ever heard! Keri and I witnessed this girl's prayer of faith. Keri can tell you...."

"So Keri is in on it too?" Dale stepped in front of Daemon and shook a finger in Barry's face. "We know she's money hungry just like you are, preacher, with her big job at the bank and all. We've heard how she butters up the rich people, hoping to fatten the offerings!"

Two dozen people stood frozen in the vestibule, their eyes glued on the four shouting men. A group of senior ladies stopped their conversation and stared. Danae's mouth hung open in surprise. Lance Adkins, entering from the office hall, had his hands on his hips.

The pastor reacted like a cornered animal. With one motion he slapped the jutting finger away. His weight shifted forward to launch his fist with all the coiled strength of his athletic frame, smashing square against the lawyer's mouth. The little man flew backward, sprawling across the carpet from the force of the powerful blow.

The crowd gasped as one, a chorus of surprise and disapproval.

Barry leaped forward to tower over the crumpled figure.

"Shut up, you idiot! Leave my wife out of your stupid lies! You can say what you want about me, but accusing her goes too far!"

The older man, Franklin, reached to grasp Barry's arm. "Now, Pastor...."

Barry jerked his arm away.

"You've been fighting me for years. I've had it with your petty games," he thundered in their faces. "I don't have to listen to your insane accusations against me and my wife. Now get out! Get out of this church and take your lies with you!"

Lance rushed into the melee, his arms spread wide to separate the warring men.

"What's going on here?"

The four men glared at one another. Barry's breath heaved from the rush of adrenalin. Franklin's mouth seemed frozen with astonishment. Sid's face glowed red with anger. A trickle of blood flowed from the corner of Dale's lip. Daemon stood, arms crossed, composed and cold. He broke the silence with knife-edged tones.

"The pastor has lost control because of things he doesn't want to hear." He reached down to lend Dale a hand in getting up from the floor. "We've learned what we need to know."

Lance kept his arms outstretched, one hand on Barry,

the other toward the pack of three men. "What does that mean?"

"You'll find out soon enough." The leader straightened his sports jacket. "Come on, gentlemen." The four men turned abruptly and marched toward the exit without further word.

Soft organ music drifted through the Sanctuary doors, hanging mellow over the motionless parishioners crowded in the vestibule.

"Tell the people in the Sanctuary I won't be able to attend tonight," Barry growled through clenched teeth to Lance.

"Pastor..." Lance grasped the pastor's arm.

"That's all I have to say." He pushed through the crowd toward the church offices.

Lauren saw his eyes sweep across the crowd, suddenly aware of the bystanders who had witnessed the stormy episode. She hurried to follow him through the doors of the church office.

"God! What have I done now?" Barry's question echoed in the office. "What will the people think?"

At his office door he turned. She stood close enough to look into his eyes. They still seethed with anger at the blitzkrieg attack, yet mourned his own violent reaction that leveled the lawyer. Then the door closed in her face. She hurried back to the stunned crowd.

"What was that all about?" Danae had positioned herself near the vestibule exit when Lauren returned.

All around the room the women could see small knots of witnesses huddled in animated conversation, rehearsing what they had seen. At the front of the Sanctuary, Lance tried to sell a hasty explanation of the pastor's absence to the group that had assembled for the mid-week worship service.

"I have no idea."

"I'd call it a well-planned ambush. I watched Daemon and his buddies leave. They worked together like a squad of hit men. Daemon even cracked a smile when they got outside. Now look at them." She took Lauren to the glass doors and pointed across the parking lot.

At the edge of the lot nearest Mt. Faith Drive Daemon, Sid, Franklin and Dale stood close together, engaged in animated conversation.

"It worked perfectly," Daemon said. He pulled open the door of the green Lincoln. "Barry's sealed his fate now."

Dale rubbed his mouth. "We didn't plan for me to get decked!"

"That seems a small price to pay for helping the church. His childish tantrum gives us exactly the ammunition we need. Mark my words: tonight the statue of the tyrant has started to topple. Some day soon a leader who can restore this church will walk through those doors."

The oldest one of the quartet tossed his half-used cigarette aside. "Let's leave," Franklin said. "I want this mess behind me as soon as possible."

"I've already started working on our next step." Daemon put the car in gear. "We must see the plan all the way through to the end."

Inside the church, the two women watched the car drive away. Danae crossed her arms. "What do you think Barry will do now?"

"I don't know. I've never seen him so angry. And I've never seen people so shocked." She looked at her friend. "We'd better let some people know about what really happened."

Keri heard the rumble of the garage door opening and put down her book. *That's strange. It's too early for Barry to get home on Wednesday night.* She stood up from the family room couch, stretched, and stepped into the kitchen.

He stood near the door, shoulders sagging like a man laboring under a heavy bundle. His mouth, usually smiling at the first glimpse of home, seemed carved from unyielding stone. Like a shell-shocked soldier, the noise of battle still ringing in his ears, he steadied himself with a hand on the knob of the door.

"Hi."

"What is wrong with you?"

"I struck out in front of the home crowd tonight. I don't know if I can ever go back again." He dropped his leather diary down on the bar and shuffled past her toward the bedroom.

"What are you talking about? How did you 'strike out?'"

The bed creaked loudly when he plopped down heavily. Bending over, his hands began slowly unlacing the black shoelaces.

"Daemon Asher attacked me tonight before the prayer meeting. Blindsided me. I can't understand how I didn't see it coming. C.K. stopped in the office today to warn me to expect problems. The news is all over the church by now, I'm sure. If only I could have anticipated this deal I could have handled it better. Instead, I blew it. Blew it big time."

"Honey, you're not making sense. What do you mean, he 'attacked' you?"

"I played right into their hands. We may be out of here, Keri." For the first time since arriving at the house he looked directly in her eyes. "I think my ministry here is finished."

With prompting, he unfolded the story of Haskins' warning, the ambush, the accusations against her work at the bank, and his own violent reaction. He finally lay back on the bed, tracing the swirling patterns of the ceiling with anxious eyes.

"I just can't believe my own stupidity."

Keri sat next to him and gently took his hand. The knuckles that had smashed Dale's jaw glared red and swollen. "I need to get some ice for your hand."

"I've haven't taken a swing at someone since junior high."

"Surely the situation is not as bad as it seems. Everyone gets upset once in a while. At the bank people stay upset most of the time. Surely the church members will understand, especially if Asher planned this confrontation."

He shook his head. "I guarantee this mess will keep getting worse. I wouldn't be surprised if the Board isn't in my office by nine o'clock tomorrow. The little ladies who saw the whole incident are probably on their phones right now. Dale may file a suit for assault. It's just going to get worse." He stood to carry his shoes to the closet. "The smart move would be to beat them to the punch and resign."

"Please don't do that. Let's wait and see what happens."

He didn't answer for a full minute. She sat on the bed trying to imagine the scene from the atrium. How could such insanity have taken place?

He walked past her and collapsed like a deflated balloon in the recliner near the window. "What did you think about that vision Kent described Sunday night?"

"I don't know. Afraid, maybe. Curious."

"I couldn't go to sleep Sunday night. I wandered for awhile, then stood on the patio. The shadows wrapped up everything. I wanted to run out of that yard and never stop."

Her eyes welled up with tears. "I'm sorry," she whispered. "I know you've felt so much pressure. I've gotten so caught up in my own world I haven't helped you."

"Don't blame yourself. I created this problem. There's nothing you can do to change it."

"Maybe this provides the direction you've been looking for about the Potter's House. We could get away from these angry, scheming people. I'd be ready to move in a minute if you gave the word."

"I've thought of that. It might feel so good to just dump all the worries and drive away."

"It's what some of them deserve. Then they could try to do the work themselves for a while. That would change their tune fast enough."

"But what would it mean for me? That I'm a quitter?" His frayed nerves tingled with anger. "Everyone would know I'm running away, quitting like a failure! What a conversation that would make at the next assembly! No one would want to hire a failure."

"You're not a failure."

"You sure thought differently last night at this time," he snapped, black eyes flashing. "You bit my head off because I couldn't answer the Morgan Dockery trivia question."

She stiffened, silent.

"That seems like all I've heard lately. One family gets mad about their wedding plans getting changed. Another guy comes up with visions about me getting attacked. You blast me out of the water over a person who's been dead six months. Then I get mugged in the hall on the way to prayer meeting!"

"I'm trying to understand."

"I don't think anyone understands!" He jumped to his feet. "I get blamed for everything. If the offerings go down, it's my fault. If the music is too loud, I get the phone calls. If I'm not the perfect husband, I get jumped. I get real tired of putting up with it all the time. Real tired!"

"It may never have occurred to you that I am getting tired of it all myself!" She stood with her hands on her hips to look straight at him. "I'm enduring the worst week of my work ever, and how much sympathy have I received? None!"

"Fine. It's my fault again, like always."

"I didn't say that."

"Let's just forget it." He threw his dirty shirt in the hamper and stormed from the room.

She sank to the edge of the bed, her eyes burning with tears once more. Long minutes passed before she could collect her thoughts. "Lord," she finally whispered, "what is going to happen to us?"

Chapter 5
Thursday

"*Waaah!*"

The piercing wail jerked Lisa's attention back to the noisy little kitchen of the New Dawn Family Shelter. Across the table, a one-year old African-American boy grunted his protests about the taste of breakfast. His mother, young and overweight, whispered obscenities with each valiant attempt to spoon cereal into the uncooperative mouth. Another mom, Miranda, hurried to mop up a glass of milk spilled on the breakfast bar, the casualty of a misplaced slap between her red-haired, four-year old twins. Unsure about the strange melee around them, Kendra and Courtney huddled quietly together.

Miranda tossed the milk-laden dishrag into the sink. She fixed Lisa in her gaze. "You gonna meet with the social worker today?"

"Yeah. She's coming this morning. But I don't know what good it could do."

"Listen, hon. When things get bad enough to bring you down here, then it's time to get help wherever you can find it. The case worker gave me some good advice."

Lisa shrugged. "Maybe. But we've got some pretty big problems."

The New Dawn shelter promised a refuge for her

anxious heart. The sprawling, two-story house with gray siding and a wrap-around porch had been remodeled two years ago by community volunteers. Equipped with six bedrooms and four baths, the rambling house provided an oasis for women and children in crisis. This morning every room overflowed with busy children and harried mothers.

After the terrible fight at the trailer Tuesday, she had searched desperately in the dark for the Shelter. The address, scribbled on a crumpled scrap of her notebook paper weeks ago, guided her furtive journey. In the darkness, the streets on the older southeast side of town had seemed fraught with danger under the moonlit sky. Even when she found the Shelter on Myrtle Street, panic gripped her throat, forcing her to circle the block twice. Finally, her desperation had pushed her through the shadows to pound at the door.

During that first night, rest eluded her. Courtney finally settled into a jerking, nervous sleep, no doubt restless from the painful knot on her head. But Lisa remained tense, jumping at every sound. *Can Cody find me here?* She debated that question through a restless half-sleep until a soft knock at the door brought a welcome invitation to breakfast.

Wednesday morning she had carried Courtney into the kitchen, not knowing what to expect. She found the house bustling with activity. Under Mrs. Jordan's watchful eye, the kitchen filled with the smell of bacon sizzling and the sound of children's chatter. The Director's deeply-lined face nestled gray eyes that seemed to know the sorrow carried by each guest.

"I've forgotten your name already," Mrs. Jordan said.

"That's O.K. I'm Lisa Burns. This is my daughter, Courtney."

"After breakfast you'll need to fill out some papers. The state wants us to keep track of everyone, you know." She pulled the hair away from Courtney's injury. "Your baby took quite a smack. Does she need to see a doctor?"

"I don't think so. I put ice on it and the swelling is a lot better. By the way, thanks for taking us in. I've never had to do this before. I... I didn't know where to go. The whole night felt like a nightmare."

"I'm sure it did, honey. But you and your baby will be safe here for a few days. Come on and eat some bacon and a pancake, and feed that little darling, too." She lifted a golden brown pancake from the grill. "We'll talk about your situation more after breakfast."

Just after lunch, Lisa had strapped Courtney in the car seat and ventured back to the trailer park to pick up Kendra. The eight-year old's trip with a friend to visit grandparents had mercifully spared her the traumatic exodus. Lisa's heart raced with fear when she entered the trailer park. The moment Kendra got in the car, Lisa gunned the engine and raced away, checking the rearview mirror every few seconds for signs of Cody's pickup. She returned to the Shelter so overcome with anxious exhaustion that she fell across the small bed and slept through the entire afternoon.

With Thursday's dawn, she felt her immediate fears settling. Even amid the crying children, she felt safe and more rested than she had in months.

Mrs. Jordan sat down with at the rough-hewn dining table. "How are you feeling?"

"Better. I didn't feel as afraid last night. With both girls here, I can feel some hope again. I'm nervous about meeting the caseworker. Is her name Ann?"

"Yes. Don't worry. You'll enjoy meeting her. She's worked with families for years. Comes by here twice a week to coordinate help for our families. A very caring person, you know."

As if on cue, the doorbell rang, bringing the director to her feet. "I bet that's her now."

Moments later, Ann blew into the room like a summer windstorm. Big-haired, clad in a flowered dress, she quickly bustled the petite young mother toward the airy back porch, leaving Mrs. Jordan to steer the girls toward the television room where the other children sat playing. The morning breeze swirled around the slender white posts of the porch, making the summer morning quite comfortable. She pulled the two aluminum lawn chairs closer so they could talk.

"Honey, let's get started with some information on what's happened to you." She removed a writing pad with yellow paper from her satchel to begin a rapid-fire interrogation.

"How old were you when you married Cody?"

"I'd just turned 17. We had only dated for a few months. He seemed to really care for me."

"Do you still feel like he cares?"

"Yes. Well, I guess so. He just gets frustrated about things. He lost his job again. He doesn't understand the kids. So the other day he blew up."

"Did he hit you? And then hurt Courtney?"

Lisa looked down at her hands for some moments. The truth seemed hard to admit. "Yeah. He did. I felt really scared the other night."

"Scared?"

"With Cody screaming at us, and everything." She looked across the yard. Tears slipped down her cheeks, wetting her blue cotton top. In the sobs she murmured, "He hurt me really bad last year, too."

"He has hurt you several times, then?"

She nodded. Her shoulders began to heave with her weeping, the pain overwhelming the control she had fought to keep. She covered her face with both hands while the sound of her heartache filled the quiet porch.

Ann leaned forward and gently drew the anguished young woman to her, like a mother caring for a daughter. She felt Lisa cling tightly for a moment, then straighten herself with deeper resolve.

"I don't think I can go back," she said with a firm shake of her head. From somewhere deep within, the thought became a resolution. "I won't go back. Not if it means being hurt again."

"No one will make you go back, darling. You have a choice about your future. All of us want to help you find a better future."

She settled back in the lawn chair. She wanted to seize the glimmer of hope beckoning through the kind social worker. But the awful loneliness of the last three days hung like a curtain of darkness in her mind. She stared across the freshly mowed grass of the little back yard, her mind churning with the rush of emotion and uncertainty.

"But what about Cody? You can't even begin to understand how he really acts. I've seen him crazy sometimes. I can't live here forever. Sooner or later I'll be out on the street again. And when that happens...."

"Lisa, women today have rights and power they didn't have a few years ago. If Cody becomes a problem, we can get a restraining order to take care of him."

She laughed in rebuttal. "Lord have mercy! That won't do any good! Cody will do what he wants to do, no matter the consequences. A piece of paper from some judge won't stop him."

The petite woman stood, flipping the strands of long dark hair over her shoulder. Her face hardened with new resolve. She walked to the kitchen door, then looked back. "Thanks for talking with me. I promise you I won't go back any time soon. But I know Cody. He's looking for us right now. That's what scares me so. He won't give up until he finds us. I'll have hell to pay because I took the girls, you can bet on that."

The slamming door left the social worker silent on the windy porch.

Drew's size twelve feet rested on the edge of his desk like two crossed ski poles protruding from a slope. The devotional book in his hand promised a dose of calmness to counteract the uneasiness that had begun to brew late last night.

After church yesterday evening, Cassie had waited at the door for him to return from walking their big yellow Lab. "I just took a call from Danae Upton. Do you know anything about the preacher getting in a fight tonight at church?"

"A fight? I don't know a thing about a fight. The preacher?"

After hearing Cassie recount the shocking story, he stepped to the phone to call Barry. Then a second thought made him decide against adding more confusion to the situation. He decided to call Lance instead. The eyewitness account he heard left lots of questions to ponder through the night.

A knock broke his meditation. Brent pushed open the door. "Are you busy?"

"No. I can't concentrate anyway. Come on in."

"Did you hear anything about what happened last night?"

Drew nodded. "Yeah. I guess you mean the deal with Barry. We got a call from Danae Upton, and later I talked with Lance. They witnessed the whole thing."

"I spent the evening in choir practice and didn't know anything until this morning. Liz and Mary told me when I came in. I've never heard of anything so stupid in my entire life. I thought the preacher had more class than to knock some guy down in the atrium of the church."

Drew raised his hand. "Now wait a minute. I'm not sure the blame falls entirely on Barry. The way I understand it, Asher and his buddies ambushed him deliberately."

"Who told you that?"

"Danae saw the fight from start to finish. Asher and three other guys stopped the preacher in front of everyone so they could embarrass him publicly over the non-issue of a child's baptism. They planned the whole thing like a terrorist attack."

"That's still no excuse to blow up."

"Probably not," Drew said. "But did Liz and Mary tell you what they accused him of doing, and what they said about Keri?"

"I didn't hear any details."

"Sit down." The youth minister waved his hand toward an empty chair. "You've only served here two years. Let me give you some unpleasant history." For the next minutes he explored the bitter opposition which had dogged Barry's ministry.

Brent ran his hand over his kinky black hair after the history lesson. "But doesn't it take two to tango? Given Barry's personality, someone could easily find things to fault. Even I've noticed he pushes hard to build good numbers."

"I see a lot of difference between recognizing a few faults and organizing a mutiny. If Asher was a sailor, he'd be swinging from the yard arm."

"I hope you're right. Frankly, our ministry at Mt. Faith might go down, too."

"I'm not worried about that." He leaned back in the desk chair. "But to be honest I do have concern about another element in this whole story."

"The vision Puckett shared Sunday?"

"That's right." He leaned forward and put his elbows on the desk. "You talk about things Mt. Faith has never witnessed before! Prophetic dreams? That's definitely a new animal in the petting zoo."

"What do you think we should do?"

"I plan to support Barry."

"Even if the bloody-thirsty men have their day?"

The square-jawed minister jabbed the desk with determination. "Bring 'em on."

Sam Lane answered the phone. "Missouri Financial Solutions."

"Cha-ching!" Barry mimicked the ring of a manual cash register. "Made any money yet this morning, buddy?"

"I'm selling yen in Tokyo and buying marks in Berlin, but still can't find the pot of gold at the end of the rainbow," Sam said. "What are you bothering me for now?"

"I've got a question for you. If a person had several thousand dollars, how would you advise them to invest it?"

"I like those kind of questions. What goal does this person have in mind?"

"Oh, long-term growth, I guess. Maybe to use it in ten years."

"That makes the answer fairly easy. The risk goes up if people try and make a lot of money in the short-term. But when you have a longer time line, all the studies show investments in stocks pay best."

"But isn't the stock market really risky?"

"Every investment has some risk. Most people remember the crash of 1987 vividly. That bloodletting set the economy back big time. But recently, stocks have taken off. The secret is spreading investments to different sectors of the market. Don't put all the eggs in one basket."

"O.K. That will help this guy a lot."

"Just have him come see me. I can guide him to success in three easy lessons," he joked.

"I don't think this guy has the courage to make the plunge yet. But I'm sure he will keep you in mind."

"That's great. Hey, I'm sorry I didn't get to church last night. I went to a friend's softball game and didn't get home until after 9:00."

Barry hesitated for a moment, not knowing how far the stories about last night's events had spread. "Oh, that's no problem. I had an interesting evening. Maybe I can tell you about it later."

He could hear Sam say something muffled. Then, his friend came back on the line. "My secretary says I've got a long-distance call holding. Better do my job. Can I give you a call later?"

"Sure. Thanks for the information. Bye."

He jotted down a note about Sam's helpful analysis. The $5,000 of mysterious cash still lay in the back of the bottom desk drawer. He had to do something with it.

"I've got to talk to someone about all this," he muttered.

As if on cue, the intercom buzzed. Lauren's voice came over the speaker. "Pastor, C. K. Haskins on line 3 for you."

Perfect. Just the person I need to see.

Steam obscured the mirror when Josh Allen stepped from his hot shower. He impatiently wiped away the moisture, gazed at the dark brown regulation style haircut, and put it in place with a few quick swipes of the brush.

Being off-duty today promised a real adventure. He started humming a Garth Brooks song while rummaging through the drawer for just the right clothes, casual, but not sloppy. Light brown cotton shorts, a St. Louis Cardinal polo style shirt, and leather loafers. No socks today for his well-tanned legs. Looking in the mirror, he judged the look acceptable.

I hope she likes it.

Lauren had occupied his mind all morning, a thought pattern that had become habitual in the last few months. Even his mother, of all people, commented on how much he had changed since the willowy young woman stepped into the picture. The single guy who would gladly fish all night had gotten too busy for a trip to the lake. Cut-away tee shirts had been replaced by colorful sport shirts. Rumors flew behind his back of wagers at the police station that he would pop "The Question" before Christmas.

His secret plans for today would confirm all their fears. Josh himself felt amazed by the plan hatched in his mind two days ago. It required just the right touch but could reveal a lot to his love-struck heart. The sun played hopscotch through the clouds during his drive north on HW 69 toward North Carmel Road. The thermometer marked a full twenty degrees cooler than the blazing temperatures recorded Monday. The green slopes of Buck Hill strutted their beauty, refreshed by yesterday's wet weather. Over the sweet-sounding motor of his Mustang, he rehearsed his plan for the tenth time.

Mt. Faith Church stood just to the left after he turned from the main highway. He had first entered the doors of the church when a fellow officer asked him to attend. Surprisingly, he enjoyed the services. Just three weeks later, he met Lauren. The memory of their first real conversation remained vivid in his mind. She had taken a seat next to him when the singles of the church went out for hamburgers after church. Her auburn hair framed her face and drew his eyes like a magnet. He kept her entertained long after the rest of the group had left the restaurant. From that day on, he found himself hooked on the tall beauty.

Mary greeted him with a cheery smile when he opened the office door. "Good morning, Josh. Not working today?"

"I don't know how the city will be safe without me, but the chief did give me a day off. Is Lauren busy?"

Mary's smile grew even broader. "She's in Drew's office."

"Thanks."

At his knock on the open door, Lauren turned around in the chair. Her eyes lit up to see him. "What are you doing here?"

"I took the day off and just wanted to see if you had time for a short break away from the sweat shop."

"I'm not sure we could spare her for a few minutes," Drew said. He winked at the secretary. "Just come back to the office sometime before 5:00, O.K.?"

Lauren looked at Josh. "You heard what the boss said. Are you buying?"

With the top down on the Mustang, Lauren's hair played in the wind, making it hard for the safety conscious police officer to keep his eyes on the road to Springview Mall.

"What's going on at the church office today?"

"What happened with Pastor Barry last night has everyone worried. I bet you haven't heard, since you pulled the late shift. The pastor and four laymen got in a fist fight last night at church."

"He did what? You've got to be kidding!"

"I wish it were a joke. I saw the whole thing." She recounted the entire incident while they walked into the mall and took a seat in the food court. "Barry must be under a lot of pressure from something. To react that way seems so unlike him. He's an energetic person, and I've always enjoyed that. But he's not an angry person. Something has really gotten under his skin."

"I just hope he can get it worked out before things get any worse."

The young man's attention turned to more pleasant topics, like drinking in the looks and wit of the beauty at his table. Her lipstick perfectly matched her hair, a feature he had never noted on any woman before. After forty minutes had flown by, he saw her glance at her watch.

"I'd better get you back to the church. Let's walk this way," he said, pointing down another wing of the mall. Strangely, his direction did not follow the most direct way to the convertible.

Near Smith's Jewelry, Josh developed a sudden interest in window shopping. He felt his face flush and his breathing grow faster. Suddenly, his plans for conducting this moment with the just the right flair and poise evaporated.

"Look at those rings," he blurted, stabbing a finger toward the case of wedding rings as if they had appeared in a puff of magician's smoke.

"They look nice." He waited, hoping she would add more to her brief reply. He wanted to gauge her response, to see if the subject of Wedding Rings would capture her attention. In his male-biased mind, even glancing at the display case had enormous ramifications. In contrast, she sounded no more interested than if she was discussing heads of lettuce at the grocery store.

"They sure seem expensive," he said. His mouth felt as if a ball of cotton had lodged beneath his tongue.

"Really expensive."

The Wedding Ring Conversation died a painful death on the tiled floor outside Smith Jewelry. They strolled on casually, with no further words added to the topic. Feigning a nonchalant spirit, he guided her back to the car.

"Give me a call when you get home," he offered when she opened the Mustang's door to return to the office.

"O.K. Maybe we can go out for a hamburger this

evening. Bye."

He drove away slowly. *How could I have blown that so badly? I wanted her to pick up the hint. Maybe she would even say, 'I love that one.' Then he could easily say something like, 'What if you had one like it?' Her response would reveal if she felt interested in marriage. Marriage?* He could feel his armpits wet at the thought. *Well, yes. Marriage to Lauren! But now, with my bumbling, I don't know what she feels.*

He had no way of knowing that, at that moment, a suddenly introspective secretary sat looking at the empty ring finger of her left hand, curious about the strange comments that echoed off the glass of the jewelry store.

The whine of the vacuum died, allowing the stereo to fill the sitting room with the soft rhythms of jazz music. David glanced out the window. No sign of her yet. After replacing the vacuum, he stooped over the coffee table in front of the couch and straightened the papers from the school district attorney for the tenth time.

The cream-colored, two-story house stood at the curve of Shadow Trail, a Victorian-style beauty distinguished by a turret with arched windows on the west front corner. Morgan had seen the potential of the seventy-year old house on the first tour with a realtor. During long weekends of labor, she had made the labors of restoration fun. Within months, her creative magic—and lots of David's elbow grease—had transformed it into a grand show piece.

A knock on the front door sent him hurrying across the room. The shadow of Keri's trim figure on the lace curtain that covered the leaded oval glass of the front door raised his heart rate. "Hi! It's been a long time since you knocked on this door. "

"I thought I'd never get here today! Mr. Johnson stepped out, and it took his secretary a few minutes to find the papers we need. Sorry to keep you waiting."

"You're right on time with me." He closed the door behind her. "I needed to straighten the house a little."

She stopped for a long moment to scan the familiar rooms. To her left lay the formal dining room, bright with the sunshine of the noon hour falling on the oak dinner set. Whitewashed cabinets, offset with yellow and white wallpaper in a criss-cross pattern, dramatized the opening into the large kitchen and breakfast nook. To her right the round sitting room, graced with antique furniture under a nine-foot ceiling, invited quiet conversation.

"The house still looks so nice."

"Thanks. You know what a great decorating touch Morgan had. I really haven't done much to improve it on my own. Here, let me take your papers. I'll put them in the sitting room."

He took the notebook and yellow envelope from her hand before she could reply and deposited them on the couch.

"Could I convince you to eat a sandwich with me before we get down to business?" He gestured toward the kitchen. "I laid out some deli meat and chips."

The unexpected invitation pleased her. *Maybe I can bring some conversation that will lift his spirits.* "I'd be glad to. My appointment book is pretty light this afternoon."

He followed her through the doorway. A sweet, flowery scent lingered in the air behind her, a pleasant sensation absent from the house for six long months.

"Sit down and I'll pour you some tea."

She let her eyes wander around the once-familiar room. Before the accident, she often came here to work on one project or another with Morgan. At the breakfast bar they had laughed over the misadventures of money-making schemes and cried over the frustrations of church problems. Her glance fell on the picture of a foggy Mississippi River morning, set off by a whitewashed antique frame, hanging above the table. The memory of the delightful find at a farm auction and the struggle to fit the heavy frame in the car's backseat brought a smile to her face.

He brought a tray of sliced meat, buns and sandwich spread to the table. "I'll let you make it the way you like it. Do you want sugar with your tea?"

"Yes, that would be great." She took some bread to prepare a sandwich. "This quick lunch is so thoughtful of you. I've always liked mixing business with pleasure."

"So, how is everything at the bank?"

"We've not had a real good week. I guess you've heard about the big fight with the Vietnamese?"

"No. What happened?"

She described the accusations and her efforts to influence public opinion, even over the objections of disdainful co-workers. Soon their laughter at her description of the dour vice-president filled the room.

"I've talked too much about my problems. I do appreciate the listening ear, though. Sometimes Barry is so busy he doesn't pay any attention." She noticed his stare and dropped her eyes. "Have things around here settled down? Any more strange sounds?"

"No. That was just my morbid imagination, I guess. Sometimes my mind does strange things. Working on this scholarship project is good therapy, I suppose." He drained the tea glass and pushed back his chair. "Why don't we go in the sitting room? I'd like you to go over the papers from the trust department before you go."

"I'll be glad to explain what I can. You do know that trust and estate matters don't fall in my area of expertise. I may work at a bank, but they never let me close to the big money."

"I'm sure you know more about it than I do."

He led the way to the sitting room. Keri found a seat on the left end of the brown velvet reproduction antique. He sat down on the middle cushion, close enough to push her elbow tight against the curving side of the couch.

"See what you can make of these pieces," he said, handing her several pages bound together in a yellow folder.

On the top lay a letter from the school district financial officer, then below a nice note from the high school principal. Someone had written a moving testimonial about Morgan and the uplifting purpose of the scholarship. The thoughtfulness of the memorial touched her deeply. Her eyes moistened.

"David, donating the money for the scholarship will preserve Morgan's memory in a way that helps many girls over the years."

"Thanks." He lifted his gaze toward the window and sighed. "Most of the time I haven't known what to do. It seems like a nightmare that won't end."

She laid her hand on his. "I can't imagine how you've felt all these months. When you told me about hearing her voice, I couldn't get you off my mind. I've prayed every day for you to work through the heartache."

His jaw muscles tensed to choke back the emotion. A long moment later he turned toward her, taking both her hands in his.

"Thank you for caring when everyone else seemed to forget me."

Keri felt limp with the warmth of his hands. His brown eyes held a depth of suffering that reached to her soul.

"I just want you to be happy again, David." Her whisper seemed as soft as the gentle music that filled the room.

He leaned forward to place his left hand gently on her

cheek, locking his eyes directly on hers. The glow of the noontime sunlight illumined her hair with a golden brilliance.

"I need your help as a special friend."

Briing! The shrill ring of the phone shattered the tender moment.

He pulled his hand away. "I'd better get the phone." The ring blasted again. He marched to the kitchen. "Hello?"

She leaned back into the couch. Conscious of her racing heart, she breathed deeply, twice. Better get my mind back to more proper business. David had tossed the papers to the middle of the sofa table. When she reached to get them, a framed picture standing on the table's edge caught her eye. The frame held an enlarged photo of herself, bikini-clad and holding a hot dog, standing near a campfire with Morgan and Barry.

He scurried back from the call and plopped down next to her. "I'm sorry. Some of my stupid clients have my home number."

She lifted the picture from the table. "Where did this come from?"

He laughed. "I found it the other day when I cleaned out a drawer. Wasn't that a fun weekend? I never knew you could ski so well."

"I've always loved going to the lake." She pointed at the scene. "I remember that weekend very well. We had perfect weather and a lot of fun."

"I really had a good time getting to know you better."

She could feel his eyes boring in on her again. With a rush, she handed him the papers. "From what I understand, we can have the forms ready for you to sign next Monday. Do you feel good about the arrangements?"

"Uh, I guess." His answer came slow. "Now that you've read it over, I do. I don't want people to think I'm on some kind of ego trip or something."

She gave a quick shake of her head. "I don't think anyone will feel that way. I know the community will be touched by the genuineness of the project."

"I'm glad you see it that way. I will go to the bank Monday. That should give the school plenty of time to award the scholarship before graduation next spring."

They listened as the Victorian mantle clock sounded, playing a simple melody and then striking a single mellow note.

"The time's gotten away from me. I'd better get back to the bank." She stood to gather up her purse and the documents.

"Thanks for coming by." He moved toward the door. "I'm glad to get this business on its final lap. I enjoyed the lunch, too. It's not every day an old widower gets to entertain a pretty girl."

She stopped in the doorway and tugged the strap of her purse up on her shoulder.

"Grieving is hard for everyone. But I certainly don't think you're old."

"Let's talk again. Soon."

"I'd like that."

He hugged her, gently, and kissed her on the cheek. "Thanks for being a friend," he whispered.

She pushed the front door open to a rush of hot air. Her heels echoed across the wooden porch and down the stairs. With a quick wave, she slid into the gray Honda. The moisture of his kiss lingered on her cheek during the drive down Shadow Trail toward the bank.

Rachel Haskins quietly closed the door of the sunlit patio room. Although the tall glasses of iced tea she left with her husband and her pastor had been received with gratitude, she could read through their subdued voices the desire for privacy in the small townhouse.

"Daemon Asher's name came to me so clearly it seemed like someone had shouted it out loud," Barry said. "Kent didn't suggest it to me. I'm sure he doesn't know about the troubles I've had with Asher in the past."

Just yesterday C.K. had carried to Barry's office the news of trouble brewing in the conversation with Ed Loomis. Now, the pastor returned the visit to narrate more disturbing developments. "Perhaps I should have acted immediately. I wasn't prepared for the ambush last night. It looks to me like Daemon and his gang planned the whole episode with the precision of a commando strike team."

"You don't think the real issue has anything to do with the Burns girl?"

"No. Not at all. That issue camouflaged their real goal." He slowly shook his head. "The worst part is knowing that I took the bait. I still can't believe I belted Dale."

The retired minister's quick laugh filled the room. "But it really felt good, didn't it? I can't tell you how many times across the years I wanted to do something like that. Or even worse! But seriously, pastor, anyone in this congregation who knows the full story will understand."

"I wish I could feel that confident, C.K. I'm afraid I've given this group one more log to throw on the bonfire that will burn me at the stake. I've already heard this morning from the Board chairman. He called a special meeting for Sunday night with the 'incident' Wednesday night as the only item on the agenda. I couldn't sleep last night without seeing Dale's sneer over and over. I don't think I'll ever get over it."

He fell silent. A robin, hopping across the green grass of the small backyard, caught their eyes. The little bird moved, listened and stabbed the ground with its beak in a search for prey.

"I guess I've come to see if you could talk me out of resigning. Keri and I talked about it very seriously this morning."

"I'm not surprised. Being burned at the stake has never appealed to many people."

"Don't get me wrong. We've seen some good things happen in these six years. Maybe the time is right to let someone else take over." He looked toward the older man. "I've been offered another position."

C.K.'s eyebrows shot up. "Another church?"

"No. Have you ever heard of The Potter's House? It's a children's home with a rapidly expanding ministry, located near Kansas City. The director has contacted me about a new position. I would be religious dean and associate administrator."

"How do you feel about it? What does Keri think?"

He leaned forward and propped his elbows on the table. "Some aspects about a move seem really positive. I'd have more time with the family. The ulcer factor of so many expectations goes way down. The extra money would help send Jason to college. Keri worries about living in a large city, but she can see the benefits, too."

The white-haired minister took a deep drink. "You realize, of course, that some people will say that you're leaving the ministry."

A slight grin lit the pastor's face. "Some will be glad to think I'm leaving the ministry! But we know ministry encompasses more than just serving a church as a pastor. Most people will understand that, I'm sure."

C. K. refilled his glass from the pitcher Rachel had left on the table.

"In other circumstances I'd be the first to suggest you go directly to Daemon and try to resolve the problem. Then, if that doesn't work, take someone in authority with you. In other words, follow the pattern of Matthew 18."

"Are you suggesting that I try that now?"

"No." He sighed. "You see, I knew about Mt. Faith Church before I retired. What I knew didn't please me."

"What do you mean?"

"Didn't the Board ever level with you about Dr. Patrick's departure? The truth is that they asked him to resign. Very quietly, of course. The members took care of every detail. Some key leaders thought he had lost his effectiveness. Three months later he announced his retirement."

"I've never heard that before! Of course, Dr. Patrick and I only talked a few times. He never volunteered any details about his leaving."

"My sister, the one who died last year of cancer, served on the Board at that time. I heard the whole story and grieved for Hiram. The tragedy drove him away from active ministry."

"Really? I just supposed it was a natural step for him to retire at that stage of life."

"This warning may come too late. Professional research has shown that churches often repeat their destructive patterns. Problems reoccur and the preacher gets all the blame. They fire one pastor after another."

"Do you think the same people are stirring up problems now?"

C. K. looked directly in his eyes. "The cast of characters is nearly the same, Barry. I'm afraid they want to film a sequel with you as the villain, instead of Hiram Patrick. Trouble is, you may not be able to hire a stunt man to handle the fight scene."

"Mt. Faith Church, Liz speaking. May I help you?"

Liz balanced the receiver on her shoulder while juggling

copies of the weekly attendance report. Her list of jobs to complete this Thursday had multiplied, producing a rising sense of frustration. Mary's absence from the reception desk did not help.

"This is Daemon Asher. Do you have a few minutes?"

"I guess I could talk for a few moments." She glanced toward Lauren's desk. Her co-worker had not returned from the education hall. The doors of the ministers' offices were closed. The setting seemed to provide a safe time to talk, without unwanted ears overhearing.

"Give me a reading on the attitude around the office today." He had wished several times today he could scurry around the office as a big-eared church mouse.

"Closed door conversations seem to be the order of the day." Her voice dropped. "Brent and Drew had a long discussion early this morning and neither of them appeared very happy about the topic."

"Perhaps the little drama in the atrium made an impact. You do know what happened last night, don't you? I should have told you about the plan before it happened."

"I had no idea what took place until this morning. Lauren eventually told me the whole story. It sounds to me like you may have finally gotten the pastor to admit the church has some problems to solve."

"Pastors bury their heads in the sand too easily. But I've always believed that the first step to a solution is honest assessment. Your past experience shows the importance of honesty, doesn't it?"

The statement caught her by surprise. "Yes, I guess it does." She couldn't remember telling him about her past dealings.

"I doubt that anyone in the office has told you about the real issue in the confrontation last night. We believe Barry intends to run up the membership, packing the rolls with young minds easily swayed to his radical ideas. The youngster, Kendra Burns, is a case in point. I confronted Barry with it, and he blew up. It's simply unfortunate the scam had to come out so publicly."

"I can't believe it. How could he try something like that?"

He could read her voice and added more fuel to the fire. "Liz, your eyes are wide open to the problems the church faces today. What you've done this week has already helped to solve this sad problem. It's vital for everyone that you continue to keep very close track of what happens in the office."

"I'll watch closely. I guess it will help the church, won't it?"

"Of course it will. By the way, if you have the opportunity, look around Barry's office. Check on the status of that envelope you placed on his desk Monday. Stay alert to anything else that looks suspicious and report it to me immediately."

Lauren opened the office door, balancing a tall stack of papers in her long arms.

Liz lightened her tone. "O.K. I'd better get back to work."

"I'll call if we see any further developments. Together our team will get to the bottom of this problem. Bye."

She quickly hung up the phone and carried the attendance reports to her desk. Daemon and Nadine had greeted her warmly the very first day she attended Mt. Faith, reaching over the pew with a friendly handshake and smile. Sunday by Sunday they grew better acquainted. Since she took the job in the church office they had shown special interest in her welfare. They had taken her into their confidence, quietly telling her of the problems Barry had brought on the church. It appeared obvious that Daemon, as a long-standing member, had the best interest of the church at heart. But his knowledge of her past troubled her.

How much does he know about me?

The leaves of the rough-barked cottonwood trees ruffled in the hot breeze high above the Eastside Community Center, throwing a dance of shadows on Keri's parked car. Dominique had already begun to unload her equipment from the television news van when Keri walked up with her friend.

"Dominique, please meet Duyen Luong, a client of the bank. Duyen, Dominique Greer works at Channel 9."

"I recognize you," Duyen said, reaching to shake hands with the black newswoman. "It's very good to meet you." Glancing toward the camera, she added, "I hope you won't ask hard questions. I'm not an actor or anything."

Dominique smiled. "If you were, I'd be loading my stuff up right now. The last thing this town needs is a professional actor interviewed for the news! Monday I came over here to listen to Van Dang, the leader of the Vietnamese Citizen's League. Now I want to hear what a genuine citizen of Mt. Carmel has to say."

"We appreciate you taking time to chase this story," Keri said. "Duyen does have an inside viewpoint that could put a different light on the situation. How hard did you work to convince your boss to send you out this morning?"

"Not too hard. He knows this is a big story. In fact, he told me this morning we could feature this piece tonight if it turns out well. But, he's skeptical about you providing the source. I want you to know that." She motioned to Butch, standing near the camera. "Let's do a sound check."

The mustached cameraman handed her the mic, stepped back, and lifted the camera to his shoulder. After a few moments, he moved them forward a few steps to escape the shadows of trees in front of the Center.

Duyen's hands trembled a bit as she brushed her hair.

Keri touched her shoulder for reassurance. "Don't worry. All Dominique needs is for you to tell what happened at the bank when you applied for the loan. Dominique, if she stumbles, could you reshoot the interview?"

"Yes, I think so. Our schedule looked pretty light today, so we're in no big rush now."

Butch turned a final knob on the camera. "I'm ready to shoot when you are."

"Fine. Let's get going. Duyen, I need you to stand close to me. I'll ask a simple question and you just tell me your story. Don't even look at the camera, just focus on talking to me like a friend."

"I'll try."

The tall reporter and the diminutive Asian faced the camera. Butch squinted through the viewfinder, counted, "3-2-1," then pointed his finger.

"A new twist in the controversy over Security State Bank has been uncovered by the Instant 9 news team. On Monday, the Vietnamese Citizens League brought charges of bigotry against Security State Bank of Mt. Carmel. But, our research has revealed another side to the controversy."

The camera panned over to include both women in the picture.

"Here with me is Duyen Luong, a Vietnamese woman who lives two blocks from the East Side Center. Duyen, how did you feel about the comments you heard from Mr. Van Dang on Instant 9 news?"

"I feel that the he and his citizen's group don't know the whole story. I'm a single Vietnamese woman, working for the Mt. Carmel Independent School District. I don't have a lot of money, but when I went to Security State, they loaned me the money for my house. The loan officer helped me every step of the way. I moved in eighteen months ago."

"But have other Vietnamese people been able to secure loans?"

"I've recommended the bank to several friends. Two others have applied for loans, and one is already my neighbor."

Dominique turned the comment backward. "so, the bank did deny credit to a Vietnamese applicant?"

"I don't think so, well, I guess I don't know what happened," Duyen stumbled a bit and glanced down. "He didn't get the loan." Her head bounced back up. "But my other friend did."

"Did you sense any reluctance or hostility on the part of Security State officials when you applied?"

Duyen shook her head. Her voice sounded adamant. "No, not at all. They even helped me clear up some credit problems from my divorce. They explained everything to me."

Dominique paused, then waved to Butch. "Let's cut here. I've got an idea. Duyen, would you mind if we drove to your house and did some cut away shots? I think they would help tell the story."

"I'd be glad to take you there, especially if I didn't have to say anything on camera again!"

Within a few minutes, she and Keri watched Butch walk around the attractive home, recording scenes that every home owner in the viewing audience would be familiar with, down to the name on the mail box. The one-story frame house, yard freshly mowed, flaunted an eye-catching coat of fresh tan paint and dark trim.

"I'll probably do a voice over with these scenes to wind up the segment," Dominique said to Keri. "Will you be available in the afternoon if I have questions?"

"I don't think I have any other outside appointments today. Fran can hunt me down, though, even if I'm out. Just call. I appreciate you having time for us today."

"Good. I think the news director can figure out that someone who drives a Tercel, not a limousine, might have a important viewpoint on this deal. I'll give you a call if I need anything."

Keri and Duyen sat down in wicker rocking chairs and watched from the porch while the news van pulled away. Duyen sighed. "Did I do O.K.?"

"Like a champ! We can't predict what will happen when the director puts the story together, but you told your side of the story perfectly."

"I'm glad to help. By the way, do you remember the last time you visited here?"

"I remember it very well!"

"We didn't finish our tea, remember? Let me make that up to you now. Would you join me inside for something to drink?"

"I'd love too—and let's not call 9-1-1 this time!"

"My Father is the gardener."

A Scripture verse perfect for Saturday's funeral message sprang to Barry's mind when he noticed the carefully pruned rose bushes beside the front porch of Harvey's home. The view of the gorgeous, crimson blossoms drinking in the sunlight of the bright afternoon lifted his spirit. He knew instinctively the theme would be just right for the service.

Verna responded to his knock on the door. "Come in, preacher. Mom's resting in the kitchen. May I get you something to drink? We stirred up some lemonade a little while ago."

"I think I will have a glass, thank you. This afternoon

heat has nearly melted me down into my shoes."

The small kitchen embraced him with the aroma of fried chicken. Under the painted white cabinets the kitchen counters overflowed with irregular mounds of food, wrapped in shiny foil. On the table lay cake pans, plastic-wrapped pies and a bountiful variety of sweets, providing the home-cooked evidence of a church family ministering through sumptuous helpings of comfort food.

Edith stood to give him a grandmotherly hug. He noticed the dark skin under her eyes, a natural tattoo of her grief.

Barry returned her embrace, then leaned back to look her in the eyes. "How are you doing today?"

"I'm doing fine, under the circumstances. So many people have come to help me. I never knew I had so many friends." She gestured for him to sit down on a creaky, kitchen chair.

"You and Harvey have helped so many people in their hour of need over the past years. It doesn't surprise me that people have returned the favor."

"It meant so much to me that Keri came with you the day Harvey died. Red and I had so many decisions to make. Knowing you both were praying made the sorrow easier to bear."

Verna poured a tall glass of cold lemonade and joined them at the kitchen table. "Red had to move some equipment to Joplin today, so he can't meet with us. But, he said whatever we wanted in the service would suit him fine."

Barry pulled a pen from his shirt pocket. "Let me write down some of the details you have planned for the funeral service."

"We don't want anything fancy. Harvey didn't carry any pretense—or much like people who did."

"We'll work to make it just what you want."

For the next minutes, Barry jotted down the thoughts of the gray-haired widow. Her ideas sounded full of the hope and faith that had strengthened her life across the years. Verna joined in occasionally. Soon the plans for the Saturday memorial service satisfied the mother and daughter-in-law.

After small talk and a second glass of lemonade, the pastor made his way down the winding streets of Buck Hill. It would only take a few minutes more to compose the message about the beauty of the roses. A message based on flowers for Mr. Flowers. He made a mental note to consult with the funeral director and talk to Brent about the music.

I might never do another funeral in Mt. Carmel. He motored slowly across the Spring River Bridge. *What would a ministry with no funerals feel like?* No sad house calls, no somber music. For years he had labored in the quiet rhythms of grief. He had grown skilled in reading the demeanor of the gathered families and parsing the attitudes of stricken hearts. *What a change it would be!*

He eased up to the stoplight at HW 60, drumming his fingers on the wheel. A strange ache of regret draped across his heart. *I've also seen some shining moments of faith in all the pain.* Hurting families usually welcomed him with open arms, valuing his unique contribution to the unfamiliar passage of life. Like a high plateau mounted after an arduous climb, ministry in the crisis inspired him in ways he found deeply fulfilling. *Do I really want to leave behind such moments of grace?*

Parking in his usual place, he looked up at the spire towering above the sanctuary. Behind it puffy white clouds drifted through the bright blue sky. *Am I rooted solidly in God's will or drifting on my own selfish path?* The high clouds kept their silence during his contemplative walk towards the glass doors.

The knob on the aluminum front door, heated by the

fierce western sun, burned his hand. Cody jerked the door open with a curse. The faint smell of baby lotion greeted him, punishing his senses with a vivid reminder of little Courtney. He flipped the switch on the front of the window air conditioner and the old motor thumped to life, blowing a musty cool breeze into the hot room. Opening the grocery sack, he grabbed a beer and dropped his heavy frame on the faded recliner.

Where in this stupid little town are they hiding?

The silence of the trailer mocked his frustration. Yesterday, he had gunned the pickup back and forth through the rainy streets of Mt. Carmel, hoping to find Lisa and the girls. Today he had tried to work smarter. Around noon he had called motels, relatives, and friends to track her down. Either everyone lied real well, or she honestly was not at any of the places he checked. Out of ideas, he finally went to the liquor store to get his favorite brand of beer. Maybe a cold one would help him develop a better plan.

A third empty can had targeted Lisa's picture on the bookcase when the sound of a car caught his attention. He jumped from the frayed recliner and peered through the front room window. A black-haired man stepped from a 4Runner. Holding a small booklet in his hand, the stranger stepped deliberately toward the porch of the trailer.

Three cans of beer in his belly soured Cody on the idea of meeting some idiot salesman.

"What do you want?"

The man stopped at the foot of the wooden stair. He looked up at the hulking, angry young man clad in a wrinkled t-shirt. "Hi. I'm Pastor Barry Peters from Mt. Faith Church."

He scowled. "I said, what do you want?"

"Is Lisa here?"

"What do you need her for?"

"I've got some material about the baptism scheduled for

Sunday. I want to make sure all her questions are answered before we baptize Kendra. Are you Mr. Burns?"

He pushed open the door. The small wooden porch creaked under his weight. "I don't know nothin' about a baptism or Mt. Faith Church. Who said you could baptize Kendra?"

"Let me explain. My wife and I came by at Lisa's invitation last Sunday night. She and the girls attended the church Sunday morning. We talked to Kendra about faith in God. We were all so pleased when she prayed to receive Christ. Lisa scheduled her to be baptized this Sunday."

He struggled to process the rush of news. Insecurity about the unfamiliar concepts added to the pent up anger from forty-eight hours of rejection. "I still don't know what you're talking about. They're not here anyway. Haven't been since Tuesday. I've looked for them all over this blasted town."

"I see. Do you expect her back soon?"

A new thought suddenly made sense. "Do you and your church people know anything about her leaving?"

"About Lisa leaving? Not a thing." He cocked his head. "I guess I don't understand. Isn't she living here anymore?"

Cody threw himself down the stairs. The beer loosened his emotions.

"I said she ain't here, mister," he shouted. "She took off with both kids. I ain't seen her since Tuesday. Something strange got into her." His finger stabbed the air. "I bet your church has got a whole lot to do with it."

Barry could smell the booze. He raised his hands to calm the red-faced man. "Hey, I don't know anything about Lisa leaving."

"Sure you don't. You come by with your religion junk and two days later she's gone. None of her friends know where she's hiding. But, I bet some of your sweet do-good women at the church do. Maybe they're the ones hiding her from her big, bad old man." His accusations sounded loud enough for the whole trailer park to hear.

Barry felt his mouth dry. He stepped back. "Now, slow down just a minute. Believe me, we didn't talk to your wife about anything like that. We only visited here a few minutes." He tried a softer tone. "I'm sorry to hear what's happened. Surely she'll be back in touch soon."

"She'd better get home, or she'll get what's coming to her." He snatched the paper out of the pastor's hand. "If she needs something from God, we can take care of it without your church women. Now you get out of here. I don't want to hear anything more about baptism or your stupid church."

The two men stood face to face, Cody breathing heavily, wild-eyed, Barry with jaw set in defiance.

After a long moment, the pastor spoke. "I'd appreciate it if you would give that booklet to her." He turned on his heel and walked back to the Toyota. Without a glance at the hulking figure, he started the car, backed away from the mobile home, and gunned the accelerator to leave the trailer park behind.

"Don't come back either!"

He stamped up the creaky stairs. Now he understood what had gotten into Lisa. Somebody at that church brainwashed her. They convinced her she could dump him and get somebody better. The insult re-ignited his fury. He swung a dirty work boot at the kitchen cabinet, caving a hole in the door.

"I'll make those crazy church people pay for this," he roared to the battered house.

The reflection of the late afternoon sun glared bright silver on the water of the Mt. Carmel Club pool. Barry squinted at the earth-toned bodies catching the rays of the bright summer sun.

Jason tossed him a large beach towel. "I'm going to get in, Dad."

"O.K. I'll wait for your mom in our usual spot."

He tucked the striped green towel under his arm to pick his way through the maze of lean young bodies. The thunder of a rock music station playing on the loudspeaker marked the time of his steps. His favorite hangout lay on the shady side of the open cabana, a few feet back from the side of the busy pool. Finding two empty plastic deck chairs, he pulled them together, parking the pool bag between them. He checked his watch. Keri should be leaving the bank about now. That should give him a few minutes to close his eyes and rest by the pool with no one bothering him. With a sigh, he sat down and stretched his sandaled feet toward the pool.

Instead of restful thoughts, however, the angry, unkempt face of Cody Burns popped to his mind. What could have caused the man's strange behavior? While driving away from the mobile home park, he had checked his rear view mirror several times as a precaution against the troubled man following him home. Why would blame for Lisa's disappearance come to rest on the church?

"Dad!" Jason's voice and a splash of water came simultaneously. His dripping face hung over the side of the pool a few feet away, wet hair plastered down across his forehead. "Mom's here!"

Keri waved from across the pool. Her arms balanced a large picnic bag and two more towels. The pale yellow swimsuit stood out against her tanned, taut body.

Barry stood to help her unload. "Hi, babe. How are you?"

She pecked his cheek with a kiss. "I'm great, since I'm not at Security State Bank. It has felt like a pressure cooker all day. Even Fran commented about the tension. She is usually oblivious to anything short of a bomb threat."

"The Vietnamese deal?"

"Yes. They've threatened to start picketing tomorrow. I can't imagine how Ledbetter will react to that. No, I *can* imagine how he will react." She started to unpack the picnic bag. "I'm not going to think about it for awhile."

"Well, at least he hasn't threatened to throw you bodily off his property. You won't believe what happened when I went back to the Burns' trailer on the way home from the church."

"Lisa wasn't there, was she?"

"No. That created the problem, I guess." Barry returned the look. "How did you know?"

"Did I not tell you about that last night?"

"No," he answered, slowly, "you didn't even mention her. And what you didn't say nearly got me manhandled by a very ugly guy, namely her drunk husband. What do you know about it?"

Keri grimaced. She bypassed the opportunity to complain about his attitude last night and instead recounted Lisa's phone call Wednesday afternoon from the shelter.

"The way Cody acted toward me today, I'd hate to think what he could do to a little woman like Lisa. If she calls anymore, we'd better take some precautions."

Jason appeared in a rush, showering water on his parents. "Dad, come throw this ring so I can dive and get it."

Barry pushed himself out of the chair. "Be back in a minute." He picked up a bright yellow plastic ring and gave it a toss. Jason dove in with a splash to rescue the sinking toy.

As her men played, Keri tried to relax. Her stomach ached with the tension of the afternoon. The problems seemed muddled with the bank and the Burns family, but another issue crowded in as well. Leaning back in the chair, she seemed to feel the fabric of the couch in David Dockery's parlor rather than the cool plastic pool chair. The laughter of the swimmers faded into the mellow tones of jazz echoing through the sunlit parlor.

She couldn't even remember the drive from the house on Shadow Trail to her parking space on the bank lot. Somehow, she had managed to get by Fran's desk without divulging the details of her lunch. Throughout the afternoon hours, her thoughts fluttered like wild birds from one perch to another.

A sense of satisfaction swelled within her about helping David achieve an important goal. The scholarship arrangement honored the memory of her best friend and even put a feather in the hat of the bank. She could talk to anyone about such positive results.

But other thoughts—ones that a happily married woman should never voice—swooped darkly. She felt again the warmth of his hand laid on hers. And his kiss. Her cheek seemed to glow with the touch of his lips. Should I be offended? No. He meant it only as a friendly gesture. But did his lips linger?

"Can we eat now?"

Barry's voice made her jump. Her eyes sprang open to see the silhouette of her dripping husband. "Sure. Dig out whatever you want."

She started to lift the bag, but it slipped from her hand and landed on the concrete. The plastic-wrapped sandwiches and chips spilled across the deck.

"I'll get it." He hurried to bend over and scoop up the food. The overturned sack sent his thoughts back to the spilled contents of the manila envelope he had discovered Tuesday, green with promise of financial reward. Five thousand dollars. Who knows the secret behind it?

"Want something else?"

"Uh, no, this is fine."

While they ate, a tired Jason came over to stretch his body on the concrete in front of them.

"Have a good time, buddy?" Barry prodded the gangly young body with his foot.

"Yeah. I did. But Dad, can we come back Saturday?"

"Sorry pal, but I don't think so. I've got to do both a funeral and a wedding on Saturday. That's going to fill up my day."

"You've got both on the same day? That's like getting two hits in one game, isn't it?"

Barry chuckled. "It sure is. I hadn't thought of it like that. And you know what? I'm doing a baptism on Sunday. So, those are the three main rituals of the believer's life, all on one weekend."

Keri joined in. "Sounds like that baseball player who hit for the cycle in the baseball game Sunday. All you need is to be around when a baby is born and it would be like hitting a single, a double, a triple and a home run!"

Jason jumped up. "Cool! Have you ever seen a baby born, Dad?"

Barry grabbed him in a bear hug. "Just one—a wrinkly, black-haired boy named Jason! Hey, listen. I hope I don't deliver a baby this weekend. That would make the headlines."

Jason seemed disappointed. "That would be like hitting for the cycle if you did, though."

Keri stood up and rubbed her son's wet hair. "Let's head home. We've got a lot to do before Dad's big game this weekend."

"Daemon!" Nadine shouted over the whine of the hand-held vacuum. She saw him lift his head over the trunk lid of the Lincoln, nod and push the power switch to kill the whining machine. "Ed Loomis is calling."

"Tell him I'll be right there." He laid the vacuum

carefully on the workbench and headed into the kitchen.

"This is Daemon. What can I do for you, Ed?"

"Sorry to bother you," the big merchant rumbled. "I heard earlier today about the, ... uh, the problem you and Barry had last night."

"The whole situation turned unfortunate, to say the least."

"I agree. I thought you might want to know that I talked with C. K. Haskins earlier this week. We've worked together on a few projects, and I wanted to get his take on Peters. But when I described the problems, he stalked out of the office mad as a wet hen."

"He was angry with all the problems Barry has caused?"

"Hardly. I mean he blew up at the accusations. Said he wouldn't play any part in an effort to attack the preacher. He stormed out and went right to Barry, I'm sure."

"You think Haskins talked with the pastor?"

"I'm sure he did. I didn't realize how much C. K. really cares about the staff members. Must be because he pastored so long. I'm sure he told the pastor all about it."

Daemon cursed to himself. For weeks he had worked to keep his plans confined to a small circle of associates. This news leak could rob the element of surprise from his plan.

"Have you talked with anyone else?"

"Just Haskins."

He hid his displeasure. "Well, O.K. Thanks for letting me know. Say, Ed, before you go, would you be able to meet tomorrow evening? We need to discuss our plans to help the church."

"I need to check with Doris. What time?"

"Seven o'clock. There'll be a few others here. We can decide what our next step should be, in light of the circumstances."

"I'll do my best to come. See you then."

He punched the off button. What had possessed him to include the big gorilla in his confidence? For weeks everything had gone smoothly. The circle of concerned members had embraced his desire to force Barry out of office. The sting money had been collected easily. Liz readily agreed to provide inside information. Small rumors planted here and there grew quickly. Over time, a good number of members came to quietly share his concerns. Even one of the Peters' closest friends had joined the effort.

He opened the sliding patio door and stepped outside. Pacing the flagstones, he tried to calm his thoughts. Loomis' breach of confidence threatened everything. If Barry's supporters were given time to organize, the fight would become much more difficult.

The ring of the phone interrupted his anxious rumination.

"Daemon? This is David."

"I wondered when I might hear from you. Did you get a tape?"

"Not yet. She's been preoccupied with a problem at the bank. I nearly had what we needed yesterday but things... uh... fell apart, I guess, at just the wrong time."

"I wish you could do something right! That tape is critical to this whole plan. I want you..."

"Hey, calm down. I'm working right now on a sure-fire deal that will give us plenty of nails to close the coffin on Barry. Just give me time."

"Time is exactly what we don't have! I just talked to Loomis. Barry's gang knows something is going on. If we don't act soon, we'll lose our advantage. I need something soon."

"O.K. I'll do my best."

"Tomorrow night come to my house at seven o'clock.

We'll settle our plans then. And bring anything you have. We can't waste even a single day."

"I may be a little late, but you can count on me. I'll see you then."

He leaned against a rough cedar post beneath the patio cover, his stomach tight with concern. If we only had one more week everything would be in place.

A moment later, Nadine slid open the door and hurried across the patio. "I wondered where you'd gone. Liz is here."

The gray-haired secretary stood waiting in the entry. She seemed breathless. "I stopped by to let you know I did find something interesting in Barry's office."

"Thanks for making the effort to come by, Liz. Now, what is this discovery you're so excited about?"

His informant settled in a patio chair and took a deep breath. "Barry left the office early this afternoon with plans of visiting that Burns family. Apparently, he intends to carry out the baptism in spite of the warning you brought Wednesday."

"That doesn't surprise me. His delusion of greatness will drive him no matter what we may say."

"I carried some papers into the office after he left. Like I mentioned on the phone, I found something very interesting. Look at this."

She pulled a single photocopied page from her purse and slid it across the table.

He read the letter slowly, holding the page at an angle so Nadine could see it. He lowered it to look at the secretary. "This truly is an answer to prayer, Liz."

"I'm thrilled," Nadine said. "I hope he accepts the position tomorrow."

He shook his head "It's not that simple."

"Why?"

"Look at the letter again. Does the president's name ring

a bell?"

Liz read the name out loud. "Stephen Richards. I don't recognize it either."

"Dr. Richards serves as the chairman of the Synod. His three year term provides tremendous leverage to control the work of the denomination."

"That means Barry..."

"Barry will have an inside track of influence upon many churches, not just ours. We can't allow that to happen." He stood up, lips drawn tight. "Stopping Barry right here, right now, is critical. The future of the conference may be at stake, too. Tomorrow won't be a moment too soon to bring our plan together."

Chapter 6
Friday

Kent checked the time on the ornate desk clock in the small guest bedroom behind the kitchen. Thirty more minutes until Beth's alarm. He shifted forward on his knees. Once again, the labor of a pre-dawn prayer furrowed his brow.

"Lord," he whispered, "Barry and Keri have grown to mean so much to us. I know You have called him to this place and appointed him to lead this church. Strengthen him for whatever he may face today. Let him live true to Your call."

After the quiet intercession carried his heart across well-trodden paths of prayer, he settled in a chair at the small oak desk near the window. The brass table lamp burned just bright enough for him to journal his work of prayer. He lifted a small wire-bound notebook from the drawer and opened the pages to his last entry.

The steady tick of the clock pronounced the value of each passing moment. Heavy with marble and glass, the treasured timepiece also resonated with the memories of Benny. His only son had purchased it six years ago in a scenic Italian mountain village. It would be the last item on his credit card, a priceless treasure packed ready to ship just minutes before the rented Fiat left the icy road and plunged down the mountain.

The grief of the sudden loss had fractured the foundations of Kent's life. Trite answers of meaning and eternity disappeared in the maelstrom of heartache, forcing him to search the dark recess of his soul. Where could the passing hours of life find any real purpose? He slogged through months of anguish until one wind-swept afternoon on a lonely peak high in the Rockies. Casting his grief into the heart of God the Father, he found new devotion to the One who works in all things for good.

What should I record about my prayer today? He flipped back through the previous pages of his daily prayer record, then took a pen for today's entry.

Awakened early with burden about Barry. Something is happening that threatens him. But still no idea what it is.

He paused. For the hundredth time he replayed the startling vision of the dark-robed men attacking the pastor.

Wasn't that just like Wednesday night and the assault by Daemon Asher? The men who confronted Barry at church brought a thirst, not for physical injury, but to discredit Barry and his ministry. They left no physical blood stain, but the emotional trauma to the pastor and the church produced wounds of the heart.

He could hardly write quickly enough to record the revelation.

Wednesday three men accosted Barry in the atrium of the church. I've never heard of anything like that before. This must have been what the vision warned about. The pastor is under attack by his own church members!

He laid his pen aside and rubbed his forehead with both hands. I see the connection now. But what do I do about it?

I should probably go talk to Barry and warn him again. Then, he can really fight this attack aggressively. That provides a strategy to meet the problem head on and be proactive.

Call people together and pray.

The directive resonated in his mind, vivid and fully formed.

Call people together and pray.

He sensed the presence of the Father, nudging him toward a different strategy than what had seemed so right a moment before. *This conflict reveals a spiritual battle. These blood-thirsty men cannot be defeated by human confrontation. The time has come for weapons of spiritual power. This house on Rolling Meadow Road must become an arsenal of heavenly power. The future of Barry's ministry and the ministry of the church hang in the balance.*

The mellow chimes of the Italian clock sounded again. The time had come for action.

The expansive breakfast buffet covered the red tablecloths of the serving line in the Pershing Room of Mt. Carmel's best hotel, the Stonebridge Inn. Steaming stainless steel trays contained yellow mounds of scrambled eggs, thin slices of ham and piles of hard biscuits. Many of the city leaders had been enticed to load their plates as if it were Fat Tuesday. Keri's uneasy stomach, however, confined her choices to a slice of cantaloupe, some grapes, and four large strawberries. Except for her assignment to represent the bank at the monthly Chamber of Commerce breakfast, no other demand could have forced her out of bed, feeling like she did. Holding her plate, she threaded her way through the buzzing crowd to a large round table set for six.

"Good morning, ladies. Do you have a place for me?"

Betsy Windle, associate director of the human resource department at the hospital, gestured for her to sit down. Betsy attended First Baptist Church. Her calm, careful manner usually accomplished the task assigned when she worked with Keri on community projects.

"Sit right here." She patted the seat of the empty chair

next to her. "How are you this morning?"

"My stomach's a little quesy this morning. This is too early for me, I guess." She reached across the round table to shake hands with the three other ladies.

"Anyway, I couldn't believe it when Kenny showed up at the party in this loud Hawaiian shirt and white shorts! He is a scream." Dana MacClansin, the owner of three antique shops, resumed her story. Keri remembered the rumor that Dana had a store for every divorce settlement. She sported platinum hair and jewelry that dangled noisily when she shook Keri's hand.

"How long have you been dating?" Danielle Gibson looked over her glasses to ask the question. She looked barely old enough to be in college, not in her second year of law practice at Hingiss and Mossberg.

"We started going out in May. His company has season tickets to the Royals, so he invited me to go with him a couple of weekends. He's a great guy."

Elizabeth Walker, the fourth woman at the table, worked in the County Clerk's office. Her large, florid face wore a perpetual blush of exertion. "My Bob would really get excited about season tickets," she said. "He likes anything that gets him out of the house and away from yard work."

"Sounds like I had better get acquainted with sports if I'm going to make any progress with the guys in Mt. Carmel," Danielle said.

"Oh, the men around here are sports, all right,' Dana replied. "But the sport they care most about isn't played on a ball diamond, if you know what I mean." She laughed loudly at her own joke. "That's what you need to practice."

Danielle giggled. "Some of my college dates were like World Championship Wrestling. But the guy I'm seeing now — his name is Mitchell, lives in Columbia — is more laid back. Not so much pressure."

Keri groaned to herself. I didn't come here to talk about men. I've enough trouble in that area already. She picked up a strawberry with her fork. Her mind wandered from the noisy conference room breakfast to the antique-filled parlor at the Dockery's. What if I had responded? For a moment she had a picture of sitting snuggled with David near a quiet camp fire.

She looked across the table at Dana. She'd changed mates, not once, but three times. Some might applaud her courage to face her unhappiness and do something about it. When a relationship had run its course, she had the initiative to look for someone who cared. Maybe I'm stuck with someone who has forgotten about caring for me at all.

Betsy leaned closer. "Are you O.K.?"

Keri shook her head. "Even these fresh strawberries don't appeal to me right now. I don't feel much like eating this morning."

"I'm sure the little problem at the bank hasn't helped you this week. Maybe the program won't last too long this morning. Do you want some antacid pills?"

The ringing of Keri's cell phone interrupted the offer. She pulled it from her purse.

"Hello?"

"Keri? This is David."

The color drained from Keri's face. "Hi. Just a minute." She nodded politely to the women and left the table to seek a quiet corner of the loud and crowded room.

"I'm at the Chamber breakfast. What are you doing?"

"I'm sitting here looking across the breakfast bar at a pretty picture."

"Oh?"

"Some dame in a bathing suit."

"From Sports Illustrated?"

"No. From a very nice day at the lake. And yesterday

even improved on the memory."

"I enjoyed helping with your project." She turned her face away from the crowd and moved closer to the wall. "It's a wonderful testimony to a wonderful person."

"I'm glad you had time to help. But the best part came with the goodbye."

She played a game. "The best part was me leaving?"

"No, that's not what I meant. Maybe I'd better explain in person. Would you mind if I treated you to some coffee when I bring the scholarship papers to the bank?"

"I'd have to check my schedule. We've got a nice coffee bar for employees, so it wouldn't be hard to arrange."

"I'd rather walk up the street to the Java Shop. I'll stop by your office after I meet the trust officer." His voice turned serious. "I want you to know I appreciate you for being such a good friend. You mean, uh, your friendship means a lot to me right now."

Her stomach tightened even more. His words suddenly seemed too serious. She couldn't think of anything proper to say.

"You know, after you left yesterday, I..."

She saw the speaker step toward the podium and seized the moment to interrupt. "I'd better go now. The program is starting."

"Oh, sure. You've got a busy schedule today, I know. My appointment is at 1:30. I'll see you later. Then we can talk some more."

"Bye." The phone clicked off. She dropped it in her purse and looked toward the friends she had left. No one seemed to notice her absence. *Good. The chamber can get along without me this morning. And I won't have to explain my phone call from a good-looking widower!* She pulled her purse strap over her shoulder and slipped out the door.

Still no sign of them anywhere. Cody turned from the

dirty window. The floor boards of the worn mobile home creaked with each heavy step he took. The irritating sound, unmasked by the absence of family patter, mocked his aimless movements through the lonely trailer.

Last night he thought the ordeal might be over. He had jumped when the phone roused him from sleep.

"Hello?"

"Cody? This is Lisa. The girls and I are safe and doing fine. Don't worry about us and don't look for us. Goodbye."

He sat on the edge of the bed for a stunned moment before reacting to the rush of words. "Lisa? What did you say? Are you there? Lisa!" The hum of the dead line gave the answer. Only later did he grudgingly admit he felt glad she called. *I heard her voice. They're all right. That's good news. They haven't gotten into trouble somehow.* It took him more than an hour to drift off to sleep again.

This morning he couldn't concentrate. He wandered through the small rooms of the rented home. The girls' empty room glowed bright with the morning sunshine. *Lisa worked hard with the little money I brought home to brighten up this little place. Why did I fly off the handle?* The broken slats of the crib gave stark testimony of the rage that drove them away.

The shrill ring of the phone brought him across the living room in a single bound.

"Hello?"

"Mr. Burns? This is Mary from Mt. Faith Church. How are you today?"

"O.K."

"Good," Mary's bright voice continued with no pause. "I'm calling to remind you about the baptism for Kendra this Sunday."

"Baptism?"

"Yes. We have her scheduled for baptism in the 10:45 service this Sunday. I know it will be a blessing for her and for the whole family. Now let me tell you what to bring."

He started to object, but Mary pressed on.

"She will need to bring a bathing suit to wear under the baptism robe. We'll supply the towels. If you can bring her to the church office about 10:30, then we'll take care of all the details. Do you have any questions?"

"I don't guess so."

"We'll look forward to seeing you on Sunday. Thanks for your time. Bye, now."

The conversation covered no more than sixty seconds. He didn't even have time to let her know that Kendra wasn't here.

Stupid, interfering church! I told that preacher to forget about baptizing Kendra. Who do they think they are? I'll go down there right now and set them straight. He grabbed his ball hat from the table, then checked himself. Kendra had talked to the pastor about God. Lisa had agreed to the ritual and had set the schedule. That could only mean one thing.

Lisa, Kendra and Courtney would be at Mt. Faith Church Sunday morning.

"Yes!" He slapped his fist into his open palm with a pop. He didn't know where they were hiding right now, but he knew exactly where they would be in just two days.

He stood at the front door, hands on his hips. *The church doors are open to everyone. There's no reason why I can't be there too! I can find Lisa. I can get hold of her and let her know how bad she's hurt me. I can set this mess right once and for all.* He marched to the streaked mirror over the bedroom chest and stuck out his chest.

"Cody, my man, you're going to church Sunday!"

Ryan examined the two fan-shaped candelabra

towering in the worship center of Mt. Faith Church. Why had Mandy ever selected such ornate monstrosities for the wedding? He stifled his objection and called to his fiancé. "Where do you want me to put this?"

"There is a storage room just through that door." Mandy gestured toward the left front of the worship center. "Carry it in there so it will be out of the way until after the funeral." The two of them had been at the church for over an hour making the adjustments demanded by the funeral's sudden interruption of their plans. As Ryan disappeared around the corner of the storage closet, the doors of the Sanctuary opened to reveal Paulette, her lips set firm in an expression that Mandy knew all too well.

"Where's Ryan?"

"He's carrying the candelabra to the storage room."

"Can the unity candle table go in there too? Everything's got to be out of here until after the funeral, you know."

"Yes, I know, mother. We'll have plenty of room. We can even put the boxes with the programs and the rice bags there. It shouldn't be a problem."

"Well, I hope not. We don't want our little wedding to cause any more of a ruckus to the church than it already has."

Ryan returned from the closet for the second candelabra. Paulette greeted the stocky groom with a quick hug. "Did you call Conrad to remind him about the rehearsal time?"

"I left a message last night on his answering machine. He'll be here, I'm sure."

"We need everyone to be here so they know what to do. Maybe we can get though this without any more problems. I told Phil this morning I just feel like something bad is waiting to happen."

"Mom, everything will turn out fine," Mandy said. "Don't let the change get under your skin so badly."

"I suppose the cavalier attitude Brother Barry had in asking us to change all our plans is what bothers me. He doesn't understand how hard it is to put together a wedding. He just expects everyone to do whatever he dictates. Pushy people like that bother me."

Ryan joined the criticism. "He can be pretty brash. He talked to us like the world's greatest expert in marriage. It made me uncomfortable to let him know so much about us."

Mandy took up a half-hearted defense. "Well, I appreciate him talking so candidly to us. Marriage is hard work, and we need all the insight we can get."

"All I want is to get everything arranged without a huge hassle," Paulette said. "Then we can get life back to normal."

"I don't think I'll be back to Rev. Peters' church after the wedding." Ryan lifted the candelabra to his shoulder. "These religious types bother me."

Mandy didn't have time for another argument about faith. She brushed a brunette lock from her eyes. "For the moment, let's just get the wedding stuff where it needs to be. Mom, you and I still need to get the presents for the wedding party wrapped and taken over to the restaurant before 2:00 o'clock."

Ryan headed toward the storage room. "I've got an errand to run, too. I'll see you this afternoon."

Mother and daughter started up the long aisle with quick steps. Paulette consulted her list, now marked over in several places. She shook her head. "I don't guess I'll stop worrying until the last handful of rice is thrown."

Lauren looked up from her computer when Liz put the folded bulletins for Sunday's services on her desk. "I'm so glad it's

Friday. It seems like the week has dragged along."

Liz continued walking toward the front of the office, her voice flat in reply. "Saturday and Sunday always seem long to me."

Lauren frowned at the short reply. What's wrong with her? Her co-worker had seemed more open and friendly since their lunch Wednesday. But this morning the same dour attitudes of the past had resurfaced. Could something have happened last night?

The door of Brent's office opened with an explosion of choir music. Brent and Drew emerged, carrying three small plastic cases with black wires protruding from the larger end.

"Lauren, we're going to the worship center to adjust these new microphones," Brent said.

"I thought you tested them a few days ago."

"We did, but the equalizer needs to be set for each of them."

One of the cases slipped from his hand and fell to the floor near the desk where Liz sat. Drew put the two microphones near the telephone on the front edge of her desk and reached down to gather up the unit.

"What does the equalizer do?"

"Every output device has its own signature of sound. Some have a lot of high frequency noise and some are overweighted in low frequencies. The equalizer can filter and adjust the sound so the voice or music is heard at the best level. If a mic is not equalized, whoever is using it may not sound natural."

"That's way too complicated for me."

"Listen this Sunday, and see if you can tell a difference."

Drew motioned to Brent. "I need to get my keys from my desk. I'll meet you in the worship center in a minute."

"Sure. I'm going to get started on the installation. We don't have much time today to work on it." He picked up one transmitter pack from the desk where Drew had placed it and headed toward the worship center. The second microphone lay unnoticed near the phone, a small green light glowing to indicate the unit had been turned on.

"Rights for all, rights for all!"

The angry cadence echoed off the gray granite pillars of Security State Bank. Twenty Vietnamese demonstrators marched in an elongated circle on the hot sidewalk, raising fists in time with their shouts. A small crowd stood gawking at the immigrants shaking signs covered with scrawled threats against the commerce of the quiet city. Business men in suits and ties hurried to cross the street away from the chanting crowd.

"Look at those Asian fools," Jack said, pointing through the window to the marchers circling on the sidewalk five stories below.

Johnson's forehead touched the window as he looked down. "The security guard told me the demonstrators arrived precisely at 11:00 a.m. in two identical minivans. Within five minutes they had set up shop and started their march. Professionally trained, I'd say."

A glint of red and blue light reflected off the window of the building across the street. They watched three Mt. Carmel police units round the corner, lights flashing. At the other end of the street, a van marked with the Channel 9 logo stopped at the curb, disgorging a hustling news crew.

"Now, we've really got a circus," Jack said. He stepped across the office and punched the intercom button. "Merylene, get Peters up here."

Johnson turned from the window. "I hope your community relations girl isn't home wiping her little boy's nose.

She might be of help today, since our story will be splashed across five states before dinner."

The protesters parted when their leader approached a portable podium with sound system that one of the protestors had pulled from the back of the Lexus. His lightweight Dockers and open-necked golf shirt portrayed a friendly, confident appearance. When he rapped on the microphone, the chants of the demonstrators stopped immediately.

"My name is Nha Van Dang. We're here today to expose some secrets this bank has been hiding for a long time."

Two men, each carrying a television camera with protruding microphone snout, ran from opposite corners of the crowd and knelt directly in front of the podium.

The Citizen's League president continued. "Security State Bank has snubbed and humiliated the ethnic citizens of Mt. Carmel. We're here to say, 'No more!' As if on cue, the demonstrators cheered, shaking their signs high above their heads.

"Hard-working residents of your city have been denied the opportunities they deserve. Years ago many of them fled war to find sanctuary here. They planted their hopes and dreams here and fertilized those seeds with sweat and honest work. But this great American dream is being shattered, my friends! By whom? This bank! The leaders of this bank...."

Without warning, four policemen burst through the front line of the crowd. Two had night sticks drawn and turned toward the demonstrators. Two others headed for the podium.

Van Dang seized the moment. "Hey," he shouted, "this is America! We've got a right to be in Mt. Carmel!"

The demonstrators picked up the chant. "America! America! We've got rights in America!"

Inside the glass front doors, Keri waved toward four Vietnamese scurrying across the lobby. "Hurry! The police are trying to break up the demonstration!" Two men and two women accelerated their pace through the crowd of bank employees.

High above the action, Ledbetter had lost sight of the policemen when they left their cars and dashed closer to the building. "Come on. We'd better get down there."

Johnson shook his head. "It's going to be messy. I don't think you'll like it."

Merylene looked up from her desk when the two men threw open the door of the president's office. "Mrs. Peters is in the lobby, sir."

Mike McCormick removed a Bible from the rack on the back of a pew and shoved the book toward Barry.

"Pastor, we've got to order some new Bibles." He flipped open the dog-eared pages. "The kids keep tearing them up." He held up a page of the Psalms decorated with a mustachioed happy face.

"Looks like we need art lessons more than new Bibles."

"Very funny. Should I order some new ones?"

Mary's voice came over the speakers of the hall intercom. "Barry, long distance call on line two."

"I'd better take that call. Look up some prices for replacements, and we'll run it by the Finance committee. And I'll speak to parents Sunday from the pulpit about watching their budding Rembrandts a little more closely."

Once in his office, he pushed the blinking red light on the phone. "Hello."

"Hi, Barry. This is Stephen Richards."

"Dr. Richards! How are you today?"

"Glad to be inside. Must be 101 here in Kansas City

today. I had a few minutes between appointments and thought I might check on your decision."

Barry's heart rate accelerated. "Well, I wish I could give you a definite answer today. Keri and I have talked and prayed about it but just aren't ready to give you a final answer."

"I understand. I'm sure it's hard to consider leaving a fine church like Mt. Faith. But, I'm more enthusiastic than ever about the possibilities of you directing our program."

"We know it is an exciting opportunity. To be honest, I had one of those days on Wednesday when I would be happy just to take a custodial position at Potter's House, if you know what I mean."

"I pastored for twenty-two years before moving to Potter's House, so I understand. How does Keri feel about coming to Kansas City?"

"She feels positive about it. We do worry about finding a good school for Jason. We've read lots of negative publicity about metro schools."

"Yes, the schools are in a mess. I can't guarantee anything, but some of our faculty have received discounted tuition rates at Anchor Christian, a top-notch, private school just three miles from us. It would be worth checking out when you come."

"I know Keri would be thrilled about Jason having that opportunity."

"I'll let you get back to your work. But I look forward to hearing from you Monday."

"Thanks for calling. Bye."

Barry hung up the phone, then lifted both arms high in celebration. His mind raced at the promise of the new opportunity. Anyone could see the benefits far outweighed the difficulty of staying here. No matter what happens in the board meeting Sunday night, if Keri feels the same way as I do, I'll nail down this decision first thing Monday morning.

On the sun-baked sidewalk in front of the bank, the fleshy, round-faced Police Captain confronted the trim Vietnamese lawyer.

"Sir, may I see a copy of your permit for a public demonstration?"

Van Dang stood his ground. "I don't have a permit, officer, nor do I need one. This sidewalk is public property, and we have violated no laws."

Around the policemen, the murmuring crowd and the rhythms of the chanting protesters added fuel to the mounting tension. The Captain's voice grew louder. "Sir, if you don't have a city-issued parade permit, I'll have to ask you to remove yourself, and those in your party, from this sidewalk."

Van Dang crossed his arms. "We aren't going anywhere until we have told Mt. Carmel the truth about this bank."

One of the demonstrators seized the moment. With a shrill, accented voice he shouted, "We won't go! We won't go!" By the third repetition, others had joined his defiant shout. The protest signs danced again.

The two officers near the protesters sprang into action, pushing the protesters from the sidewalk with their nightsticks. At the same time, the Captain jerked the defiant leader away from the podium. In the melee, Dominique Powell pushed through the front line of the crowd on the sidewalk, holding a long microphone in front of her to catch the words of the Vietnamese leader for the evening news.

Keri rushed through the heavy glass front doors as the confrontation ignited. With all eyes on scuffling police and protesters, she seized the moment, hustling her diminutive friends to the unguarded podium.

"Listen to me, everyone!" Heads turned at the sound of Keri's voice booming through the speakers. "The Vietnamese Citizens League has organized a protest to say this bank has hurt the Asian citizens of our city. But I have evidence that shows the exact opposite!"

"Hey, wait a minute!' Van Dang struggled to get back to the microphone. The officers held him firmly, just ten feet from where Keri had seized the stage.

"These friends will tell you that the accusations of the Citizen's League are nonsense." She gestured toward Duyen Luong. "This is Duyen."

The middle-aged Vietnamese woman stepped to Keri's side. The confused protestors stopped chanting.

Duyen raised her lips to the microphone.

"Last night on Channel 9 I told my story of how the bank helped me buy a house on Myrtle Street, near the East Side Community Center. Not only did they loan me the money for my first house, but some of the employees went out of their way to help me. There is no bigotry here!"

Van Dang shouted again. "Quit lying to the people!"

Someone in the crowd yelled, "Let her talk!"

A small Vietnamese man hurried to the mic. "I worked at this bank for three years. When my car was stolen, the people who work here donated a thousand dollars to help me out!" He turned and pointed to Van Dang. "This man doesn't speak for the Vietnamese of Mt. Carmel! He's from St. Louis!"

The huddle of protesters surged toward at the lectern. A tall protester shouted in Vietnamese and grabbed the man speaking, pulling him backward and down to the sidewalk. Swinging his night stick, the police captain dashed to break up the new conflict. The crowd cheered loudly.

Keri's other witnesses refused to be frightened. They

jumped together toward the vacant lectern.

"We have our money at this bank! Let's get these strangers out of Mt. Carmel!"

"Go home! Go home! Go home!" A lone voice from the citizens started the chant and many others followed. The fight on the sidewalk subsided with the tall protestor clamped tightly under the knee of a sweating Mt. Carmel officer.

The red-faced Captain approached Van Dang and pulled his handcuffs from his belt. With heavy breath, he barked at the lawyer. "I'm asking you one last time to leave the sidewalk on your own, or I'll arrest you and remove you by force!"

Van Dang surveyed the chanting bystanders, now turned against his carefully orchestrated plan. He glared again at the Captain. "All right! I'll call them off." He gave an abrupt wave to the tightly bunched demonstrators. Within a few moments their signs drooped. He jabbed an angry finger toward Keri. "I'll be back! You and this filthy bank haven't heard the last of this!"

The partisan citizens cheered their approval at the call for retreat. Dominique moved toward the Vietnamese friends who had given testimony for the bank, her microphone ready.

Several bank employees ran to Keri. "You did it!" Fran shouted above the hubbub.

Just outside the tall, bank doors, the bank officers stood with arms crossed. Ledbetter looked around the crowd roused by Keri's counter-protest. He smiled broadly and joined the applause. Walking toward her, he stuck out his hand. "Congratulations, Peters!"

Keri pulled herself from Fran's hug and shook his hand. "Thank you, sir," she said, a smile lighting her face.

Johnson stood near his elbow. "Jack, I don't know if this Broadway show...."

"Get a life, Johnson," the president said. He turned abruptly and waded into the swelling crowd, leaving the sour-faced vice-president standing alone near the door.

"Testing, testing, 1... 2... 3." Drew's bass voice filled the speakers of the Mt. Faith worship center. He towered above the pulpit, the new wireless mic clipped to his shirt and the earpiece in its place.

"Keep talking," Brent called from the console of the sound system. "I need to adjust the levels."

"I see that hand," Drew responded, offering his best imitation of Billy Graham's distinctive crusade invitation. "Those of you in the upper level will only need two minutes to come here to the platform. Your bus will wait for you."

Brent laughed and continued turning the small knobs on the audio control board. "Now let's check the new stuff. Stay at the pulpit and turn on the intercom. A green LED should light up. I'll turn the main unit on back here."

Drew pulled the clip-on plastic case from his belt and flipped the switch marked 'Receive' to the 'On' position. Instantly he heard the whisper of Brent's voice in his ear.

"Hey! It sounds like you're sitting on my shoulder."

"I know it. The quality of sound is amazing. When we're wearing these, we can coordinate people in the worship service. The staff can even use it like a walkie-talkie in the building."

"That will be...." Another voice, muffled but distinct, interrupted their conversation. "There's not much going on around the office now," the voice said.

"We must have some citizen's band interference," Brent said.

The woman continued. "No. We haven't heard anything about a called board meeting."

"Sounds like a woman." Drew left the pulpit and walked

toward Brent.

The woman's voice sounded in their earpiece again. "but, I did find out something interesting in the pastor's office."

Brent cocked his head, straining to listen.

"I slipped in there this morning before anyone else arrived."

Brent looked toward Drew. "That sounds like Liz!"

"Are we picking up the telephone or something?"

The woman's one-sided conversation continued. "He doesn't have a special key, just the same one all the ministers have."

Brent glanced around the sound booth. "Hey, where's that third mic and receiver I had?"

"You had two in your hand when we left your office. Then, we stopped at Liz's desk to answer her question."

"I must have left one on her desk. I bet it's turned on right now. We can hear what she's saying while she talks on the phone!"

As if on cue, the secretary's voice came through the earpieces again. "He had left a letter laying on his desk from a children's home called the Potter's House. It was an offer for a position." She paused. "Yes, sir. They want Barry to come and be on their staff." Another pause. "It's in Kansas City."

The two ministers held their breath as if Liz could hear them. Brent pushed the earpiece deeper.

"No, I don't think any of the staff knows about the money." Another woman's voice came across the line, but it was too muffled to understand. Liz spoke again. "I've got to go and help Mary. I'll talk with you later. Bye."

Brent slipped out the earpiece. "Sounds like Liz has enlarged her job description to include spying on the pastor."

"That's unbelievable."

"Liz is reporting to someone what is going on with the

preacher. That says to me that someone is trying desperately to dig up some dirt on him." He processed the idea. "I guess you were right about the mutiny."

Drew crossed his arms. "You mean Asher? Do you think he's putting together something against the preacher?"

"I'd bet money on the fact that he is behind Liz snooping in the preacher's office." He began to gather up the new microphones and receivers.

Drew's lips set in a hard line. "Do you think we should tell Barry?"

"Let's do a little snooping of our own first." He reached across the control board to the telephone.

"Lauren? This is Brent. Could you come to the worship center and help me for a minute?"

Soon the three staff members huddled in a tight knot at the front of the worship center. Multi-colored light from the stained glass fell across the pews. In hushed tones, Brent and Drew shared the disturbing discovery about Liz.

Adding to their insights, Lauren said, "The pieces all fit together. I think Daemon Asher, with who knows how many others, intend to drive Barry from this church. We need to talk with C. K. Haskins. He's close to the pastor, and he's survived other church wars. I think we ought to tell him what we know and see what he suggests."

"Do we have enough time to do that?" Drew's forehead knotted with worry.

"I think so," Brent said. "Daemon may even choose to wait it out and see what Barry decides about this Kansas City deal before he makes a move."

"Maybe," Lauren said. "But, let's not waste any time. I'll contact Haskins today and work out a meeting."

They sat silently, minds turning with the reality of the crisis.

"I think we need to pray right now," Drew said.

Two heads nodded in assent. With linked hands they bowed to pray for God's direction in the strife-torn church.

"I'm going to the hospital to check on the Loomis girl and her new baby." Barry pulled the door to his office closed. "After I finish there, I'll head over to the baseball field for Jason's game."

Lauren turned from the computer screen. "Do you know whether Jenni plans to place the baby up for adoption?"

"Not that I've heard. To be honest, though, I haven't talked that much with Jim or Sandi about it. They've kept a low profile."

"I heard that Jenni hated every day of her pregnancy. Maybe she can get a new start now that the baby is here."

"I'll know more after I visit her today. If Keri calls, let her know my plans. Her line has been busy every time I've called. See you later."

Barry felt the broiling heat of the late afternoon sun singe his neck on the brief walk to the car. He mulled over Lauren's comment. *A new baby is such a tremendous responsibility. I don't know if I could raise another child.* He drove out of the parking lot and turned south on HW 69 toward the medical center. *Was it seven years ago we tried to have another baby? Now it seems too late, really. Keri hasn't mentioned trying for another baby in a long time.* He smiled to himself. *If I can just get one boy raised, I'll be doing good.*

The air-conditioned atrium of the hospital provided respite from the heat. On the second floor hall, he checked the name holder beside the closed door to see, "Loomis/ Dr. Hopkins." He knocked and pushed the door open slowly. "Jenni?"

The dark-haired girl lay on the bed, her small figure dwarfed by the immense white sheets. She managed a weak smile, "Hi, Brother Barry."

He left the door open and reached out to shake her hand. "Congratulations! We heard the good news in the church office. I wanted to be one of the first to congratulate the new mother. How are you doing?"

"O.K., I guess," the teen said in a quiet voice.

"When was he born?"

"About 8:00, I think. But my labor started last night after dinner." She brushed a lock of dark hair from her eyes. "It felt like a long night."

"Babies just seem to have their own schedule, no matter what we may plan. What's worse, today is just the beginning. You may have several long nights ahead."

"Yeah, I guess that's right," she replied, looking away from Barry's smiling face.

He tried another tack. "Have you and your mom fixed up a nursery at the house?"

She brightened slightly. "Yeah. It's not a whole room, but we moved some things in my room and bought a baby bed. I like it. I hope Benjamin will, too."

"Benjamin? I like that. It's a Bible name, you know."

"It is? You know, my grandma Doris suggested it. She really knows the Bible."

A sudden grimace twisted her face. She groaned under her breath. Her face puckered with worry as she slowly dropped her gaze from Barry to the rumpled sheets.

"Oh my God! What's happened to me?" Bright red blood glared like a flashing neon sign from the pale sheets near her hips.

Barry's eyes locked on hers for a moment, then looked down again at the blood. The stain had spread. He couldn't hide the alarm in his voice. "Push the call button for the nurse!"

She fumbled with the sheets. "I don't know where it is! Oh God, I'm bleeding!"

Barry followed the white cord that led to the red emergency call button clipped to the bed rail. He pushed the button hard, then again, and again.

Jenni gathered up the sheets around herself, as if she could escape the spreading flood of crimson. Her fearful breathing filled the room.

"Yes?" The voice of the nurse sounded mechanically from the speaker on the wall behind the head board.

Jenni moved her mouth but no words came out. She looked at the pastor, eyes wide with terror.

"We need some help down here, nurse. Jenni's bleeding."

"I'll find a nurse and send her down to your room."

"This is an emergency! She's bleeding heavily. Get someone down here now!" His voice became a commanding shout that echoed from the hospital walls.

"Uh, yes sir. We'll be right there."

He looked at Jenni. "It's going to be O.K. They'll be here in a moment."

Her face, a pale mask, blended with the sheets. She closed her eyes, her breath coming in short, labored pants. The blood oozed from under the rumpled bedcover.

With a rush, two nurses rounded the corner of the open door. The RN, a tall, black woman, took the lead. "What seems to be..." Her eyes focused on the ominous crimson circle.

She barked an order to the aide, a middle-aged redhead. "We've got bleeding. We need to get her to the OR right now!" She punched the red call button, activating the intercom once again. "Call surgery and Dr. Hopkins for emergency surgery. It looks like the patient has a uterine hemorrhage."

The nurse threw back the sheets and began to massage

Jenni's swollen abdomen. The aide wrapped a blood pressure cuff around the young girl's upper arm. The frightened teen screamed in pain.

"O.K., Hon, listen," the nurse said in a no-nonsense voice. "You shouldn't be bleeding like this. We need to do some surgery. I'm going to get you ready and down to the operating room."

Jenni nodded slowly, her wide eyes welling up with tears.

The nurse turned to Barry. "Who are you?"

"I'm her pastor. I think her mom has gone to run some errands. I stopped in to congratulate her and see the baby."

"You can help us, sir. Can you find her mother, or someone, who can sign some papers?"

"I'll try."

The aide jerked the foot of the bed toward the door. The call button popped from where it was clipped to the bed and smacked against the wall. Jenni reached toward Barry with a mournful groan. He squeezed her hand tightly as she rolled past.

The nurse threw her weight against the bed to navigate through the door. She called over her shoulder. "Get her family down to the surgery waiting room, please!"

"Yes ma'am. I will."

He turned and looked around the room. In the drawer of the small bedside table he found a phone book and scanned the names for Jim Loomis' law office.

"This is Pastor Peters. I need Jim Loomis. It's an emergency." The secretary put him through and in a moment Jim answered.

"Jim, I'm at the hospital with Jenni, and I've got some bad news."

"What's wrong?"

"She started bleeding while I was visiting here in her

room. The nurses have just taken her to surgery. They said to get you up here as quickly as possible."

"I can't believe it! She seemed fine this morning."

"It came on very suddenly. Just get over here to the surgery waiting room, and I'll meet you there. Do you know where Sandi is?"

"She may have gone home for awhile."

"Have your secretary try to find her. I'll meet you at the waiting room."

"Thanks. I'll be there as soon as I can."

Barry looked around the room. A small teddy bear with brightly-colored balloons sitting on the window sill caught his eye. He thought of little Benjamin tucked quietly in the nursery. A wave of fear twisted his stomach. *Lord, watch over that operating room, so Benjamin doesn't lose his mom.*

"Should I fix lemonade, too?" Nadine had busied herself most of the afternoon preparing for the secret gathering of concerned church members. A chocolate cake and a plate of decorated cookies from the bakery sat on the kitchen table. Years of experience had taught her that difficult church business could be handled better if some tasty snacks smoothed the way.

"That's an excellent idea," Daemon said, "considering the humidity this afternoon."

The list of carefully screened guests invited for the council of war lay near the telephone. She scanned it to count the number expected. Sid and Claire should arrive soon with a coffee cake. Ed Loomis had declined because of his granddaughter's new baby. Franklin and Marilyn Blue had agreed to come, as had Dale and Donna Galloway. Fred and Kitty Campbell, who had been present Sunday night to hear Daemon's announcement, planned to bring Fred's younger brother, Mark. Mark had served on the Finance Committee but had resigned when he refused to agree with buying a new sound system for the worship center. Sad little Liz, the secretary, indicated she would attend, too. The young widower, David Dockery, seemed enthusiastic about the invitation. Two other couples brought the total to sixteen.

The water splashing in the glass pitcher released the pungent smell of pink lemonade mix. After a vigorous stirring she loaded it on a tray and handed it to Daemon. "Here, carry this down to the patio room. While you're there, count the chairs. We'll need sixteen to accommodate everyone."

He frowned about the distraction to his business but dutifully took the tray down the stairs. The patio room provided plenty of space and privacy. The pleasant view across the lush flower beds in the backyard, colorful now with petunias, always caught the eye of guests.

By 6:30 the patio room had filled with conversation from the animated visitors. He called the meeting to order. "I am truly grateful that each one of you has come to our home this evening," he said, interrupting the murmur of conversation. "I know you share our feeling that the church is in crisis. So, let's have a prayer and get started. Dale, would you lead us in prayer?"

After the lawyer offered a brief invocation, Daemon adjusted his chair for better position and began.

"A common concern for the church has brought us together tonight. Some of you attended the fellowship at the Simpson's on Sunday night when I shared publicly my feelings about the crisis we face. My honesty may have shocked some, but with the work of God, the truth is always best."

"For others, let me bring you up to date. We have a crisis in leadership at Mt. Faith Church. Signs of it are everywhere. The Pastor has promoted changes that have taken us away from the great traditions of our faith. Untested leaders have gained control of key areas. Money is spent on unnecessary projects without church authorization. The great pastors who built Mt. Faith Church, like Dr. Patrick, would hardly even recognize our divided fellowship today, so dramatic have been the mutations that Peters has produced." He spit the pastor's name like a curse word.

"Now, I do realize not everyone may share these opinions. Our church attendance over the years has actually grown. So there are many who can't, or won't, see the problems like we do."

Sid interrupted. "Won't Barry's outburst Wednesday night prove his true colors to everyone?"

"Perhaps. Anyone who looks at Dale's jaw can see evidence of his immaturity. How do you feel, Dale?'

"Terrible. I had it X-rayed, just to make sure nothing is broken. But I haven't been able to sleep more than two hours a night."

"Obviously, Barry has lost control of himself. Punching Dale like it was a fight on the streets of New York confirms the suspicions I've had for months. He would never have lashed out unless he feared the truth about his selfish goals might be exposed for all to see."

Daemon paused and took a drink of the lemonade. He leaned forward. "For that reason, another part of the plan began this week. David, you can explain your part."

The stocky insurance agent looked across the room. "Before her tragic death, my wife was a good friend of Keri's. I've watched the pastor and his wife many times as they tried to get along. To be brutally honest, he really is a poor husband, inattentive to the needs of his wife. If the church really knew the truth about them, you can bet attitudes would be different."

"But should we drag Keri into this...?"

David cut off Marilyn's question. "All I want is for her to

talk about the problem — when I've got this little microphone turned on." He slid a small recording device from his shirt pocket. "That's all we need for the truth to come out."

"That hardly seems enough to get the pastor relieved of his duties." Fred crossed his arms and waited for a response. "Lots of marriages sail on rough seas at times."

Daemon nodded. "I agree. But David's plan is just a small piece of the puzzle. Let's look at another. We've watched the materialistic desires of the pastor grow through the years. It's obvious that he has developed an insatiable appetite for the finer things of life. He's pushed his salary to the highest amount ever."

"I can vouch for that after serving on the Finance Committee," Mark said.

"All this prompted an unusual action. We wanted to help everyone see the true motives of the pastor. As I mentioned, what you might call a test is underway right now. With Ms. Emory's help, an unmarked envelope containing $5,000 in cash was placed in the pastor's office."

Marilyn gasped. "Five thousand dollars?"

"Exactly. Now, I think all of us agree that any honest person would conclude that the money was a gift for the church. The cash would be immediately placed in the hands of the church treasurer. Our little test had a specific purpose, however. We wanted to know: Is that what Barry would do?"

The question hung in the air. Daemon surveyed every person in the silent group before answering his own question.

"He kept the money."

The pronouncement hit like a thunderclap. The crowd erupted in loud questions and shocked exclamations. Sid stood, his large girth dominating the room. Over the hubbub he bellowed, "He stole $5,000 of our money?"

Daemon shrugged. "He hasn't reported it to the treasurer. I checked at noon today, and Sam hadn't heard a thing about any special donation."

"That makes me furious!" Marilyn said. "I can't believe something like this could happen in our church."

Fred nodded vigorously. "He's really gone too far now!"

Sid turned to Liz. "Did you hear anything this week in the church office about this money?"

The face of the quiet secretary flushed red. "Yes, well... a little at least. Barry asked if anyone knew anything about an envelope that had been lost. But nothing more was ever said. I do know the envelope is gone from his office."

A hubbub of displeasure swept the room. When the swell of indignation paused, Marilyn spoke for all. "What can we do about this?"

Dale had an answer, supplied by Daemon before the meeting. "We do have some recourse with the congregation. In Mt. Faith Church, the people have the power. We must give them the opportunity to make a decision."

Mark shook his head. "We can't do that. Barry's people have got every committee sewed up tight."

"We don't have to go through a committee," Dale said quickly. "We can go directly to the church. With careful planning, we can make sure everyone knows the truth and acts on it."

"You mean at the board meeting Sunday night?"

Daemon seized the moment. "I think Sunday morning is the time to act! If we are willing to work together, we can make sure the truth is known and solve Mt. Faith's problem once and for all."

Fred raised a hand. "But there's no business meeting scheduled then. How can we do this on Sunday morning?"

"It's really very simple, if we'll work together. We can get control of the service and bring these facts to the attention of the people. That will be all it takes to solve our little problem of leadership!"

"Let's do it, then," Claire said. "We may lose our church if we don't stand up now."

Every head bobbed in agreement. A spirit of adventure filled the room. The plan to risk everything in a coup of church control had hit the mark. David stood. "Each one of us needs an assignment, don't we? I'll make a list of everyone's duty."

"Good." Daemon pushed forward in his chair, eyes bright with excitement. "We need to expose the maximum number of people to the truth we've uncovered. Working together, we can commandeer the microphone at the end of the service. Within ten minutes the facts will be clear to everyone. Then, nothing can stop the people from solving the problem!"

"You go report to the coach and I'll park." Keri watched Jason pull his bat and glove from the car trunk. "Good luck!" she called, twisting in the car seat to see him, a small version of Barry outfitted in a baseball uniform. He tore across the asphalt and disappeared through the gate of the Ozark Youth Ballfield.

With this heat, I'm glad I had time to change clothes. She glanced in the visor mirror to check the fit of a green-checked ball hat and the matching cotton blouse, then followed her son's path toward the home-team bleachers of the small ballpark.

Sitting alone on the aluminum bleacher gave her a few minutes to reflect on the dramatic events at the bank. The atmosphere had throbbed with excitement all afternoon over the protest and dramatic turn of events. At three o'clock Fran organized an impromptu celebration in the break room. When Keri stepped through the door, the crowd of bank employees celebrated like a winning team pouring champagne in the locker room. Even Ledbetter attended, actually mingling with the workers. Merylene reported, with a serious tone, that Johnson had left on urgent business an hour before.

Keri decided to stretch her legs and made her way to the concession stand for a drink. *I wonder where Barry is? Lauren said he had gone to the hospital. Surely he'll call if something has happened.*

The announcer's scratchy voice over the old loudspeaker system began announcing the action on the field. "Batting first for the Giants: Evan Dockery."

Keri started at the name. *I didn't know there were any other Dockery's in town.* She had not paid any attention to the adults gathered on the visitor's side, but now she scanned the faces quickly. *Wouldn't it be something if this kid were a relative of David's?*

She returned to the bleacher, now comfortably full with eager Dads and enthusiastic Moms poised to cheer the team to victory. Her mind wandered. *What could David be doing on this warm summer evening?* A picture of the beautiful restored house and the antiques in the sitting room came to her mind. *I wonder if he's there, alone again? Would he be thinking about me?*

A routine fly ball became the third out and the teams changed places. Jason would bat first. The coach looked at him from the third base coaching box and clapped his hands. "Get us started," he yelled.

Jason stepped up to the plate. The pitcher, a tall twelve year old, blazed the first pitch across the plate for a strike.

"You can do it!" Keri shouted.

The ump called two balls next. On the fourth pitch Jason connected solidly, ripping the ball down the third base line. The tubby left fielder moved slowly toward the ball. The base coach hollered, "Second, second!" Jason hustled down the base path and slid in safe for a double, bringing Keri up from her seat, clapping with delight.

She looked again through the gate to the parking lot. What's keeping Barry? The thought brought a trace of anger. That's his only son out there. He should get out here to cheer him on, too. Instead I'm the only one sitting in this heat.

The next batter hit a line drive that rolled all the way to the right field fence. Jason scored standing up. Keri pumped her arm when the young ball player looked toward the bleachers. "Way to go, slugger."

She dug in her purse for a small mirror and checked her makeup. Would David call again? A few days ago he seemed broken and deeply in need. But now his strength seemed to be growing. She remembered his caring brown eyes, focused on her, when they stood at the door.

A two-out rally in the third inning brought Jason to bat again. The first pitch hung over the plate and Jason jumped on it, slapping a line drive over the head of the second baseman for a single. He stood proudly on first, smiling when the coach patted him on the back.

Barry's missing the best game of the year, Keri groused, crossing her arms. He's turned so selfish lately that he doesn't think of Jason or me. I'll have to sit through this whole game by myself.

"I can't believe what I'm hearing!" Lance threw up his hands. "How could members of a church attack their own pastor like he was evil incarnate? I know I'm a new Christian, but anyone would know that's wrong! Wednesday night I just thought someone's temper had gotten out of hand. But those men deliberately planned to attack the pastor!"

"That's what it looks like," Kent said. "If our

information is right, this group has worked for several months to spread rumors intended to discredit Barry."

"That stinks." Lance crossed his arms and sank back in his seat. The other friends lining the Puckett's family room, Jean Adkins, Josh and Lauren, the Upton's and Cassie Carter, nodded in agreement. The story of their host had pulled back the covering that hid a dark conspiracy for months.

"It's amazing to me that their work stayed secret for so long," Danae said.

"Let me make sure I'm understanding this right." Josh held out his hand and began to tick off each point on his fingers. "First, we know that some people in the church have been unhappy about changes since Barry became pastor. Second, this past Sunday, Daemon Asher took advantage of a home prayer fellowship to discredit the pastor. Third, rumors are circulating about Keri using her bank job to manipulate church members."

"That's what I heard," Brad said. "But that's not all."

"O.K." The policeman resumed counting on his fingers. "On Wednesday night Asher and his buddies verbally attacked Barry. They baited him by attacking Keri, and he lost his temper, hitting Dale Galloway. Is that all we know?"

As if to answer his question, the door bell sounded. Beth answered and returned with Drew. Anxiety marked his long face.

Kent stood to greet him. "Glad you could join us. We're trying to understand what's happening at the church so we can mount a defense of prayer."

Drew pulled a chair close to Cassie. "I might be able to add more to this sordid story. Lauren, did you tell about the intercom incident this afternoon?"

"Not yet. I didn't know whether to share it or not."

"Yes, I think we should." He surveyed the group. "Lauren, Brent and I had a most interesting experience today. We were in the process of testing the new wireless microphone intercom we plan to use Sunday. That's how we discovered Liz Emory is a part of the conspiracy, too."

Jean turned to Lauren. "She was here for the prayer meeting Sunday night!"

"Yes, indeed she was. She's worked in the office a little more than a year. I think Daemon befriended her for his own purposes." He quickly explained the misplaced microphone and the surprising phone conversation that implicated Liz in snooping through Barry's office. "And what she found disturbed us, too. Barry is considering an offer to leave Mt. Faith and go to work for a children's home in Kansas City!"

Lance spoke out. "They really are on the verge of driving Barry and Keri away from the church!"

"Now wait," Kent said. "We don't know that Barry really plans to leave, do we, Drew?"

"No. At least he hasn't talked to any of the staff about it. But if I were walking in his shoes, I would jump at the opportunity to move after the incident on Wednesday!"

"We've got to get on the phone and let everyone know what's happening," Lance said. "When people hear the truth, it'll make the difference."

"I'm willing to do my share of calls," Josh said.

But Kent raised a hand to slow the rush to action. "Is a political campaign really what we need?" He pulled on his salt and pepper whiskers, waiting for a reply. "I think we need to remember that God has been at work already. Remember, He gave the first alert to something amiss through my vision Sunday night. Then, He worked today through strange circumstances to reveal more of the conspiracy. I think we should really seek God and discover how He would want us to handle this. He may have something better in mind than anything we could plan tonight."

"But we know Daemon and his band of pirates are working right now to spread rumors," Brad said. "The Church

Board has called a special meeting for Sunday night. Anything can happen in a meeting like that. I don't know if we can afford to wait!"

Cassie turned her wide-shouldered frame toward Brad and spoke for the first time. "You know, we've served here longer than any of the other staff members. Through the whole time, there has been a whisper of controversy, like a conversation behind a wall, where you could hear the voices but not make out the words." Drew nodded his agreement. She continued, "This time something has changed. It's all coming out in the open, but not because we've done anything. I think Kent is right. The Lord is working in a powerful way to deal with this problem. We ought to get on our knees and seek what He wants."

Drew looked around at the group. "I've been in Barry's office every day. Monday he seemed fine. I doubt if Asher and his group are planning any more high jinks soon. We've got time to listen to the Lord before we take action."

"Of course, prayer is action—and the most important one," Jean said. "We need to agree that what we know will stay in this group for now. And we must be serious about prayer this week. Really serious."

"We could meet back here next Friday to see what our feelings are then," Beth said.

Kent saw heads nodding agreement. "O.K. That will be our plan. We'll pray diligently, but sit on what we know for now. We'll meet next Friday." He stood up. "Let's all join hands and plead for the Lord to act as a mighty warrior in our church this week."

In quiet murmurs of prayer, the circle drew close together, interceding for the future of their church and the pastor who led them.

The chairs of the hospital waiting room sat empty, save

for the Loomis family. They huddled close to one another, like a flock of frightened birds, limbs drawn tight to their bodies. Barry returned from the snack bar with a soft drink in his hand and sank down in the chair near Sandi.

"Maybe the surgery won't take too much longer," Doris said, reaching over to stroke her daughter-in-law's dark-brown hair. Sandi smiled but quietly continued to twist a crumpled tissue.

Two hours had passed since they rushed to the waiting room. Jim had arrived first, then Ed and Doris, and finally Sandi. To each one Barry recounted the sudden eruption of blood, the nurses' frantic rush to surgery, and the confidence he had in the surgical team.

Sandi took the news especially hard. "Jenni felt so unsure about all this. I didn't do much to help her, either."

"She told me about a dream she kept having," Doris said. The others looked at her curiously. "She kept seeing herself holding a dead baby."

"Oh, my God! I didn't know that. She never told me."

Doris nodded. "She had lots of fears."

"That is a shock, but let's not lose sight of the fact that Benjamin's doing fine. We can be grateful about that." Jim said.

Doris patted Sandi again. "Being pregnant at sixteen is terribly difficult. I guess all of us have suffered in some way."

"But Jenni's the one in danger now. If I had only stayed here this afternoon, things might have been different." Sandi continued to castigate herself. In a few minutes, Jim stood up and took her hand, pulling her from the group. Out of the corner of his eye, Barry could see them standing close together, crying. She seemed stronger when they returned to the family circle.

A few minutes later a surgical nurse, clad in her scrub greens, rustled through the door. "The doctor wanted me to let you know that everything seems to be going fine. He found the source of the bleeding and has started to take care of the problem. The surgery will probably take 45 minutes to an hour more, then he'll be out to speak with you." Before they could even think of questions she disappeared through the door marked with a large, red sign, "Authorized Personnel Only — No Admittance."

Ed smiled broadly at the news but Sandi could hold her fears no more. She leaned against Jim's chest and began to sob, shoulders heaving. Jim wrapped both arms around her and tenderly pulled her close. They stood awkwardly together in the middle of the room, the burdens of nine months of worry, pain, and heartache pouring out in hot tears. Barry signaled to Ed and Doris. Together all five of them drew together. Barry prayed earnestly for Jenni, for the doctor, and for little Benjamin.

Fifty-two minutes after the nurse had disappeared, the same door opened with a rush. A dark-skinned man stepped through to greet the family.

"I'm Dr. Naqvi," he said in clipped, accented English. He reached forward to shake hands around the circle of anxious people. "I was on call for Dr. Hopkins when your daughter required surgery. It seems she retained part of the placenta that should have been expelled. It could have turned much worse, but since we were able to act so quickly she has come through very fine, very fine."

"Why did it take so long?" Doris whispered the question.

"The surgery was a delicate procedure. We removed the placenta by curettage. She needed two units of blood. Her vital signs remain strong. Within about two hours we'll move her back to her room."

Sandi had tears in her eyes again. "Thank you, Lord. Thank you," she whispered.

"I'll continue to monitor her progress. I'm sure Dr. Hopkins will look at her carefully, also. It seems that she will be just fine now, just fine. Thank you." Without waiting for more questions, the physician disappeared through the door.

"I just knew the Lord would take care of my little Jen," Doris said.

"Pastor, God used you to watch over that little girl this afternoon," Ed said. Thanks for your help."

Barry looked up with a broad smile. "Maybe she won't have to worry with those bad dreams any longer. In fact, with a new baby, she may not get enough sleep to dream at all!"

His humor broke the ice. They gathered their belongings for the short hike to Jenni's room. Barry said his good-byes, shared a final word of encouragement with Sandi and hurried to the car. His short visit for good wishes to a young mother had turned into a marathon. He looked at his watch. Jason's ball game must be half over by now.

The lights burned brightly over the Ozark League field when he pulled into the parking lot. He spotted Keri sitting on the home team bleachers.

"Hi!" He sat down beside her, draping his arm across her shoulders for a hug. But her body felt like a green checked rock.

She kept her eyes focused on the playing field. "Where have you been?"

"I've been at the hospital."

"Since 4:30?"

"Yes, since 4:30. The Loomis girl..."

"Well, I've been sitting here alone. And your son has played his heart out for a Dad that wasn't even here!"

"Now what a minute." He tried to keep his voice down. "Jenni started bleeding. They rushed her to surgery. I had to stay...."

Keri stood up. "This was a great day for me, until you decided you didn't care enough about us to show up at the game." She reached down to gather up her purse. "You can enjoy the rest of it by yourself!"

"Keri! Wait a minute!" He watched her step down the

bleachers and follow the sidewalk to the parking lot. He started to chase her, then caught the turning of nearby heads. Embarrassed, he sat back down.

"Batting for the Mariners, Jason Peters," the announcer said.

Jason kicked dirt with his right foot and planted himself in the batting box. The first pitch sailed outside for a ball.

Barry stood again and looked out to the parking lot. The Accord pulled quickly out on to the street. He put his hands on his hips. What in the world had gotten under her skin?

The crack of a bat jerked his attention back to the field. He saw Jason digging his way up the first base line. The right fielder headed back toward the fence and watched the ball sail over his head. A home run! The crowd jumped to their feet. Jason's fist stabbed the air as he rounded second, then his stride eased into a confident home run trot. His team mates greeted him with high fives when he skipped across home plate.

Barry made his way to the fence by the door of the home team dugout. "Hey, man! Congratulations! You belted that thing!"

Jason's grin stretched from ear to ear. "Dad! Guess what? I've had a double, a single and now a home run! Do you think I can hit for the cycle, just like Carmichael?"

"I had to stay at the hospital and didn't see what you've already done. Sure you can do it! Just keep your eye on the ball and get a hit. Don't worry about it and do your best."

Jason grabbed his glove to take his place on the diamond. Barry turned and walked to the concession stand. He felt torn and frustrated. *Jason's hitting for the cycle, and I've struck out with Keri. What do I do now?*

The house on Highview stood dark under the deep purple twilight when Keri cruised down the hill. She waited impatiently for the garage door to raise. Her frustration at Barry's self-centeredness had hardened to a painful lump of rejection during the drive home. Stuck at the hospital. Sure. He could have at least called. The loud slam of the car door in the empty garage expressed her irritation. She hurried around the rear of the car toward the kitchen door.

"Keri!"

The unexpected voice made her blood run cold. She whirled around to see a man's form outlined in the darkness beside the open garage door. He stepped slowly forward, the light shining from the garage climbing up past his khaki shorts and blue shirt like a slowly rising curtain until the beams illuminated his face.

"David! You scared me!"

He stepped still closer, now fully inside the garage. His hand jiggled nervously inside his shorts pocket.

"What are you doing here?"

"Oh, I saw you turn off Mt. Faith Drive and followed you. I thought I might steal a few minutes to follow up on our visit." His eyes flickered around the garage. The slot where Barry parked his car stood conspicuously empty.

"We've been watching Jason's game down at the Ozark Ballfield."

"Is Barry still there?"

"Yes." She caught herself. "Well, I guess so. The game was nearly over when I left."

David took two steps in her direction. "I came by hoping we could talk some more. Like I said on the phone, I really enjoyed our time together."

"I guess I did, too."

He cast his eyes toward the concrete floor. "I've wondered if you've been able to see through my brave front. Honestly, my life has hardly seemed worth living these six months. The house that Morgan built looks beautiful, but it's empty. I've tried to keep myself busy. My commissions have never been higher." He shrugged and looked in her eyes. "But every night I sit by myself. I swear that old house has a thousand creaks—and I've heard every one of them!"

"Your heart's still broken, isn't it?"

"I've visited her grave nearly every day. I just haven't known what to do to get past it, you know."

She looked closely at the broad shouldered man. His hair lay tousled from the wind. Was it lighter than just six months ago? His words had revealed more this week than she had known in months. Her voice grew tender. "David, this may be painful for you to hear. I don't mean it to hurt. But maybe the time has come to push past the pain. It might be time for you to start dating. No one loved Morgan more than I did. I've missed her, too. But, I know I must reach out and make new friends. You should, too."

The light timer on the electric garage door clicked and the light went out, throwing the garage into darkness. The warm air of the August night wrapped around them. Outside the silent garage, the song of the cicadas harmonized through the hills. She took another step back toward the kitchen door, the spot where the shadows lay deepest.

"Lots of really nice single ladies attend church. You could start by going to the new singles' class we started last year."

"It's hard for me to think about taking that plunge. I don't want to settle for someone second-rate. In all these months, only one person has taken time to listen and understand how I feel."

He felt the cool plastic case deep in his pocket and moved a switch slightly to activate the machine. With a quick step he moved forward until he stood face to face with her.

"I think you have your own emptiness, Keri. I've noticed it for months. Barry seems so preoccupied with running the church he hardly pays attention to the prettiest woman in the pews. Am I right?"

"You must have seen me sitting by myself at the baseball field tonight." His gentle words disarmed her. "I wondered over and over again why he didn't show up. Sometimes he neglects me with all the other demands."

She felt his arms encircle her waist and gently draw her closer.

"Don't fight. You have needs just like I do." He pulled her closer, his lips brushing her neck. "Don't you want something better than loneliness?"

The warmth of his touch excited her. His strong arms offered wings to carry her far beyond the painful disappointment of the days just past. Her heart felt longing to help, to mend, to comfort.

His strong kiss took her breath. The green-checked ball hat tumbled unnoticed to the floor.

She turned her head and whispered a protest. "Don't do this."

"I have to do it. You're the only one who understands. I know it." He pressed close to kiss her again.

"No. I... I can't. It's not right, David."

"Why?" He tightened his grip. "We need this, Keri."

"I don't know. I care... I want to help. But..."

"Don't think about it now." His hand gently pushed her head toward his lips. "Forget Barry."

"No!" The word exploded from deep in her soul. Her hands pushed against his chest with all the strength she could muster.

Caught off balance, he fell back, allowing her to slip from his grasp. "Keri? Don't run. We need this, both of us."

"I won't do this, to you or to myself!"

She pivoted to jerk the handle of the door and bolted

across the threshold. With a crash the door slammed, throwing the linen curtains back and forth. Her hand flew to slam the deadbolt solidly in place.

His muffled voice came through the door. "Keri! Please! Don't do this to me." The hurt in his voice stung her soul.

She pressed her face close to the curtains, shouting. "I can't, David. I'm sorry. I didn't mean... I thought you..." Her breath came in short gasps. "Please just go away. Now!"

She stumbled away from the door. The lingering sensation of his embrace felt electric on her body. With shaking hands she straightened the cotton blouse. Her heart fluttered wildly, torn between two worlds. Trembling, she retreated to the dark living room until the roar of his car racing away echoed through the neighborhood.

"God, what's happening to me?" The stillness seemed to absorb her shout. The desire she felt for the wounded man soiled her soul like tar. Hot tears filled her eyes. "I don't want to feel like this. I just wanted a friend. How did this happen?"

Maybe the problem wasn't in her heart.

"It's not fair! You took Morgan from me and when I try to help David he takes it all wrong!" The sweep of her anger grew larger.

"I don't have anyone who cares about me! My mother didn't care about me. Ledbetter just wants his stupid bank to make money. Barry's so busy he can't even come to the ball game. The people at the church are attacking us."

Her angry scream filled the darkened parsonage. "God, you can have this trash! I don't want it any more!"

The house felt like a cage. She didn't care if David lay waiting somewhere or what Barry might think. She snatched her purse from the bar and fumbled for her keys. The garage door still stood open, an escape route from the storm of anguish sweeping across her heart. With a squeal of tires, she backed the car away from the dark house and fled into the darkness.

Two miles down Osage Highway, Barry and Jason wrapped their tongues around double dips of ice cream from the Frozen Fancy.

"Do you feel sad you didn't hit for the cycle tonight?"

His son nodded. "I guess. No one else on the team had even heard of doing that."

"You almost pulled it off. And hitting four for four is still a great night."

Jason nodded and licked at the drips running down the side of the cone.

Barry leaned back in the hard plastic chair. Out the window he saw the parade of car lights speeding down the busy street. *I guess Keri went home. Why did she get so upset? Something else must have happened at work.*

"Did you ever hit for the cycle when you were playing ball, Dad?"

"Um, I don't remember, buddy. It's been too many moons ago." He crunched the cone. "But I may be hitting for one this weekend."

"Really?"

"This afternoon I went to the hospital and helped a new mom who had trouble after she gave birth. So, we could count that like hitting a single, you know, to get on first base in the game of life. Then, on Sunday we've got a baptism scheduled, so that would be like a double to get to second base. My triple would be the wedding I have to do tomorrow afternoon."

"What's the home run?"

"I guess a funeral would be like a home run, because then a Christian gets to go to Heaven and all the angels in Heaven cheer! You remember Mr. Flowers, don't you? His funeral is tomorrow morning."

Jason's face glowed with pleasure. "That's just like Carmichael did for the Rangers!"

Barry stood up. "But he gets paid a lot more than I do!"

Chapter 7
Saturday

Lisa hurried down the oak stairs to the kitchen, every footfall marked by a different creak, groan or pop from the old boards. She carried three rumpled cotton sun dresses. When she turned the corner of the staircase, she found the director wiping down the breakfast bar.

"Mrs. Jordan, do you have an ironing board and an iron?"

The easy-going woman raised her voice over the Saturday morning cartoons blaring from the television in the living room. "You can find them in the closet by the refrigerator, honey. You gettin' ready to go out?"

"Tomorrow we're going to church. My little Kendra's going to be baptized. I want each of us to have a dress that looks nice."

"Where do you go to church?"

"Mt. Faith Church." She unwrapped the black cord from the heavy silver iron. "We just started going a few weeks ago. I really like the pastor and his wife. They even came to the trailer to talk with me and Kendra."

Mrs. Jordan stopped her sweeping and leaned on the broom. "Are you sure it's O.K. to go? Won't your husband be there?"

The comment brought a smirk to the young mother's face. "Cody wouldn't be caught dead in a church. I don't even think he knows we've attended there. He's always working, or fishing, or hung over on Sunday morning, you know? I might be afraid to go to the mall but not to a church."

"I wish I could go and see Kendra's big day."

"I do too. I am going to call my sister and let her know. Kendra wanted her to be there."

The shouts of red-haired twins fighting over a toy interrupted the conversation. Mrs. Jordan turned to help referee the dispute, leaving Lisa to the ironing board and three colorful dresses. She methodically turned the thin fabric, pressing the iron hard against the wrinkles. The director's comments ran through her mind. The threat of Cody discovering where she was and what she had done began gnawing at her stomach again.

Long before dawn, she had awakened in the small upstairs bedroom. She could just make out the shadowy forms of the girls sharing a twin bed. Their slow, deep breathing brought reassurance about the daring flight to the Shelter. Instead of the loneliness and fear that filled her last days in the trailer, the days spent in this secret refuge had lifted her spirit. She felt safe and relaxed, even with the unanswered questions that hung just beyond the dawn of another day. Lying on the warm, rumpled sheets, she vowed, whatever might happen, never to place her girls in danger again.

But what do I do next? Could I turn to Dad? No. Not with his move to Pensacola eighteen months ago. We've only spoken twice since Christmas. He and his new wife might be willing for me to visit for a few days, but that would be all.

In the soft green glow of the street light through the window, she had leaned back against the wooden headboard. God cares for us. The revelation surprised her like the appearance of a beacon boring through the fog. In the middle of this quiet night, in this refuge, His eyes are watching over us. That's what the preacher's wife had prayed. Her thoughts soared from the room to imagine God's great eye far above, seeing them, tiny and helpless, in the Shelter's bedroom.

"Lord," she whispered, "We need your help. It's just me and these girls. Please get us through this and on our feet. Keep us safe from Cody. Thank you, God." The words that formed her first prayer radiated a deep pleasure through her soul. The anxious beating of her heart slowed. Soon she had settled back to sleep.

"I like the colors in your dresses. All of you will look beautiful at church."

The Director's words brought her mind back to the ironing board. "Thanks. We don't have many nice things, you know. I figured dressing up would help Kendra understand how special baptism is for a Christian."

Remembering the presence of God made her steps seem lighter when she carried the newly-pressed clothes up the stairs. *I won't go back to the way Cody and I lived. The change will be tough. But with God's help, the girls and I can make it. Tomorrow will be the first day of a new life for all of us.*

A pickup piled high with a green mountain of grass clippings stood sentry in the church parking lot when Barry pulled into his parking space. He could hear the deep roar of the small tractor in the front of the church laboring on the thick, bermuda grass. *Mike will be pleased that the lawn looks nice. The double duties today, with the funeral scheduled for 10:30 and the wedding at 4:00, are making everyone's work harder.*

In one way, he felt relieved to get away from the house. Last night had turned sour with the misunderstanding at the ball park. His anxiety had grown when he discovered Keri's absence. For more than an hour after Jason went to bed, he had paced through the house, waiting for her return. The mantle clock had already chimed eleven before she returned.

He waited in the darkened kitchen, arms crossed. "You had me worried."

"I just needed some time alone." She stood with shoulders slumped, her voice husky from crying. "I went up on the ridge just to be by myself. I'm feeling better now. Is Jason in bed?"

"He laid down about an hour ago. We went out for ice cream after the game."

"Did he get his last hit?"

"He did get a hit but it was only a single. So, he didn't hit for the cycle."

"That's too bad." She dropped her purse on the breakfast bar with a weary sigh. "I'm going to clean up and go to bed."

He reached out his arm to gently stop her. "I love you," he said and kissed her cheek. "I'm sorry I wasn't there for you and Jason this afternoon."

"I know. It's O.K." She ducked by without looking at him.

This morning he had eaten his breakfast alone. He stopped to look closely at her, still sleeping, before leaving to take care of his early chores. Her quiet breathing drew his compassion toward her wounded heart. He vowed that he would make some time for serious talk after his duties of the day were past.

In his office at the church, he quickly removed the fat manila envelope from the lower desk drawer. The solution for the mysterious money had come to him during the anxious hours last night. Compelled by the new plan, he tucked the bulging parcel under his arm. The time had come to visit Sam Lane in his office at Missouri Financial Solutions.

He motored at a leisurely pace along North Carmel Road. The crystal blue sky, unmarred by a single cloud, promised a productive day. On impulse, he lowered all four windows and let the breeze fill the car. The fresh morning smell of the wooded hills buoyed his spirit. Over the log fence to his right a green and yellow tractor sauntered under the black oak trees, pulling a small flat trailer piled with brush and limbs. Boyish cheers attracted his attention to the vacant lot at the corner of Ridge Lane, where a large dirt pile hosted a bike jumping contest for a gang of school kids. The pleasures of a great summer morning in the Ozarks surrounded him.

Why would he want to leave Mt. Carmel? The reasons to stay seemed obvious. This city needed a church with vision. The county presented solid opportunities for a growing congregation like Mt. Faith Church. The small town attitudes provided a great place to raise a kid. Keri seemed happy enough at the bank, at least most of the time. If they moved, she might find difficulty in landing another job with such substantial compensation. Staying put in their beautiful home seemed to fit as comfortably as a summer t-shirt.

He waited for the stoplight at Mt. Faith Drive and Union, elbow cocked out the driver's window and fingers drumming on the roof. Why leave? This time the negatives leapt to his mind. Dissatisfied members actively maneuvered to disrupt his work. They had won a battle through his own stupidity just three days ago, and Sunday's Board meeting might bring serious repercussions as a consequence. Keri could use a new start of friendships to take her mind off Morgan. Jason could benefit from the opportunities a larger school could afford. He could escape the pressure cooker of endless demands. It all made perfect sense. A new start could do them all a favor, it seemed.

In the next few days he had to find an answer. He looked up at the azure dome of sky far above the ridge. Lord, show me which way to go.

A block off the Square, he slid the Toyota into a shady parking place. Sam's office occupied a brown brick, one-story building. First built as a clothing store after the war, it had been remodeled as an office building in the 1970's. When Sam bought it five years ago, he added a dark brown awning and a double glass door entrance. The engraved bronze plaque mounted by the door announcing 'Missouri Financial Solutions' added a professional touch to the appearance.

The carpeted reception room, paneled with oak wainscoting and topped with dark blue wallpaper, stood empty.

"Sam?"

"I'm back here," a voice answered from the end of the hall, where a small counter near the bathroom held a coffee pot, microwave, and tiny sink. In a moment, the tall, sandy-haired accountant came around the corner, holding a cup of coffee. "Well, Brother Barry! What's going on this morning?"

"I'm out enjoying the morning and wishing I had a tennis racket in my hands." He stroked an imaginary forehand. "I'd love to play a match before the temperature gets up."

"I should have taken you out to the golf course yesterday, pastor. That's a sport where you don't have to work up a sweat." He waved his arm. "Come on back and sit down."

The simple office held a black metal executive desk, a credenza, and three chairs. A cork bulletin board under the high window overflowed with pictures of his wife, Lynda, and three children. A red 4H ribbon, evidence of endless labors by the youngest child, hung proudly beneath a picture of the boy standing next to a golden Arabian horse.

Barry settled in one of the tan guest chairs and looked across the desk at his friend. "I've had some weird things happen to me this week."

"I heard about one that happened on Wednesday night.

I hope you haven't been bushwhacked like that again!"

"No more muggings in the church hallways, thankfully. This presents a different challenge." Barry tossed the plump, wrinkled yellow envelope on the broker's desk. "Take a look at this."

Sam gently lifted the envelope and bent open the wings of the metal clasp. He looked in, then up at Barry. Upending the envelope, an avalanche of green bills spilled on the desk.

"Lord in heaven!"

Barry winked at the startled businessman. "Like to do some business today?"

Doris Loomis straightened the tiny blue t-shirt stamped "Grandma's boy" and laid the sleepy infant on the soft quilt in the clear plastic bassinet.

"Did you get enough to eat, little man?" As if to reply, the black-haired newborn stretched out his arm for a last wiggle and gently closed his eyes.

"Thanks, Grandma," Jenni said. She buttoned her robe and leaned back on the raised bed. She felt exhausted. Benjamin's appetite seemed to grow by the hour, waking him twice during the night to nurse. The sleepless hours had painted her pale face with dark bags under her eyes.

A rap on the hospital room door broke the stillness. Jim swung open the door, a small piece of luggage in his hand. Sandi and Ed followed.

"How are things going in here?"

"We're doing fine," Doris said. "Benjamin has just finished his second breakfast."

"That's quite an appetite," Sandi said, putting down her

purse. She turned her attention to Jenni. "Do you feel any stronger this morning?"

"Not really. I feel like a truck hit me. I didn't eat breakfast because my stomach feels sick."

"The surgery will set you back a few days, I know. But we'll help you get back on your feet." Sandi kissed the forehead of the sixteen-year old. "I'm just glad Brother Barry had come to visit yesterday. His timing was perfect."

Ed sat down in a chair by the window. "I have to admit I felt pretty nervous when Barry called with the news. But he stayed calm through the whole thing, no matter how worried the rest of us became."

"I appreciate the fact that he stayed with us until the doctor came out to give us a report," Jim said. "Maybe he felt a little concerned about the surgery, too."

Jenni twisted on the raised bed to get comfortable. "Grandpa, when I looked down and saw all that blood, I couldn't even talk! Barry pushed the call button. The nurses ran in and had me rolling to surgery before I could say anything."

"When we were sitting in the waiting room," Doris said, "I couldn't help wondering what really motivates those people who speak so critically of Barry. Here he sat, on a Friday evening, for two hours, when I know he had many other things to do. In all the years he has served as pastor, I don't think I've ever heard someone complain about him not caring. And that's the most important thing a pastor can do."

Benjamin snorted in his sleep and wiggled his legs to get comfortable in the bassinette.

"Are you voting for Brother Barry, too?" Sandi said in baby talk, pulling on the blanket. "I bet you want to keep your mommy strong and healthy, don't you?

"Well, as far as I'm concerned, Barry can count on being

around to see Benjamin hit his first home run," Ed said. "I think he's doing a good job as pastor."

The skilled fingers of LuAnn Sweete softened the booming organ melody when Barry approached the pulpit. Edith Flowers, supported on Red's arm, stood in the atrium, ready to lead the Flowers' family procession down the east aisle. The simple steel casket of Harvey Flowers, surrounded by ornate sprays of fresh-cut blossoms, lay at the front of the church, a silent centerpiece in the tableau of grief.

With a rustle, the congregation stood to watch the somber faces of the grieving family follow the funeral director toward the second pew of the center section. Red's forehead carried beads of sweat, while Verna twisted a tissue in her right hand. The band of mourners soon filled five pews. When they were in place, Barry motioned for the entire congregation to be seated.

At the gesture, LuAnn keyed the organ to the hymn that Brent had selected for a solo. His strong voice filled the house with the words of 'Amazing Grace.' The old melody quickly brought tears to family members who had heard Harvey whistle the tune countless times.

Barry waited until the final note fell silent, then stepped to the pulpit. "We've gathered today to remember our friend, Harvey Flowers. Harvey meant so much to each of us. We can't take away the pain we feel with this sudden loss. But we can share it so the load will feel lighter. Join me in grateful prayer for the gift God gave us in the life of Harvey Flowers."

Heads bowed across the large crowd. The family huddled together, old and young, tattered and tailored, united in sadness. In the center of the group, attired in his Army dress uniform, sat the grandson, Danny, who had arrived just yesterday from Germany.

"In front of Harvey's house bloom a multitude of beautiful roses. Cream, red, yellow—they share their beauty and their fragrance with the world. As I walked past those roses this week, I thought of the care and love that Harvey had lavished upon them. Years ago he planted them. Through hot summers and frigid winters he nurtured them. Today they testify to his caring hand."

Edith smiled in assent. She loved the beauty that surrounded her home, most of it the product of Harvey's busy hands.

"God cares for us much more than even Harvey cared for his roses. With the skill of the Master Gardener, our heavenly Father has daily provided for our best. He feeds us through the Bible. He supports us through the church. He may even prune us through circumstances to make us blossom lavishly."

"If we could hear Harvey today, his words would boast of God's care. Across the years he sat in these very pews to learn of God. Then, he rose from here to put into practice the commands he learned. All of us need to understand the wonder of God's care in our lives. At this moment Harvey holds the comforting hand of the Master Gardener. And perhaps even now, Jesus is walking with Harvey through places of such indescribable beauty that his heart cannot contain the joy."

"Today our hearts feel sad. We miss the smile of this saintly man. But let's use our grief to grow stronger. Let each one of us make sure we know Christ as Savior, so we can look forward to seeing Harvey and his new garden someday."

Solemn "Amen's" rose across the congregation. Brent signaled them to stand while LuAnn swelled the organ with the notes of "Blessed Assurance, Jesus is Mine." The funeral director and his associate stepped smartly forward, grasped the ends of the dark casket, and pushed it up the aisle toward the atrium. Once the casket sat in place outside the worship center door, the director opened the lid and smoothed the thick fabric cushioning Harvey's earthly remains.

Barry took a place near the head of the casket to comfort those who passed by. One by one the people walked in silent procession, some stopping to gaze somberly at the still form, others staring straight ahead, perhaps afraid to look so closely upon their own mortal future.

The Flowers family approached at the end of the slow procession. Red grasped the side of the casket, speechless in tearful grief. Verna gripped his shoulders, frozen-faced. Finally, he pulled away, surprising the pastor with a sudden hug. "Brother Barry, thank you for everything. What you said about Dad seemed to fit him so well."

Verna joined in. "Harvey had just planted some new roses in the backyard. I said to Red after your message that we ought to transplant them to your yard, if you had a place."

"I'd be honored. I've got a spot by the front fence that would work perfectly. I'm not much of a gardener but maybe enough of Harvey's magic is around to help them grow."

Red shook his hand. "I'll call you next week after things have settled down and bring them over. Thank you again."

The parade of cars in the long funeral procession had left the church parking lot for the cemetery when Brent noticed Keri standing near the door to the church office. "Hi, Mrs. Preacher."

"You did a great job with the songs."

"Thanks. We can always count on the old hymns to carry a great message of comfort. Barry did a fine job, too. By the way, I heard he had an exciting time last night at the hospital."

"Really?"

"With the Loomis girl, you know. The whole family

feels like he nearly saved her life."

"We had a... uh... ballgame to watch. He didn't say much about what happened at the hospital."

"Jenni Loomis started hemorrhaging while Barry talked to her. His quick reaction got her help just in time. The doctor did surgery and she's going to be just fine."

"I'm glad it turned out all right."

"Me, too. Your little preacher is having a really busy weekend. I'd better run. See you later."

The quiet atrium left her alone in her thoughts. She steadied herself with a slow breath. *How could I have reacted like I did, with so much on Barry's mind?* Her face flushed with agitation. *If another thing happens, I may go crazy. If I just had a quiet place to go.*

No sooner had the thought come than the picture of a peaceful spot flashed in her mind. Her heart jumped at the idea. *I can sit there by myself and think for awhile.*

"Liz? Hi. This is Nadine. Any success with your calls?" She paced through the cluttered kitchen, the checklist of names the women had agreed to telephone fluttering in her hand.

"I'm not sure," Liz said. "I'm not very good at calling people I don't know. But everyone has acted very interested."

Nadine groaned inwardly. *I should have just called everyone myself.* "Did any of them promise they would attend church tomorrow?"

"Everyone except the Dittmers and the McNeils. Both couples have other commitments."

"So, that means six can be counted on?"

"Seven. I reached seven families. The Ingram's had

questions I couldn't answer. That bothered me."

"I'm sure Daemon can provide all the details."

"Nadine, this is nerve-racking. I've never been involved in a situation like this." She seemed on the verge of tears. "I'm worried about what will happen to the church."

She didn't have time or interest to discuss the feelings of a worried secretary. "I really appreciate your work, hon. I'll let Daemon know how it's gone. We'll talk to you later."

Daemon entered the room to hear her close the conversation.

"Is our little network making any progress?"

"Liz contacted the seven families on her list. With Claire's calls and mine added in, our little enlistment campaign reached nineteen families. Here's the list." She handed him a yellow pad with names checked off.

He scanned the collection of disparate members, stockpiled from months of backroom conversations. All shared a common dissatisfaction with the work of the pastor. With proper guidance, the group could march together into the decisive battle for the future of the church.

"I just talked with David. I don't know how he did it, but he got the words on tape direct from Keri's mouth, words that will seal their fate. His editing of the audio tape is nearly finished. He did say I need to have a friendly hand at the controls of the sound system to play it. Isn't Len Freeman the one who helps with the sound system?"

"Most Sundays, I think. Why?"

"I need his help at the end of the service. If I have a microphone and he is guarding the volume, then we can make sure everyone hears what we have to say. I'm going to call him personally and work out the details."

"Don't take too long. The Simpsons will arrive for

dinner at 5:00 and I need you to get the grill and patio ready."

"An army fights best on a full stomach, I suppose. It shouldn't take me long to get this last detail worked out."

He snatched up the phone. The momentum of his campaign seemed to grow with every passing hour.

The bright, fuchsia-colored blossoms of crepe myrtle waved over the clipped green hills of Hopewell Cemetery. Only a few visitors meandered through the ordered rows to mark the resting places of loved ones. A grey-haired woman slowly carried a bouquet of flowers to a tall granite marker. A heavy man in overalls stood unmoving near the simple white cross that named his youngest son as a hero fallen in a muddy rice paddy half-a-world away. Under the shade of a cottonwood tree, Keri's feet moved out of her control, pulled inexorably toward the black granite stone etched with Morgan's name.

Morgan Dockery 1960 - 1994.

Her eyes moved slowly to trace the chiseled gray letters. She gazed closely at the finely etched picture of lilies to the left of the name, a feature she hadn't noticed before. Her senses sharpened further. She saw a small imperfection, a chip in the upper corner of the stone. She heard a blue jay give a raucous call from the branches high above her head. She felt with every pore the soft wind rustling past her face and dancing up the hill. Even her soul seemed elevated, throbbing with the grand, immense rhythms of a deeper realm.

Transfixed, her vision penetrated past the black dirt to glimpse the white steel of the casket, adorned with gold. The lid became transparent, revealing the folds of Morgan's favorite lavender dress. Her artistic hands lay pale in peaceful repose across her waist. Keri's attention moved to the tawny hair, flipped under the chin, as her friend had always kept it. And then, for the first time since that tragic spring day, she could see the face of her friend, silent and fixed in death.

"Morgan!" Keri dropped to her knees next to the black stone. Like a flood, the ache of her soul burst forth. "I miss you so much," she sobbed. The cold stone pressed against her tear-stained cheek, unyielding to the pleas of her grief.

Twenty yards away, David crouched behind a thick privet hedge, eyes narrow with concentration. Since the service ended he had carefully tracked her every move, always far enough away to be unobserved. Minutes before, he had stolen around the perimeter of the cemetery to a concealed place on the little hill that looked down on the plot.

He fingered again the black button near his collar. The words Keri spoke in the dark garage, captured by the recorder, had echoed in his ears a hundred times. Each syllable could be a testimonial that would destroy Barry.

Her sudden motion to kneel by the grave lifted his eyebrows in surprise. The sound of weeping revealed the anguish wrapping her soul. A wave of compassion swept past the hard crust of revenge. *Maybe I should go and help her. I can help take away the pain.* He started the tape machine and advanced quietly through the trees toward the weeping figure near the headstone. *This time, I know she will respond to me.*

Keri dabbed at the rivulets running down her cheeks. The face of her silent friend swam before her weeping eyes. "Why were you taken, Morgan, why? Why didn't God leave you with me?"

"Keri?"

"Oh, God!" She spun away from the unexpected touch and cast her eyes upward. "Beth! What are you doing here?"

"I came to find you," Beth said, kneeling down to draw Keri close. "Kent and I have had you on our minds all morning, like you were in danger or something."

"How did you know I was here?"

"I went by your house. When you weren't there, I put two and two together. I got here as quickly as I could."

"I... I don't know what to say. I don't know what happened. But I could see Morgan in the casket. I could see her face. You probably think I'm crazy. But I've missed her terribly." Her tears welled up in fresh sobs.

Beth wiped the tears away with gentle fingers. "I do understand. You're not crazy, just a friend with a broken heart. That's why you've come here."

They sat together on the grass near the headstone. The wind stirred across the green leaves high above them.

"I've come here a lot in the last few weeks. Life has seemed so crazy. The bank is so demanding. Jason is growing inches every day. Barry worries about something at the church every day. I've been so lonely since Morgan died."

"Grieving is hard. When we lose someone we love, it changes more than just one relationship. It affects our whole world. We change in unexpected ways."

Keri took a deep breath and let it escape her lungs. "Beth, I need to tell you something. Would you listen? Listen without judging me for what I'm about to say?"

"What is it?"

"It's about David. Since Morgan died I've tried to be his friend. His heart has ached, too. I spoke with him Sunday night. He said he'd even imagined hearing Morgan's voice! Wednesday, I went by his house to take some bank papers. I felt so... so tender towards him. But last night he surprised me in our garage, when I was getting home from Jason's game. At first, I felt pleased he came. He needs to work through his pain. I care about him. But he...he misunderstood my feelings."

"Your feelings?"

"Yes, I guess. I didn't even know I had feelings. But everything's been a mess this week. Barry and I have fought, and the bank crisis worried me sick. When David took time to care for me...."

"You were drawn to him?"

"Don't think I'm terrible, please! He kissed me so tenderly. But I pushed him away and ran! Oh, God, I'm sorry. Beth, I need help with all this!"

Beth took both her hands and looked directly at her. "That's why God brought me here. You don't have to feel guilty for caring about someone, or how he took it all wrong. What he tried to do is beyond your control. You're human. You're a woman. You've been grieving for months, holding it all in. But not any more."

"Can God still love me? Or Barry?"

"Yes. And you can even love yourself as a living, breathing, normal child of God."

"I'm so sorry this happened. I don't even want to talk to David—or even to Barry."

"But you can. And I'll walk with you every step of the way."

Keri leaned her head against the granite, her eyes closed, her hands touching the cold stone. The dancing shadows played across the hillside, a hint of the vibrant life creeping back into her heart through the caring love of a friend.

"But I can't stay here. Morgan loved life and adventure. I've got to go on."

Beth nodded. "You're right, and Morgan would want you to do just that. She's with the Lord, and she's happier with Him than we can possibly imagine." She squeezed Keri's hand. "I'll help you." She stood and reached down a hand.

Keri pulled herself up and brushed the grass from her dress. "I'm so glad God sent you here to find me."

"You and Barry mean a lot to us. We know you've been thrown into the fire. But God's at work. We've just got to see all this through to the end."

In his nearby hiding place behind a large, granite mausoleum, David muttered a curse at Beth's interference. He had gotten close enough to the distracted women to hear every word. Now, he watched the women walk slowly toward the parking lot, arms encircling one another's waists in friendship. Rage boiled in his heart. He slammed his fist into his palm and turned his back to the sun-dappled grave.

Ryan glimpsed the tremor in Mandy's hand when she brought her slender candle forward. He focused intently on keeping his own candle steady while she twice missed the stubby wick on the white unity candle. Finally, the two flames became one. With a sigh of relief, the bride and groom replaced their thin candles in the holders on the tall gold candle stand. The single bright yellow flame, burning for all to see, symbolized their matrimony.

His family, Mandy's mother, step-father and the church hostess had rushed to decorate the worship center in the five hurried hours that separated the funeral and the wedding. Only a handful of people would ever know that, just hours prior, a casket had been parked at the very place where the bride and groom now stood.

He continued to stare at the small flame, wondering if the vocalist would ever finish. The song hadn't seemed so long last night during the rehearsal. What's supposed to happen next? He looked at Mandy. She smiled radiantly from beneath the white satin hat and veil.

The music finally faded. With a rustle of stiff fabric, the

bride turned away from the candle stand. Cinnamon, the maid of honor, moved forward to arrange the train of the wedding gown so the bride could move back to the center of the platform.

He didn't understand the sound at first, a sudden intake of collective breath from the congregation behind him. In a moment, the gasp became an "ooh-ooh" whispered from a dozen voices. Then, his eyes glimpsed the tottering candle falling toward Mandy's beautiful dress.

When Cinnamon helped her move, the front of Mandy's immense bridal gown had billowed forward just enough to catch the curled metal foot of the candle stand. The tug of the hem jerked the stand forward, once, and then again. One of the slender candles toppled over directly toward the beautiful satin gown. The congregation's exclamation had sounded the warning of an impending disaster.

Barry reacted instantly. Stepping toward the stand, he caught the candle in mid-air as it fell, flame down, toward the bride's dress. At the same moment, he stepped on the hem of the gown, preventing the unsuspecting bride from causing further damage.

No one breathed as the ceremony teetered on the verge of disaster.

Ryan recovered first. He reached forward to stabilize the candle stand. The pastor gestured downward and the groom stooped over to unhook the snagged dress. When the dress cleared the foot of the stand, Barry set the fallen candle back in its place.

An audible sigh of relief washed across the crowd, replaced momentarily by a twitter of nervous laughter. Mandy stood frozen for a long moment, then calmly reached toward Cinnamon to take the bouquet of bridal flowers. Ryan patted her hand tenderly. Barry winked at Mandy to say, 'I've got it under control!' He turned to the next page of his wedding book and resumed the ceremony as if nothing out-of-the ordinary had occurred. At the back wall of the worship center, the photographer smiled broadly, knowing he had captured the moment like a priceless Pulitzer Prize winning photo.

Hours later, as they winged their way through the night sky from Dallas to Honolulu, Ryan laughed out loud.

Mandy glanced toward him. "What is it?'

"I don't know how Barry caught that candle in mid-air."

"I didn't even know what was happening. When I looked at you, your eyes were bugged out like you'd seen a ghost."

"I couldn't react fast enough. But Barry handled it like a pro. You know, later, he just brushed it off. He wasn't upset or anything. Before he left the reception, he said, 'I'd really like for you to attend church here when you get back from the honeymoon.'"

"What did you say?"

Ryan took her hand. "I told him I would. He's a neat guy."

"Good. I'd like for us to do that together." She leaned over and offered her lips to her new husband. "I love you," she whispered. Their kiss lingered long with the promise of the future.

A chorus of cicadas filled the dusk with a melodious, natural symphony as Barry and Keri strolled hand-in-hand along the broad concrete walkway beside Spring River. No matter what the time of day, the city park adjoining the gentle waterway offered a quiet refuge. After a long, silent walk they stood shoulder to shoulder, gazing at the rippling reflection of the tall, rocky bluff which towered beyond the broad, green stream.

Barry leaned on the steel railing. "I hurt you this week. I want you to know I'm sorry."

"You don't have to apologize. We're both at fault," Keri said. "I jumped to a conclusion because my feelings were hurt."

"I guess we've both had our pain this week, haven't we?"

"I should have seen how Kent's vision bothered you. The attack Wednesday night added even more confusion." She linked her arm in his. "You've worked so hard to lead the church, but some of the people will never be happy."

"You know, I enjoy helping people. This weekend has actually been satisfying, with this whole 'cycle of ministry' that Jason has invented. The birth, the wedding, and even the funeral fulfilled what I've always felt called to do."

"It feels good to me, too."

"I rediscovered some of the old joy today. I felt like I did on that beach years ago, when the Lord spoke so clearly."

A gray egret swooped low over the water and landed in the trees along the bank. The whispering river flowed dark in the deepening twilight. While they stood arm in arm at the railing, a calm and healing energy seemed to flow around them.

Keri looked at her husband's face. *I can recount his faults easily. His mind wanders. He worries too much about money. He tries to please too many people. But, there's something deeper. He's the man who once stood at the altar and looked into my soul, giving me his solemn vow. He's never held me back from following my own, sometimes foolish, heart. He fathered my son and cheers his every step of progress.* She turned toward him and pressed herself close.

"I need to tell you something."

"What's that?"

"I don't want you to be angry, because some of it is my fault."

"Now, you've really got my curiosity up." He saw her

blue eyes heavy with concern.

She took a deep breath. "David tried to seduce me this week."

"He what?"

"Now listen to the whole story," Keri said, holding his arm firmly. "Don't get upset. It's all over now, and nothing really happened. But I need to tell you about it." She closed her eyes and turned her face out toward the river. "Two vulnerable people stumbled into each other this week."

Her story tumbled out under the darkening sky, soaked with tears, revealing the soul-rattling rush of sympathy and anger that had carried her like a roller coaster through the week. At last the words gave way to sobs, her blond hair pressed against his chest.

He listened without comment. When she quieted, he kissed her tear-stained cheeks. "If I had been paying attention to you like I should have, this never would have happened."

"I repeated the wedding vows today, just to myself, and just for you."

He stroked her soft hair. "I always think of you, too, when I perform a wedding ceremony. But now it's my turn to tell you something."

"What?"

"I've kept a secret this week, too. Or maybe I should say, 5,000 of them."

She leaned back and looked in his eyes. "What does that mean?"

He took her hand and pulled her further along the walkway. He recounted the chain of events around the envelope of mystery money and the action he had taken that morning.

"Do you think it could be stolen, or maybe drug money?"

"I think someone's conscience got the best of them. But I have no clue as to how they could get it to my office."

"Could someone have come in without being seen?"

"Sure," he said. "I've come through the office many times and not seen any other workers, simply because of errands that take people out of the office to other areas of the building. It's not good, but it happens."

The shadows of the great oak trees threw dark outlines across the walkway. Barry draped his left arm around her slender shoulders.

"Do you want to leave Mt. Carmel?"

She shrugged. "If that's what you feel we should do."

"But how do you feel?"

She set her lips and sighed. "Five days ago I would have jumped at the chance. I felt lonely and angry and frustrated. But I feel different now. The PR success at the bank this week made a big difference. The job won't get any easier, but I know the climate of the bank has changed. Even old Ledbetter may have learned something."

"He needed to!"

"Something else happened today when I went to the cemetery. I had a very strange experience, a vision, like Kent's somehow, of Morgan in her grave."

"You saw Morgan?"

"Yes. I know it sounds bizarre. It was like I could see through the ground and the lid of the coffin to see her face again. But the vision helped me. I can accept the truth that she's gone now. We shared so much, yet I know I must move forward with my life. I won't forget her. Then Beth showed up."

"Beth Puckett?"

"Yes, completely out of the blue. As we talked, I felt like I had found another friend. I didn't think I would ever know someone like Morgan again. Beth's different than Morgan, of course, but I think she's just the kind of friend I need right now."

"How does that make you feel about leaving?"

"I feel better about things. I could stay for several more years, if that's what God wants for us."

They had reached the end of the walkway. The statue of Lt. Throckmorton, Mt. Carmel's hero from World War I, towered above them, his bronze eyes forever set on the horizon of a great battle. Barry leaned his back against the statue's base.

"In that case, I need to let you know what I just found out. Drew and Lauren caught me at the office after the wedding reception. They think that a group of people, led by Daemon Asher, want me out of here. That's what prompted the Wednesday night incident. Lance called it an ambush. They've even got Liz involved."

She put her hands on her hips. "Just how many people have joined this little mutiny?"

"I don't know. I've felt uneasy all week, like an animal, nervous before a big storm hits. We may not have a choice about leaving. God might be opening the door to Kansas City at just the right time so we can get away without the pain of more conflict." He looked up at the weathered statue towering above them. "Unlike Lt. Throckmorton, I don't think I'm hero material."

She squeezed his waist. "You are a hero. More people than you think can see what God has done here in these six years."

"But is it worth the pain to stay and fight? The people who have organized against us will stop at nothing. If they planned an ambush in the atrium and are spreading lies about you, there's no way to guess what vicious trick they will try next. Daemon wants to run the church, and we're in the way."

"I just have a feeling we can't see the whole picture yet."

"You mean the picture of life flashing before our eyes just before the end?"

She laughed. "That's not what I meant. We're not alone against these people. Drew and Lauren prove that. Besides," she lifted her head and looked at his deep, dark eyes. "It doesn't matter where we are, just so we're together."

He wrapped his arms around her neck and stroked her golden hair. "I need you." A gentle kiss fell on her forehead. "I love you."

The bronze bullets felt cold in Cody's palm. He rolled them back and forth, then closed his fist, satisfied. "Yeah, these'll do the trick," he whispered.

He turned to the counter of Ernie's Sporting Goods, pouring the bullets back in the box. They would be more than he needed to fill the chamber of the old gun he had borrowed from Clyde, the bartender at Harry's Place. He nodded to the bearded clerk. "Ring these up for me."

"Sure. Looks like good weather for target shooting."

"I need the practice. It's been a while since I shot a handgun." He pushed the box and the change in his pocket. "See you later."

Now, where can I get some clothes? He fired up the old Ford in a roar of smoky exhaust. "Even if it is church, I'm not wearing a starched shirt and a tie," he mumbled over the roar of the engine.

What about that white and red western cut shirt? Lisa bought it for him not long after Courtney's birth, so the four of them could make a family picture. It should still be hanging in the closet. I need to dress so I don't attract the attention of those hypocrites at the church.

When he turned the corner to Mt. Faith Drive, his determination mounted. I'll get her attention this time. She won't be able to hide any longer. Those girls are mine just as much as hers.

The plan seemed foolproof. Tomorrow morning, while Lisa watched Kendra's baptism in the sanctuary, he would arrive at church and go straight to the nursery. Since he would be dressed like any other Dad, he could check Courtney out of the nursery, on the excuse that they had to leave early. Then, he would high-tail it out of the building with the baby. When Lisa found what had happened, she'd have no choice but to come back home.

He glanced at the box of shells on the torn seat of the truck. Why do I need a gun? Just call it insurance, in case someone interferes. I wouldn't really use it, but it could keep some idiot from messing up the plan.

The deserted church parking lot provided time to plan his route. He pulled in and drove slowly near the building. The stately church towered like the hull of a mighty ship, with the tall, stone, worship center wall the bow sailing north toward Mt. Faith Drive. The main glass doors came next, opening to the vestibule at the center of the facility. Further toward the south stretched the two-story education building. Entrances marked by double steel doors stood on the east and the west. On the south end, the stern of the ship, two more double doors could be seen at each corner. Short ramps and stairs descended to the level of the south parking lot. On every side, well-tended shrubs stood close to the building, with towering black oaks hanging over the sidewalk. He could see that a directional sign hung at each entrance. Above the southeast door the word 'Nursery' stood out in large letters.

The location looked perfect. He could leave his truck running at the curb, not twenty feet from the door, dash in and get the baby, then return to make his getaway. In and out, maybe two minutes max.

"She'll never know what hit her," he said with a smirk, and gunned the engine to a satisfying roar. Tomorrow, Cody Burns would show the world how a real man fights to keep his family.

Chapter 8
Sunday

Soft notes from the carillon at Trinity Methodist Church floated on the morning air over Mt. Carmel's rolling hills. Barry heard the melody of Old 100 when he opened his front door. He strolled down the walk to retrieve the Sunday paper, quietly singing the familiar words of the hymn, "Praise God from whom all blessings flow." *Will I be singing that after all this mess is over?* The question still hung in his thoughts when he pulled the door closed.

Keri padded into the kitchen, pink night shirt askew on her shoulders. She raked her hand through her hair. "I thought you'd left already."

"I just stepped out to get the paper. The weather feels great this morning." He laid the Globe on the breakfast bar.

"Your new sport coat looks nice. You'll be the best dressed preacher at church today."

He chuckled. "I may not even be the preacher after today. But I'll look good riding the rail out of town, anyway." He slid his diary into the inside pocket of the blue blazer and kissed her lightly on the forehead. "See you in the service."

She gripped his arm and looked directly in his eyes. "No matter what happens today, the Lord will take care of us. Don't worry about it. Just do what you're called to do."

"You're right. I need to remember that today. We've

both lived through a terrible week." He wrapped her in a warm embrace. "It's taught me that I couldn't live without you."

The tan stone facade of the sanctuary, glowing with the golden, morning light, welcomed him as he rounded the corner of Mt. Faith Drive. A silvery dew lay across the trimmed green lawn. Barry saw Mike and Brent standing together when he opened the door to the atrium.

"Morning, guys. How are you?"

"I've got two air conditioning units dead this morning," Mike said. "I've already called the service guy. He's going to start leaving his phone off the hook for Sundays if we don't replace these units soon."

"In six months he'll want that extra money. How are you doing, Brent?"

"I feel like I've got a hangover after yesterday's schedule." The musician held the new intercom units in his hand. "After a cup of coffee, I'll get these units hooked up. Yours will be in the sound booth by the lavaliere microphone. You can put it on just before the service."

"Wearing that intercom should be interesting. Did you remember that we'll start the service with that Burns baptism?"

Brent nodded. "Right. Come out in the baptistry when you are ready and LuAnn will lower the volume of the prelude. After you finish the baptism the choir will sing."

"Roger, wilco." He walked through the office. His Bible and sermon manuscript lay on the desk. He had more than an hour to review the message again before the congregation began arriving for Sunday School. The worship service would follow. By 11:00 the Sanctuary should be filled with people.

Am I ready to meet them? Faces floated before the eyes of his imagination: Daemon, Dale, C.K., and little Kendra. *Some accuse me while others trust me.* His heart turned upward in a whispered prayer. "Lord, be with me down this difficult path today."

A half-mile from the church, Cody stood on the creaking wooden porch of the trailer. The morning light hurt his eyes, though, and his head pounded from the booze consumed the night before. Retreating inside, he glanced at the kitchen clock. Just 9:30. *Good. I've got more than an hour to clean up and put on my church clothes.* He ran his hand over the stubble on his face. *Better shave, too. I've got to look just like the rest of those pious fools.* He turned on the shower and laughed loudly at the thought of himself strolling the holy halls of Mt. Faith Church.

Daemon eased the green Lincoln into his regular parking space, the wide vehicle aligned perfectly between the yellow stripes. "This is it. We've waited a long time for this day."

Nadine slipped the carefully annotated list of friends in her purse. "I hope everyone shows up like they've promised. I'm ready to get it over."

"You sound like you're worried."

'No, not worried. But I've seen things go wrong before."

He closed the door behind her. "Not today. Too many things have gone our way this week. Even Ed's foolish words have helped our cause. Barry won't get away this time. The evidence is all on our side."

Nadine's heels clicked loudly on the concrete sidewalk. She slipped her hand in his. His palm felt ice cold despite the warm morning sunshine.

"Come on, hon. We need to be at church in fifteen minutes. Let me get your barrette in," Lisa said. "Are you scared about being baptized?"

"A little," Kendra said. She backed closer to her mother

and held her brown hair up to be styled. "Will the water be cold like a swimming pool?"

"No, it's warm. It'll be just like getting in the bath tub." She skillfully pulled the hair in place and squeezed Kendra's shoulder.

"Will you be in there with me?"

"No, I'll be out in the congregation watching."

Courtney stood in front of her big sister and swung her hands against the starched fabric of the ironed dress.

"Courtney, can you get your bag? We need to leave to go to church." She looked directly in the eyes of her oldest child. "I'm really proud of you, sweetie." A lump rose in her throat. "This is a big day for you, and I hope you'll remember it the rest of your life."

Courtney accepted her mother's kiss. "Will you help me change clothes after I get all wet?"

"You bet."

Courtney dragged the pink and white bag to the door. "Go!"

"Watch your step going down the stairs," Lisa called. And I'll watch over my shoulder all day, she thought to herself, for dangers far more threatening.

LuAnn played the last verse of "Majesty" with a deliberate beat, filling the worship center with thunderous tones. Daemon and Nadine found their familiar pew on the east side and settled in the seat. He touched the folded paper in his suit pocket for reassurance. On it were the words he knew would get the church back on the right track.

"I think everyone is here already," Nadine said over the music.

"I saw Sid and Fred Campbell in the foyer."

"When will you go to the podium?"

"When Barry calls for Mike to give the announcements. I'll be talking before anyone even realizes what is happening."

LuAnn lowered the volume of the organ music at precisely 11:00 a.m. Barry waded slowly into the baptistry. At his side sloshed the tiny form of Kendra Burns.

"Good Lord!" A dozen heads turned at Daemon's outburst. "Can you believe that? He's got that little girl from the trailer park. What gall!"

"Welcome to this morning of worship at Mt. Faith Church," Barry's strong voice boomed through the speakers. "Our praise to God begins today with the observance of baptism. Jesus said, 'Go and make disciples, baptizing them in the name of the Father and the Son and the Holy Spirit.' Standing here before you is Kendra Burns. Kendra, last Sunday did you pray to receive Christ as savior?"

Her voice seemed small. "Yes, sir."

At her affirmation, Barry lifted his left hand up, palm-forward, to express the time-honored vow. "I baptize you in the name of the Father, the Son and the Holy Spirit."

He pressed a white cloth against her face and lowered her backward into the water. In a moment she emerged from the rippling pool, frog-eyed and gasping for a breath.

"Amen!" Several voices echoed through the worship center. The youth on the third row twittered with laughter at her expression. Lisa turned to her sister, Becky, and beamed with pride. Becky dabbed a tear from her eyes and nodded. Barry draped a gentle arm on the trembling new believer and escorted her from the water.

At Brent's command, the choir stood. Thirty pairs of eyes locked on his lifted hand, waiting for the signal to begin. On the downbeat, LuAnn launched vigorously into the introductory bars of the call to worship.

C.K. took Rachel's hand when they stood to sing the opening hymn. For decades of ministry he had been the minister standing in front of the church while Rachel sat in the pew. *Did she ever feel as helpless as I do now? The mutiny is looming, and I can do nothing to stop it.* He looked at Barry. No evidence of nervousness there. *But I know in the pit of his stomach he feels something's got to give—and soon.*

Lauren's smile made it hard to keep singing when Josh sat down on the pew beside her. His crisply ironed, dark blue uniform made him look professional—and heart-stoppingly handsome. She placed a hymnal in his hand and patted his arm, delighted he could use an early lunch on a quiet Sunday morning as a perfect excuse to be together.

His strong presence against her arm allowed her tension to drain away. She had awakened early, taut as a bow string. Her first glimpse of the church brought an involuntary shiver. On the surface nothing seemed amiss. The parishioners crowded near her seemed happy, raising their voices to follow Brent's lead. Sunshine illuminated the stained glass with a glowing symbol of God's blessing. Any observer would be quick to recognize the wholesome strength of this congregation.

But something else, something sinister, crouched on the periphery of her spiritual vision. The first cold breath of evil had blown across her neck while she prayed with Drew and Brent in this very room. The foreboding faded a little on Friday night, during the prayer meeting at the Puckett's. This morning the icy uneasiness haunted her again.

She glimpsed the gray pompadour of Franklin Blue just three pews in front of her. *How many more people are involved? What plans have they hatched for today? I feel like something is growing, like a cancer spreading beneath the skin to destroy a healthy life. But what can I do about it now?*

"Pastor, can you hear the monitor all right?" Len's voice sounded with clarity through the earpiece of the wireless intercom.

Barry touched the 'Talk' button on the small plastic case. "Sounds great from up here on the platform. The balance is perfect."

"The sound out here is good, too." Barry could see Lance standing at the usher's station behind the back row on the left side.

Brent stood at the pulpit, his expressive hands coaxing more sound from the parishioners. He turned to mark the music for the choir, then slipped his left hand down to the intercom pack.

"Let's do 'Majesty' one more time from the first before I dismiss the kids."

The organist and pianist nodded at the voice through their earpieces. Still keeping the beat, he turned around to lead the congregation through the chorus.

Barry scanned the faces of the congregation. He could see a long-haired, teenage girl whispering to a friend. One pew behind them a mother chased an errant crayon for her preschooler. Two blue-haired widows stood close and shared a hymnal. He gauged the crowd to be larger than normal for a Sunday in August. He didn't look toward Daemon. *I know what he's thinking about that baptism. How anyone could question the simple faith of a child is beyond me.*

Lisa stroked Kendra's hair, still damp from the baptism. "How do you feel, sweetie?"

"The water went up my nose."

In a moment, the music ended, and Brent invited all the children to move to Baxter Hall for the children's worship service. Kendra stepped on her mother's toes as she scrambled from the pew. Lisa placed the hymnal in the pew rack and watched her leave, her heart glowing with joy at the youngster's faith.

  I feel completely different than I did a week ago. The nightmare feels like it's lifting. Kendra has started a new life. In a way, all of us are starting over. She folded her hands with a sigh of relief. I know my problems haven't ended. But God is real. Even the problems with Cody can be worked out if I have enough faith.

  David sat alone on the back pew. Beads of dew glistened on his shoes from his morning stroll near Morgan's grave. His thoughts wandered from Barry's comments to the children to focus again on the graveside encounter yesterday. Visualizing the sheen of Keri's burnished gold hair against the cold black stone caught his breath. Glancing sideways, he glimpsed her sitting near Lauren.

  He looked up to see Barry dismiss the children and approach the pulpit with a Bible in his hand. The words of Psalm 51 rang across the crowd.

  'Have mercy on me, O God,
    according to your unfailing love;
  According to your great compassion
    blot out my transgressions.'

  A flash of anger blazed across his heart. Listen to your own words, you hypocrite! Your sins have nearly wrecked this church and broken the heart of your wife! You're not worthy of having either one!

  His mind flashed back to the electric moment in the shadows when Keri's warm lips touched his. Surely that expressed her true feelings.

  But she had to be set free from this shyster. Today it would happen. He ran his hand across the small tape machine hidden in the pocket of his sports coat. The echo of her own words, deftly edited, would liberate the church and her own oppressed heart. He stared at the black-haired minister. *Enjoy your last sermon, pastor.*

Daemon's Bible remained on his lap, sealed tight. *I want nothing to do with that hypocrite standing behind the pulpit. Everything about this service feels wrong. The music director used those simplistic choruses again. And who is that tall man on the second row of the choir? I've never seen him before. He must be a new member that doesn't have a clue about what we believe. It's time to solve these problems. We'll be far better off then.*

The halls near the southeast entrance of the church stood empty. A battered pickup, puffing blue smoke, sat just outside the door. The burly young man, dapper in the red and white striped shirt, glanced nervously around the building. He could hear the laughter of children in the nearby rooms. A wide hall, carpeted with a multi-color of blue and brown, stretched in front of him. Unsure of his direction, yet trying to look confident, Cody sauntered toward the voices.

Each door along the hall had an identifying sign, with a picture of a flower and the ages of the children attending the class. The first sign read "Ages 4 - 5." He kept walking, forcing a smile in case someone appeared. He passed three rooms, then came to an intersection of hallways. *Now which way?*

"May I help you?"

He whirled to see a broad-shouldered, young woman wearing a name tag that read, 'Cassie.'

"Uh, well, yes, I guess," he said. "I'm lookin' for the room where my one-year old girl might be."

"You're almost in the right place," Cassie said. "Her room is right this way." She turned and walked quickly up the hall. Cody hurried behind her. His breath felt short and small beads of sweat appeared on his upper lip. She stopped at the last door on the right.

"Just knock and they'll be glad to help."

"Thanks."

He looked at the closed door. The gun felt like a brick in his right pants pocket.

Daemon's thoughts drifted to the past. *Years ago, I sat in this very pew when God's glory filled the church. I can still hear Dr. Patrick's gentle voice masterfully teaching the Bible. His words challenged adults, rather than being simple stories that entertained the children, like the babblings of the man in the pulpit now. Mary Ellen, always lovely as the pastor's wife, sat next to Nadine and would keep us informed about the inner life of the church.*

Where had the golden days gone? Barry had thrown it all out to be replaced by disco music, strange doctrine, untried leaders, and a wife who had sold herself to money like a whore.

He glared at the black-haired man in the pulpit. *I swear this will be the last time he ever stands in this pulpit.*

"Do I need to be forgiven? Confronting that single question could bring a new start for your life today." Barry took a deep breath. His voice softened. "I know it's true for me. This week I asked God to forgive me for losing my temper on Wednesday. Right in this very church I struck a man in anger. I regret what I did. I apologize to you as a congregation and to Dale Galloway. I plan to discuss with the Board tonight what I can do to make this right."

Every eye focused on him as he stepped to the right of the pulpit, leaning forward, to plead with the congregation.

"Like the refreshing spray of a shower that cleanses the

grime and restores the muscles, forgiveness from God has touched me and let me begin anew. The same is possible for you today. As we bow together, make the words of Scripture your personal prayer. Say in your own way, 'Wash away all my iniquity and cleanse me from my sin.' God is listening right now. Let's pray."

LuAnn softly stroked the keys of the organ. Barry voiced a prayer for the people. His words contained a depth of honesty, born from the trials of the week. As one forgiven, he now prayed for others to know such grace. For some, the moment of prayer marked a turning point toward a cleansing that would refresh their souls.

"Amen." With his final word, the pastor turned and took a seat in the chair at the right side of the small platform, directly in front of the choir.

Mike McCormick marched his portly form towards the pulpit. "Thank you, pastor. Each of us needs God's forgiveness. Anyone who would like to speak with Brother Barry about this, or about church membership, is invited to do so before you leave. Now, before we go, let me direct your attention to the announcements you see printed in the worship folder." He lifted the printed bulletin and two other papers slipped from podium, sailing toward his feet. He stooped down to pick them up.

At that very moment, Daemon bolted from the pew toward the platform. Every eye in the choir loft tracked his unexpected advance. Without hesitation, he stepped between Mike and the pulpit to grab the microphone.

"Please give me your attention. I have something very important that each member of Mt. Faith Church needs to hear."

Shocked, not a person in the entire sanctuary stirred. Conversation ceased and the shuffling of paper died. Youth stopped fidgeting. Mike gave way to the bold intruder. Beth gripped Keri's arm. Barry froze in his chair.

"Our congregation is deeply troubled today. The time has come for people who care about the true work of God to stand up and face the issues." His voice climbed a notch with the tension. "I speak for many today who feel the time has come to deal with the problem by declaring this pulpit vacant and seeking a true man of God to be our pastor!"

An explosion of startled gasps and murmured questions engulfed the crowd. Franklin, Sid, and Dale moved as one to close the doors from the atrium to the worship center. Only Lance, preparing for the offering, and David, returning from his car with new batteries for the tape machine, were left outside.

Brent stood near the organ. He touched his intercom and whispered, "Len, turn off his mic."

Len glanced at Dale. His hand never moved toward the controls of the sound board. "Maybe the people need to hear," he said over the intercom.

Daemon continued his tirade at full volume. "It's my duty to speak out today, though some of you do not want to hear my words. A large group of faithful church members believe the trouble in our church springs directly from the policies of this pastor. He has tried to pad the membership and changed our practices from the ways that made our church great. He has changed, without a vote of the people, the way we worship God. He has held money for his own selfish ends that belongs to God. I believe you should have the freedom to decide whether we will continue to be lead astray, or whether we will return to the true ways of God!"

The vitriolic words assaulted Barry like a gang of hoodlums. Instead of fear, however, a strange, powerful armor of peace settled upon him. He folded his hands and calmly directed his attention to the agitated man who had taken over the service.

"Father, it's in your hands now," he whispered.

"I'll need to see your card, sir." The hefty matron standing behind the half-door of the nursery balanced Courtney on her left hip.

"What card?"

"The Childcare Security Card that we gave to your wife. It has a number that matches the one we've pinned to the baby's jumper."

"Uh, I don't... I mean, she didn't give it to me."

The caregiver shook her head firmly. "We're not supposed to release the children unless the parents have the card."

He looked down the hall. The supervisor who had escorted him to the door turned and started walking back toward him. She must know something is wrong. His thoughts raced in confusion. The only chance to bring his family together could disappear in an instant. He had to get his baby—now! He whipped the gun from his pocket and jabbed it toward the woman holding Courtney.

"Give her to me!"

The woman's face filled with a wide-eyed fear. "I... You..."

"I said give her to me!" He screamed the words and lunged over the half-door. Grabbing her arm, he pulled the two of them closer. "Now!" He tore his daughter roughly from the woman's arms.

Cassie had drawn within a few feet when Cody whirled to face her.

"Don't come any closer!" His menacing gray revolver loomed inches from her face.

She stopped in her tracks, lifted her hands to her face, and screamed. Her piercing cry resonated down the hall like a fire alarm.

"Shut up!"

Cassie gathered her breath and screamed even louder. The woman in the nursery shouted too. A door down the hall flew open and another woman stepped out.

Cody panicked. Without getting his bearings, he started running with Courtney held tightly to his chest.

"Stop! Help, someone help!"

Cassie's loud shouts reached the atrium where Lance and David stood outside the closed doors. Lance turned to look down the hall. "What's going on?"

Lance turned on the wireless mic clipped to his shirt. "Barry! Brent! A woman is screaming like crazy in the preschool hall!"

At the second scream, David bolted from the atrium toward the sound.

Daemon's words riveted the people to the pews. "Some of you may think these accusations are just my opinions and that the pastor has done nothing wrong. But I can give clear evidence that corruption infects the highest level of our church! Liz Emory, a secretary who works in the church office every day, wants to report some startling news."

Liz trembled as she stepped to the platform. "I placed an unmarked envelope with $5,000 in cash in the pastor's office on Monday." Her voice quavered. "The pastor took it without telling anyone."

The congregation gasped with one voice. Daemon pressed ahead, cross-examining her like an attorney. "Is it standard practice for the staff to remove large sums of church money from the office for personal use?"

"No. That would be misappropriation," Liz said, sticking verbatim to her carefully scripted lines.

Daemon turned and pointed across the platform at Barry. His voice trumpeted victory. "That should settle the case for everyone! This pastor has sold his soul to the love of money and taken $5,000 from the church!"

Boom! The sound of a gunshot pierced the congregation with a stiletto of fear.

David staggered from the nursery hall, his hand clutching the front of his blood-stained sport shirt. He looked at Lance with a question on his lips, took a half-step, and fell across the information table. The heavy wood piece overturned with him, spilling papers everywhere and dumping his limp body on the carpet.

Lance's shout blasted across the wireless system. "David's been shot! Someone with a gun is running loose in the church! Call an ambulance!"

Cody felt his hand vibrate with the recoil of the pistol shot. That fool had surprised him by appearing directly in the path of his headlong rush down the hall. Now he could see the atrium and the crowded worship center just beyond the crumpled body. He cursed his own stupidity. Which way to run now? Got to get to the pickup.

Terrified by the gunshot, Courtney began to scream and push away from his iron grip. His confusion mounted. Then he saw another exit across the atrium to the west. That's the way. He gathered his breath and sprinted past the bleeding man. At the hallway entrance, he half-turned and fired a warning shot, intentionally too high to hit anyone, then lumbered down the hall with the screaming child over his shoulder.

Boom! The second gunshot shattered the window high in the wall between the atrium and the worship center, raining shards of glass down on the people inside. A woman screamed as glass sliced her shoulder. Daemon and Liz flinched and stepped back, not comprehending the events that had interrupted their carefully crafted assault.

The shots launched Josh from the seat beside Lauren. Drew followed. Together, they dashed down the side aisle toward the atrium.

Brent jumped across the platform to the pulpit. "Get down! Everybody, get down in the pews!" He turned to the duo near the pulpit. "Both of you get down!" The musician shoved them roughly behind the chair where Barry had been seated just moments earlier.

The pastor had reacted to Lance's warning by rushing from the platform through the fire exit tucked at the front east corner of the sanctuary. He could get to the atrium by going through this door to the outside, bypassing the confused congregation in the sanctuary. *Daemon's mutinous accusations mean nothing now. My people are facing a greater danger.* He burst through the door into the bright midday sunlight.

Drew and Josh pushed Franklin aside and crashed through the closed Sanctuary door. David lay in a pool of blood near the overturned table. Lance crouched beside him, grimacing at the blood-soaked shirt and David's ashen face.

The officer jerked his walkie-talkie from his belt. "Dispatch, this is 89. Shots fired at Mt. Faith Church. I need backups and ambulances. Code 3."

"MCPD," a voice crackled back on the shoulder speaker. "Confirm your location."

"Mt. Faith Church. We have a casualty. Code 3.

Backups needed now."

Lance pointed down the open hall to the west. "I saw a man in a red shirt run that way. He had a baby!"

The policeman pulled his gun from his holster and ran cautiously across the atrium. Drew, stooped in a half-crouch, trailed behind.

At the entrance to the hall the policeman slowed, assumed a ready stance, then stepped around the corner, weapon stretched forward. The hall went south from the atrium for fifty feet, then turned to the right toward an exit on the west side of the building. He saw a large man clutching a screaming child make the turn.

Drew called over the intercom to update the staff. "The guy's holding a kid hostage! He's run down the west hall. Josh and I are following him."

Brent pulled the mic closer. His voice boomed over the loudspeaker in the sanctuary. "An armed gunman has a child hostage in the education wing. Please stay down in the pews where you are. The police have been called. Everybody, just stay where you are and pray. We'll be safe in here."

Huddled down in their pew, Keri, Lauren and Beth held hands. Beth looked across at Lauren. "Oh, Lauren, Josh ran out there."

Lauren's lips trembled. "I know."

Keri squeezed their hands. "Let's pray right now." The women drew close, gripping one another in fear.

Cody opened the glass door on the west side of the

building cautiously, squinting in the noonday sun to locate the old pickup. The curb sat empty. Another glance revealed the terrible mistake. He had run the wrong direction again. His truck sat idling at the corner on the south side of the building.

He cursed loudly. It's too risky to go back in the building now. I can get there faster by staying outside.

He pulled Courtney closer and headed down the sidewalk to the south. "I've got to get you to the truck," he grunted, clutching the little girl closer.

Josh and Drew saw the door closing when they rounded the corner of the hall.

"He's gone outside! He's probably got a car waiting," Josh said. He moved close to the exit, readied his gun, and pushed the door. "There he goes!"

Drew reported the developments on the intercom. "He's outside now. I think he's running toward the south parking lot."

In the atrium, Barry saw Brad crouching beside David and Lance. The off-duty fireman jerked a bullet-mangled electronic device from David's coat and threw it to one side. His probing fingers found the wound and pushed firmly against the red-stained skin. Then Drew's report crackled in his ear. He turned to Lance. "I've got to get to the south side of the church." Leaving the men, he ran from the atrium down the preschool hallway, passing Cassie and the sobbing worker who had been caring for Courtney.

Turning at the southwest corner of the building, Josh and Drew saw the big man struggling to hold a slightly-built child in a blue dress. He had slowed to a fast walk to handle her frantic movements.

"Shut up!" Cody clamped Courtney tighter. She wiggled

even more fiercely and wailed again.

"Police!" Josh shouted. "Stop now! Right where you are! Don't move. Put the girl down now!"

Cody whirled to look toward the unexpected voice. Where'd the police come from? He looked again toward the pickup. The old Ford sat idling over a hundred feet away. Too far. Then he realized the large trees and heavy shrubs between the sidewalk and the building might offer a shelter. Clutching his daughter, he abruptly dove behind the trunk of a huge red oak tree.

The two pursuers took cover behind the brick wall of the stairs that ran from the southwest door down to the edge of the sidewalk. The man crouched in the shrubbery not thirty feet away. The captive he held screamed again.

"Leave me alone or I'll hurt her," Cody yelled, pointing the revolver at his daughter. His heart pounded in his ears.

"No one is going to hurt you." Josh peered over the wall. The safety was off his gun. "Just throw out your weapon and let the child go."

"She's my daughter. My wife stole her Tuesday." His boiling anger pushed his voice to a roar. "I ain't givin' her up."

Josh pulled his head down and ripped the mobile radio from his belt. "Dispatch, this is 89. Tell the backups to set up a perimeter around the south parking lot. Repeat: set up around the south parking lot of the church. The suspect is hiding in the shrubs on the south side of the building. He has a hostage."

Drew squatted near the officer, his tall figure bent safely behind the wall. Barry's voice came through the church intercom.

"Drew! Where is the guy?"

"He's on the south side of the building hiding in the shrubs. Where are you?"

"I'm just inside the southeast door of the nursery hall."

"O.K. He's got his back toward you and is looking at us.

He's got a little girl in his arms." The youth minister whispered to Josh, "Barry is behind the guy, just inside the far door."

"Tell him to stay put. The backups will be here in a minute and we can talk this guy down."

"Barry, Josh says to stay where you are!"

Courtney wiggled harder against Cody's iron grip. A full minute slipped by. The heat from the noontime sun brought rivulets of sweat pouring down his face. He could see the policeman's head peeping around the brick wall.

"Throw out your weapon and step away from the building," Josh commanded. "Now!"

Courtney got a lungful of air and screamed again. The big man crouched lower. *The cop will call for reinforcements. I can't wait here.*

Barry quietly pushed open the door. Slipping outside, he crouched close to the wall of the church where he would be hidden by the heavy shrubs. He crept slowly toward the sound of the crying child. From behind a large evergreen bush he caught a glimpse of the man's brightly striped shirt.

Josh leaned around the edge of the stair. "You don't want your daughter to get hurt. Throw down your gun and let her go."

His words faded with the wail of a siren from Mt. Faith Drive.

Cody jerked with fear. Glancing down the sidewalk, he saw the pickup waiting, still chugging a cloud of blue smoke. *No time to lose.*

"Don't try to stop me, man!" Leaping from the cover of the bushes onto the sidewalk, he leveled his gun toward the pursuers shielded behind the low brick wall.

Boom! Boom! Chips flew from the masonry wall with the impact of the bullets.

He whirled to dash for the pickup and freedom,

clutching the baby.

"Oomph!"

The big man crashed down on the concrete, his legs knocked awry by Barry's lunging tackle. Courtney rolled away from his grasp, flopping like a rag doll.

Barry lay across the sidewalk, knocked flat by the daring maneuver to stop the fleeing gunman. Scrambling to his knees, head spinning from the collision with the massive legs, he located the baby. He crawled crab-like toward her, hoping to scoop her up and escape before the kidnaper could regain his wits. He grabbed her sun dress and pulled her close.

Cody stirred from the concrete. He still held the gun. In the corner of his eye, he saw Barry pick up his whimpering daughter. Staggering to his feet, not six feet from Barry and his child, he focused his fury on the man who had foiled his escape.

In one motion, he jerked the gun up and pointed it at Barry.

Boom!

The colors of the Sanctuary whirled as a kaleidoscope of walnut, blue, and cream, mixed with bright shining spots of light and deep chasms of darkness. Through the spinning hues, Barry recognized the front of the church. A long, dark box lay in front of the platform.

He discerned a line of people moving slowly toward the box. The whisper of their voices drifted to his ears.

"He called me the night after my divorce, just to say he was praying for me."

"I looked up from the bed in the emergency room to see him."

"He drove 50 miles to see John's basketball game."

The ashen faces turned to look in the box. A black-haired man lay in the long box, silent, eyes closed.

Through the swirling colors Barry saw his own body, framed in the dark wood casket.

Josh sprinted toward the trio after the crack of the gunshot.

Cody lay spread-eagled on the sidewalk. Blood spread across his chest where the policeman's 9 mm. slug had entered a split-second before his own finger could jerk the trigger to fire at Barry. A convulsion rattled his arm just before his eyes closed a final time. From beneath the twisted body a red trickle of blood began to stain the gray concrete.

The officer drew close, arms extended to hold his revolver in a firing position, watching for movement. He knocked the gun away from the kidnapper's hand with his foot.

When the officer lowered his weapon, Drew ran to Barry. He knelt down and wrapped his arms around the pastor and the screaming child. "Are you O.K.?"

Barry tried to focus on his friend. "Drew?"

"Yeah, pastor, it's me. Are you hurt?"

"I don't know. I... my head hurts." He rubbed the side of his head.

Drew followed his hand to see an angry red abrasion, marked with purple. "Looks like you cracked your head pretty good."

A shrill scream snapped their attention to the youngster laying next to Barry. Courtney had an ugly scrape on her left arm and another jagged line across her temple. She bellowed with fear and pain, coloring her cheeks red with exertion.

Drew stepped closer and gently ran his hand along her

arm. "I don't think it's broken. She's hurt for sure, but mostly just scared out of her wits."

"I think I am too, now," Barry said.

At that moment, police cruisers rounded both sides of the building. Two officers threw open the car doors and crouched behind them, guns drawn.

Josh holstered his pistol and signaled to them. "The suspect is down! Hold your fire!"

From the second police car a tall captain slowly emerged. "What happened, Corporal?"

Josh took a big breath to steady his trembling muscles from the rush of the pursuit. "We've had a kidnapping by an armed suspect, sir. The witnesses said this man took the child from the church nursery. He shot a man in the church who tried to stop him. I pursued him until he took cover in the bushes. He threatened the girl, who he claimed was his daughter, then fired at us when he made a break for the truck. The pastor here tackled the gunman, sir. He pointed his gun at the pastor and that's when I fired."

"The preacher tackled the gunman?"

"Yes, sir. The pastor hid in the bushes and upended him when the man broke for his truck."

The wail of an ambulance interrupted the debriefing. The captain waved to the crew in the cab to signal permission for the emergency team to examine Cody. Beneath the flashing emergency lights two men bounded from the vehicle, carrying bright-blue nylon bags. The leader knelt near Cody. Pulling on latex gloves, he felt for a pulse, then bent close to listen for respiration. Lifting his head, he said to the assistant, "Get the cardiac monitor."

Josh left the crew at work and turned toward Barry and Drew. He stood above them and jabbed a finger directly at Barry. "You're the stupidest preacher I've ever known."

Barry nodded, looked at the big body sprawled across the pavement, then turned back to the policeman. "I'm glad you're the best shot I've ever known." Drew stood and helped the pastor to his feet.

Nearby, the emergency technician pulled a heart monitor, cords flopping, from the bag. The leader worked quickly to place the leads on Cody's chest. The display flickered to life. For several moments they watched a flat, red line trace across the screen.

"Patient registering asystole," the leader finally said. He looked at his watch. "Mark 1226 hours." He stood and walked toward the captain. "The patient has no pulse or electrical activity, sir. There's nothing more we can do for him. We'll clear out and let you work the scene."

The captain looked around, reminded that they stood on a church parking lot on Sunday morning. He gestured to the other officers. "A lot of curious people are going to be around here in just a minute. Get the barrier tape strung up to keep them back while we work. I want the body covered but not disturbed."

Drew held the shaken girl close to his chest, stroking her hair. Her wide eyes looked uncomprehending at the still form of her father.

Barry looked at the captain.

"Officer, do you need me here right now? I probably should go back in the church and try to calm the people. The mother of this girl is inside. I think she can be of help to you in understanding what has happened."

"We will need to ask you some questions, Pastor, but I understand the church people need you right now, too. I'll send an officer in to get you when we're ready to hear some answers." He extended his hand. "Let me be the first to commend you for an act of courage that might have saved the life of this baby and Officer Allen."

Barry returned the handshake. He nodded toward Josh. "I think this officer needs the commendation, sir. He saved my life. I'm just glad this nightmare is over."

Barry could hear the pandemonium long before he entered the atrium. Well-dressed men and women pressed toward the exits like animals fleeing a fire. Fear-stricken mothers rushed down the hall to find their children. A gang of adventuresome teenagers bolted outside to gawk at the ambulance crew loading the gurney with David strapped to it. A large woman in a turquoise dress fainted when she saw the blood stained carpet, causing a gridlock at the office hallway. The din of noise reverberating through the hall made it impossible to communicate with the panicked crowd.

Seizing a chair near the wall, Barry stood up on the seat to gain a view of the crowd. He waved his arms over his head. "Stop!" Nothing changed. He shouted louder, "Stop! Everybody stop where you are right now!"

Anxious eyes looked his way. A few nearest him slowed. His demand started to make an impact.

"Stop right where you are," he yelled again. "Listen to me."

The roar of the confusion slowly diminished. A few helpful souls tried to hush the crowd.

"Listen to the preacher, everyone," Drew shouted. His deep voice finally brought a semblance of order to the packed atrium.

"The danger's over now. We've had a terrible crisis. But God has helped us. The kidnapped baby is right here, safe in Drew's arms. Where's Lisa Burns?"

"I'm right here." Her voice from the back of the crowd

sounded high-pitched with fear.

"Your baby has a few scratches but is O.K.," Drew said. The crowd parted for the petite woman. At the sight of her mother, the quivering child reached out her arms and burst into tears again.

"The father of this little girl tried to take her from the nursery." The voices rose again but Barry gestured for calm. "He had a gun and fired the shot that wounded David, but the danger is over now. The police stopped him and rescued the baby."

"Oh my God!" Lisa shouted. "You mean Cody kidnapped our baby? How did he know where we were? What happened to him?"

"Maybe we'd better go talk to the police, Mrs. Burns," Drew said, wrapping his arms completely around the mother and sobbing child. "Come on with me." His massive hug overpowered her resistance. He turned them from the atrium and down the hall towards the south parking lot. Cassie pushed through the people to lend her support.

"I know everyone's upset...." Barry stepped down from the chair.

"But we've still got business to take care of here," an angry voice demanded from the sanctuary doorway. Dale pushed his way through the crowd toward Barry. Daemon and Franklin marched behind him. The three squared off like a gang of gunfighters directly in front of Barry.

"This tragedy can't stop the real business the church must confront," the attorney called out loudly. "Daemon started to tell us exactly what many people have suspected for months. The pastor is fleecing this church! Did you hear what the secretary said in there? Five thousand dollars are missing! We never got an answer from this man about that. I want to know what happened to it. So do a lot of other people. We can't let crazy gunman distract us from the issues Daemon raised."

The crowd fell silent. Barry stood alone, arms crossed, looking at his accusers.

"I did find five thousand dollars in my office," he said in an even voice.

Lauren stood in the front row. "Oh no!" she whispered, lifting her hands to cover her mouth. A murmur of astonishment swept the crowd.

"So, he did keep the money!" Daemon raised his hand over his head and shook his notes toward the crowd. The hubbub grew louder. He shouted again, "That's all we need to know!"

"No, it's not! What we need to know is the whole story!"

Another voice turned the heads of the crowd as one. Sam Lane had climbed on a chair at the far side of the atrium. "The pastor found that money, all right! Now, everybody, listen to the rest of the story!" He thrust a slip of paper defiantly in the air. "Barry found that money. These men accuse him of misappropriating it. But look right here. This is a deposit slip for five thousand dollars."

"He did steal it!" Franklin sounded gleeful.

Sam cut him off with a swipe of the paper in his hand. "Wrong again, Franklin! The pastor brought the money to me yesterday. This deposit slip is not for himself. He deposited the money in a fund for needy children to attend church camps! Now boys and girls from all across the city can go learn about our faith. The pastor gave the money to help the kids!"

The crowd erupted in confusion, a hundred voices talking at once. The color drained from Franklin's face.

"I wondered a thousand times where that money came from," Barry said. "Never did it even cross my mind that a member of my church would intentionally try to trap me with a pile of cash. It tempted me all right! Who wouldn't be, with a windfall of secret cash? But God showed me that money isn't going to make my family happier. Our city is full of kids who have real and desperate needs. Now, Daemon, your filthy money can go to some of those children you felt so concerned about Wednesday night—kids who need to know about Jesus!"

Sam raised his voice over the hubbub of the crowd. "In my book, that's not misappropriation. That's the heart of the best pastor I've ever known!" He pointed directly at Daemon. "There's a problem in this church. You bet there is. And he is standing right over there. Daemon Asher is the problem! He and his buddies planted that money to trap the pastor and drive him away from where God called him! I think it's time to say enough is enough." He waved the deposit slip high again. "This provides evidence enough for me to say Barry deserves to pastor this church. And pastor, I'm with you all the way!"

"Amen!" Lance shouted. Other voices joined in the chorus of affirmation. Dale and Franklin stood silent.

Lauren took up the cry. "Let me tell you even more. Liz Emory and Nadine Asher spent an entire day calling people to spread lies about the pastor and his wife. Those people want to take over control of this church. I'm with Sam! I think our real problem is standing right over there and if we don't do something, this crazy plot will split our church."

"Now, wait a minute," Daemon replied, stepping toward Barry. He had to gain the upper hand before the crowd got out of hand. "The money has only confused the real issue. We've got a problem much bigger than a few dollars given to charity. I've been watching this church go downhill for a long time. Can't anyone see who is the real cause of it? Over the last six years this man has changed the way we worship and what we believe. He's let a bunch of outsiders take over the church! He's neglected your needs to make a fast buck! I'm telling you stupid people, you don't know half the story...."

"Yes we do, Daemon, we know a lot more of the story than you think." A resounding bass voice joined the debate. Ed came from the nursery hallway and stood near Barry.

"My family feels like we know the truth. In the past two days, Barry spent hours at the hospital ministering to my family. His care and quick actions saved the life of my granddaughter! Just this morning she looked at me and said, 'I wouldn't be here without Brother Barry's help.' Daemon, I've been a member of this church as long as you have. Take a look around. This church unites people from all across the city. The only problems I've heard about have come from a small group of people who won't accept the future. You're wrong about the leadership of this church, Daemon—terribly wrong."

The towering man draped his arm across Barry's shoulders and looked around the atrium. "I think this is God's man for our church."

Dale jumped forward, his face red with anger. "You idiots! Can't you see God's trying to warn us? A mad man shot up the church today. What more of a sign from God do you need? If David hadn't been shot, his tape recorder would tell us something about Barry and his marriage that would make our hair stand on end! This pastor needs to go!"

Another figure slipped to the side of the pastor. Edith stood next to the minister who had walked with her to Harvey's grave just twenty-four hours ago. She raised a firm voice that captured the attention of the confused crowd.

"Daemon, you heard Harvey's warning last Sunday night. You tried sowing the Devil's seed of dissent among the people then. Harvey told you not to touch God's anointed man. Those were his last words to the church."

Her voice caught with emotion. She brought a hand up to wipe a tear from her eyes. "Harvey loved Brother Barry, and most of us do, too. We know he's not perfect. He struggles with problems and, like all these kids today, probably spends too much money. They need to live through a Depression, like

Harvey and I did! But he and Keri love this church and have cared for us time after time."

She took Barry's arm and wrapped her gnarled fingers around his hand. "Daemon, this world is changing. We can't hold it back. The real problem has grown up in your own heart. I hope you can get over it. But even if you can't, Barry is the one God has chosen to be our leader."

Keri pushed forward through the crowd. She embraced the senior saint, blond hair against white hair, standing in the crisis together.

"We're with you, pastor!" Kent's hearty voice sounded above the crowd.

"You're all fools!" Daemon pointed a finger at his own chest. "I've tried to show you what's happening to this church. But you won't see it. So now, you can have your future. I don't want any part of it!"

He turned his back to Barry and Keri, and marched toward the front doors. Without a word, Franklin, Dale, and Liz followed him. A few others joined the group. The crowd pulled back silently to let them pass.

After the glass doors thudded shut, Kent raised his voice to the hushed assembly. "A warning came to Barry a few night ago, direct from the Psalms. We couldn't understand all of it then. Now I do. That same Psalm says, *God will go before me and will let me boast over those who slander me! You, O God, are my fortress, my loving God!'"*

The police had already placed the barrier tape reading 'CRIME SCENE DO NOT CROSS' in the south parking lot when the Channel 9 news van lurched to a stop. Dominique hurried toward the officers. "Captain, I'm Dominique Powell. What happened?"

"We've had a kidnapping and two people have been shot. We're talking to witnesses and trying to piece the story together."

"Where is the kidnapper now?"

"We'll have a spokesman here in a few minutes, ma'am. He'll be able to answer your questions. But I can say that the kidnapped child is safe and has been returned to her mother. We're interviewing her at this time."

The reporter looked past the officer. A white sheet of plastic covered a large figure laying still on the sidewalk.

"Was someone killed?"

The officer nodded toward the covered body. "That's the kidnapper. But please wait until our spokesman comes before releasing that information."

"Sure. I'll be back as soon as the spokesman arrives." She turned toward the camera man. "Butch, let's go to the main entrance of the church. We'll come back here when they have a statement."

Drew stood outside the front doors when the TV crew approached. "May I help you?"

"Hi. I'm Dominique Powell from Channel 9. We're trying to cover the story here today. Does the church have a spokesman I could talk with?"

"I could answer a few questions. I saw the whole thing," Drew said, shaking her outstretched hand. "It was terrible."

"And who are you?"

"I'm Drew Carter, the minister of youth at the church."

"Would you be willing to answer some questions on camera? We'd like to know what you saw happen."

"I'd be glad to help."

"Butch, are we ready?"

The cameraman steadied himself and squinted through

the eyepiece. After some adjustments, he pointed toward the reporter and the minister.

The Worship Center held scores of church members, knotted together in anxious huddles, their plans for Sunday dinner long forgotten in the stomach-churning crisis. Barry and Keri walked among the shaken parishioners, seeking to comfort mothers clutching children in their arms or to hug stunned senior adults.

Brent took a place on the platform and waved for attention. "Mike McCormick just called from the hospital. David Dockery, the man wounded by the kidnapper, is now in surgery. Let's stop and pray for God's mercy to help him through this."

"Brent, we also need to pray for Lisa and the girls to make it through this tragedy," Beth said. "I'm sure everyone knows by now that her husband was killed in the gunfight with Officer Allen. She faces a huge load of grief, plus the challenge of being a single mother."

Heads nodded across the crowd. Brent lifted an earnest prayer for David's healing and for the young mother. Keri's eyes brimmed full of tears when the petition concluded.

Barry pulled her close. "I know the Lord will see David through," he whispered.

Brent called from the pulpit. "Pastor, what do you want us to do now?"

"I think all of us should make our way home. The police have a lot of work to do. They want to question me about what happened. I'm sure they'll want to collect evidence, so we ought to get out of their way. I think it is important for some of you ladies to help Lisa when the police finish talking with her. For all of us, today we saw a dark shadow fall across the church. It's time now for us to pull together again. Before we go, let's all do that in a physical way. Form a big circle, everyone holding hands, and let's have prayer."

From all sides of the room the somber people surged to the front of the Worship Center, reaching out to one another, sharing gentle hugs of reassurance, and linking hands.

"Pastor! Wait a minute." Lance stepped quickly down the aisle. He held something shiny in his hand.

"We have a special presentation for you, Brother Barry. On behalf of the little girl you saved and from the whole church, we present you with this medal of honor!"

He lifted a silver wad of aluminum foil, shaped like a star and hooked on a paper clip, and hung it dangling from the pocket of Barry's shirt.

"Thank you, pastor," someone called.

"I don't think I deserve this. That big guy made me mad, so I had to do something!"

"You did the right thing," Lance said. He turned to the crowd. "Dumb—but the right thing!"

Laughter filled the air. Like a wave, the people thronged near, engulfing the Peters with a warm embrace.

"Amen." The voices of a dozen Mt. Faith members spoke in unison after C.K. finished asking a blessing over the evening meal. More than twenty people stood together in the kitchen of the Peters' home.

Beth hugged Keri close. "What an incredible week since the prayer meeting at my house."

"I can't believe everything God has done." Keri looked closely at her tall, dark-haired friend. "Thanks for being there to help me."

The ring of the doorbell sent Barry towards the door. "I'll get it. It might be Drew and Cassie."

The youth minister's wife bustled into the crowded kitchen moments later, bearing a cake pan. "Sorry! I couldn't get this cake to bake fast enough."

"It smells great to me," Barry said, walking in with Drew. "I don't think you should bring it in here where all these gluttons are!"

Keri offered Drew a glass of tea. "What's the latest report from the hospital on David?"

The tall minister shook his head. "Not very good. His condition is still serious. The surgery went well, but the bullet tore up his stomach. The doctors wouldn't make any predictions about the speed of his recovery."

The scene of the blood-stained carpet played through everyone's mind in the quiet moment that followed.

"He showed a lot of courage when he ran down that hall," Lance said. "I'll go see him tomorrow and anyone here can go with me. He needs us now."

"Can I have a sandwich?" Jason stuck his head around the kitchen door.

"May I have a sandwich, please?" Keri corrected his grammar. "That sounds like a good idea for everyone. Come on and let's eat. Then we can make plans about helping David and some of the others in the church."

The sandwich buffet assumed the center of attention. Danae stepped to the front to fix a small plate for Tyler. Lauren took a playful swipe of Josh's Jell-O salad on her finger and stuck it in her mouth, drawing a mock protest from the off-duty officer. Rachel stuck a glass under the ice cube dispenser in the refrigerator door, filling one glass for herself and the other for C. K. Others began making sandwiches from the deli tray on the island.

Soon the guests settled in the family room. C.K. took a place in Barry's overstuffed recliner. "No Board meeting this afternoon, pastor?"

"The chairman called it off. He felt we needed time to sort out everything that happened. He set the meeting for two weeks from today. Sam will bring a report on the money that I deposited. We also hope to make some plans about helping Lisa and the girls by then."

"I'm sure they will support your decision about the fund for kids."

Jason sat on the floor, Indian-style, next to C.K. "Dad hit for the cycle this weekend, didn't he Mr. Haskins?"

"I'm not sure, Jason. What do you mean?"

"Well, everything Dad had to do this weekend copied hitting for the cycle in a baseball game. At least that's what I told him. Hitting for the cycle in baseball is when a player hits a single, a double, a triple, and a home run, all in one game."

"I'd say that's quite an achievement. How did your Dad do that?"

The young man's eyes gleamed with pleasure. "He did it in a minister's way. Saving the baby's mother at the hospital is like hitting a single. Then baptizing Kendra became the double, you know, like the second step in life. The wedding would be like third base in life. The funeral is the home run that gets a person safely to Heaven. That takes him all around the bases of life. Isn't that cool?"

Drew lifted a tea glass like he was making a toast. "The way I see it, your Dad did one more thing. Stopping the kidnapper should be like winning the Most Valuable Player award!"

"Yeah! The MVP! Way to go, Dad!"

Barry held up an open palm to receive a high five from the bright-eyed teen. "I didn't think very well before tackling that big guy. I felt like I'd butted heads with a bull charging a red flag. Drew knows I wasn't exactly myself for a minute or two."

"You're telling the truth, preacher. When I got to you laying in that parking lot, your eyes were swimming around like turtles in a pond!"

"I guess I had my own vision while my head was spinning. I saw the church filled with people attending a funeral. The casket at front held a black-haired man—me!"

The room grew quiet.

"I heard people talking about my ministry. They told stories of their experiences with me, like when I visited the hospital, or helped them with a problem. The strange part came when I noticed no one mentioned a sermon, or a committee meeting, or even the growth in attendance! I've thought all afternoon about that dream. There's so much more ministry to do here in Mt. Carmel. Touching the lives of the people is as exciting as any home run I've ever hit."

"Shhh, everybody!" Cassie gestured toward the television. "Here's a news report about the church."

The screen held a close-up shot framing the face of reporter Dominique Powell.

"Both tragedy and heroism touched the congregation of Mt. Faith Church this morning. The congregation, one of Mt. Carmel's largest, was holding their regular worship service when gun shots rang out."

The camera panned the atrium and zoomed to the large bullet hole in the upper window of the worship center back wall.

"Police say that a twenty-six year old unemployed car salesman, Cody Burns, attempted to kidnap his own daughter at gunpoint from the church nursery. He had separated from his wife and children earlier this week."

The face of Lisa Burns appeared on the screen. Her eyes appeared red from crying. The caption at the bottom of the picture read, 'Wife of kidnapper.'

"Cody and I had only been separated for a few days. I knew he was looking for me but didn't feel I could move back in yet. I had no idea he planned to do something like this."

"Her whole life has been marred by tragedy," Keri said.

The camera showed Dominique standing on the south sidewalk of the church. Behind her yellow police tape fluttered in the wind.

"Cody Burns tried to run from the church with his young daughter. His flight took him through the atrium, where he shot and wounded a church member. A uniformed officer of the Mt. Carmel police attending the church service, Corporal Joshua Allen, followed the suspect when he ran outside toward a pickup."

The scene shifted to officers clustered around the body of Cody Burns.

"As witnesses describe the scene, the pastor of Mt. Faith Church, Barry Peters, joined the chase. Rev. Peters actually tackled Burns in an attempt to rescue the baby. Burns recovered and pointed his gun at the pastor when Officer Allen fired a fatal shot."

The police spokesman came on next. "Officer Allen will be placed on routine administrative leave while the investigation is being conducted. The results of the investigation will be given to the grand jury for review."

Dominique returned to the screen, her face serious.

"A hospital spokesman told me this afternoon that the church member wounded in the shooting is in stable condition following surgery. The members of Mt. Faith Church I spoke with today are shocked at this tragedy but grateful that no wider bloodshed occurred. Reporting for Channel 9 news, this is Dominique Powell."

Keri turned down the volume of the TV.

"Whew. I never thought our church would be on the news with that kind of story, " Cassie said.

Lauren nodded. "Today could have turned into a disaster."

"It's just like I said, boss. You're the MVP."

"Drew, I think Josh deserves the honor. I wouldn't be around tonight without that crack shot he made. That's what I tried to tell the detectives this afternoon."

Josh waved off the suggestion. "The Lord watched over us all today. He helped me do my part with the kidnapper. Remember though, we faced two threats today. Without the courage shown by Mrs. Flowers, Sam, and Ed, Daemon's schemes might have carried the day. We'd be here tonight filling moving boxes! I see God's hand at work to protect us and give our church a new beginning."

"Pastor, we talked about praying for David. I think we should do that, plus thank the Lord for taking care of you and our church body," Kent said. "I think our worries about blood-thirsty men are over!"

C. K. stood. "I feel the same way. Come on, every body. Let's stand up and hold hands for prayer. "

Chapter 9
Monday

"Ma'am? May we visit with David for a moment or two?"

Drew and Kent stood in the intensive care unit of Magill Medical Center. A thin nurse with weary eyes sat behind a large counter crammed with five computer monitors, two telephones, and a bookshelf of notebooks. Three other nurses in blue uniforms stood behind her, busy with a balky infusion device on a stand. Around the perimeter of the ward, glass walls with sliding doors and pale green curtains separated the patient beds from the central nurses' station.

"Are you relatives?"

"No. I'm a pastor at his church," Drew said.

"Sure, but only a few minutes, please." She stood and walked across the room to bed 4. Pulling the curtain back, she softened her tone. "I heard what happened yesterday at your church. It's just unbelievable that could happen here in Mt. Carmel. A short visit might be good for him."

Two IV towers, hung with bags of clear liquid, stood above David's head, dangling tubes that dripped life-giving chemicals. Wires for the monitoring equipment ran from under the sheet across his body. A tube filled with a slow moving, dark liquid snaked to a collection bottle on the floor. The green plastic oxygen line draped across his pillow and cheek, then disappeared into his nose. Hanging in the corner, a television monitor traced two glowing lines with peaks and valleys, framed by the dance of numbers recording vital signs.

"David? It's Drew Carter."

David's brown eyes flickered open, blinked again, then focused on Drew.

"Hi." The smile seemed weak.

"Kent Puckett came with me. We wanted to check on how you were doing this morning."

"They say I'm doing pretty well." His words had a slow and sticky sound.

"That's great news. The whole church is pulling for you."

Kent overcame his reluctance and moved closer to the bed. "We're all sorry this crazy thing had to happen to you."

David nodded. "It all happened so fast. I don't remember much after I heard the woman scream. I guess the guy just went berserk."

"The pastor told us last night that the man had abused his wife and daughters until she hid at the Women's Shelter. It's crazy, but I guess he thought he could get the family back together by kidnapping one of the girls from the church."

"I just happened to get in the wrong place at the wrong time, I guess."

Drew laid his hand on the patient's bare shoulder. "David, we're believing that God is working right now to turn this tragedy around. He never wastes anything that happens to us."

The patient glanced away without making a reply.

The curtain rustled behind the visitors. An older man and woman entered the crowded room. The man's broad forehead and brown eyes formed an older version of David's own face. He extended his hand. "I'm Ray Dockery."

Kent shook his hand, introducing himself and Drew.

"We came to cheer up this hero."

David's mother walked to the far side of the bed and gently took her son's left hand. "Are you hurting as bad this morning?"

David shook his head. "They're keeping me doped up and that helps."

Ray turned to the tall minister. "His surgery had just finished when we got here. We found the surgeon and quizzed him pretty good. In his opinion, the prospects look good for a full recovery. The bullet tore up part of his stomach and lodged near the spine. Just a half-inch difference, and this terrible experience would have been truly tragic. From what the doctor said, we hope that in a few weeks he'll be back to full strength."

Kent gave a thumbs-up sign to David. "You can be glad to have such great cheerleaders, pal."

"I guess I do have something to be thankful for."

Drew grasped David's right hand. "You're going to get over this tragedy. Now that your folks are here, we'll get out of the way. Let me lead us in prayer, then Kent and I will take the good news back to the church."

Hands came together in a circle around the bed. Drew voiced their concern and faith to God, seeking grace for healing. From the control desk, the nurse saw their bowed heads and added a silent petition of her own for the pale, wounded man.

The slender leaves of the willow trees lining the parking lot of Mt. Faith Church fluttered in the gusty morning breeze. Liz parked beneath the branches and walked with slow, deliberate steps toward the glass doors. The keys of the church office felt cool in her hand.

"Liz!" Mary greeted her when the office door opened.

She certainly had not expected to see her co-worker after the confrontation yesterday. Ed Loomis, chairman of the Personnel Committee, had called the office this morning to inform the staff that the employment of Liz Emory had been terminated by the Personnel Committee, effective immediately.

Liz lifted her chin. "I need to turn in my keys and pick up my last check."

"I'll tell Mike you're here so he can write the check," Mary said. Her co-worker's Monday morning chutzpah impressed her.

Lauren saw Liz and hurried to the front desk. She leaned over to hug the gray-headed associate.

"I want you to know I've enjoyed working with you, Liz."

"I've enjoyed getting to know you, too." She pulled away from the embrace. "I need to get the pictures from my desk."

"Do you have any ideas where you might look for another job?"

"Not really." Sadness tinged her voice. "Would you give my keys to Brother Barry?"

Lauren took the ring of door and cabinet keys. Her own heart felt heavy. "I'm sorry this all happened, Liz. For all of us."

Liz turned to face her, shoulders slumped. "I am too. I...I never intended to harm anyone. I didn't see what Daemon had in mind until it was too late. He seemed like a nice man that had a genuine concern about the church."

"He used you, didn't he?"

Liz slowly moved some personal items from the desk drawer into her bag. "Yes, he did. When he called last night, I just hung up on him. He said several families planned to leave the church. But I don't care if I ever see him again."

"I can understand your feeling," Lauren said.

Mary came from Mike's office with an envelope in her

hand. "Here's your check."

The three stood awkwardly around the bare desk. Liz pulled her purse strap up on her shoulder. "I guess I'll be going."

She started toward the door. At the reception desk, she turned and looked at Lauren. "I wish you and Josh the best. He's a neat guy."

"Thank you. I'll tell him what you said."

Liz slipped the envelope in her purse and put on her sunglasses. She stepped out the door without looking back.

Mary walked across the office toward the workroom. "What a heartbreak she's going through."

"We need to keep her in our prayers."

"I'm going to put her name on the list for the Wednesday night service for a few weeks."

"I don't think Barry would mind that at all."

"Do you want some coffee?"

"I'd love some. I guess so much has happened, I'm having trouble concentrating this morning."

While the coffee brewed, they took a seat in the work room.

"How does Josh feel today?"

"I talked to him about an hour ago. He reported at 8:30 to the police station for an interview. He felt nervous about it. The usual procedure after a shooting is to put the officer on a paid administrative leave. One of the supervisors reassured him about the process. After hearing that, he told me he hoped to be cleared within a couple of weeks."

"Good. If they do what's right, they ought to give him a medal for saving Brother Barry's life!"

"I think so, too!" Lauren laughed, pulling her long hair behind her ear. "I just thank God both of them are around this morning. I'm going to need them, you know."

With that, she held out her left hand. A ring with a

small diamond sparkled brightly.

"Oh, Lauren! He proposed? Congratulations! How wonderful!" Her words poured out. She reached across the table to embrace the willowy associate. "When did this happen?"

The glow on Lauren's face matched the bright stone of the ring. "Last night after we left the Peters.' He came up to my apartment and just blurted it out."

"When's the wedding?"

Brent entered the workroom. "When's the what? Did you say 'wedding?'"

"Just look at her finger," Mary said, pointing proudly. "That's the real thing!"

Brent took Lauren's hand and held it close, eyeballing the ring in a comic fashion. "That's beautiful! So when is the date?"

"We don't have a final date yet. We want to talk to Brother Barry about his schedule in March. And we want you to sing for the wedding."

"I'd love to. I'm thrilled for you guys! Barry will be delighted about it."

"He and Keri should be back from Lisa Burns' in a little while. I'm going to tell him about it when he gets here."

The faded blue-green trailer house rocked slightly in the gusty wind, giving the effect of a boat on gentle seas. Inside the walls, however, a storm of emotion raged. Lisa, convulsing with sobs, sat huddled between Barry and Keri.

"I can't go look at him! He's dead!"

Keri tried to calm the young widow again, whispering in her ear. "You don't have to, honey. The funeral home doesn't require it."

"I saw him yesterday when they took him to the funeral home." She continued to cry while Keri stroked her black hair. "A huge pool of red blood lay right there on the sidewalk for the girls to see. It looked horrible! I can't take anything like that again."

Barry slipped off the couch and knelt down in front of the grieving woman. He took both her hands in his strong grip, his face just inches from hers.

"Lisa, we'll be with you every step of the way. I know the funeral director, and I promise that I'll speak to him about what you want. In today's world, many families don't open the casket at the end of the funeral."

"They don't?"

"No. In fact, when a tragedy has occurred, that's normal. Everybody understands how hard it is on the family."

Keri shook her head. "Don't worry about making a decision now. Let's just wait until your Dad gets here. Then, tomorrow you'll have someone to help you with all this."

"O.K., O.K. I'm sorry to be such an idiot," she whispered. "I just still can't believe it all happened. I feel so guilty and so ashamed. He would have killed you, pastor, and it would have all been my fault."

Barry looked at her, face to face. "Now Lisa, don't do that to yourself. You didn't cause anything. Cody made his own choices every day. You had to protect those precious girls. You couldn't control what he did."

"I guess so. I'm just so confused." She wiped the tears from her cheeks.

"That's why we're here," Keri said. "In just a few minutes some of the ladies from my Sunday School class will be here. They care about you and don't want you to be alone. They will help with everything. Someone has already given money to get the girls new dresses for the funeral. If it's all right, they can go out this afternoon and find something that will fit just perfect."

As if on cue, a knock at the door brought Barry to his feet. He waved through the storm door to Cassie and two other women. "Hi, ladies." He opened the door. "We were just talking with Lisa about you coming by to give her some help."

"We'll do everything we can," Cassie said. They made their way to Lisa and pulled her close in a motherly hug.

While the women talked, Barry stepped outside. To the north, the gentle, forested slope of North End Hill towered over the trailers. The strengthening wind whirled around him suddenly.

"I will look to the hills, from whence cometh my help," he prayed, quoting the Psalm. Lord, I'm going to need your help as much as Lisa to get through this funeral. That man shot David and then tried to kill me. He beat his kids. Help me to do this job.

The screen door slammed behind him. He felt Keri's arm encircle his waist. He looked over at her and nodded back towards the door. "Is she doing O.K.?"

"Recovering from this will take years, I'm afraid. She's in shock now. The anger she felt against Cody will bring an even deeper grief. I hope we can help her through it."

"Does that 'we' mean us specifically? Are you saying you want to stay at the church?"

She looked up at him, her blue eyes luminous. "God still has a lot for us to do here, together, with His help. She's only part of it. Most of the church is ready for a new day. You heard what the people said yesterday."

"Did they mean it?"

"They did. And I meant what I said, too."

"I know."

The creaky porch groaned as he hugged her close. The buzz of the women's voices filtered through the old door, tinged with tones of caring for the grieving family. The rays of the sun bathed their embrace with warmth.

He pulled back and locked her fingers in his strong hand. "Come on. Let's go back to the church."

"Another yellow envelope? He will go bonkers when he sees this!" Lance roared with laughter. He opened the rumpled, letter-sized packet and looked inside to see it stuffed with money. "Hey, this is real money!"

"Sam Lane collected it last night from some of the elders," Brent said. "There's one thousand dollars and a brochure about Jamaica. He thought it would be a great joke and a great gift, too."

"Let's just put it in his office," Lauren said. "Then he can discover it just like he did the other envelope."

The delighted conspirators agreed to the mischievous plan.

The high-pitched whine of the carpet cleaner quit when the pastor and his wife entered the atrium. Barry saw Mike rubbing his hand on the carpet.

"Has the blood-stain come up?"

"Not really," Mike said, standing up and putting his hands on his hips. "The police kept us away all day yesterday, so the blood had dried before we started." He nodded toward the older man standing with his hands on the carpet cleaner. "Billy worked for an hour last night with some pre-soak and came in at seven this morning to see what he could do. We've made some progress but still have a ways to go."

Keri turned her eyes from the darkened spot. "I'm going to the office," she said.

"I'll be there in a minute." Barry bent down to touch the wet fabric. "If we need to call a professional cleaning service, let's do it. I'd like for everything to be ready for Wednesday."

"If one more treatment doesn't take care of it, that's what we'll do."

Billy caught the pastor's eye. "How's Mr. Dockery this morning, pastor?"

"I heard he came through the surgery real well. The doctor says he ought to recover fully in a few months."

"He sold my boy some insurance a few years ago. Fine man. Just too bad, with his wife dying and all this year."

Barry pursed his lips. "We never know what tomorrow will bring, do we?"

"Barry, you have a call on line two. Barry, line two," Mary said over the intercom.

The pastor turned to go, then paused. "Thanks for the hard work on this, guys. And keep David in your prayers."

A buzz of conversation filled the office when he opened the door. Mary and Lauren sat at their desks, while Keri, Brent and Drew stood talking with Lance near the work room door.

"Good morning, Brother Barry," Lauren said.

"Looks busy around here."

"We've had a lot of action this morning already. I'll fill you in when you've finished with this phone call."

Barry hurried to his desk. He wasn't surprised to hear the voice of Dr. Richards.

"Barry, I just had to call to check on you this morning. The story about your church appeared in the <u>Star</u> this morning. Are you all right?"

"Yes, I'm fine. I think I'm still in shock about everything that happened yesterday. We had more going on here than the media could ever understand."

"Did you know this man who tried to kidnap his daughter?"

"I'd met him only once just a few days before the incident. Keri and I have helped his wife. She left him earlier in the week after repeated abuse."

"It's a terrible tragedy, and my heart goes out to all of you," the director said. "I'm sure all of this has taken your mind off our conversation and the children's home position. If you need to take more time...."

"Actually, Dr. Richards, all this has helped clarify our decision." Barry stood and stared out the window. His mouth felt dry. Beyond the parking lot he could see the houses of Mt. Carmel and the bluff of Osage Hill. The face of the limestone glistened in the morning light. Once he had stood at the crest of the bluff, gripped a gnarled oak branch, and gazed across the small city, thinking of the people living in the valley. Now, he knew more strongly than ever the call of God to touch their cycle of life.

"Keri and I feel the Lord isn't done with us here quite yet. Our ministry has turned a corner. We want to be around to see the best part of what He is doing at Mt. Faith Church."

"Really? Well, frankly, I'm surprised."

"I don't think my answer would have been the same before the things that have happened this week. But we know what God has spoken to our hearts.

"I know you've done a good job there. I'd hoped to bring your energy to our organization."

"Your desire to have us at Potter's House means quite a bit to both of us. Now is just not the right time. We've survived a war, sort of, and I want to stay around and enjoy the parade."

"Is there a change I could make in my offer that might cause you to reconsider?"

"No, that's generous of you, but our minds are made up. I think some of the best days of the church are ahead."

"In that case, I promise that my prayers will be with you and Keri. Let us know how you're doing in a few weeks. And thanks for considering the offer. Please pray for us here while we try to fill this position."

"I will. Thanks once again for your offer."

Barry slowly placed the phone back on the hook and stretched back in the chair. A feeling of relief flooded over him. *Earlier, I wanted so badly to escape from the pressure. But not now. The church needs us right here. I'll play this game until the last inning is over.*

"Did you decide to take a day off, Keri?" Brent handed her a doughnut from the box in the workroom.

"Yes. Last week seemed to last forever. I just couldn't face it this morning. In fact, I've decided to look for something else."

"You're kidding!"

"No, that's really the way I feel. The excitement of the bank doesn't appeal to me like it once did. I want to devote some more time to the church and to Jason."

"Nothing wrong with that," Drew said. "I'll let you teach a great little class of ninth grade girls!"

A shout from across the room interrupted their laughter. Barry bounded from the door of his office. "What is this?" He shook the yellow envelope above his head.

"More stolen money!" Lance yelled, lifting his hands in mock alarm. "The pastor found more stolen money!"

"Where did this cash come from?"

The conspirators began to snicker. Keri's brow knitted in confusion. "I don't know what's going on," she said to Drew.

Lance waved his hand for silence.

"Brother Barry and Keri, on behalf of some folks who

think you guys had more than your share to put up with, let me explain." He reached in his pocket to get a glossy brochure, covered with provocative pictures of blue ocean and white beaches. "Yesterday evening, Sam took up a collection to send you two off for awhile to relax. This really is a gift, not a trap." Laughter broke out again and he waited to continue. "There's one thousand dollars in here and this pamphlet about Jamaica explains exactly what to do with it. We want you to get away and enjoy life for a few days without worrying about mutinous church members and hurting families!"

Barry put his arm around Keri's waist. "You guys are the greatest."

Lauren stepped forward and held up her left hand. The diamond of the engagement ring sparkled. "You wouldn't mind if Josh and I went with you for our honeymoon, would you?"

The little crowd erupted with approving applause.

Barry shook his head. "I'm calling a time out! I had to plan for a funeral a few minutes ago, and now you're asking about a wedding. I'm not sure I'm ready to hit for the cycle again!"

Study Guide for
Mt. Carmel Memoirs: The Cycle

This study guide to MT. CARMEL MEMOIRS: The Cycle may help you bridge the gap between the pages you've just read and the everyday world you'll walk in tomorrow. Use the questions for private reflection or with a discussion group to develop a more authentic journey of faith.

1. C. K. revealed to Barry the ugly secret that Mt. Faith Church had a history of conflict with ministers. Research in congregational life shows congregations may become 'repeat offenders,' terminating one minister after another. Discuss in your group whether that pattern has been shown with any congregation in your community. Can congregations change?

2. Barry felt at one point "like a drab billboard, weatherbeaten and dull..." This is a classic description of vocational burnout. The experience certainly isn't limited to the clergy. Consider your own vocation. Have you ever struggled with this same condition?

3. Painful encounters sometimes bring an emotional backlash that forms a grievance. In our hurt we place blame on someone else. Daemon suffered a broken relationship with his son, Jack. Yet he accused Barry of failing in ministry when Jack attended just one Sunday. How can someone who has held a grievance move past it?

4. Lisa fled an abusive husband. Is that a biblical

response? What would you have told her the night she left to find the women's shelter?

5. David and Keri each felt the laceration of grief over Morgan's death, yet reacted in vastly different ways. How have the shadows of mourning and grief affected your life?

6. Keri actively tried to integrate her vocation and her ministry. Is that really possible for a minister's mate? Why?

7. God used Ken's vision to warn Barry. That's unusual. Or is it? What has been your experience of surprising communication from the Lord that helped you in a difficult situation?

8. Consider your own walk with God and involvement in a congregation. Which character in the book reflects some of your experience, character, motives, or struggle?

AFTERWORD

The dream to help churches and clergy...

has been in my heart for more than a decade. First, it took the form of study and research. Next, it became the vision of writing fiction that would inspire and support. Finally, it lead to the founding of JOURNEYSOUL CHRISTIAN MINISTRIES to nurture authentic, holistic spiritual development.

Through the Mt. Carmel Memoirs, I desire to help the body of Christ face the reality of church conflict and clergy distress. Each book in the trilogy will tackle different issues in this frightful epidemic. Professional research has examined the problem, critics have glorified it and ministers and their families have paid the price. We must never forget that just today 10 clergy were terminated from their positions in American churches! It's my hope that the Mt. Carmel Memoirs will address the issues through inspiring and hope-filled fiction.

Please contact me at www.journeysoul.org. Let's work together on the journey of faith!

I want to express my heartfelt thanks to...

- My loving and talented wife, Jan, who has always offered the right mix of support and patience through the years of my writing, hoping, and absent-mindedness, and who ultimately added her expertise to the project;
- My wonderful children Bethany, Josh, Drew and Lauren, who believed in their old man and his ideas;
- My congregations in Beaver, Oklahoma, Lawton, Oklahoma and Amarillo, Texas, who showed so much that's

right about the Body of Christ;
- To readers Candy Marshall, Cindy Copeland, Debbie Morris, Dana Moore, Gene Shelbourne, Jan Fisher, Janie Lowe, Kay Durbin, Kim Chapkan, Laquita Shaw, Lynda Queen, Matt Tullos, Marilyn Trook, Nancy Harris, Ronnie Shaw, Ruth Junkins, and Sherri Briggs for your precious time and valuable insights;
- To consultants James Perdom, Jeff Gilbertson, Jerry Neufeld and Jock Morris for your knowledge that made the scenes come alive;
- To artist Kendra Weldon, and the talented staff of C and B Printing;
- To my parents, Carl and Julie, and my father-in-law, John, even though your years of serving the Lord on this earth never saw a word of this manuscript, your legacy is an imprint on everything I've done;

...For all you've done to bring <u>Mt. Carmel Memoirs: The Cycle</u> *to the Body of Christ.*

Larry Payne

ORDER TODAY

ADDITIONAL COPIES OF
Mt. Carmel Memoirs: The Cycle

Share this tale of suspense and hope with a friend, a distressed minister, or a church leader!
335 pages. With Study Guide.
$14.95

AVAILABLE NOW BY LARRY PAYNE

The Matrix of Spiritual Assessment: A Practical Tool for Ministry

A clinically-informed, indicator-based tool for assessing the spiritual needs of a patient or parishioner. It provides a record of assessment which can inform pastoral interventions and communicate with other professionals. The MATRIX utilizes the theoretical and clinical studies of nurses, chaplains, physicians, and counselors to assess the patient's spiritual needs by observing seven psychosocial-pneumatic dimensions. The dimensions are Meaning/Faith, Affect/Emotion, Trauma/Grief, Ritual/Practice, Intimacy/Social, Anxiety/Fear and Self-understanding. Each dimension is further developed through four levels of intensity: Well-being, Concern, Distress, or Despair.
31 pages. Spiral Bound. With bibliography and Patient Record.
$8.99

Developing A Lifestle of Prayer: Devotional CD

Take an amazing pilgrimage of prayer experience. Based on Dr. Payne's original research, the 30 short devotions can prompt a greater depth of prayer than you ever thought possible.
CD. With Workbook
$9.99.

25 Greatest Verses of the Bible

Inspiration from the mountain-tops of Biblical revelation to accelerate your journey of faith. Each challenging chapter is two pages in length, with exercises for personal application. Read one a day, or one per week.
Ring binder for easy accessibility.
$9.99

COMING SOON!

Miracle of the Plunger: True Stories from the Parish Zone

Why was a toilet plunger standing in the middle of the road and what did it mean to 40 screaming teenagers? Explore the wild and glorious stories of one ministry family and the tales of church life they've never told before. Twelve great episodes to delight and amaze.

Mt Carmel Memoirs: The Voice

A mysterious and powerful prophet is drawing large crowds to a hidden cavern with the promise of spiritual experiences like few have ever known. Keri's mother, afflicted with Alzheimer's disease, must be cared for. And Jason is in love! Pastor Barry and Keri will stretch to the limit of their endurance to save everything they love. Volume 2 in the Mt. Carmel Memoirs.

LOG ON TO

www.journeysoul.org

OR WRITE
JourneySoul Christian Ministries
3300 S. Coulter Dr, Ste. 3-155
Amarillo, Texas 79106